Nuts & May

First published in 2022
by the Bruges Group

ISBN: 978-1-8380658-3-6

Nuts & May

Ten short stories

Jeremy Nieboer

www.brugesgroup.com

Published in 2022 by The Bruges Group, 246 Linen Hall,
162-168 Regent Street, London W1B 5TB

Follow us on Twitter t @brugesgroup, LinkedIn in @brugesgroup,

GETTR f @brugesgroup Facebook f @BrugesGroup,

Instagram @brugesgroup, YouTube @brugesgroup

Contents

These ten stories are all to an extent concerned with consolation and reflection. Since they relate to the distant view of life that age confers many begin with accounts of early youth and adolescence since the impressions of those years are often the brightest and most enduring.

Page

MISS SIDDONS

Miss Siddons had never been inside an aircraft before.

Her nephew, Piers Strutte, had arranged all the tickets, the taxis and fares. Miss Siddons had gone by taxi from Kericho to Nairobi. She did not want to fly until it was really necessary. Piers was aware that the flight from Kisumu to Nairobi meant over an hour by car to the airport with the added stress of the customary chaos when she got there. Whatever she chose was fine. The trains were no longer running from there to Nairobi. So taxi it had to be. As so many of her generation and background she thought it most extravagant – but what could she do? She would not admit to her relief at not having to rise miles in the air for longer or earlier than was necessary to get her to Gatwick.

In Nairobi she had stayed in the Sarova Hotel.

It was most comfortable. It was a bit too magnificent for her she thought – more for sheiks and millionaires. Her nephew said that he always stayed there when at his Nairobi office. At least it fortified her for the coming ordeal of flight.

A taxi arrived to take her to the airport. She protested at first when a wheel chair was offered to her as she alighted. The steward explained that the wheel chair was a passport to a charmed passage to the departure area. He took her stick and suitcase – she kept her bag. She was still in the wheel chair as they raised it up on a kind of lift platform into the cavernous interior of the vast structure of the aircraft. She clutched her straw hat digging her fingers into the cotton flowers sewn into the ribbon as the draught from the engines loosened its hold upon her small head.

It seemed to her preposterous that such a leviathan could even move.

She found that she was one of the first to embark. The stewardess seemed most attentive. When finally Miss Siddons turned up her boarding card from the depths of her handbag she was shown to a seat next to the aisle on the window side to the left as she came in.

Her nephew had solicitously explained that this would mean she could more easily stretch her legs. He hinted also that it would allow her more freely to wash her hands.

She gripped her stick as the stewardess moved to take her suitcase. She was adamant that no policy of the airline or attempt at persuasion or coercion would induce her to release her grip. She laid the stick on the floor by her side.

It seemed quite cool in the cabin after the relentless dry heat.

A long interval passed. Embarkation, which was at first diverting, continued without incident or interest as the endless line of expectant passengers were drawn inexorably in to the 747. Miss Siddons' head tilted slowly by degrees to the side of her head rest. Her stick slipped unguarded into the aisle.

She woke abruptly – her stick was being pushed sharply against her ankles. She found she could not move her legs. A passenger in a full length colourful long dashiki was lying awkwardly in the aisle beside her, his feet caught in her stick. He had a round flat little hat -like a small cake – which had come off and fallen in her lap. The stewardess had run out of the kitchen area just behind her. She was vainly trying to raise him from his involuntary posture. He knelt forward over the stick and crouching on his knees raised himself slowly to his feet.

It was clear to Miss Siddons that she had somehow contributed to this mishap. But before she could attempt to redeem herself the booming voice of the fallen passenger claimed her complete attention.

"Miss Siddons? – surely it's Miss Siddons? Don't you remember me? Lindwall Benza-Cobuko – rather a mouthful I know but my father loved his cricket. He was a supporter of the Australians - England the 'old enemy'!"

Miss Siddons blinked, looking startled. "Oh do please forgive me...." she started. Then with delighted astonishment she continued

"Why B-C – is that really you? I'd never have known. You look so colourful. How extraordinary. It must be 20 years since we you came to see us at Kericho. Yes all of that I think. Well! Meeting you like this. Lindwall Benza -Cobuko – indeed. Yes, yes indeed. You were B-C to us do you remember?"

The large but kindly passenger smiled, leaning down as he put his hand on the back of the seat in front of her.

"Ah yes – so I am to many friends and colleagues now – particularly as my age is showing"

"We often saw you" she continued "when you brought your children to our little kindergarden. They all went on to Kinango did they? Or was it big school in Nairobi?. Your eldest son I well remember - another cricketer - Bradman was his name wasn't it?

"Yes indeed – what a memory. Yes, he had a short time at Kinango before going on to Nairobi. I don't think you'd have recognised me now from how I appeared to you and your sister as a 4 year old. Larger I fear – much larger as you can see all too clearly Miss Siddons."

As if needing to explain his presence Lindwall said

"I'm in London tomorrow for an arbitration – a dispute about shipping – I get quite a bit of international work from the Mombasa container shipping lines. Don't be deceived by my dress – I find a Dashiki much more comfortable for a long flight than lawyer's black serge. The arbitrations are often held in London as your English law applies to many of the disputes. But what, if I may I ask, are you doing on this flight? What is it that takes you to England?"

Before Miss Siddons could gather her thoughts he continued

"No - one moment - before you tell me -I've an idea – why not come and join me in Business class! You'll have 9 hours in that seat. I wouldn't like to think of you cramped and unable to sleep or see anything of the world below. I always take 2 seats – not just to spread my ample self but for the documents I need to review. It's very comfortable up there. They have wide reclining window seats with wonderful views beyond the wings. Food and wine excellent – a very good way to go to work. Would you find a way to accept? Do please – it'd be delightful for me to hear how things have been for you these past years".

Mrs Siddons was of that generation that were reluctant to feel indebted. But B-C was the father of no less than 4 children who had gone through her school and had himself been in her care. It seemed churlish to decline his invitation.

She settled in the large seating of the spacious interior to the front of the 747 with her handbag, hat and stick whilst the stewardess stowed her suitcase. She sat on her seat belt and got up – Lindwall helped her to complete the exercise.

"Now! Tell me. How was it that you came to Kenya at all Miss Siddons?"

"Well, you see, Papa had been a tea planter in India as a young man. He was asked by Lord Amersham to manage his tea estates in the Kericho hills. That was well before the second War – in 1932 I think. He met my mother going out on the steamer to be a nurse in Nairobi hospital. My twin sister and I were born in Nairobi in 1934. We loved it in the hills there and we made many friends – all settlers at that time of course. But we all came back in the summer of 1939 when things began to look black at home – Papa wanted to do his bit. He was too old for active service – he was recruited by the Ministry of Food."

"We spent the War in my uncle's large house in the Surrey hills. My mother's brother, you understand – it's now my nephew's. It was convenient for Horley station – Papa took the train to Victoria from there."

"Now where was I?….Oh dear…"

"Going home? In the Surrey hills?" suggested Lindwall.

"Oh yes – that's right – only to us little girls it seemed more like we were actually leaving our home."

"I remember that we went up the Nile in a steamer, then from Egypt to Marseilles and on up through France to get the Folkestone ferry. When that War ended he we all came back – in 1947. It was hard in England then – no opportunities and too many young men and women looking for them. My father just wanted to get back to life in the hills and the sun of Kenya. We, of course, went with him. He only had just over 10 years here before he died. My mother couldn't put her life back together in the Kericho hills without him. Constant reminders of her loss got her down and she missed her friends and family in England.- So after a few years my mother went back."

"Well B-C, we were still in our twenties – Kenya was home for us but like so many young ladies of that time quite untrained for anything. It was arranged that we should become governesses to the daughters of a wealthy English family who had a home in the Kericho hills and knew Papa. They had construction and shipping interests in Mombasa. They wanted to open a school for the very young children of their employees in the country outside Kericho – in the hills, you know– such lovely country there. It was partly for education but also to help the mothers who had to work to get by."

"We were so surprised when they asked us to be teachers – such a compliment we thought – one each, you see, for the girls and boys. The company owned a house on the west side of the hills and had put up two small school rooms with a verandah. So there we went. It was nearly ten years before independence but when that came it really made no difference. The authorities seemed content with how we were getting the children ready for their big schools".

"I should think they were Miss Siddons" broke in Lindwall "What a beautiful world it is in the Kericho foothills. And for the children to pass through your care like that - well - what a start in life."

"Yes - Oh yes. It was heaven for us. Heaven on earth. The lovely soft air and gentle climate. The great Mau reserve next to us, lush fields and woodlands. And just forty miles to Lake Victoria. How did we deserve such fortune my dear B-C?"

It seemed intrusive to break into the silence as Miss Simmons dwelt again in the Kericho foothills looking out from the frail verandah.

The colossus of the air began to roll slowly backwards releasing Miss Siddons from memories. By her expression she looked as if she had to be very brave. She clutched her stick and bag. She fixed her gaze upon her feet. Without moving or looking up she endured the terror of the rising of the giant into the heavens.

To distract her Lindwall asked loudly

"Tell me about your family. Did they all spend their lives in the colonies? It seems your father and sister thought of Kenya as home. What about your grandfather and earlier?"

This acted like a shock for she quickly turned to him.

"Well one of my great grandparents– or was it great great? . One of my great great grandmother's sons. What does that make him I wonder?"

"A distant relative?" said Lindwall hoping to untie the knot of her story.

"Any way" she carried on "he did spend much of his life, I believe, in India. He was in the Customs or the Indian Civil Service"

"But what my family was known for, at one time, was being on the stage. You see we twins, my sister and myself were descended from Mrs Siddons."

"That would be normal my dear Miss Siddons I think."

"No. So sorry. No, so sorry dear B-C - I suppose people, after so very long, have forgotten her. She was a very famous actress. So was her brother. On the stage I mean. Not the cinema. She was so celebrated that many famous artists wanted to paint her portrait. Did you know she was painted by Gainsborough and Reynolds and that Lawrence painted her twelve times -first when he was only thirteen?"

"I take your word for it. I don't remember seeing a photo of her."

"Oh dear me no. No! You see B-C she started acting 100 years before the British arrived in Kenya and 180 years before they left.

"Puts it all in perspective doesn't it?" said B-C.

"What's that B-C?" I fear my hearing is a little bit unreliable"

"The Empire of the great white queen."

"Oh but she wasn't a queen – just a tragic actress you see. And she played mostly at Drury Lane. The Tragic Muse. - she was known as the 'Tragic Muse'"

"Now where was I ?…Oh dear!"

"With Mrs Siddons?"

"Ah yes – do forgive me dear B-C – I fear I forget things when pottering about in the past".

"Well" she rallied and continued "We three were descended from Mrs Siddons - did I tell you that?"

"Oh- I can see from your smile that I have".

"You see she had two sons. Henry her first son was also on the stage but we think that George Siddons, her second son, must have been our great grandfather. Did I tell you that he went to India in the ICS? I believe he got leave to come home to look after his mother when her health declined – she was all of 76 when she died – a great age then."

"Do you know" she said as if disclosing something of importance "my grandfather came into the world on May 24 1819 and left it on January 22 1901 – exactly as did Queen Victoria - so my father used to say."

B-C waited to see if Miss Siddons had more in her mind – then seeing her pausing for thought he enquired

"She never went to Africa did she? Wasn't she Empress of India? I remember hearing that the sun never set on her Empire but she never went there – except if you count Ireland and I don't think the Irish would, now would they?"

As if to conclude their exchanges the 747 flew into the sudden turbulence over Sicily. Miss Siddons clutched her hat with one hand and the arm of Lindwall Benza-Cobuko with the other.

In a kind deep voice he soothed her

"Just some potholes on the road dear Miss Siddons. Nothing more."

It seemed to settle her.

"How silly of me – holding your hand – I don't know what use it would have been if we had dropped out of the sky. Do forgive me B-C. So girlish and silly."

She had lost all recollection of what she had been saying and lunch trays were being distributed with little bottles of wine. It was all very nice.

But as the Alps passed to the right of the 747 she seemed to catch the thread of memory again.

"You see there was a great scandal with the Siddons girls – No, no not what you think – not my sister and I – no nothing like that – dear me no."

"It was Mrs Siddons' own two girls Sally and Maria. You see Lawrence – that is the painter who was so struck with Mrs Siddons –well, he fell for Maria. They used to meet in his studio – it was in Greek Street.

"Ah yes" said B-C "that's in Soho isn't it. I had an attic bed-sit there in the 70s - in Bateman Street it was."

"I don't know I'm sure. I only went to London a few times and Soho – well it had a reputation then didn't it."

She continued

"It seems a Miss Bird arranged Maria's trysts **there** with Lawrence. He asked her to marry him I understand. But do you know he then broke it off – a terrible thing at any time but in that age a cruel act. You see it risked social scandal. And, dare I say, showed a young lady as if she were rejected goods. Maria was just 19. Lawrence painted them both and more than once. But he treated them very badly or so it seems".

Miss Siddons paused – it seemed as if she was recollecting events she had herself witnessed.

"Poor Maria died 6 months later from what they called 'consumption' in those days – it was tuberculosis of course. On her death bed she made her sister Sally promise her never to marry Lawrence. Sally did not. Ah- so sad - poor thing, she herself died just 5 years later."

"Oh dear I'm rambling again. You must forgive me B-C – it seems to help me take my mind off the thought of sitting on a chair all these miles up in the air – you've been so kind to listen to me – I'm sure you would rather have had a restful sleep after your lunch."

"Dear Miss Siddons, it's a privilege to be in your company. You gave so much to the children you taught – English, the Bible and loving kindness - all together. One could not fail to see in you a rare devotion to our people – and for so little reward."

"Goodness me B-C. I didn't think you would find our little school would seem at all important"

"I never thought I'd live to say such things of our colonial warders or that I'd feel keenly a loss at your departing. I'm glad that the tide of Empire ebbed away from my country but we were lucky that it left you for a while on our shore. You'll be missed my dear Miss Siddons. You sisters showed me as a little boy the gentle grace of England as much as the woods and downs I saw years later when I came to study law over there."

"My dear B-C. How very kind… Most poetic…We just had a little kindergarden – I don't know what to say…so kind."

"All my children started out there as I did and all from our village. How can I forget."

"But now you're going back?"

"Yes - but not really going back. I only remember England as it was just after the War you see. Kenya and the Kericho hills are really my home. I just thought I couldn't manage on my own after dear Hermione went."

"So", continued B-C, "if you don't mind me enquiring, how will you manage? It is going to be very different – and I think much more expensive isn't it?

"No of course I don't mind dear B-C. You see what happened was that my sister and I bought an annuity with our share of Papa's estate. My cousin arranged it all. But that's not been enough for us here for some time – I mean in Kenya – so I don't quite know what will happen. Even with my sister gone. She died, you know, a year ago."

Miss Siddons broke off but B-C did not feel he could add any condolence as it would distract and might disturb her.

"But my nephew has a house in the Surrey hills – did I mention that? – and he has so kindly let me have a cottage in the grounds. His firm has an office in Nairobi you know. He has done rather well it seems."

"I see." Lindwall waited on her in silence not wishing to press his concern.

Miss Siddons reflected for a while, distantly gazing ahead - then waking to where she was

"But Papa did leave us various things. He wanted us to draw lots for them as it seemed the fair way. There was some silver – quite a lot of it- and a great number of wooden boxes of wine I remember – all gone now of course. There were also a few things which Papa told us that his grandfather had bought at the studio sale of Sir Thomas Lawrence after his death – it was in 1831 as I remember him saying.

"Would the silver fetch much?"

"Well no B-C – you see we took what we could when we left England but had to sell it all to keep the little school going – books and desks and things like that. I think there might perhaps be a few bits left as my cousin put our things in store. He might have taken them out – I don't know really."

There seemed little that B-C could say but Miss Siddons resumed with a bright start.

"Oh yes – I have quite forgotten – so silly of me. Of course…quite escaped me…. Yes, there is of course the portrait by Lawrence."

"Really? The one who painted Mrs Siddons?"

"Yes indeed. You see I got the portrait and Hermione got the other things Greatgrandpa bought at the sale - mostly bric a brac but a few bits of jewellry and clothing he used for his subjects. Papa left instructions for the three of us to draw lots – so that is what we did. Did I mention that? We were twins you see so we always did share everything."

"What happened to the jewelry – that must be worth something today surely?" said Lindwall kindly.

"Well no – you see my sister and I could not pay Millie very much – Oh…. do you remember Millie B-C?"

"Do I indeed. She was our shield from you both when you got cross – dear Miss Siddons I fear that we were very unruly – Millie gave us our school lunches and we didn't have to speak English to her."

"Dear Millie" reflected Miss Siddons. "So very sad at having to leave her – she is perhaps the most precious of all my memories of a life spent in Kericho. So many years. It was a wretched and tearful parting for each of us."

"I left Kenya with just my suitcase of things and what was left in the Bank – very little I fear – my nephew gave me the ticket home. Most kind. You see all I had of any value was the few bits of jewelry left by my sister. I gave them to Millie so at least she had something she could sell."

"But the portrait you spoke of – what about that?" asked Lindwall. He was a famous painter surely? Your great grandfather must have thought so."

"Oh no I think he bought it for sentimental reasons – family reasons."

"How do you mean Miss Siddons"

"Well you see the portrait is of Maria Siddons, my great grandfather's sister. He was only 16 when she died. But it was also a remembrance of her mother the great Mrs Siddons - our famous forebear you see. A link with past fame. My father was very proud of it – he had a little gilded panel fixed to the bottom of the frame with Maria Siddons' name and Sir Thomas Lawrence Pinxit in black script on it"

"Pinxit? I regret that I'm only familiar with legal Latin"

"Oh – so sorry B-C 'Painted by' I think is the English translation"

After a while Miss Siddons' head gradually fell a little to one side on the headrest. She closed her eyes. The flight had unsettled her and she felt tired after so much talking. B-C felt able to recline his seat. After a while he too fell asleep.

He gently touched her as the 747 made its descent through the autumn darkening sky. As she collected herself and her things she explained to B-C that her nephew had arranged for a car from his West End office to meet her at Heathrow and take her down to the house in Surrey. B-C commented that it was kind of him to ensure she did not have to cope with such crowds, rush and confusion as she would never before have witnessed.

She had only her suitcase, bag and stick. B-C helped her through to Arrivals and saw her safely into the hands of her driver. As she took her seat in the back of the car he opened the door saying, as he looked calmly into her watery grey eyes,

"When you decide to come back to the Kericho hills you will let me know Miss Siddons. Promise me that please, you must promise me."

"Oh B-C, but I don't see how I could possibly manage to come back now do you?"

"The flower returns to the bulb does it not".

The door clunked and he walked slowly away down to the waiting taxis.

* * *

The driver took the M 25 leaving it for Reigate then on to Leigh and Norwood Hill. It was raining. The grey rain sinking from grey clouds so unlike the April and November rainstorms of Kericho. The journey seemed interminable. She was shocked by the intensity of everything. Nothing was slow or quiet. Cars and vast lorries hissed past ceaselessly. There was no sunlight nor did it seem possible that any should break through the solid, even, heavy mass of cloud just above. Garish signs highlighted the dismal scene. Nothing of the natural world came to view.

Miss Siddons recoiled from all that she had so far seen on the journey. Sitting deep in the back seat of the car she began to reflect on what she could recall of her uncle's house -now of course her nephew's.

Morley House stood in 40 acres of garden, woodland and pasture off Partridge Lane near Newdigate. It was of the late Victorian age. It had been laid out with two drives. The furthest one took you to the rear entrance of the house past the cobbled yard area enclosed by stables, dairy, feed store and implements building. It gave access for tradesmen and staff to the kitchens, larders, scullery, coal and wine cellars. The other was the formal entrance. Mature woodland stood deep around the house dominating all but the South elevation. The trees were mainly oaks and hornbeams – they had grown to a great height for the heavy clay had made it easy for them to thrive.

The gloomy aspect of the architecture was unrelieved by sunlight except in the south facing rooms. For most of the year sunlight was excluded in the yard and outbuildings. All that was despondent about Victorian respectability seemed to invest the spirit of the place.

The entrance hall was large. It was entirely faced with stained oak panelling. There was an imposing staircase rising to the first floor next to a high stained glass window depicting scenes from the lives of the first owner and his wife. A substantial stained glass lantern in the roof admitted a little light through its coloured glass panes.

The first floor landings ran in the form of galleries overlooking the atrium below with arches and columns to the sides intersected by balusters. All was stained dark oak and richly carved.

Such were the impressions and images she had formed as a 13 year old girl now beginning to re- appear in her mind. All as it was over 50 years ago. Now in Millennium year.

As the car rose up Stan Hill the rain dispersed to reveal at last, in the evening light, the gentle English fields and woodland. The road narrowed between grass verges and field hedges unlike anything she had seen since a girl.

Arriving at Morley House she was greeted Piers's wife, Jane. After such a journey Miss Siddons was anxious to settle in and get her bearings. She had rather hoped it would be all right if she could just have a sandwich and go to bed. Jane explained that Piers would be late getting back.

"Well now Aunt Alice what a wrench it must have been for you - leaving Kenya. I know the shock of arriving in damp Surrey after the heat and beauty of Kenya. I well remember seeing where you had lived in the lovely Kericho hills."

"It is so very good of you both to let me take the cottage" said Miss Siddons. "I know it's something of sacrifice. Piers mentioned that it's one of your holiday cottages. I do hope it will not be any hardship for you?"

"Oh Aunt Alice how too absurd. Of course not. We think it's wonderful that you should have found your way back to Morley. Piers was getting so worried about you, what with Hermione and everthing. Now would you like to see the cottage and perhaps have a hot bath? It's just a few minutes walk down the back drive. There are knee high light stands all the way and it's all tarmac."

She found the cottage was a conversion of some of the stables. There were two other cottages which were let for holidays a week or two at a time. It was just the end of the season. The buildings round the yard were built of bright red and slightly glazed large bricks with steep slate roofs and gables. There was a little belfry over the dairy building. The yard itself was laid with dark Victorian grooved tiles sloped slightly to a drain in the centre. No one was there. It had a desolate air in the dismal twilight drizzle.

Her cottage had two bedrooms, one with bath and the other with shower. There was a sitting room with an open fire and the kitchen was beautifully fitted out with startling bright white walls and cupboards. It was all quite modern. The rooms were small but it seemed very warm and comfortable. Jane had put out a bottle of milk, butter, cheese and fruit and other supplies. Miss Siddons decided to have the bath suggested by her and go to bed.

Piers called unexpectedly at the cottage much later that evening explaining that he would be back for the whole of the following week end. He left with her a copy of the inventory of things that had been put in store by his father many years ago.

*   *   *

When over the next month or two she looked back on how it was that she had left the Kericho hills for the solitary confinement of the Morley House outbuildings and the endless sunless Surrey winter she realised that what she had done was to forfeit all that was familiar and safe. It was nothing particular which she could, as it were, pin in her memory. She had expected some sense of dislocation but as the weeks passed she came to realise how her contentment had rested so much on the goodwill and kindness of the village people in the highlands of Kericho. It was a constant of a lifetime spent with them – a life indeed - especially with Hermione had gone. She had seen so many generations of children pass through her care. Every day would bring a wave or greeting, a lift in a rusty pick-up to the shops or to church, a gift of the abundant Kericho hills fruit.

It was borne in upon Miss Siddons that what she had expected to find in England was a restful security. Now with deepening she realised that she had severed those unseen arteries of gentle benevolence that had sustained her for all those years. She had a kind of security but, lacking familiar humanity, its confines pressed more closely upon her with each passing day.

She did not at all expect how much she would miss the fertile gracious hills of the highlands country. They shared with the Surrey downs a lovely undulation, it must be said, but they were not compressed within thunderous roads. The silence borne in the clear and temperate highlands air was not disrupted by the roar of aircraft – there was no Gatwick. The Cape Ash and Cape Chestnut trees were as mature as their namesakes growing in the Surrey hills. The Kericho plantations were of the rich deep green of growing tea. Distant woodlands of the higher hills set off the flowing fields and clumps of trees. Constable himself would have marvelled at the beauty of the changing forms of clouds over the Kericho hills.

As she sat in late October alone in the twilight in her brightly lit sitting room looking over the empty yard down the misty and dismal back drive she was overcome with a profound sense of loss and despair. She saw herself as if in an alien world excluded now for ever from her true home.

* * *

"Now Aunt Alice" said Piers putting down his tea cup "have you been through the inventory of your things? My father brought them out of store when he realised you would not be coming back from Kericho. They're in the North attic – we converted the South attic to a flat for William the gardener and Muriel - his wife that is. She's our housekeeper as you've found out. Why not come up when you finished tea and have a look?"

"Well, dear Piers, that's most kind but I'm not sure I'll have much use for any of them. But it would be nice to see what there is from those times. I would particularly like to see the portrait of course. You see my dear Piers I've been thinking – it's been a great worry to me - about my staying here with you and Jane. You see I simply could not take advantage of your generosity once I've been able to supplement my pension to provide for my needs – I'm sure you'll understand. And the house and holiday lettings and grounds are far too demanding for Jane and Muriel to spare time looking after me."

"But Aunt Alice that surely is…"

"Now Piers! I was sure you would protest and that is why I am adamant". Miss Siddons paused to nod her head to emphasise her intent. "I need to explain to you what is in my mind. You see you've both been so kind and concerned. But when dear Hermione went I foolishly fell into the trap of forgetting how lovely was my life in Kenya actually was – in the present as it were. Once I was on my own I allowed myself to be oppressed by thoughts of the future, ill health and extreme age. I came to believe that I needed the haven of security and care you sweetly conjured up in my imagination."

"But Aunt Alice we're delighted that you eventually agreed to come back. Kenya's not really home is it however long you may have been there surely?"

"Oh but it is you see, it is. I know that now. It is. I wanted for nothing there. It's not just medical care – that is very good even just in Kericho – it's the goodness of the people and the loveliness of the land you see. It's all I know. I do miss it all dreadfully. Most dreadfully."

"But…"

"No, Piers, I must explain. I am so, so sorry dear Piers – so very sorry - and that is why you must listen now most carefully to what I propose as it will resolve everything."

"Well of course you must let me know what you think is best, but….."

"I shall sell the Lawrence portrait. Also I will ask Millie to come over, if you'll allow it, and she can have the other bedroom in the cottage. There! I've got it out. It's been preying on my mind for many anxious weeks. I'm so glad I've been able to say it. It'll mean I can help with the cost of keeping me, as it were, and Millie will be such a comfort to me. You do see don't you?"

Piers was unsure what to say to her. She was resting so much hope on Millie who would surely not wish to be pulled up by the roots. But, more than that, he did not know how he could break it to her that the Lawrence was only an attribution not a certain original work by the artist himself.

His father, on taking her things out of store, had sent the portrait to Sothebys in order to settle both the matter of whether it was indeed by Sir Thomas Lawrence and also if it depicted one of the Siddons sisters. Sothebys were uncertain, it appeared. They had consulted a recognised expert. They would only say that they could attribute the portrait to him. At least that is how he remembered his father's account. That would be all of 30 years ago now.

Thinking it best not to present his Aunt with an instant dismissal of her proposal – the disappointment as to the value of the portrait would have been cruel if not managed tactfully over time – Piers simply said

"Yes dear Aunt – yes I do see of course. Well, why not come up now and see the portrait?. I expect you've no very clear recollection of it and it's rather lovely. And as to Millie – well what do you think is the best way to put it to her? Wouldn't she find the flight too frightening? What about her family?"

"Oh she would not be frightened, I am sure. She's not timid at all – Oh no – not at all! She would see it all as an adventure. After all, so many have gone to England from the highlands. She has a good many siblings, cousins, nephews and nieces of course. But she lives on her own in the room that comes with the housekeeping post she was given at the care home in Kericho – I helped get it, you see, before I left".

They walked slowly together up to the main house. The trees were dripping, leaves still not really falling. It was dim and damp so that the 'courtesy' lights on the drive were reflected off the shiny tarmac. They passed a dark pond in the wood which looked like the slough of despond in the gloom.

The staircase to the North Attic rose from an opening in the panelling on the first floor gallery landing. It was a modern steel affair. It seemed out of keeping with the house. Miss Siddons trod with great care fearful of grazing her shins. Lights in the Attic came on automatically as Piers opened the substantial entrance door.

The North Attic was not just a cramped roof space. It was very large indeed. It extended the entire length of the house broken only by thick struts and trusses. The rafters ran up to the underside of the ridge at least 10ft above the deep floor joists. Piers extolled it as a minor masterpiece of carpentry. He explained that the timber was pine but straight grained and free of knots – he said it was Siberian pine. There was even a faint perfume of pine within the airless confines of the rafters.

Large plywood sheets had been laid on to the floor joists over half of the Attic's extent covering the lath and plaster ceilings below. Piers thought that they were in crude contrast to the magnificence of the structure. Upon them stood two metal black boxes on which 'MR RICHARD STRUTTE' had been painted in what originally would have been gold script. There was a trunk with 3 wooden semi circular bands bent around it. There were a number of framed paintings which appeared to be water colours. A few prints or etchings were stacked next to them.

Leaning against a massive timber roof strut was what was obviously a large gilded picture frame visible at its edges under a discoloured linen sheet. It could only be the Lawrence portrait. Piers carefully removed the sheet.

The portrait depicts a lady who has not quite reached the full glory of her beauty. The face is shown half facing turning to her left. She has a focused look of intent as if her glance was held for a moment on some fixed point. The lustrous dark brown hair is vigorously worked, parted and drawn back from the middle forehead, with a ribbon tied behind and under her chin. She has a generous top filling her low cut but full white blouse edged with a modest frill. Her figure is set off by a pink ribbon tied under her breasts. Her graceful neck is long and set off by a coral necklace clasped at the front. There is a powerful sense of presence emanating from the work.

Miss Siddons was disturbed and enchanted by the portrait. The frailty of earnest youth was so skilfully disclosed by the artist. The sitter had a guileless beauty which displaced any hint of the voluptuous. Lawrence – if it was he – had caught an instant of time with astonishing perception and power of execution. She was certain that she was beholding an image of her ancestor.

Piers sat down on the trunk as his Aunt stood quite still in quiet reflection. She sighed deeply turning to him.

"Ah yes – quite perfect. What passion must have stirred him to such a delicate but forceful work. Most moving. Thank you so much. I wonder that you haven't hung it in the drawing room or the library?"

"Oh I have no literal works of art – I mean those that depict what the eyes see. I suppose the claims of abstract forms that dominate architecture in my practice have taken hold of all my taste in paintings -not just paintings but, I suppose, all objects – after all where does art stop and utility begin?"

"Most interesting Piers. Yes – well…. most interesting"

And so it was arranged that Aunt Alice would go up with Piers to Sothebys in New Bond Street. Piers made the appointment with the head of British Pictures department. He booked a table at his Club just down across Piccadilly in St James's Street. He reassured her that it was just five minutes walk down Bond Street. If the portrait was a Lawrence this would justify celebration. If it was not then champagne would perhaps mask disappointment.

They were directed to the Sothebys St George Street entrance where they were shown into a small room whilst they waited for the expert – Mr Wynne.

"Ah yes, the Maria Siddons!" he said at once seeing the portrait now revealed resting against and easel on the floor as he entered. He had under his arm a large volume of what looked like a coffee table book of coloured prints which he put on a table against the wall opposite the door.

"I never look at a Lawrence without this Bible of his works – the last word" he said.

Mr Wynne with great care lifted the portrait on to the easel. It was like a school blackboard but used for display.

"We have seen this before – as you mentioned, I think, Mr Strutte. Some years ago now. Yes it definitely could have been executed by Lawrence. It must have been done – if it was done by him – before March 1798 as he stopped seeing her for good by then – when he broke his engagement, you know, before reverting his attentions to her sister Sally. He first fell for Sally you know and was then, it seems, overwhelmed for a while by Maria."

"Yes" said Mr Wynne looking meticulously all over the canvas "Yes indeed…It is very good isn't it. Very good indeed."

There was a long pause as Mr Wynne sat down with the portrait facing his gaze on the easel.

"You see we are very diffident about giving authenticity to portraits said to be by Lawrence. He was so popular in and for many years after his time – he died at the very end of the classical period a few years before Queen Victoria came to the throne. He was not only frequently copied but he was also imitated by very able artists producing most convincing works."

"In this case I see from our records that we were indeed disposed to credit it as a Lawrence. He was almost obsessed with the Siddons ladies – he did over twelve portraits of the girl's mother – she was of course the great Mrs Siddons the tragic actress - and it's most probable that his well known passion for each of the girls themselves – Maria and then Sally – would have impelled him to his easel. We know of course of at least two that he did of Maria. There is no reason at all to suppose it ended there."

"Please forgive me if I appear impertinent but how did this come into your possession? Provenance is so important you see. Have you acquired it since we last saw it? That would have been some 30 years ago. Unfortunately there's no note on the file as to ownership – you see we had to give it at our opinion that we did not think it was by Lawrence and it never came into our rooms to be offered for sale."

Piers turned to his Aunt. She was holding her bag on her knees looking at the portrait. She turned to the expert.

"On no, nothing like that. You see I am Miss Siddons. Mr Strutte here is my nephew. Mrs Siddons was my great great grandmother. It has been in the family ever since it left Lawrence's studio I believe."

"Well" said the expert "that is very interesting indeed – we know there exist a few Lawrences with no known home as it were. I did not realise this was a family piece. That is very good provenance indeed I have to say."

"You see, Mr Wynne, my aunt Miss Siddons has only just come back from Kenya" Piers explained. "It was my father who brought it in – Richard Strutte."

"Ah yes. I see. Well we do know that Lawrence had painted at least one complete portrait of Maria. There is also an unfinished work showing her in full face. He worked very quickly - he had a superlative gift and technical mastery of course."

"And another thing – I must tell you that there is a lovely – really enchanting – painting that he did of a gipsy girl. It was done in 1794 - it's in the Royal Academy. I mention it because the likeness of the gipsy girl to the Maria of the known portrait is unmistakable. You see on that basis there is good reason to think that it's Maria when she was just 15 – exactly the age depicted for the Gipsy Girl. The expression and form of the face are as in the later portrait."

"But Mr Wynne" said Piers "you seem to think it is likely that this is a Lawrence".

"We actually did think it was when it first came in. It was such a fine example and the subject took it to a higher level than many of his portraits – the Siddons sisters you know – the scandal – the celebrated mother and so on."

"Well, so far as I can tell from the notes at the time, Professor Curry was of the opinion that the coral necklace gave it away as a very good original work of another artist – done not long after Lawrence died. You see the coral necklace was used by Lawrence in his famous Tate Gallery portrait of Mrs Siddons which he started in 1803. And I think it is also to be seen in the National Gallery portrait of Emily Lamb – also done that year. But the necklace doesn't appear in any earlier portrait as far as is known. What Professor Curry advised was that whilst in every other respect all the pointers were to Lawrence his conclusion was that the coral necklace was added by the artist to give the work authenticity – the connection with Mrs Siddons, you see. We think that Lawrence himself did have a coral necklace at some time as a studio prop and used it to give emphasis to the delicacy of the neck and enabling him to raise the head over the shoulders a fraction further then strict perception allowed. But it does not appear in his work until 1803 as far as we can tell."

"Such a small detail Mr Wynne" protested Piers "surely that can't be enough to displace your original conclusion – before you asked Professor Curry?"

"Oh but you see Mr Strutte it's just such small details that the artist thought would be overlooked. That's why he inserted the necklace. But why is it that Lawrence appears to have used the necklace as an enhancement of his portraits twice in one year but never before – if he regarded it as such an aid to excellence? We simply couldn't risk our reputation by a clear statement of authenticity. Lawrence portraits of beautiful or famous ladies are highly sought after – very few ever come on the market. An attributed work would, I fear, be a mere fraction of the value of a true original."

He paused, allowing his opinion to settle in the minds of Miss Siddons and her nephew.

"You see if it was indeed by Lawrence we would certainly recommend a reserve of £1.25 million perhaps a little more – the provenance is really so good and the Siddons connection as well. As it is, well you could perhaps expect around £5,000."

It was obvious that the judgment of Sothebys was final. Any appeal to higher authority had been foreclosed by the opinion of Professor Curry.

Piers got up to thank Mr Wynne who arranged for a porter to wrap the portrait with a carrying handle. They walked down to Piccadilly and on down St James's Street. The Club hall porter took the portrait. There was a smokeless coal fire burning in the hall. Miss Siddons found it welcoming and gracious. All was so restrained and quiet.

Nothing had changed for Piers. He had been sure that Sothebys would not alter their opinion. His concern was that Aunt Alice should not be too dismayed. He feared that she would feel as if she had lost a decisive battle to preserve her independence. So many elderly slipped from there down upon the slope of final decline. How could he help. She would never accept any form of allowance if he offered that.

He ordered a half bottle of champagne. That would permit some gaiety perhaps. With his second glass he was struck with what seemed a most elegant solution. It would arrest a slide into despondency and resignation of his aunt and she would not realise it was fictitious. He found himself proposing that, whilst he was dealing with the delays and complexities of applying for her State pension, he would see that she was paid the amount due to her – he assured her that there would be a payment of arrears from the time she had become entitled so he could recover it all then.

Miss Siddons seemed to be quite stoic about it all. She had determined to think only of getting through the winter. With Millie coming over she would not have to endure those dark evenings alone. Perhaps Piers and Jane could help her find work baby sitting and teaching the very young.

She had not for a moment thought that she might be entitled to a pension. It was very good of Piers and Jane to take this up with the authorities. It would help very much with Millie. And having Millie would lift some of the burden of her care from their shoulders. Also the portrait would fetch something after all – Sothebys had thought about £5,000. Piers seemed so concerned about how disappointed he thought she must have been about the portrait. So what she would do was to accept Piers generous offer and repay him if he was out of pocket when pension actually came in.

"My dear Piers – that is most kind. Are you sure about that? Really. Thank you so much – really very kind. But only if you are sure you can recover all that you spend from my pension arrears. You are quite sure about that?"

Piers raised his glass "Quite sure. To the Siddons sisters -past and present!"

*　*　*

The care home in Kericho put his call through to Millie in the day room. She was told it was a call from England and spoke loudly to make herself heard. After a while she got used to it and ceased to bellow. The news of Miss Alice and the cottage in England brought her to the edge of tears. She felt a sudden deep sense of relief and joy as if she had found a precious thing that she had lost. Warmth and relief overcame her. She stuttered with disbelief. She did not understand all that Piers was saying.

She found it difficult to utter anything when asked if she would like to come in time for Christmas.

Piers said it over again so that each word could register in her mind "To be with Miss Alice in her cottage in time for Christmas". Christmas again with Miss Alice – and in a cottage in England. She heard him say he would send to the Care Home all the tickets and money for the journey. He would arrange for the taxis and would be there with Miss Alice when she arrived at the airport in London.

He said it was just as Miss Alice had done. Millie wiped her eyes as she tried to explain to the Matron of the ward. Miss Alice again. God be praised.

Millie appeared in the Arrivals hall at Heathrow like a fishing smack coming into port with a billowing sail. She was blessed with generosity in her form as well as spirit. The large plastic shopping bag and a brown parcel she bore seemed bent on escape as she clutched them in one hand and then the other while she pulled at the loose, brilliantly coloured African garments that fell over her worn trainers causing her to progress in trips and jerks across the shiny squeaking marble floor.

"Miss Alice, Miss Alice. Am here Miss Alice! Am here!" she boomed with relief and delight. She set sail towards them, her bow wave parting the crowded hall. Piers stood in front of his aunt like a mooring fender awaiting the crush of a ferry boat.

Miss Siddons' pleasure at seeing her dear Millie was concealed by the folds of garment, arms, bag, parcel and ample bosom that enveloped her.

It was impossible for Piers not to be feel uplifted by the evident joy of his diminutive aunt and the jubilant, bulging Millie. Moving because so strange.

"Now Millie is this all you have?" said Piers "just this?". "Yes Mister Piers – and the parcel here".

"Well we can get anything you need in Crawley – Muriel can run you both over tomorrow, if you'd like, once you have settled in – don't you agree Aunt Alice?"

"Oh quite – yes indeed. So kind."

A certain continuity of life returned to Miss Siddons with the arrival of Millie. She had always been discreet and respectful – as was expected of her in those times when the Queen's head was still on the postage stamps. It was as if they each reminded the other of what had once been so familiar at home - relics of a past existence now slowly receding in memory.

Gradually a ritual of life evolved for them both at the cottage so that the days passed easily and scarcely noticed.

When Millie first arrived she spoke about Kericho at times. But she saw that Miss Alice found this unsettling. After a while neither spoke of those days unless Miss Alice mentioned them. It was as if she had suffered a bereavement. Thus it was that a dam arose to hold back the vague and deepening sense of sorrow that slowly began to overwhelm Miss Siddons. For it was the very presence of Millie that brought daily to her mind those days in the distance enchanted.

*　*　*

It was on Boxing day that Miss Siddons found Millie's parcel.

Millie had left it on the table in the sitting room. Miss Siddon found it when she got back from her lunch at the house with Piers, Jane and a few friends. She picked it up as Millie came in, stumbling a little, roused from her afternoon rest.

"Oh Miss Alice – I bring 'em back". "I leave 'em under the bed with my bag - forgot about 'em you see. I couldn' sell 'em Miss Alice. No, no I couldn'".

"They're Miss Hermione's. S'not for me to sell Miss Hermione's things –couldn' – like it was stealin' and she looking all the time at me – no Miss Alice so I just kep 'em in the parcel for to give you when you come back one day."

"What things Millie – what are you saying? Giving me things from Miss Hermione?"

"But Miss Alice I did'n take em I just kep em….."

"Oh Millie – yes of course. I remember now. Oh yes. But of course. But dear Millie - you should have sold them. Hermione would've wanted it. It was all we could give you, dear Millie. So little for all that you did for us. It was for you to put something under the bed for rainy days when we were gone. You should've sold them."

"No Miss Alice – you mus' take 'em – they're not mine – Miss Alice – no."

Millie seemed relieved to put the parcel on to Miss Siddons lap. As if she had owned up to some default and had wiped the slate clean once more.

"Well dear Millie if you will not take them."

"Miss Alice can you see 'em on my thick neck?. They no go round at all. I don' go out 'cept for the shops an' that would make me silly - me in jewllry an' shopping. An I don' need anything now am with you again".

"I put the kettle on now Miss Alice. Time for your tea".

She stumped into the little kitchen.

Miss Siddons began to pick at the knot of the string that held the brown paper. It fell away. She saw that it had covered a cardboard box which had once been filled with swabs – from the care home she supposed. It had Sellotape round it which peeled off quite easily.

Inside it was a much distressed long thin box of faded and mottled leather. There was also a small gold chain and two pearl like necklaces she remembered Hermione wearing.

They appeared to her as pathetic remnants of a long life.

She looked out on to the empty darkening yard. A kind of desolation descended on her as she reflected that she could not effect even such a token provision for Millie.

The kitchen clatter drew her back into the room. Millie would be bringing in the tea tray and would need the table.

Hurriedly seeking escape from her thoughts she pulled out the faded worn box and released its little hook. She raised the lid. Inside was her sister's necklace. It was longer than she had imagined. It rested on a cream velvet bed, now discoloured. There was quite an elaborate clasp. It had an oval label on the underside of the top but the writing had become indistinct.

Hermione had never worn it. It was like a lock of hair – just an object from another age. A testament to a former life long gone. Miss Siddons doubted if it had been ever been taken out since their father had died.

She tried to close the lid but could not close the box. The hook was caught on the underside of the velvet bed. She saw that something underneath the velvet bed was catching the hook. She found that that the bed itself was loose.

It came off quite easily to reveal underneath a folded yellow paper. It had three folds.

It was a yellowed receipted Bill of Sale. It read:

> *Messrs Hennells, New Bond Street, London*
>
> *Thomas Lawrence Esquire   Date: 12th September 1797*
>
> *57 Greek Street*
>
> *Soho.*
>
> *To our charges incurred in   12 Guas*
>
> *connection with making necklass*
>
> *of warm water Coral and clasp.*
>
> *Reciept gratefully acknowledged*

Miss Siddons became quite still.

In an instant – immeasurable in time – the dismal thoughts, recollections of the past, dread of the future, the long passage of the years, what had gone, what was yet to come, the banishment from home, the futility of hope – all receded and then were gone. It was as if she was suspended in celestial calm.

Of a certainty it came to her that all was well – all would be well.

THE BOTTOM LINE

The shop was on the corner of Brownlow Street and the Whalley Road to the south west of the town. It had a little garden at the back – larger than next door's but not much larger. Its great amenity was the lock up long shed at the bottom of the garden, reached from Brownlow Street.

The town itself lies in the valley of the River Ribble. It has some historic structures including a small Norman Castle. There are a number of Victorian stone buildings in its main street, three stone churches, many chapels and a few simple early 19th century buildings. It has an ancient and excellent Royal Grammar School. Until 1968 it had a considerable and dominant gasworks by the railway station. Nothing about the town could fairly claim national distinction. Its outlying shops and houses are at best modest and multiplying.

But for those who seek happiness in places– if that is even possible – there can surely be no better sanctuary than Clitheroe and the villages that it serves with its limited but sufficient services. For national statistics show that of all those who live in England none are happier than those those who live in the Ribble Valley of which Clitheroe is the centre.

The inhabitants of the small hamlets of the Forest of Bowland, through which flows the sublime Hodder River, would claim, rather, that heaven lies within its valley. After all, does not the River Ribble course down for 40 miles so determined is it to share the beauties of the Hodder by their union just to the south of Cromwells Bridge? You have as good a chance of finding the rainbow's end in Bashall Eaves (not a roof) or Bashall Town (not a town) or Cow Ark (neither of them) than in any other place in England on which the Sun's rays fall.

The Forest of Bowland was before the War, at the time this story opens– and remains today– of such natural beauty as to put it beyond the reach of description or comparison. The peaks and lakes of Cumbria and Wales have imposing scenes of natural beauty but none surpass the Forest of Bowland for simple loveliness. It lies immediately to the north west of Clitheroe. To the east is majestic Pendle Hill whose graceful slopes release countless streams and rills into the Calder River, Sabden Brook and Pendle Water.

The town is beyond the immediate reach of Blackburn, Preston and Burnley. Yet it is just over an hour by bicycle from the Whalley Road shop to Whitewell, lying below Hall Hill, where the Hodder perfects a graceful flowing turn under towering beech trees before slipping easily into a slow deep glide to reach long fast runs between narrowing steep sides thickly forested with beech and ash.

Prosperity and change have wrought changes to Clitheroe since June 30 1943 when Stanley entered the world in the Coplow View Public Assistance Infirmary. There are now many thousands who find such solace and rest in the town as their free time allows but the flows of visitors have not disrupted its essential character. It has stumbled reluctantly into the modern age but remains ancient in its appeal, traditions and spirit lying as it does in the lap of heaven.

* * *

The shop was essential to the life of those who lived in the Whalley Road and its side streets. People would also come from the other side of the town and nearby villages. For in the 1940s and 1950s expectations of comfort, convenience and ease of living were very different to those prevailing today. Mains electricity was a prized amenity and there was a still large minority of householders whose homes were denied it.

Things that were of utility were conserved as if they were stores of wealth – which indeed they were to many. Waste was worse than blasphemy to those who had weathered the storms of War and of want since birth.

It was with gratitude and wonder that the Whalley Road received the advent of the age of electrical domestic goods in the mid 1950s. Table lamps, wireless sets, vacuum suction cleaners, refrigerators, cookers, bar heaters, toasters and kettles began to lighten daily toil. War time rationing – itself the cause of the shortages it was intended to relieve – had just ceased and the light of optimism that illuminated the Festival of Britain cast its rays as far as the Whalley Road and beyond. When the good people of Clitheroe, in Church or Chapel, thanked their Lord for his blessings they did so with them evident in their very homes.

So it was that when Stan sat down to his 6th birthday tea and treat, life in Clitheroe for his father and mother was better than they could remember it ever being. His father Will had started work in his father's bicycle and electrical goods shop on the corner of Brownlow Street at the time of the closing of the Workhouse. That was in 1930. Will used to say he started work when the others had packed it in. It was turned into the Infirmary.

Will's widowed father had only just died so there was a room for Stan at the front of the house. Gertie, Stan's mother, had a little room at the back for sewing and ironing. She had a linen covered model for dressmaking. The room was opposite the bathroom. That was so small it was as if the walls had been erected around the enamelled bath and cast iron lavatory cistern. Like the sewing room, its door had to open onto the passage. Will and Alice had the room facing Whalley Road. - opposite Stan.

There was a sash window in the each of the end of the passage walls looking over Whalley Road and also above the stairs looking over the back garden. They had little squares in each corner of ruby coloured glass into which had been etched a delicate star like frosted shapes. The window at the back came down lower, to just above the half landing on the staircase. It had coloured squares in the corners of the middle rail as well.

The front door led directly into the shop. At the back of the shop was the kitchen and a lean-to addition for the scullery, open to the kitchen. There was a back door under the stairs which opened on to the garden and path to the large shed. The back door had etched plain glass for most of its height with the same little squares of coloured star patterned glass in each corner – only these were sapphire blue. Stan liked the blue stars that the sunlight cast on to the distempered cream wall below the under side of the stair treads. The staircase run up at the back of the house with a dog leg half way up.

The shop was called Whalectrics. It suggested some automotive leviathan of the deep but Will would not change it. He had thought rather good when he took over. Whalley and Electric.

"After all's said and done your E.K. Cole called 'is shop EKCO and he's done all right han'ty" was one of Will's retorts when chided about the name. He would insist that the banter and chat it seemed to promote was good for business so why change it.

"What's wrong wi' bringing a smile on when thinking of coming to the shop I'd like to know "You're not yer name after all." he used to say when Gertie started to pick at that scab. "What's in a name that's what I say. What's in a name if it brings in trade!"

Whalectrics had mains electricity and company mains water. It also had gas from the Corporation Gas Department, once the Clitheroe Gas Light Company, about to become the abstraction called the North West Gas Board.

The glory of the site was the shed.

It abutted the pavement in Brownlow Street. It was wide enough for a large wagon for which it had originally been constructed. It ran the length of the garden's south boundary and at its west end it formed the boundary in line with the fence by the next door garden. It was made of wide overlapping planks of pine as could be seen on the inside. The outside had been doused in creosote over many years and was completely black. Its walls were much higher than a man, with gables and a roof now covered in black painted corrugated metal sheets laid on to felt which over the years had perished save just under the rafters.

There was a floor, half way along under the rafters, reached by a ladder which had to be fitted into a recess made for it. Along the top under the slightly projecting roof sheets was a line of windows - both sides. They had hinges at the top but were never seen open. Years of dust grime and labour had rendered dim what light could penetrate the panes.

The floor area was generous. It was enough for three benches on one side and racks of drawers and shelves above benches on the other. Towards the back stood engineering lathe, grinder, pillar drill and other machinery of the pre-war period but of great quality and endurance.

On the upper half-floor were the relics of Stan's grandfather's business. What could seen from below were bicycle wheels and frames stacked chaotically. A pile of spoked and tyreless wheels had spread themselves over the planked floor with sundry items including hurricane lamps, large glass jars, and a large stuffed pike in a case beginning to lose its bowed glass front.

The principal objects were the large carboys of sulphuric acid in wire frames packed with straw round their bulbous glass bodies. They were deemed to be too hazardous for storage on the ground. These were stacked along one side of the shed half floor. Beneath the joists below were struts bearing down on to the upright posts that carried the roof.

Below them on a long bench stood rows of Exide, Cossor or Oldham Accumulators. At that time, without mains electricity, the way in which the valves of the wireless sets were heated was with a low voltage accumulator – only 2 volts. There also had to be a high tension dry battery to provide low current but high voltage supply for the actual set. The accumulators had thick square glass containers about 1ft high and 6" wide. They were filled with diluted sulphuric acid for the electrolyte and had heavy lead diodes. They normally were taken to Whalectric for re-charging once a week. The names of the owners were painted on the side. They had wires from their terminals carrying the slow flow of power from the round pin power sockets fixed along a panel which was bolted above them to the shed wall. Above the power sockets was a rack on which were the HT batteries for the wireless sets. These lasted for months but then expired and could not be resurrected.

The shop itself was what is today described a "service industry". It is curious how so often the root original meaning of a term has so recently been lost to common use. The Cambridge dictionary defines 'industry' as *"activities involved in the process of producing goods for sale especially in a factory or special area"*. If you look at the Latin root it is *"industria"* and that means *'diligence, activity and zeal'*.

The enterprise of Whaletric was of service. It would not be stretching meaning to describe it as a communal benefit. To the Whaletric shop came those with wireless sets to charge or new valves to fit, fire filaments to replace, irons which would not heat, kettles that would not boil, motor bike and car batteries that were flat and toasters which would not come on or even worse would not turn off. And it was from the shop that Will bicycled to repair and fit parts to refrigerators, electric stoves, fires, fuse boxes and household circuits and new fangled twin tub washing machines. No one had dish washers –not in the Whalley Road.

No money value could be attached to the gratitude of his customers for these small acts of diligence and zeal. The attentive care Will gave to the repair and mending of these valued objects was a gift to those who brought them to his shop or called him out to their homes. Their thanks evoked in him an underlying benign sense of goodwill. Strange it is to set down, but these small exchanges, though gruff and bluntly expressed, were of humour, benevolence and mutual regard. Coins and sometimes notes were laid upon the mahogany counter but the true experience was otherwise.

'Bloody nonsense' he would have said if he or anyone had tried to express it.

* * *

Stan went to St James C of E primary school when he was five. It was first left up the Whalley Road so it was only a 3 minute walk. After the first few days he ran up there on his own. He knew everyone in the houses he passed.

It was on his 6th birthday that there opened for Stan a door to the grown up world.

Will announced at breakfast that he had bought a second hand pram and was converting it so that it could easily be pushed by Stan. As he explained, it had good springs but the handles were too high. He was replacing these. Stan was to use it to collect Accumulators from customers who did not have mains electricity and bring them in for charging in Will's shed, taking back re-charged ones to the customers. He could keep 2d of the shilling that Will asked for re-charging, collection and delivery. There was still a good demand for recharging and topping up of acid in the accumulators used for the valves of wireless sets that brought the world into many Clitheroe homes, Music While You Work for mothers and Dick Barton Special Agent for children.

"And on Tuesday and Friday you can get on up to the gas works, lad, when you've done and bring back the coke for the fires. It's a short trip down t' station yard. There's another 2d for you when you get back – but mind! Filled right up now!"

Looking back over his early life Stan would say that the years spent in his father's workshop, before he entered the Royal Grammar School, were great days spent as if in the distance enchanted. The intense silent pride in helping his father merged with his astonished discovery of unimaginable things about electricity – a magic unseen force in tiny dots called atoms. How could things so small be so powerful. With a simple switch you could admit the force of the universe into your bed side light. How was it that what could not be seen made seeing possible?

Then there were the immense carboys of the sulphuric acid. What would that do to you if it got on your face or hands. A boy in his class had told him he had read in the Eagle comic of a gangster who had caught his foot in the straw of an acid carboy when running out of a warehouse for the getaway – in falling the acid took all the skin of the side of his face. The carboys seemed to be waiting like bottled demons in the dark recesses of the roof threatening him with unspeakable horrors. He did not look up there for long.

Then one Sunday lunch time, when Stan was ten – just before his 11 plus – Will said that after Stan had done the washing of the dishes and after he himself had had a rest, he would show Stan something he had been working on in the shed.

On the far end bench stood a contraption of sorts. With the overhead fluorescent light it could be seen that it had two glass plates close together with metal slips stuck on them. On each side there were two arms opposite each other attached to fixed horizontal rods. The arms had little brushes on the end resting on the metal slips. There were two vertical rods with round metal balls on the top. These rods were connected at the bottom to what looked like two glass jam jars. The balls were at least 6" apart. There was a large wheel with pulleys so that, when turned, one glass disc when round one way and the other went round the other way.

"It's for making electricity that is lad" said Will. "Turn the wheel and see what happens. Gu on lad it won't bite you!"

Stan put his hand on the handle of the wheel.

"Gu on lad – wass the matter wi thee! Have a go. You'll like it or I would'nt 'ave made it for thee"

Stan tried to turn the wheel. It needed more strength than he expected. With two hands he was determined to revolve the glass discs. Immediately an intense blue white spark leaped across the gap between the round balls. The spark flew across repeatedly for as long as he turned the wheel. It made a 'crack' each time. Stan was entranced. It was beautiful and also incredible. A spark from an endless and unseen store of power and light.

"That there's an induction electrostatic generator that is" said Will in measured tones. It takes electrons off the atoms or summat' like that. That there's 70,000 volts lad. The pressure of the power it is. Marvellous in'tit. Bloody amazing is that. Nature you see my lad. Nature."

It was the Wimshurst machine.

Stan stood quietly looking at it, his hand resting on the wheel. With just one turn of the handle there would appear immediately before him a power and beauty otherwise invisible. With almost fearful respect he regarded the contraption that drew on forces far beyond the reach of imagination.

When in later years he reflected on his journey from the Whalley Road into life he saw that it was the Sunday afternoon in the shed with his father and his Wimshurst contraption that had set his course.

* * *

Shortly after Stan's tenth birthday, after the Queen's Coronation, Miss Jane Jeffs, the Headmistress of St James primary, called in on Will and Gertie. It was about Stan she said. She explained that she was not sure what they were both thinking about Stan's secondary school.

They all sat down round the simple kitchen table – It was tight in the kitchen with the gas cooker and the new fridge. Will got up and pulled table and chairs noisily over the red quarry tiles back into the scullery to give more room. He turned off the dripping tap and sat down close to Gertie. Stan was in the shed his head over a bench.

"Well the lad's very bright in't he Gertie" said Will loudly while turning towards her.

"I c'dn't do without him at times in the shed. He's that good at soldering and making simple circuits as well as run of the mill repairs and such like".

After a brief silence,

"Well Gertie and I were thinking of some technical school or other to bring him on so he can start with me full time– it's a lot for me on my own as it is"

"Well" said Miss Jeffs "He is really an exceptional kid"

She paused, looking at the table top as if realising the importance of the moment. She noticed Will taking Gertie's hand. A car door slammed in Brownlow Road. There was quiet.

"He's small and he's reserved like" said Miss Jeffs. "Doesn't push himself forward you see. But he always gets in the top two or three when we mark our little tests – not for the kids mind, just for ourselves. He can work out sums in his head. He got hold of multiplication and division quite soon after he came to us. He has such an imagination – like he lives in his head. And he's so good with his hands – I mean making simple toys and the like - and his drawing – well you have seen what he can do" she said, looking up at the pictures stuck on the board on one of the scullery walls.

"Well we are that pleased with how he's making out" said Gertie. It's good of you to take such trouble coming over to shop like this – isn't that right Will?"

"It is that"

"You see" continued Miss Jeffs diffidently "we think he would pass the exam for entry into the Royal Grammar School. It's getting so much harder for kids of working folk to get in there now. What with the growing numbers the standards have got so high that more and more it's middle class folk who are getting the places from outside the town from up the Ribble valley."

Will turned to Gertie. They looked in silence at each other until Gertie sighed and, smiling, slowly nodded her head as it to acknowledge what they both realised.

"Well Gertie and me want what's best for the lad don't we lass and he's that bright he'll surprise us all I'll be bound."

Miss Jeffs' enthusiasm lit up her face. "You couldn't find a better school than RGS. It's one of the best in all the country and older than most schools – 250 years before public school Stonyhurst just down the road, would you believe it. And here in little Clitheroe – what a thing eh! Yes what a thing."

Then, as if to warn them both, she added softly "He's a little lad mind. He could be picked on – it does sometimes happen in big school. But if he can't get in then no one should."

"He's a half pint yer right a' that" retorted Will. "But he's that tough I tell you. He can take six of them lead filled Accumulators in his pram and bring back a hundred weight of coke and then go back for more if wanted – and he won't think anything of it will he Gertie?"

"No that's Stan all right. He'll not be put down by owt" added Gertie.

Miss Jeffs appeared to be delighted.

Gertie and Will bought Stan a new Raleigh bicycle – at trade discount - when they heard that he had been awarded a place at the RGS. It was deep green with gold lines on the frame. It had three Sturmey Archer gears and shallow drop handles shining with chrome. Will dropped the seat right down.

* * *

On a Sunday in May of his last summer at St James little school Will took Stan into the shed. He said he had something he had been waiting to show him when the time was right for it. Getting down the ladder from the half floor he had with him an aluminium tube, a canvas bag with long shoulder strap and a rucksack.

He placed them most carefully on the large bench beyond the accumulators and batteries. The tube had a screw cap. Taking it off he shook the tube to release a khaki coloured sleeve containing what looked to be long sticks in sleeves. From these Will gently withdrew the two parts of a split can fly fishing rod. It stood just higher than a foot above Will when assembled. It had little rings of tied silk every few inches and glass edged ringlets that ran down to the shaped cork handle. Its shining varnish caught the light from the table lamp as he laid it full length on the bench.

"There my lad. What do you think of that! Beautiful that is. Beautiful my lad. Got in the sale at the big house in Downham years ago. It's a Hardy Perfection Palakona Fly Rod. The finest ever made." Will fitted the two lengths together holding the cork handle and pointing the rod tip up above the half floor. He whipped it backwards a little so that it flexed down its full length with a slight whisper.

"I'm going down to river now and you're coming with me. This is one of the great things of life lad – it is that and no mistake. You're old enough and canny so you're in for a treat my lad you are that".

"We'll walk down to Edisford Bridge on the Ribble – it's just through Eshton Terrace and Thorn Street opposite and then 15 minutes down the Edisford Road. Not so good as the Upper Calder but you'd need your bike for that".

They started out through the double doors of the shed into Brownlow Street.

"Yes this evening you'll come back with the gift of a lifetime young man. You'll 'ave cast your first fly on moving waters and see it float upon their skin"

As they walked together down the Edisford Road, Stan very proud to be carrying the fishing bag over his shoulder, Will began his fisherman's tale.

"This is not about catching fish yer see, or for getting a meal or for showing how much better at it you are than other folk nor anything else like that lad.

No, no, nothing at all like that. The secret's finding a way into Nature without making her disappear you see."

It seemed to Stan that his father was speaking a foreigner's language. It made no sense at all to him. He did not dare utter anything.

"What I found when my Dad first showed me how to fish was that I c'dn't think of anything else but getting one on the bank and then another and another. It was always the next one and the next one and the next cast. Sometimes by the time I'd finished the day I'd have far more than Dad and Nan could eat in a week. It was so easy using worms and maggots. You did'nt need to wade or get tangled casting artificial flies. I mean why would you bother lad – no point! That's 'ow it seemed to me."

"But then one day I met a man sitting on the bank with a little fly rod. He seemed really very old to me as young snapper. He had an ancient tweed jacket which was torn in so many places you would'nt believe it. You see, he kept his favourite flies hooked into it - his jacket, see - so when he was wading he could get at 'em easily when he needed a new one to match the different flies rising off the water."

"He was sitting on the path in my way along the river. But it di'nt seem right to ask him to move. I just walked round him next to the river. I asked if he was having any luck."

'Oh yes' he said 'it's very good this evening. Lots of fly life. Trout rising everywhere. Had a lot take my olive duns before I had to put on the black gnat as the sun lowered. Lovely evening isn't it – perfect in every way'

So I says to him 'That's good – should be OK for me further down should'nt it?'

'Oh yes I'm sure'

I saw then that he di'nt have a net and then I noticed that he had no fish at all on the bank.

'Where are your fish?' I said to 'im.

'Oh they're in the river. I don't use a net you see.'

'Well how d'you land them then'

'Ah that. Well I don't often do that. What I do is cut off the barbs from the little hooks and so when I get the fish by the side of the bank I bring the tip of the rod down to its mouth and give a quick push. The hook just pops out you see. Don't take the fish out of the water at all you see.'

After a bit this old man looked up at me. He started to say to me 'I have found over the years – I first fished this stretch before the Great War you know.....'

He had turned his head upstream where a trout had risen noisily flailing at a Mayfly.

'What was I saying.. Dear me.........Oh yes What I found, you see, was that the more I wanted to get fish the less I was with Nature. I could not find a way to be part of her beauty and also grasp for her rewards. So after a long life I now use fishing as a kind of excuse for just being here.'

"Well lad I was not sure at all what he was meaning like. Never forgot it. And now - well I still can't explain it".

"Some things you can't".

* * *

Stan could not start at RGS until the summer term – the parents of a boy were taking him to Germany on his father's posting to BAOR in March and that would make the place available.

He was 12 years old and 10 months when Stan with his father walked down Queensway and Waterloo Road to York Street to enter the Clitheroe Royal Grammar School for the first time.

The RGS was founded in Bloody Mary's reign but it expanded and its buildings were extended in the Victorian Age.

It had always been a strict school founded on the principle that discipline was essential to learning. The 19th century fostered notions of hierarchy and subjection of inferiors to the will of superiors as part of the culture of the age. No less than Rugby School the RGS had applied Victorian discipline and turned its eyes from excesses committed by its senior pupils on new or troublesome underlings, unless under the very eyes of a master.

Each such school it seemed had its Flashman.

Such traditions had not altogether been abandoned when in May 1956 Stan sat down on his first half holiday to watch the RGS cricket 1st XI play the Stonyhurst 2nd XI.

It was a simple ground. There was no pavilion. The score board was a class room blackboard. There were no seats around the boundary. On one side there was a modest stand with a series of benches rising in 3 levels so that the top gave the best view of the game. The view from the lowest bench was frequently obscured by spectators and passing visitors. The benches were thin and long years of wear had raised up splinters. Only the boys used them.

Stan's class broke earlier than the VIth form. The match had started at 11.00. Stan took one of the spare places on the top bench with an hour to go before lunch.

Shortly after he had sat down the boy next to him, much older but kindly, spoke quietly in his ear

"You're a new bug aren't you – you must be as you wouldn't sit here – these here are for the upper school - fifth and sixth formers – you can tell who they are as they're allowed to wear their jackets without buttons done up. Watch out for Breedsley. If I were you I'd get down while you can…"

His advice could not be concluded. Bursting upon them from below came a bellow from below, so loud that the umpires turned to see what had disturbed play.

"You – yes you" the large boy and obviously senior boy yelled pointing an arm and thick finger up at Stan.

"Coomdownere! – Coomdownere! - Now!"

Stan felt rising panic seize him, wanting to flee but fearful of the height of the fall to the ground. Nor would it assure him of his escape.

Awkwardly, under the eyes of the boys who had now filled the remaining spaces on the benches, he picked his way down the rows until he was on the bottom bench. As he was stepping down a large hand seized the collar of his new school blazer and wrenched him off his legs from the bench so that he fell on to the cinder path in front of the stand. His face was grazed as the large and furious boy dragged him by the legs away from the benches.

Then

"Get up – I said get up - NOW!.

Stan felt the blood beginning to creep down his cheek, salty on his lips.

"Look at me you little runt. Look! My name is BREEDSLY. Spelt BREADSLY What is it?"

"Breedsly"

"Louder"

Again

"BREEDSLY".

"You don't speak to me unless I speak to you. What's your name?

Stan told him.

"Well you miserable little half pint I'll warm your bottom well enough if I get any lip from you. You're just small fry. That there bench at the top is for Seniors. Not for the likes of you. Next year I'll be Head of School and I'll have the Head Boy's Malacca Cane. I warn you little squit - from now on you keep out of my way – or I'll heat your arse like you'll never forget – that I will."

The bully boy pushed him away, the two boys with him sniggering in support.

* * *

Gertie was shocked to see Stan's bloody grazes. She took him to the scullery, sitting him on a chair before the sink. The iodine pricked him sharply as she dabbed the injuries. She made a cup of sweet Typhoo which Stan sipped as she fried slices of thick white bread and two eggs. Stan was finishing toast and chocolate spread as Will came in and sat down for his tea.

"Now then – what's all this with yer face lad?" he said quietly.

Stan looked down at his plate.

"I just slipped on the path round the cricket field, Dad. It's got cinders all over it. So my face got it!"

Will looked up at Gertie. She shook her head very slowly.

"Eh lad. Listen carefully now. You're right brave. What's more you're not going to tell and I'm not be making thee even if I could."

Stan looked up. In his father's quiet grey eyes Stan could see that the tissue of his words had not concealed the sharp and shaming reality behind.

Gertie put the teapot in front of Stan. The sound of pouring of the tea seemed friendly – almost comforting. Will sipped his cup of tea between blowing on it. He put it down in the saucer very slowly and then looked at Stan.

"There's a good story I must tell thee. I heard it from my Nan when I were about your age"

"She said to me that the huge Giant strikes terror in you when you see him up there on the hill. But as you take the first steps and keep your eyes down on the path right there in front of you that leads up the hill you can't see the booger. And when you do 'appen to look up he's got smaller. So you keep going and every time you look he's even smaller . When you are almost at the top you look up and by 'ec the booger's gone."

Will turned to take a noisy sip and put down his cup missing the saucer with a clatter. Gertie quietly took Stan's cup and plate and turned on the sink taps.

* * *

It was Stan's name that the big bully would pick on when taunting him.

"Why's yer bottom cold yer shrimp" "Blue Arse!" "Frosty Fart" "Icybum" and the like. Puerile but irritating. Vicious for any defenceless boy. With the dulling effect of repetition by the end of the first year - with no effect or response from Stan - the big bully Breadsly realised that it was no longer funny for his followers nor did it seem to bother Stan – he seemed to relish the taunts. There were occasional attempted wounds and slights but the malice was only faint and Stan's retorts became more cutting. He accepted it now as fact that his name would always invite ridicule.

There was one final outburst, however, in early April 1958, the Easter term before Breadsly's last Summer term.

It was on the half holiday in the week before end of term. Having had his lunch Stan had taken his bicycle out of the cycle sheds to get down to the river with the short rod he used for pike just above Edisford bridge. As he rode over the yard to York Street past the old school house the large form of Breadsly and two others suddenly came out of its side door immediately in front of him. Collision was inevitable. Stan skidded into the two boys but they absorbed the shock without falling. The big bully was unscathed but incandescent. Raising his Malacca Cane he advanced on Stan.

"You bloody little half pint. I told you never to get in my way."

Breadsly was repulsed for a moment when Stan yelled at him

"You bloody Breadloaf. I'm growing - but you can't stop can you - you Fat Fart."

Stan shot out into York Street just as the cane descended. He could hear the big bully's fading call as he gathered speed on his way down to the river.

"We'll get you, see if we don't"

Stan fished the stretch of the Ribble half a mile above the bridge casting upstream with a devon minnow spinner so that it covered the deep water close below the opposite bank. He worked his way down the river with careful precise casts each falling just within the water's edge.

Towards the evening he hooked what he thought must have been a good pike but it did not show itself before the cast broke. He had no fishing tackle bag with him so made his way slowly down the bank looking at the swims of the river where fish might lie.

He had left his Raleigh just down the side of the stone bridge.

It was gone.

Leaning over one of the stone recesses on the bridge Stan could just glimpse the chrome of the handle bars - a dull peat colour in the depths caught by late afternoon sunlight.

* * *

Breadsly's last term began on 10 May 1958.

Stan devoted his Easter holiday in April that year to perfecting a device which would bring down upon his tormentor the ridicule of 300 boys and scandalise the Governors.

He was 14 years old.

As it revealed *'diligence, activity and zeal'* some account of Stan's settlement of scores deserves to be given.

He procured two large syringes of the type used in the RGS laboratories for experiments. They came with clear flexible plastic tubes that could be fitted to one end. He took two battery operated small electric motors from the shop's stock and converted the rotary motion to oscillating motion by winding a stiff wire round the rotor and fixing the motor to a base board with the new wonder Araldite two part epoxy resin glue. The wire from the rotor was extended and then bent at right angles and again at the end to fit into a hole at the end of the piston rod in the syringe so that when the rotor turned the syringe took in air and on the return cycle expelled it. The length of the extension of the wire gave a wide enough arc to bring the syringe back and forth as the rotor revolved. Thus if connected to plastic bottles they would gradually fill with compressed air.

He fixed to the board two plastic half pint bottles connecting them to the plastic tubes inserted at the base. At the bottle neck end he fitted a crude valve. He made this by cutting off the top of the screw cap. He then made a small square out of a party balloon rubber which was held in place by a skin of rubberized glue round the sides of the cap. A battery was glued to the board next to each of the motors with a breaker switch responding to an electromagnetic impulse.

After repeated experiments he realised that he needed to drill a hole at the end of each syringe to allow air in so permitting the bottle to be compressed by the piston. He then sealed all joints with smears of Araldite.

However what seemed to be an insuperable hurdle was getting the valve balloon rubber to burst quickly and completely. The secret was to match the pressure on the valve with the maximum tension that it would endure. He found that stretching the balloon rubber down the neck of the bottle enabled him to secure it firmly whilst the rubber glue took hold.

He planed to keep the second bottle for a later use. Thus it was necessary to ensure that its balloon rubber valve did not burst with the valve of the twin bottle. Stan found that the simplest solution was to insert a fine needle into the side of stretched balloon rubber valve of the first bottle where the tension was least. He did not do so with the second bottle.

When the tiny terminal wires were connected to one of the motors he found that the balloon rubber burst with a sharp explosive pop in a little over 30 seconds under the pressure of compressed air. The other one burst in just under a minute. He repeated the process with almost precisely the same outcome.

Stan's triumphant whooping could be heard from the shop.

He was now able to complete the device. He fitted a Jubilee clip round the neck which held a tube with slots cut into it holding 3 strips or sheaths of balloon rubber in line with the tube so that the air exploding out of the bottle when the balloon rubber burst would pass through them. The ends of the strips were glued along the top sides of the tube. The whole thing fitted on to a 9" square board.

The wireless remote control was a challenge.

It required the use of the very latest technology. But transistors with demodulating diodes and early primitive circuit development meant that it was possible to fashion a battery powered transmitter and receiver. The essentials were to create electromagnetic radio waves. Diagrams of the circuitry and parts were available from amateur radio fans. His father, despite his suspicions, helped him across the finishing line. Setting the waves at a particular and discrete frequency that was picked up by the receiving antenna enabled a signal to be given to the electric motor operating the device. With a long receiving antenna sufficient power could be transmitted remotely over the equivalent length of a cricket pitch.

In the shed Stan found a wooden souvenir box with a printed outline of Clitheroe Castle which had at one time been filled with chess pieces and dominoes. It was now filled with long bolts. It could have been purpose made for the transmitter.

Diagrams of the circuitry and parts were gathered from amateur radio fans. His father, despite his suspicions, helped him across the finishing line. Setting the waves at a particular and discrete frequency that picked up by the receiving antenna enabled a signal to be given to the electric motor operating the device. With a long receiving antenna sufficient power could be transmitted remotely over the equivalent length of a cricket pitch.

In the shed Stan found a wooden box with a printed outline of Clitheroe Castle which had at one time been filled with Chess pieces and dominoes. It was now filled with long bolts. It could have been made for the transmitter.

He had a remote controlled air compressor. He was armed to strike.

* * *

The 1622 Statutes of the RGS provided that there " *shalbee a comemoracon of the foundation of the said Schoole with an exhortation to the said Governors Schoolmr and Usher that they faithfully and diligently p'forme their duties"*.

Thus on 21 June 1958 the Governors of the RGS convened in the Library building in York Street with the boys, Prefects, Head Boy, Masters and Headmaster to offer prayers for divine guidance and to give to each of the leaving boys a leather bound Holy Bible with the crest of the School and its motto *"In Saxo 1554 Condita"*.

The Library had been cleared. Chairs had to be put out. This was a tiresome chore and thus fell upon the boys of the middle and junior forms. A raised platform had been erected by the groundsman-cum-carpenter at the east end of the hall covered at the front with a dark blue beize felt drape to conceal the struts below the platform boards. Stan and his class brought in the chairs from class rooms and arranged them under the supervision of a Prefect. Behind the raised platform a pair of doors opened on to a corridor with a door to the side, just beyond the Library itself, leading to the school yard and York Street. There was a wash room with lavatory the other side of the corridor.

No notice was taken of Stan as, with his school satchel, he went behind the platform to the wash room. Behind the locked door of the lavatory he mixed the Araldite using half a tube of each of the adhesive and hardener. He applied the whitish gunge to the base of the pump device extracted from his satchel. As the glue began to adhere he let himself out and slipped under the platform. It was the work of a moment to press the device in position under the boards above towards the front of the platform and keep it in place for the two more minutes needed to ensure strong adhesion. He crawled back and got up behind the platform. Stan quietly resumed moving chairs. He had not been noticed.

* * *

Mr Breadsly was the junior partner of Warley and Breadsly solicitors of Market Place, Clitheroe. He lived just outside Pendleton. He was proud that his son Gilbert had been head boy in his last year – it made up somewhat for the loss of face he conceived that he had sustained in being unable to afford the fees of Stonyhurst even after he had converted to Catholicism to secure his son's entry to that Jesuit public school.

To mark his son's leaving the Royal Grammar School as head boy he had bought him a second hand but clean Hillman Imp car. This would confer a bit of status he thought. Gilbert would drive himself to his big occasion. Mr Breadsly was clerk to the Justices and a Governor after all – it would only be fitting.

They would be noticed he was sure.

The boys assembled in the hall. Stan sat towards the back as far back as his seniority permitted – he would be starting his fourth year in September. All the leavers were to sit behind the Governors on the raised platform to come round in turn to receive their Bibles after the Headmaster's speech of welcome to the Governors and prayers. Following the presentation it was the tradition for the Head Boy to thank the Governors.

Stan had time to rest two squares of hardboard under his chair. Araldite glue held them to a bamboo sticking out underneath. He put it under his chair next to his satchel.

The Headmaster led the Governors through the double doors from behind the platform up the wooden treads at its the side. The leavers on the platform and the rest of the school stood up. Eventually all were in their places. Silence fell as the Headmaster started his speech of welcome. It was mercifully unmemorable and brief. Calling for all to bow their heads in prayer he recited the traditional imprecations.

As all raised their heads, pushing back in their chairs, Stan extracted the chess and domino box from his satchel. Slowly each leaver left his place to receive his Bible and shake the hand of the Headmaster. As one returned to resume his seat the boys clapped briefly and the next began to come round in a cycle.

There were 20 leavers. For Stan it was an interminable purgatory of suspense before the last was called.

"Gilbert Breadsly – Head Boy" called the Headmaster, relief bringing on a smile as he reflected with pleasure on the evident success and dignity of the Founder's Day proceedings.

Breadsly rose to receive his Bible and plaudits. His ponderous gait suited his large form. He had something of the pantomime Emperor about his bearing. Slowly, smiling at his father sitting with the Governors as he approached the Headmaster he came to rest before him.

The Headmaster raised the Bible and held it out. Breadsly leaned towards him to accept it.

At that instant the first plastic bottle blew out its balloon rubber valve with a definite pop. It was succeeded by a deafening BOOOMMPHpherrrrpuPHBAAAAPHfffffffWWWWARRRREPH-PPHWOOOARRRRffffffffffffff as the first bottle's compressed air burst explosively past the rubber sleeves inside the tube clamped at its end.

At first all was shocked silence. It was as if some most unfortunate mistake had been made in the programme. A few of the Governors looked at each other. The Headmaster's emotions were evidently confused but deeply felt.

Breadsly looked like Lot's wife.

The Headmaster sought to reclaim control of the sails and rudder as his ship was blown towards the reef.

He handed the Bible to Breadsly as if nothing at all had occurred, on the principle that you may have to walk in the gutter but you do not have to notice it. In the hubbub he was able to direct that Breadsly to take the Bible and move to the lectern at the end of the platform to read his speech of thanks which had been prepared for him and which rested there.

The older boys were slow to realise that they were witnessing something they would never forget. Most could not believe the fortunate turn that events had taken and were accordingly unsure of their response. The younger ones were not thus inhibited. Snorts and squeaks of suppressed mirth broke out among them like spurts from a leaking pipe.

But, with the partial restoration of order to the proceedings and the glowering of the Masters, chaos retreated.

Breadsly's face glistened with perspiration as he laid his Bible on the sloping face of the lectern. He was thankful to be occupied – no longer a standing figure of ridicule. He picked up the typed script of the brief vote of thanks, his hand shaking, his voice cracking.

"Governors, Headmaster…er…it's my duty and…. my privilege… mmm… to offer you this day……."

A wave of sound, as if a dozen open necked balloons had been released, burst upon the fragile air as the second plastic bottle blasted aside the frail rubber valve and escaped with violence through the waiting rubber sleeves.

It was too much for the 300 boys.

Their spurts and snorts were but the sounds of the dam wall weakening and then failing utterly. Excited by the earlier departure from the order of events, by the holiday spirit and by hormones, there arose in the hall such a cacophony of unrestrained hilarity as to foreclose entirely the formal proceedings.

It was just when the boys began to rise cheering and hooting that Stan, remaining seated, raised the little bamboo stick with the hardboard on top. On it was the following notation

"FATTY FARTER"

It was as if a massed boys choir had been reminded of its lines. The strains of the repeated chorus could be heard inside the Old School House across the yard as the Governors sought refuge from the storm, some jumping down from the edge of the platform to gain the open air through the double doors.

Stan kicked the bamboo stick and board into safety further down towards the platform and slipped out with his satchel under cover of the pandemonium he had unleashed.

* * *

The Harris College at Preston was just under an hour by train from Clitheroe. It offered courses in electrical engineering. Stan enrolled immediately after he left the RGS.

The new entrants had to gather in early September in one of the large ground floor lecture rooms for the welcoming address of the Principal. Stan found he was sitting next to a tall awkward looking young man wearing what looked like an RAF tunic. He had a kind of American accent. He was tall and spread his legs loosely under the chair in front of him. Stan had to touch him on the shoulder to ask him to move his arm from the seat of the chair he was to sit on.

"Hi there! – pardon me - I'll shift myself. My name's Max – siddown!"

Max wound up his long legs shoving his back higher up the chair.

"Hello – thanks – you American?"

"Could be - but not – Canadian -Toronto."

"Oh really? Gosh So why in Preston?"

Before Max could respond the Principal called the room to order. Stan leaned towards Max

"I'm Stan" quietly in his ear.

The first day at Harris College was devoted to explaining the curriculum and touring the laboratories, workshops, stores and lecture rooms. There was a large canteen for staff and students alike. Max strolled easily round with Stan seeming vaguely amused. They sat down for lunch together in the noisy canteen.

Max lived near Warton Aerodrome. His father had been stationed there in the War when it was a transit airfield for US bombers arriving for combat over Europe. He had stayed on when English Electric took over the entire site and then its successor British Aircraft Corporation. He'd been there now nearly eighteen years

Max explained that his father had helped develop heated flying suits for bomber crews. He was then involved in design of the electronics of the English Electric Lightning fighter and the BAC interceptor - the TSR2. Max could not tell him much about the work – just that these were the latest - and his Dad thought the last - of Britain's independent supersonic strike aircraft.

His Dad was planning to get back to Toronto soon. He had been getting repeated offers from new electronics businesses which were taking off there and over the US border at seriously generous salaries, benefits and stock options.

As Stan sat on the train making its way beside the Ribble back to Clitheroe he became conscious of a deep excitement at what was opening in his mind. What could he say when he got back to Whalley Road ? On his very first day at the Harris a window had opened for him on what life might offer that he could never have otherwise imagined. By accident or providence he had stumbled near at home on a much larger world far, far from home.

* * *

One afternoon the following summer at lunch with Max in the canteen Stan said he was going to try for salmon on the Hodder above its junction with the Ribble. Max seemed electrified by this news.

"I'd no idea there were salmon in that mud bath! Down at the airfield the Ribble is a mess -mud banks for miles and weeds and reeds. Say Stan I got to tell you there's no salmon fishing like New Brunswick or Gaspé peninsular – no Sir none!"

"Sounds fantastic. Are they the local rivers Max"?

"Hell no! Need a flight and then a float plane to get to them. Canada's big, Stan – really big. Best local fishing is for pickerel and bass in the lakes above the city – Toronto that is". -

"Pickerel?"

"You call them pike over here – get them spinning with June bugs or Jitter bugs – that kind of thing. "

"You know Max, you're right. The Ribble estuary is all mud banks. But upstream it's clear and fast. The sister river, the Hodder is smaller and easier for casting and wading if needed. It runs through wonderful country. It has grayling, trout and migrating salmon – Atlantic salmon that is. Not much feed or slow water for pike – pickerel to you"

"Look, Max, why not come up with me – they allow spinning so I bring a rod for you. I'll stick to flies."

56

"Great – let's do it. Say why don't we go up in my Dad's pick up – good for all the fish we'll get."

So began those lovely days and evenings of late summer and autumn with Max on the Hodder. Max at first found the river rather 'cute' and 'neat' but soon succumbed to its beauty. He gradually lost the impulse to hurl his metal devon minnow spinner onto the opposite bank. After a few outings it was landing at intervals in the river.

Their visits sometimes used to end up in the evening at a pool known as the Froth Pot a mile down from Whitewell. It was a small fast but deep pool just by the bank sheltered by a large boulder. The fly was best for it as it veered round across at an angle rather than the straight line of the devon minnow spinner. It was difficult because you had just two or three casts as the pool was so short and the stream so fast but you had to get the fly well down.

Max would not forget their first time at the pool.

Stan had only his small trout rod. He put on the largest trout fly he had - a "Bloody Butcher" with peacock blue and black wings, a silver body with a red tag for tail. The fly sunk quickly with the sinking line. One cast was all that was needed. The fish moved a fraction – a heavy dead weight in the flow of the river. Then feeling the restraining pull of the line it moved quite slowly out of the fast water until it felt the shelving gravel shoal beneath it in mid-stream. An enormous tail fin broke surface as with colossal force it moved inexorably, but with no haste, downstream. The little rod and reel were powerless as the salmon bored steadily down the river taking every stitch of line which pursued it harmlessly, now entirely free from the reel.

Stan's shocked disappointment faded when he saw Max slapping his knees and whooping.

"Gee! Stan did you see that goddam fish! – how did the damn thing ever get up here – it was some critter of a fish – God almighty I'd never have believed it. It was all of 20 pounds. And with that cute little rod and dinky reel. Why did you let it go for heaven's sakes!"

"I did'nt - I ran out of line did'nt I."

"You mutt – Your reel's too small and your line's too short – like everything over here. Not big enough hells bells!"

They would park at the Inn at Whitewell early in the morning on week ends and before the season closed they had walked the Hodder up to Dunsop Bridge and down to Doeford Bridge. The water was higher in those days as the demands on the water of Stocks reservoir, above gentle Slaidburn and its Hart to Bounty Inn, were less than today. Water levels were not so depleted as to impede the runs of salmon - as later happened.

The winter week ends found them on the Ribble above and below the town. Max was the dominant partner after years of trapping Canadian pickerel. Monsters, green and gold, surged from the depths to seize their rubber lures and gold spoons. All were returned to the river. There was no need to wade and the biting wind did not deter at all.

There were crumpets and strong sweet tea with Gertie and Will.

* * *

One evening in late February after Gertie's crumpets and boiled eggs and a day together on the river, Stan took Max into the shed at the back of the garden. The fluorescent lights flickered before shining a pallid weak light over the shadowed contents of the space. Stan nodded to the far end letting Max approach it alone.

He saw that upon the bench at the end was a solid heavy rubber ring about 12" inside diameter. It had been cut precisely through its centre into two half rounds. At one end, fixed to a wooden plate, was a simple wire wound resistor. It had been fashioned out of a chrome horizontal rod at the top with a slide or spindle attached to it which could be moved back and forward along its length. Underneath the rod was a large tube wound along two thirds of its length with thin wire along which the spindle on the rod could pass. At each end of the rod was a terminal with more terminals at the ends of the wound wire section. There was a 12 volt battery on the floor below the bench. A negative lead lay at one end of the rod terminal and a positive lead lay by the wire section but at the other end. The positive lead passed through a switch connected to an array of insulated wires wound round the rubber ring tied down with insulating tape.

Max studied the device. He lifted the insulated wire carefully at is junction with the battery lead looking intently at it for a long time. He then sniffed the rubber ring.

"Like everything over here it's too small" he said quite quietly as if reflecting.

Long pause.

"But hell, Stan, I've got to hand it to you. This is some simple beauty. How in God's name did your work this out!! It's brilliant. It won't work of course as you won't feel it through your bum. And the bum is everything. But Boy it's something. Dad needs to see this – he sure does! Why you might not even need a thermostat!"

"Well" said Stan "I thought that if you can calculate the electrical current in a circuit by dividing the voltage by the resistance then does that not mean current is directly proportional to the voltage and inversely proportional to the resistance?"

"Boy - if you say so Stan – if you damned well say so boy!"

"So the variable resistor effect on the current will control the temperature in the wires but can also measure the body temperature and that will also control the wire temperature"

Pause.

"Or so it seemed to me".

"Good God Stan!. Time you came up to Warton – you big Shrimp!! Dad has just got to see this"

Stan attached the leads and pressed the switch. One of the terminals was loose and sparked until he clipped the lead securely. The insulated wires gave off an initial smell as the dust of the shed burned off. It was not for quite some time that a feint odour of warm – but not burning – rubber could be detected. It did not intensify.

Stan then moved the spindle along the rod and the smell became slightly more noticeable. When he ran the spindle the other way the smell disappeared altogether since, as they both well understood, the current was less able to navigate the resistance of the wound wires.

Stan pressed the switch. The device retired. Stan looked at Max.

"Another cup Max?"

They went back in, to the warm and bright kitchen, for more tea.

Glenn and Jessie Baxter lived down Bank's Lane off Lytham Road in Warton. It was just beyond the end of the main runway of the airfield to the south. It was a company house and suited them well. It was very convenient for Glenn's work and for Lytham St Annes' shops. They had been there for 10 years after moving out of wartime housing. It was bit tight now that their son was nearly twenty but they managed well enough knowing that it was only for a few more months.

As they came into the sitting room Stan could see the distant endless mudbanks at low tide looking like mirrors in the bright June sunlight. In the vast estuary expanse the shining mud and distant sea merged in the brilliant light, the glare of the sky dissolving the horizon's edge. It seemed all limitless and still.

Max and Stan sat in the sitting room facing the airfield and wide receding estuary beyond. On the oak extending dining table Stan put down his rubber ring, resistor device and switch.

"Good to see you Stan – heard good fishing yarns about you from Max Well now – what have we here" said Glenn as he stood over the little contraption.

"Now look at that. You've made a rheostat - that's mighty clever."

Glenn moved the spindle along its arm then ran his fingernail along the wound wires.

"Neat – very neat – you're one smart guy Stan. Neat! I tell you - that's neat."

Glenn lifted the top segment of the rubber ring which was lying loose on the lower half.

"Very good. I've got to hand it to you. The rubber is not best for this – but you'd not easily get hold of the thermo polymers that are just being developed"

Glenn sat down resting his eyes on the small figure of Stan holding his hands round his knees and leaning forward out of his arm chair. The silence let in the noise of cars going back to Lytham from the airfield after work.

"Max, here, tells me you made this all yourself. And he said you had made a miniature compressed air widget – with a remote switching no less. And when you were only 14. What was that for?"

"Oh – well I just wanted to see if I could – for another boy."

He paused as if that was too bland an explanation.

"It was a surprise for someone at school".

"Max" said Glenn "Get those beers in the fridge will you? I've a proposition for Stan which you need to hear so let's settle down and be comfortable"

Glass in hand Glenn began

"You see, son, I'm mighty interested in getting a heated seat for trucks and tractors to market in Canada. It'll be too slow over here. No one'll think it necessary – they'll just laugh at it – even car heaters are still thought luxuries – they're still not standard even on high cost sedans. But in Eastern and Northern Canada a warm seat is not just nice. It's what makes working in sub zero just so much more tolerable. And its good for circulation and muscular pains and can ease lumbar conditions."

Glenn took a swallow of light ale.

"I've been offered a ground floor opportunity in a new start up venture in my home town – Toronto – you may have heard of it Stan – Max will have told you I expect. The money is being put up by some ex RCAF guys –air force – who want to bring me on board – they found out that I had perfected a system for heating flying suits in the War when I was stationed here."

Another drink of light ale.

"Yeah, that's what I did for the first few months of my posting. I didn't invent it of course but I worked up some improvements and got the suits to plug in to 12 volt batteries for the B-24 Liberator which were being flown in from Canada and the US"

"So I can cut down these guys R&D time and costs – and by some margin. That's why I got them to agree who should be on my team for getting out a marketable heated seat for tractors as the first product line. And it's why I get options for 50% of the stock rising in stages with profits plus buy out option after 10 years with a minimum floor price."

"Max was going back with me but he's now been offered a spot in Avionics at BAC which is too good to pass up so he's staying on"

"You see – I know it seems crazy – but you are just the sort of guy who it would take a spate of interviews to find – and damnation! – don't you just turn up here in my house with Max for God's sake. Can you beat that! You bring your rubber ring and resistor and well – it's just what we need – someone with a gift for it - I mean the invention side of it. There are a lot of tight corners to get round and if we can get your sort of ability at a low start out cost – well son we're well off the grid".

His words hung in the air.

"I'm rushing my fences here I can see. Hec! I don't know you but what Max has told me – all good, son – all good I tell you – but you must think I'm a bullshiting Yank or off limits in my head. Why don't you get Max to take you back to Clitheroe and let me know what you think – you'll want to square things at home of course if you feel like taking me up on this."

Glenn stood up as Max made for the door.

Nothing to say arose in Stan's mind which he thought would be at all adequate. Thanks seemed too trivial a response to such a life changing offer. He realised that Glenn's praise was no party piece or jollying along.

"But hear me young man" said Glenn as if to seal the offer, "I may be a bit over the top with my enthusiasm but I'm not with my sincerity. If you can find the way forward to come over with me to Toronto I know you'll never regret it son - never - and I'm sure as hell that I won't."

It was instantly borne in upon Stan, still sitting in that bright little sitting room in Bank's Lane off the Lytham Road at Warton, that providence had laid at his feet a glittering prize. He could not attempt to envisage how it would be but all that could come later.

He stood up. Looking at Glenn he said, quietly

"I don't think I will either".

* * *

The Governors of the Royal Grammar School of Clitheroe directed, at their meeting in September 2003, that on the 450th anniversary of the founding of the School – on the Founder's day of 21 June 2004 - a dinner should be held in what was now the VIth form college of the School in what used to be the old Library. The occasion was to mark, officially, the gift by Stanley Warmbutt of the cost of an electronically operated scoreboard for the School cricket ground. The scoreboard was designed with rows of 30 fold back seats each in three tiers on either side reached by gangways adjoining the wall of the new scoreboard.

Work was to start on 1 May 2004. Mr Warmbutt had arranged for the drawing office of Warmbutts Inc to prepare indicative drawings for the Governors to review and these were now before them.

There was, in addition, the gift of an endowment of £250,000 to be expended on providing cricket whites, cable stitch sweaters, pads, bats and cricket boots for those who could not afford to buy them. These were to be returned when the boys left the school and replaced when no longer fit for use.

The Governors had arranged that a private room be set aside for them and the Headmaster to entertain Mr Warbutt after the celebration dinner at which he was to be the sole guest of honour.

Mr Warmbutt had arrived at Heathrow from Toronto two days before Founder's Day. The Chairman of the Governors had invited him to stay – his house overlooked the Ribble near Sawley Abbey. After departing from Browns Hotel Mr Warmbutt took the first class Inter City to Preston. He had not been to Preston since his mother's funeral – Will had been the first to go.

A taxi had been arranged by the School to take him to Sawley. It was waiting at the top of the long ramp up that ran next to the station. Once in the back he asked the driver to go up Corporation Street. That was where the Harris College had stood – it meant going a roundabout route to get down it due to the one way restrictions. Nothing seemed to have changed. He brought to mind coming down the twin flights of front steps with Glenn on June afternoons to get Max's pick up out of the car park. For an instant he sensed the pull of the river and the smell of that pick up.

He was still tired after the flight which had disrupted his sleep. The traffic on the Clitheroe Road was thunderous. Great slices had been cut into the countryside to accommodate it. Yet the journey seemed far longer than he remembered it in the pickup. He reminded himself that of course that was a lifetime ago – or nearly so.

The taxi avoided Clitheroe taking the A 59 and, after coming close to the left bank of the Ribble, took the turn to Sawley. He arrived in time for an early supper. It was a pleasant evening. His host appeared to be much older than himself. Avuncular he thought – fitting for Chairman of the Governors. He was a solicitor in the town – Richard Fitzhugh. His wife had recently died. Apparently he did not remember any Breadsly – no one of that name had been in practice at least since he could remember – he himself had started as an articled clerk more than 40 years ago. Old James Harding – the oldest Governor – would know he said.

After supper he asked his host if he would join him for a short walk down to the river before bed. The crossed over the graceful stone bridge with its three shallow arches. The river was rather low – usual for mid-summer – and long shingle shoals stretched out from the points of the thick piers. A farm gate just on the other side opened into a deep green field adjoining the wide river. As they slowly progressed along the top of the bank the delicious sound of the flowing stream prevailed over the intermittent hiss from the little road.

No one could deny the inexpressible loveliness of this place. It was the more so because it was not special – it was the glory of all the Ribble valley and the Forest of Bowland whose distant purple hills watched over it.

Mr Warmbutt was able to arrange a taxi for himself for the following day. He would go up the Hodder valley. The taxi office was delighted at the fare that he had proposed. He first went to see the little marble slabs recording the period of existence of his mother and father. The carved inscription or the stone could not evoke the humour, courage, devotion, care and love of whom they each were living incarnations.

He thought he would go up to the Inn at Whitewell but as they went over Doeford Bridge he called the taxi to a halt. There would be time before lunch to walk down the river. He could take the path back up to the Dunsop Road T junction they had come through on the way.

It was a warm day. He sat down on a grass bank by the river. There were stone rills running across the stream leaving shallow pools below. The music of the running water was so restful. He laid down on the soft grass beneath a branch of a wide oak tree in full leaf. A few flies visited him before he lapsed into sleep.

The driver found him still asleep after searching first above the bridge. They made their way back up to the taxi and turned back to Clitheroe. It was after tea time but the Swan Hotel said they could prepare some teacakes and two boiled eggs.

He had not realised that the Governors would dress for the occasion. Mr Fitzhugh had offered him his dinner jacket. Mr Warmbutt assured him that he himself was the one who should look out of place and it was a comfort to his host when Mr Warmbutt assured him that the suit was many sizes too large.

He wore a dark blue blazer and grey loose trousers to minimise any affront to the dignity of the assembly. He had rather hoped he could merge discreetly with a few of the Governors at a time. As he approached the imposing entrance of the old Library he realised that there was no cover for him. A sudden recollection burst upon him of the last time that he had passed through these heavy and imposing doors seeking refuge from apprehension for the chaos he had caused on this very Founders day now well over 40 years ago. For a fleeting instant he felt short of breath as he was pricked by a sharp pang of panic.

"My dear Stanley" said Richard Fitzhugh, "Let me lead you in" as he stood for a moment on the top step.

"I'm sure this will bring back fond memories for you."

"Ah yes – it does rather."

The Governors all stood – arranged behind the table on the platform draped with dark blue baize to which was fixed the school shield and motto. They applauded as Mr Warmbutt made his way cautiously up the treads of the little stairs picking his way to the seat next to between the Chairman and the Headmaster.

He had prepared a few words of thanks. His host had suggested this would be welcomed assuring him that he was. after all. one of the distinguished alumni of the School. Mr Warmbutt was accustomed to these sort of speeches – it was necessary at shareholders' meetings at times for him to speak of optimism for future profits and to applaud or gloss over past results.

He would then present the cheque to the Chairman.

Mr Warmbutt thanked the Governors is the warmest terms. His address to them was brief but most generous in his praise for the standing and achievements of the historic School. He seemed to be utterly sincere as he expressed his fulsome gratitude for the blessings it had conferred upon him when in its care.

The Governors rose as one to applaud him as he concluded:-

"It was here, in this hallowed hall that I was put upon the path which led to my modest fame and prosperity. You could say that indeed I owe it all to the RSG – yes I can honestly say that without what I discovered here fortune would not have smiled on me so sweetly."

The ovation intensified with the clinking of knives on glasses and fists on the table as Mr Wambutt formally handed to the Chairman his cheque for £250,000.

* * *

Port was served in the adjoining day room. There were cigars and cig-arettes. Around the walls stood upholstered upright chairs and some armchairs. Mr Warbutt took one of the armchairs. He accepted a glass of port. A feeling of benign benevolence came over him. He thought he would have a cigar.

"May I introduce myself Mr Warmbutt. My name is James Harding" said an amiable face.

"Ah yes, Richard told me you are the senior Governor"

"Oh well, that's what time does isn't it. And for you? Has time blurred memories of your years here – is there anything that still stands out in your memory?"

Mr Harding sat down in one of the upright chairs. A few of the Governors moved closer to hear Mr Warmbutt as he began to respond.

"Well you see I was a little squit for most of my time at the RGS. Half pint I was called. So I came in for a lot of ribbing from older boys. There was also my name you see. I couldn't help my name any more than I could make myself grow taller. I got picked on a lot for my name. So life's early lessons were rather stern - at least for the first two years or so. But I have never for a moment regretted those times. You see it taught me to find ways to get up to the Giant and see him disappear.

"The Giant?"

"Just a story my Dad told me – the Giant gets smaller and smaller the closer you get to him. Helped me a lot."

Mr Harding sipped at his little glass of port before asking

"Was there any one in particular that stands out in your memory or a group of them. I might just remember. I was a master here before I became a Governor – you'd have been here in the late 1950s I would think – if so would then have been in my late 20s - that's all."

"Well I don't know as how I should mention names -but I suppose name calling is no crime. And any way you look at it it's very long ago."

Mr Warmbutt paused, sitting there once more at the scene of retribution .

"There was one boy" he said at last. "He was called Breedsly but he spelled it BREADSLY. Particular he was about that. His father was, I think, a solicitor. He tormented me for quite a bit. My name you see. He was a bit rough with me. I was a shrimp then – not that I'm a big fish now. It was hard for a long time until I found a way to finish him off, as it were"

"Oh yes" said Mr Harding, enthusiastic at recollection of those distant times.

"I do remember Breedsly - Gilbert Breedsly. Yes indeed. Only because of the uproar. In fact it was at a Founder's day assembly that it happened. You must have been a boy there at the time"

A chorus came up from those around. Mr Warmbutt could clearly hear Richard Fitzhugh demanding of poor Harding

"Come on James, what happened – tell us – you can't leave us pegged on the washing line like that"

"I regret I must disappoint you, Richard, as to the details which decency forbids me to reveal. I can, however, say that there was indeed a shocking uproar at the prize giving on Founder's day in this very building. It seemed like an eruption until the chanting started and that seemed channel the flow as it were. The cause of the outbreak then was revealed by a notice on a board raised by some boy at the back of the hall. It convulsed the assembled school. The boys could be heard far out into the yard and the Governors took flight. More than that I cannot say – except that Breedsly's father gave up his practice shortly after that I understand and with his family moved to Burnley."

Mr Warmbutt realised that propriety and goodwill demanded that he retreat with grace from any possible invitation to clarify James Harding's opaque account.

"Well yes, of course" he said evasively "It was all any of my friends would talk about. But there was the Asian flu then if you remember. I heard about it from them before the end of term. It must have been serious for the Governors to leave prize giving must it not?"

Mr Warmbutt thought he had slipped out of the knot by being correct and misleading.

"James" said Richard, "Did they ever get to the bottom of it – so to speak?".

"No, but some time later the groundsman reported that when dismantling the platform after Founder's day he had found an old chess and dominoes box under the boards with some batteries and wires but had pulled it off and taken it to the School bins."

Mr Warmbutt could hear other Governors rising from their chairs expecting further revelations. He resolved to change the ominous direction of these exchanges.

"But you see, it was my name that might at times bring an uneasy smile. More often it was open ridicule. My Dad thought a smile was good for business. But I could never get used to it. I used to cower inwardly when it was spoken."

"Surely it was very valuable to your business though" suggested Richard. "I mean the name "Warmbutt" for heated lorry, car and tractor seats. It's become almost as famous as Formica or Lucozade. So you couldn't change it – it might be said you were rejecting your own brand wouldn't it. But other than that, Stanley, wouldn't you just have changed it?"

"Oh but I did Richard! Yes you see I did. After all, as my Dad would say 'Have a name that's good for business'"

"What was it that you did?. Not sure I understand you"

"I did change my name. It was in Canada when I applied for citizenship you see. I changed it – my name".

He paused until the very silence of the group compelled him to explain.

"I changed my name to Warmbutt – from Chillbottom."

A moment's silence enveloped them.

"It turned out to be very good for the bottom line - as you might say" said Mr Warmbutt.

K.80

I was staying for the week end recently with my old friends, Paul and Gaye Thompson, at Burford, Oxfordshire. I would usually take them to the Bay Tree for supper on the Saturday evening but on this occasion they insisted on taking me to the Bell at Aston Water just a little way down the A40.

It was the experience of once again being in that lovely village that brought to my mind the afternoon when, many years before, my father began to tell me of how a family who owned a small estate near there, had shaped his childhood. He had given me an account of events that took place now over 70 years ago which were so singular that they had remained bright in his memory.

The next day, after attending morning service, I was sitting on the verandah with Paul Thompson on creaking cane chairs overlooking the river Windrush below the town. I mentioned the Aston Water family to Paul who guessed at once that I was talking of the Withebys.

"But my dear Tom" he said "how curious that your father should have known the Withebys. My parents knew them well. But of course the estate was sold when the old people died. We didn't know the son ourselves but I remember reading one of his books - on tank warfare it was. I'd be most interested to know what became of him."

He pressed me to tell him what I had heard from my father and so, having an hour or so before lunch, I pieced together the remnants of my recollection of that afternoon and evening spent with my father – it must be nearly 30 years ago.

I had at that time just completed reading a Life of Churchill which was both scholarly and perceptive, portraying the many apparent contradictions of his thinking and actions over a long life full of incident and controversy. I had been much taken with the inclusion by the author of many glimpses into the intimate family treatment of the young Churchill which had so affected his restless ambition and grasp of life's opportunities.

Among the more striking of these passages was that which told of a dream or vision that the great man described of the appearance of his father Lord Randolph Churchill when, after the War, in 1947, he was in his garden studio preparing to paint a copy of his. So detailed was the recollection of the event and of the conversation that flowed between father and son, and so unimpeachable was the source, that when I next drove over to join my father for Sunday lunch at his home in Wolcombe on Glynde near Woodstock, shortly before Christmas, I brought our discussion round to the subject of visions of the departed appearing to those who are left.

I hesitated before embarking on my account since my father, then nearly 80, was evidently frail and I did not wish to appear morbid. Moreover, his life in the law had embedded in him a logical and practical approach to all questions. It thus seemed probable that he would dismiss such notions as fanciful and of no value or interest.

However, when I had described the passage in the Churchill biography my father moved slowly back in his chair, putting his knife and fork gently on to his plate. He brought his hands lightly down to his lap, turned his head easily towards me holding me with a watery but steady eye. There was a momentary still pause – I recall hearing the cracking of ice under the footfall of someone coming in from the garden.

He brushed a few crumbs from his patterned pullover. He was still in his now oversized tweed jacket and trousers that he had worn that morning to Church for he was still a churchwarden at St Mary's. His shirt collar was too large for him. He was wearing a plain green wool tie.

"My dear boy" -he started – "as you know I'm not in the way of giving much attention to dreams and fancies. It"s always seemed to me that one can imagine anything – but just because some ephemeral genie of our invention summons spirits to our minds it's folly to suppose that this signifies anything. Except, perhaps, approaching senility."

I was about to retreat, with a mumbled assent, from further ventilating the subject when my father continued as if he was addressing himself, so detached did he seem. His eyes rested on a faded old tapestry that hung precariously above the deep mahogany of the sideboard to my right. He was quite still as if waiting for words to give form to memory.

I was sure that any interruption of mine would dispel the scenes and names that were passing before his inward gaze. But you may be surprised when I tell you that it was not until daylight had failed that he finished telling me all that follows - as far as I can now recall it, for my father died a few months later. He spoke slowly and with many pauses – but with the icy clarity of a fine legal mind. His phrases may seem now a little pedantic but that was his way. In a few instances I am able still recite his own words but for the most part I record his account below as best as I can now remember.

"Last October, he said, I attended the memorial service for George Witheby MC at Trinity College Oxford. The obituary columns of the principal daily newspapers only cover but a few of those young men who had fought with gallantry in the last German war and their sometimes long and honourable later lives - denied to so many of their colleagues in arms."

"Perhaps I would not now myself be able to recall the events of George's life if I had been able to explain adequately how they came about, or at least had found the means to release their grip on my memory."

"My firm had for many years acted as solicitors to the Witheby family. Indeed there was a Witheby who had been a partner in the late 19th century. That was unusual, however, for the Withebys were a military family and almost all the sons of the various branches of the family joined one of the cavalry regiments. Normally the 14th/20th Hussars, but latterly the Sherwood Rangers and then the Royal Yeomanry. They were not conspicuous in distinction or achievement but were a family which took for granted the bonds of duty and fidelity".

"It's perhaps not overstating matters to describe them as representing the continuum of English upper middle class values and beliefs that appeared to be so enduring and constant before the War. They had the scattering of great aunts left by the decimation of the young men of the late Victorian age in the first War. The sons of the family went to one or other of the Berkshire boarding preparatory schools, on to Wellington College. In those days it was for sons of military families as, I believe, to some extent, it still is today. Then on to Oxford where they read Modern History or English, not wishing to waste their time equipping themselves with any professional or technical utility".

"The family lived near Aston Water on the Windrush and their private means assured for them a life of ease and comfort. George was born in August 1918 shortly after his father was seriously wounded defending Amiens having survived for the 4 years of that hideous conflict as a regular officer. George had an elder brother but he died in infancy. I was born two years after George. We were thrown together by our mutual love of tennis and fly fishing. I spent many summer days with him over at Aston Water. I cycled over from Wolcombe. He would often come over to us to try trapping little silvered dace in the Glynde with very small black flies which we tied ourselves."

My father paused again this time for a good while, softly wheezing.

"Those far off days" he said looking up at me his eyes moist and blinking. Slowly he returned to me and the dining room. He took out a handkerchief from his cuff and blew his nose.

As the forms of the past gradually took shape in his mind there opened for him a window on the vanished world he was depicting. He seemed enlivened and enchanted at his recollections.

"My dear boy", he said– "let's get comfortable in the study – there's a fire laid in there – I'll ring for Mrs Parsons to clear these things and we can have tea later – only if you can stay for it of course? Let me press the bell and we'll go through"

I cannot now be sure of my recollection of all that he said that winter evening. His account was so full of incident that I am only able to set it down in my own words with the essential narrative.

* * *

There was bell on the dining room floor in front of my father's chair. It had magnetic powers of attraction for us as young boys since it used to get stuck if you pressed it at an angle. The idea being to get Mrs P into the room and avoid discovery by legging it out of the house, our innocence resting on the fault of the bell.

It was astonishing that Mrs Parsons was still there.

We went into the study before she came in, as my father quaintly put it, 'to chide me for ancient mischief'. I stumbled as I went in. The ceiling was much lower than the dining room. It was once an outhouse. There was a step down but if you were not used to it an instinctive instant duck of the head, coupled with stepping into void, projected you towards the arm of the huge round arm of a sofa which was low on the stone floor immediately in front of you. I don't think he kept it there for safety but it was more useful than comfortable.

We sat for a while whilst Mrs P clattered next door. The study room was cold – it was a converted outhouse. The sloping lean-to roof was immediately above. We could hear the tiles cracking faintly as the ice retreated.

My father almost knocked over a table lamp on his desk as he felt for it in the dark. He bent down to pull out a single bar electric fire switching it on at the wall.

We settled ourselves before the open fireplace. Bracing himself, my father began to tell me about George Witheby.

George left Wellington in July 1937. He was an accomplished young man. He secured a scholarship to Trinity College Oxford reading Modern History with his special subject being the war of the First Coalition against France 1792 – 1798 – he later published a history of that campaign. He was a careful and determined opening batsman whose limpet like adhesion to his wicket ensured him a place in the College XI.

In his first year at Trinity he was elected to the Claret Club - regarded at that time as the best dining club of all the colleges, though Oriel's Ran-Dan club claimed superiority. Certainly Trinity's claret coloured velvet coats trimmed with gold braid excelled in magnificence the apparel of any other.

The summer of 1938, when not on the cricket field, was largely spent on the Cherwell punting or lunching from hampers on its banks. George had a pair of Holland & Holland 20 bores and in the Michaelmas term, when not shooting on his family's Aston Water estate, he joined shoots in the Chilterns and Berkshire Downs.

In those days intellectual brilliance created a sense of slight unease if it intruded on social occasions. It was normal – indeed it was expected – for it to be concealed by social banter and humour. Success on playing fields was acceptable but only within the confines of modesty and deference to the spirit of the game – a nebulous code, but none the less universally accepted by those of privileged upbringing, just as were forms of chivalrous behaviour towards ladies and elders. So it was that George, despite his brilliant intellect, earned and fostered a reputation for bonhomie and good living.

My father turned to look out of the small window to his left set back from the chimney breast. He gazed over the frosted lawn and into the past.

Without turning round he continued quietly:-

How incredible now it is to reflect that such a life was normal. And that it should vanish almost in an instant.

His chair slipped a little on the stone flags as he turned to me once more and continued:-

The bursting of the Munich bubble in March 1939 - upon Hitler's seizure of Czechoslovakia - turned the minds of Oxford's gilded generation irreversibly to preparation for the coming war and combat with German forces which each would have to endure according to his post

George and I joined the Territorials. Just five months of spring and summer were left before the catastrophe of war befell us. All the certainties that our backgrounds and upbringing had grafted on to us now seemed ephemeral. The measured steps in career and of private life and family, which had been our assured future, no longer lay before us or our generation. It was as if we were suspended in time with nothing remaining definite or expected. The experience of normal daily events and scenes could no longer be assumed. It seemed that they were perceived for the first time like first arrival in a foreign country when everything claims equal attention and interest. I remember that the days seemed long and bright.

Pausing and shaking his head a little as if to come out of a reverie, he continued:-

It was on a day in May, just a few weeks before his final examinations that George noticed the Holywell Music Room, as if for the first time. His normal route back to Trinity from his tutorials in New College was along Holywell Street's south side into the Broad past the Sheldonian. But the pavement was up so he crossed the road directly in front of the Music Room. It was set back some distance behind a small lawn fronted by railings. It appeared to him as a most imposing structure. He had not realised how large and dominant was the classical pediment. The building had an apparent importance informing its modest dimensions.

George found himself regarding this small Palladian hall wondering as to its origins and design when a young lady emerged from it carrying a violin case. He was struck by her pale almost sallow skin and her very dark and long hair. She was dressed in black – a pullover and skirt and with a little silk scarf around her thin neck. He did not move. As she came through the cast iron gate he noticed that she had a poster in her hand.

Realising that he was both staring at her and also in her way he came to and with a sudden movement stepped out of the way only to stumble backwards into Holywell Street and then to tilt forward over and on to the pavement. The young lady had finished pinning her poster to a triangular shaped board on a post at the far end of the railings. She turned towards him but could not get past the embarrassed and flailing George engaged in getting to his feet.

"I hope I should be flattered by the effect I seem to have had upon you and not dismayed?"

"Oh not dismayed – no certainly not that. I say, no, no– not that at all".

As he struggled to regain a standing posture, and being anxious to continue the exchange he said:-.

"I was just wondering what this building is used for - I haven't really noticed it before……..it's really rather a lovely classical cameo isn't it "

"They perform musical works."

"Who do?"

"Well I do. And also Handel and Haydn. But they did it a little while ago".

"Oh I see. I'm not…. I don't know much about music but…"

"You don't need to know about it – just listen to the sound it makes"

She laughed, lifting up her hands as if throwing something in the air.

"It's invisible you see. You can't describe music or see, taste or feel it – only its effects"

"Gosh…I see.... well…..I mean………..how extraordinary."

"What is?"

"Well …to hear about Handel and Haydn and the food of love whilst rising from a recumbent posture on a pavement at the feet of a complete stranger."

"Well do come to the poster concert. I sing and play the viola in a string quartet. - not, so far, at the same time. The viola is ideal for me as it is much easier to hide my wrong notes in its middling soft tones. I also play the piano but only in soundproofed rooms. I'll look out for you – but won't need to if you're usually off balance."

At which she trilled good bye, crossed Holywell and turned out of sight down Bath Place.

George had never heard any 'chamber' music – he had not even heard the term. Despite this and his intense revision studies for Finals he slipped along the Broad across ton Holywell the following week for the concert. He sat at the back so that he could escape if it was all too far over his head

He was slowly entranced by the scene and the sight of Constance – for that was her name: Constance Benn – playing with such apparent ease and diligence. She was raised up with three other performers on a platform within the semi circular apse at the far end under the gilded pipes of the 18th century organ. Below her were elegant rising hand-rails adjoining the shallow tiers on each side which accommodated the audience. All was graceful and fine.

There was the usual hub bub after the performance. Hoping to see her George remained near the entrance doors for Constance only to find, as the hall had almost cleared, that she had left.

He felt a pang of loss - more than a simple disappointment. He had not expected anything of that kind. He made his way towards the double doors but had to stand aside to let a couple pass ahead. Then hurriedly he pushed open the closing door to let himself out only for his head to collide with Constance's hat and curls as she appeared from behind it.

"Did you like the Mozart? It was his first string quartet – Köchel no 80 - written when just 14 you know" she chirped.

George's acquaintance with classical music was limited to 'Zion City of Our God' roared out in Chapel by the boys of Wellington. He had no idea who had written the music. It might have stunted any further interest in Joseph Haydn had he known that Zion hymn was taken from his "Gott erhalte Franz den Kaiser" – though the paradox would have intrigued him.

He slipped gracefully out of the knot of his ignorance.

"Come on let's have tea at the Randolph" he said – if we're too late then what about crumpets in front of the electric single bar in my rooms – it'll chase away your little coughs."

* * *

George returned to his hermetic existence in College preparing for his assault on the nine examination papers that would confront him over 5 days in the second week of June.

He did not immediately return to Aston Water at the end of that Trinity term. He was able to persuade the College to let him stay for a few weeks during the long vacation given the likelihood of conscription and the end of normal Oxford life. Constance lived with her father next to the Covered Market off Cornmarket where he kept what she described as a musicography shop.

George found a used car dealer on a vacant lot in St Ebbes and acquired a 1934 Singer 9 Le Mans 2 seater with a slab petrol tank and wire wheels. The level of exhaust noise was in inverse proportion to its performance so the sense of speed at 40 mph was exhilarating.

Thus George and Constance took off on sunny trips to the undisturbed Cotswold villages of West Oxfordshire during those precious and never to be regained days. In August George invited Constance to meet his people (as parents were then called) at their Aston Water home. The last of the summer was spent playing tennis with evening cine shows on the whitewashed walls of the outer hall or family concerts with George and his father singing out of tune Victorian music hall hits recalled by Constance on the piano.

Sometimes, after resting on deck chairs by the river after lunch, George would roll up his flannels and lead Constance, her hand in his, along the shallow Windrush disturbing small crayfish as they lifted flat stones and letting the long slow silent winding reeds trail against their legs while the silky mud, soft and cool, oozed cool through their toes.

It was on 27th August a few days after the announcement of the Nazi Soviet pact that he opened a letter from the Dean of Trinity informing him, with his congratulations, that he had been awarded a First honours degree in Modern History and offering him a research fellowship "should the present emergency allow for it".

George played his last peacetime game of cricket on the Parks with Constance dutifully on the boundary. The editor of Wisden said of those days that it was "like peeping through the wrong end of a telescope at a very small but happy world".

The end of summer came that year on 3rd September. George and Constance each now realised that they had become inseparable.

* * *

George went through a very long period of training starting with basic general military instruction, moving on to training on obsolete tanks, then on to elementary gunnery with further specialist courses after that. Six months were spent at Bovington in Dorset followed by a Warminster War Officer Selection Board assessment. He then was assigned for further Pre-Officer Training at Alma Barracks Aldershot. On arriving for officer training at Sandhurst he had to endure a repeat of his earlier basic and general military training before instruction on leadership of a tank troop began. Formal training was concluded in North Wales with simulated battle tactics and field exercises.

Leave was sufficiently generous to enable George to have time with Constance. By November 1942 with the pursuit of the Axis into Tunisia drawing of all reserves of mobile armoured divisions it was obvious that George would be posted there at any moment. Having leave due to him George arranged to stay at Trinity for three days.

The Broad Walk between Christ Church and the Meadows affords the summer visitor a view of pasture bordered by the River Isis (to you and me the Thames) through to the slopes of Boars Hill beyond. It is matched only by the view from the other side of the river back towards the 'dreaming spires'.

It was the fourth winter of world war. The November rising mists of the Isis were claiming the Walk as Constance waited for George at its gate below Tom Tower opposite Alice's shop. He cut through St Ebbes from the Station and emerged from Pembroke College lane immediately opposite Constance rushing to her over the silent abandoned road.

In the descending twilight, their steps along the Walk were muffled by the mist. They did not speak at first as they moved together below the naked elm trees.

"You'll think I have changed my name to Pandora" said Constance brightly.

"I'm no Capulet and certainly no Juliet!" quipped George. "You may have a new name every time we meet - they all will smell as sweet. I can then be both faithful and wayward in unblemished constancy!"

"How pretty!".

They walked on silently into the dark until the gatekeeper's calls brought them back to Carfax.

Constance took George to tea at the Mitre Hotel on the High Street.

"They've an open fire there to take the cold out of your bones after the struggle you must have had to get here. And I need to be sure you are quiet and resting so that I can tell you about Pandora."

They settled into two low armchairs that were warm to their legs with the heat of the fire.

Constance began:-

"You see, I know that you've come to say that we may not meet again"

"That's true - but it's not at all how you think. You see…"

"No my darling George.."

"But I insist - you must hear me out. It's because we may not meet again that I have determined to see you to make sure, if you are willing, that if we do that we shall not then again be parted."

"But I'm Pandora. If you open my box you will find many things that may repel you".

"Impossible, inconceivable……."

"No, George ………you must let me tell you – so that I can be sure you're not deceived by any disguise of mine you've imagined to be true. You see for one thing I am a bit Jewish".

"But how can that possibly…"

"My grandmother was murdered in the awful Odessa pogrom of 1905 when my grandfather and father were with relatives in Kiev. They got to Egypt and the British authorities put them on cargo steamer on which my grandfather worked passage to England. He re-married some years later– to a music teacher St Edwards School here in Oxford."

"He himself taught the violin and piano and together they opened a small shop off Cornmarket selling musical instruments, sheet music, books on music, prints and other musical bits and pieces."

"My father took on the business after they died and expanded it to include gramophone records. When he married my mother she was working in a print shop in the High Street. I came along - much later for some reason."

"And my father's family name is Benjamin. Not Benn. Joseph Benjamin. My grandfather changed it when he got away from Russia".

Constance paused as if giving herself space and time to witness the disturbance that she expected her disclosures would inflict on George's composure.

He was looking into the fire -quite still. He seemed to be intent only on getting his hands warm, so she continued.

"And it also seems that I have a rather unusual affliction - to add to my distinctive attributes – No I don't mean being smitten and love lorn!"

"I've been coughing a lot more than before and at times – don't listen! – spitting or "suffering from increased sputum production" as it is reported. So my father dragged me to the doctor who referred me to the Radcliffe Infirmary who made lots of tests and who eventually told me I had early stages of Cystic Fibrosis - which is what they call it – though why I can't tell you".

"Think of it as rather tiresome asthma – as my alto singing is anyway deep wheezing it won't keep me out of the choir".

After a long pause she added, speaking quickly,

"So you see the fable of Pandora letting out death and pestilence from her box is really quite a good one isn't it?"

A log rolled out of the fire. George watched it smoking for a while. He pushed it back with his boot. Constance coughed a bit. Someone came to clear the tea things. The revolving door to the High Street clunked.

"My dearest Constance – he said softly – we both are moving nearer to the abyss".

"I am sure to be in the fight very soon".

"But now is the moment. It's always all right now".

George moved his hand over to the arm of Constance's are chair pulling them close together. She quickly clasped her hand over his – the shiny leather of the arm chair squeaking as she did so.

George turned sideways towards her, his face now close before her, resting his other hand on hers.

"You see, my dearest Constance, you've not mentioned what was left in Pandora's jar, for a jar is what it was".

She lifted her eyes as if to speak but George continued, almost with a whisper, resting his gaze upon her

"It was Hope".

* * *

My father stood up, straightening his thin and weary body by stages. He looked out over the garden, now completely dark beyond the perimeter of the low study wall lights. I could not help being moved by his words. The silence and stillness in the little room seemed intense. I remember the slow scraping of the thorns of the bare climbing roses against the glass of the window panes.

Unsteadily he turned, looking down at me for a moment, as if to signal that he had drawn a curtain across the scenes and actors of the past.

There was sharp "Clack" of the wooden latch as the planked oak door of the study swung out violently and banged against the inside of the wall – then swinging back again on to Mrs Parsons as she turned on the glaring ceiling light.

"There you are -giving me such a fright – and sitting in this bitter cold – what's come over you – and the fire not even lit – in the dark and all – well Master Tom you should know better than keeping your father talking when he should be having his rest - and the curtains not drawn and all and him standing there – I don't know really I don't."

She muttered to herself as she pushed past my chair pulled out a spill from a little vase on a tripod table by the log basket and, with a few curses at the unwilling matches, bent with her knees to light the fire, her other arm resting on the brick sides of the fireplace as she did so.

Rising heavily she moved to draw across the window curtains and with another "Well I don't know, I really don't Master Tom" she navigated her way to the open door turning off the ceiling light and with a another "Clack "of the latch concluded the performance.

It was rather like the effect that a sparkling tuneful aria has on an operatic audience after a sad and poignant scene. My father sat down again.

I don't know what I'd have done without Mrs P after your mother died, he said. Fortunately I am closer to the Departure lounge than her – she has not reached the Terminal yet.

He looked at me intently before resuming - as if he had come to the next Act. .

Gathering the threads he continued:-

You must realise that George's experiences as a tank commander were moulded how he came to look at life.

So, as if preparing me, he told me that, for the sake of his close friend's memory, he could not shrink from the attempt to piece together what George had revealed about them at various times.

The Sherwood Rangers Yeomanry had fought at Alamein and in the pursuit of the Germans and Italians along the North African coastal belt. George's squadron disembarked there in February 1943 taking part in the encirclement of the Axis when the 8th Army got in behind the Mareth defences in March 1943. After the Axis forces surrendered in May that year George took part in the invasion of Sicily and thereafter mainland Italy. However in February 1944, after the stalemate at Anzio, he was recalled to England to prepare for Overlord.

So it was that he arrived on leave in Oxford at the end of March 1944. The wedding of Constance and George took place in Trinity College Chapel with the reception in in the Dining Hall. But only three days of honeymoon could be arranged and these were spent at Aston Water.

George's war resumed in April.

His troop's Shermans ground upon Gold beach on the day after D-Day itself. For over 2 months they were in close and bitter conflicts with the Wehrmacht from the beaches right down to the line of the River Noreau near Falaise where the final destruction of German Army Group B west of the Seine was accomplished.

George's troop were seconded to support 214th infantry Brigade as a reserve for the advance to the Seine. This took them through the small town of Chambois at the neck of the Falaise salient in which the bodies of up to 30,000 men of the Wehrmacht – who knows how many really - had been reduced by artillery, rockets and bombs to hideous mounds of dismembered flesh and limbs. Entrails had spilled out of severed carcases while the air shimmered and buzzed with countless flies in clouds hovering over the putrefying scene. The devastating shock of witnessing the concentration of slaughter of young men - those still recognisable as men - lying in heaps, contorted in ghastly attitudes and the grotesque fixing of their last moments, inflicted on the 26 year old Witheby an ineradicable remembrance of horror and futility rendering him for many hours incapable of speech.

The late summer of 1944 glowed as Witheby and his troop crossed the 'smiling fields of France' cheered by the gratitude and gifts of the liberated - a salve for the horrors of Normandy. In early September the Sherwood Rangers followed the 6th Guards Armoured Division into Brussels with its ecstatic crowds – as autumn passed and Christmas approached only the Rhine and the final thrust seemed to remain.

But the Ardennes through which burst the German onslaught of May 1940, again erupted with violent armoured assault as Panzer divisions intent on crossing the Meuse and breaking through to Antwerp, thrust through with complete surprise and devastation. By Christmas Eve 1944 2nd Panzer Division had reached Foy – Notre- Dame within sight of the Meuse.

To meet this threat a scratch British armoured group, including Witheby's tank squadron, took up positions on the East of the river bridge at Dinant. As Battlegroup Bohm approached the bridge the British group ambushed its Panzer column destroying three Panther tanks and halting all further advance. Witheby as troop commander of the lead Sherman tank was able to get off 2 rounds before losing a track. Despite being under fire and immobile he covered all his men as they evacuated and continued to fire Very lights to illuminate the Panthers for the rest of the squadron until wounded in the head and rendered unconscious by shrapnel. He was awarded an immediate MC.

With the rank of Captain he was invalided to the Radcliffe Infirmary and being unfit for further service was honourably discharged in April 1945.

My father had paused, appearing to verify silently that his account so far had been complete. It was as if he was inwardly reciting the facts of a case to Counsel in conference.

I could hear Mrs P clearing the dining room muttering still. I leaned forward to put on another log on the fire and settled back deep in my arm chair. We sat in the late evening stillness together listening to the murmur and flutter of the flames of the fire.

My father's words floated quietly over my drowsy consciousness. This is my somewhat misty recollection as he continued,

You know of course that I was in an infantry division, first under Montgomery in North Africa and then under Alexander in Italy. So I didn't get back into civilian life until 1946. My father thought that before I joined the family firm I should do my articles of clerkship at Clifford Turner in the City to bring some quality commercial and corporate law experience into the firm. As it turned out, after my articles and a period as an assistant at CT, I was offered a partnership in a firm in Chancery Lane which was most rewarding as they opened an office in Brussels when it looked as if we were going into the Common Market in 1962. I only returned to Oxford in 1965 when my father wanted to take on less work.

Accordingly, for the period of 20 years after the War my account relies partly on what George himself told me and also on matters that, as senior partner of a long established firm of legal advisers to a number of Oxford colleges, Dons and professional people in the City, drifted into my comprehension - if I can so put it.

George and Constance lived at Aston Water where they converted a range of stone outbuildings adjoining the yard formerly part of the home farm. It was obvious that she was not well but in a curious way her pallor suited her appearance. She was not gaunt but far from bonny. To the delight of George she fitted out the stables as a music room in which she gave piano and viola lessons and little chamber music evenings.

After publication of a paper on Amphibious Warfare 1782 – 1802 in 1952 George had accepted a tutorial Fellowship at Trinity in Military History. Over the next 8 years he worked on his major *opus* "The Practice of Armoured Warfare" – a truly exhaustive study of the development of armoured conflict from the American Civil War to Korea.

It was during this time, to their great delight and surprise, that Constance conceived. Their son Benjamin was born in January 1955 and they moved in to the main house at Aston Water, George's parents taking the converted cottage.

One could hardly exaggerate how delightful their life together had become for George and Constance.

As my father said the rays of the pre-war sun still shone over the 1950s.

* * *

Mrs Parsons opened the door ajar but remained in the dining room as she declared she had taken the tea things into the dining room and the cake from the larder and she had made up the fire which she had lit and she had left out a rug for my father's knees and there was some cold chicken with sprouts from lunch which just needed to be heated up in the Aga so we should have everything we needed until tomorrow and she would be going back down the village now before the snow started if that was all right.

The latched clacked back. We heard her slapping steps over the stone flags. The front door banged. All fell quiet within.

My father got up. "I must say a hot cup of tea would be just the thing don't you agree?"

He stumbled at the little step up from the study into the dining room. I held him by his arm. It was like a cricket stump. But his determination was clear as he sat down on his favoured chair. He looked at me whilst I poured the tea.

He leaned over intently towards me as if he had come to the last Act. .

"I don't know if you have read about the Lynmouth flood disaster of 1952?

It seemed a curious follow on from what he had been saying.

"I remember you telling me about it once or twice" I replied – it figured frequently in his conversations with me, more so in recent years, but I did not wish to imply any weakness of mind.

"You see, my boy, I drove through it when the roads opened – I remember my car boiled on Porlock Hill"

"What had happened was that 2 little rivers which combine at that little seaside town became devastating torrents after 9 inches of rain fell in one day above it on Exmoor - and in August! A wall of water rammed down trees damming the bridges and impelling great boulders down the confined main street. 100 tons of water burst upon houses, shops, chapels and halls leaving them exposed as if severed as if by an axe. 40 buildings collapsed."

He paused, absorbed in his recollection.

"Now where was I?"

"Oh yes…. You see that is what happened to George. I mean that two of the same events combined to destroy utterly the precious fabric of his life with Constance and their son you see".

I can only paraphrase what my father next told me putting in his mouth as it were what I remember.

He began:

You may perhaps know that Cystic Fibrosis is an affliction with no cure? It's genetic.

It is possible to manage it so that life is not immediately under threat. But within 2 years of Ben's birth it was clear that Constance was gravely ill. She had concealed from George the deepening severity of her condition with vomiting of blood and mucus, loss of weight and excruciating pain as the pancreas ceased to function.

It was obvious that Constance could not long survive but George rented a house in Museum Road to be as close as possible to the Radcliffe Infirmary and also the University Parks. He arranged for a full time Nanny to take charge of Ben at Aston Water. Joe and Ida Benjamin were able to see their daughter every day. Visits for hospital treatment with breathing aids and inhalation medication became daily but after a few months intravenous antibiotic drip catheter treatment alone kept her alive. She was compelled to move into an intensive care bed for her last few weeks of life which she finally left in 1958.

She was spared the knowledge that her son was now showing undeniable symptoms of the cruel affliction.

I saw a good deal of George and Ben after I returned to Oxford some seven years after her death. Ben was not growing at a normal rate. He was always short of breath. His temperature fluctuated for no clear reason

and he had an almost continuous wheeze. I remember his rather large
nose was always red, poor chap.

By the time he was six he was showing great promise as a violinist.
George decided to bring him and his Nanny to live at Museum Road
realising that without constant care, medication and airways clearance
treatments Ben's love of life would be overwhelmed by suffering.

Ben got a place at Magdalen College Junior School and by the time
he was 9 years old was playing first violin in the full School orchestra.
He passed the entrance examinations for the Senior School and was
awarded a Music Scholarship. He saw himself following his mother and
grandfather Benjamin into a life of music.

For George the consuming task of managing the disease deprived
him, by degrees, of his academic life and work. He'd given up his tutorial
appointment before Constance died but had then been voted an Emeritus
fellowship. He began some initial research in preparation for a major
work on Napoleon's Italian Campaign against the First Coalition's forces
on Italy in 1796/1797. It was his special subject as an undergraduate so
that eased the burden of new research.

However when Ben started at Senior School it was clear that he
was unable to do more than attend morning classes. His body could'nt
support the exercise that would have helped a little to dissipate the
mucus blocking his lungs. He ceased to go down to Magdalen except
for rehearsals and concerts. His limited energies were wholly absorbed
by study of the O level curriculum subjects.

George bought Ben a new Hi-Fi record player. Joe Benjamin gave
him a stock of LPs. I'd often walk in the evening down to Museum Road
after leaving our office in St Johns Street and sit with Ben and Joe as
they listened to classical music – mainly for strings I think it was. Ben
wheezed and coughed – but still would'nt allow Joe to hum the tunes.

Sometimes I'd find Ben sitting in his father's winged arm chair in
front of the fire in the first floor front room – it had double doors to a
room overlooking a small garden at the back. He'd be bent over his books
on a board resting on the arms. He wore his father's Claret Club velvet
maroon dining coat rather incongruously over a roll neck fine cream
coloured cashmere sweater. This seemed odd but George took me aside

when I first saw it whispering that these were the safest clothes for Ben to wear as he could'nt risk breathing in wool fibres.

There he was – looking up at me arrayed in gold braided velvet with his pale round face, his father's fine fair curled hair and deep set eyes – too deep by then I feared.

I last saw Ben on his 14th birthday. George found that Constance had kept the Holywell concert poster with his letters to her. He arranged with Magdalen for the boys of the School string quartet to surprise Ben on his birthday with the concert piece that she so loved - it had been a kind of serenade to her days of joy with George. Joe and Ida sat with Ben and his father in front of the fire at Museum Road while I opened the dividing double to reveal the players already assembled. Ben could not take part – he was too weak to raise his violin. He sat motionless, smiling as they played the Adagio. It's the first movement you know.

It was to be his last birthday. He had a month to live. His decline was shockingly rapid but merciful.

* * *

My father suddenly got up looking dismayed and exclaiming,

"Oh it's quite dark -good Lord it must be well past five. I've kept you far too long. You must get back to Oxford while the roads are still passable. Do forgive me dear boy. I was lost in the past. Quite forgot you here for a while - quite forgot you see".

"I thought perhaps you'd told me all."

"No, no – not at all!. All I've been telling you is but the prelude to what I was going to describe".

"Well then would it be all right if I were to stay the night?" I proposed, as I could not allow my convenience to disrupt his moving account.

"We could heat up Mrs P"s supper. I could'nt go back now without hearing the end of the Act – it would leave me suspended for days and the tension of the tale would be lost. And there may be ice on the road out of the village."

My father seemed delighted. He rose unsteadily and moved to the sideboard . Pouring 2 glasses from the Sherry decanter he shuffled back and set them down, shaking a little and tinkling on the side plates of our tea things. He sighed as he resumed his seat at his chair at the table.

"Of course - yes you must! – I am so pleased my boy – I am sure there are spare night things and Mrs P will do us an excellent breakfast."

"You will, I think, begin to see how all this was brought to my mind by Churchill's dream - so bear with me my dear."

He continued:-

'A few months after Ben's funeral George arranged to see me professionally. It was at the end of February or first week in March 1970. He'd decided to sell Aston Water subject to his parents remaining in the cottage for life. He wanted to order his affairs so that his estate was divided equally between Ida and Joe jointly, Trinity and the Army Benevolent Fund. He asked me to prepare the necessary legal dispositions.

We then discussed his future plans.

"Look here" George addressed me abruptly –"I don't want to appear maudlin or unbalanced – I've not much time for people who talk of the spirit that survives death. I can tell you this - seeing the mangled remnants of humanity in Normandy drove out any ideas I might have had about the soul or spirit. So it's nothing at all of that sort."

He took out a large red and white spotted cotton handkerchief from his breast pocket. He held it for a moment over his face before blowing into it with decision.

Then, almost explosively, he tried again.

"How it is… is this…" Then silence.

Seeming unsure of what was expected of him he moved his chair forward a little. He looked at me for an instant before raising his head slowly, as if his attention had been caught by something on the wall above me.

Without looking down he eventually continued with a voice strained and barely audible.

"Well …what with one thing and another you see Tom. Well, it has been rather a tiresome time for me".

"Rather trying."

"You see, what with poor Ben, I didn't really have the time to feel the pain of losing Constance. No – not quite that - more not having the solitude and the time– more like that - if you understand me."

He allowed his eyes to rest for a moment in mine. It was as if the words he was seeking were heavy rocks to be lifted from his path as he sought to explain himself.

"There really was never more than an hour or so when the needs of Ben did not dominate and force into exclusion everything else – one's feelings and thoughts"

"Trinity was more than understanding."

"My few times at High table in Hall and over port afterwards were priceless moments of ease and goodwill in that terrible time before Ben's death."

"But after Ben left us…."

"Well, you see Tom, the chill and emptiness of existence slowly overwhelmed me"

He hurried on as if getting out the words before remembrance swamped them.

"There came over me an almost tangible grief and longing for Constance - as though released from being suppressed. At first it seemed unendurable. Far worse than the sight of the violent dismembering of friends I witnessed in France and Belgium.

"And war made friends of us all. In that troop, you see…"

"Everyone"

"Now you see…. Tom …"

A door closed in the passage outside. It broke upon the intense still presence in the room. It seemed to launch him into the last things he had to say.

"In each street, alley and lane within walking distance from Trinity I find I'm still sensing her steps next to me. I know nothing about classical music - particularly what they call "string music" - , but whenever I hear it now, however distantly, she's there - around me."

"I can feel her by the Windrush at Aston Water and her presence when I stop in the Cotswold villages beyond."

He was now speaking in clipped tones and gruffly, as if to detach himself from feelings that he could not explain or dispel. His speech was interrupted. He seemed to need an inward breath for each utterance.

Any comment I could make would have been trivial in the context of the struggle my gallant friend was enduring. Slowly he emerged from his deep reflections. I could see him gently resuming his place again in the present.

At last he simply said

"I'm going to northern Italy to do research for my book – see the venues, if you know what I mean. The actual scenes of manoeuvre and combat and manoeuvre".

"I'll keep you posted with my addresses from time to time."

He got up – standing for a moment, quite upright, looking at me with sudden great calm – then, holding out his hand he thanked me and left.

I could sense an emptiness in the room. My father had fallen quiet as if to let Witheby go.

"You know my boy", he said, "that was the last time I saw George Witheby. But what followed was so remarkable as to confound any attempt of mine at explanation".

"You see I got a letter from George 3 months later – in March 1970. It was such an extraordinary letter that I kept it. It's in one of the little drawers in the fall front bureau in the study".

He started to gather his legs to get up but I forestalled him. I stumbled into the study and found the bureau opposite the fireplace. The flap was open. On the top at the back were a number of curved drawers on each side rising above the desk top each receding in depth. I opened the bottom drawer of the right hand tier. It contained an unmarked envelope under some book matches which I assumed were for the fire as he did not smoke.

My father was resting another log on the dining room fire as I got back.

"Ah you found it! Look here - why don't you sit comfortably in the study - put a log on the fire and read it undisturbed. It's quite long and the script is not that easy to follow. I'll be in the kitchen getting Mrs P's supper together. We could have a bottle of Burgundy if there's one at the back."

I put the tea things back on the tray and returned to the study again still uncertain about the step down. I could hear the oven door closing, the moan of the tap before a sudden splashing and my father's distant "Dear me" as I closed the study door.

The envelope was quite thick. It contained a few sheets of blue letter writing paper. I took them out. There were two other documents which

I left in the envelope. The letter was in a clear firm hand. It was dated 16 March 1970. I will do my best to paraphrase it.

George began "I must let you know what happened yesterday before it disappears from my mind. You were so close to Ben and Constance as was Joe B himself."

He explained that he had intended to follow the campaign path of Napoleon in north Italy in 1796 from Piedmont along the Po River to Codogno and then on to Lodi – quite near Milan. The battle of Lodi was of particular interest to him as it was an action in which the Austrian forces were repulsed as they sought to re-take the bridge over the Adda River. George Witheby, as my father had mentioned, had been decorated for his repulse of German Panzers approaching the bridge over the Meuse at Dinant in December 1944 in a similar action.

Arriving at Lodi he had taken a room with bath at a Pensione Inn - a substantial 18th century house near Porta Cremona by the river. The inn had not suffered from modernisation. It had an open central atrium or courtyard, too confined for cars. Its rooms were distributed evenly over four floors united by a stone staircase whose shallow treads rose continuously to an attic fifth floor. The handrail was wrought iron and cold to the touch. It was elaborate as were the supporting balusters some of which were loose in the stone.

There was no lift. However half way up each flight of stairs was a generous mezzanine level break. This gave on to a modest room set in the large bay built out from the side of the building into the small garden below, rising to the top floor. There was a seat against the atrium side of the mezzanine, below a double window which opened on to the little courtyard . The window had a projecting Juliet balcony on which were pots of budding camelias.

There was no Bar. However the Signora served drinks in the early evening from a large walnut table at the entrance to the dining room which looked over the river reflected vaguely in the grey glass of antique mirrors set in panels on the interior walls

Witheby's room was on the fourth floor below the attic.

He was addressed as the 'Professore'.

The whole was very pleasing.

On the day of his arrival at the Inn Witheby had hired a Cinquecento with the help of the Signora. Early the next day – it was the 15th March 1970 - he drove the 16 miles to Codogno returning to Lodi making short excursions on foot and following by car the route taken by Napoleon in May 1796. He returned to take lunch in the dining room. Intending to rest after lunch he embarked on a bottle of sparkling Franciacorta with his tagliatelle. The sun was low in the sky and shone directly on to his table. He pulled apart the flour dusted coarse bread dipping it in the shallow dish of balsamic oil.

A sense of ease came over him. He would rest for a few hours and then make up his notes of the morning's expedition. After that perhaps a Campari soda on the bridge terrace before supper.

He ascended to his room up the stone flights to the third floor finding the slight rise of the steps gracefully easy to tread. As he mounted he caught sight of the atrium below him with its large terracotta urns each planted with cherry trees now in full white blossom. He stopped on the mezzanine half way up to the third floor to look down through the lace drapes framing the long double windows over the little iron balcony. The clattering from the kitchen below as doors swung open and shut seemed far distant. He sat down on the cold cast iron seat pushing his legs out unevenly over the stone flags. He noticed little flakes of whitewash which had fallen from the high sloping ceiling. All was well.

There was a door opposite to him which had been left slightly open - on his side. The declining afternoon sun still filled the room beyond. After a while, from within the room came a sound of quiet scratching followed at intervals by what sounded like humming. Witheby rose unsteadily, crossed over the stone flags and rested his palm gently on the door handle. Waiting for a while he eased the door slowly towards him. There was window before him. He released his hold but the door noiselessly continued to swing open.

The sun was directly in his eyes. He could make out that in front of the window there was a leather covered writing table. It took up most of the room. On it was a pile of what seemed small sheets of coarse linen. There was a loose page on the middle of the table - it was filled with signs or symbols along successive groups of lines. As he shaded his eyes from the sun he realised at once that these were sheets of a musical score.

Leaning over the table was a figure of a youth whose head was turned slightly away from him. The scratching came from a pen of sorts which he was moving without hesitation over the page advancing swiftly along the lines. The figure hummed snippets of sounds as he wrote. He was engrossed by the music that he seemed to hear as if he were setting down the notes from an invisible score.

Reaching for more ink from a well set in the table the boy changed his position so that the sun caught the gold trimming on his deep cuffs and collar. A movement of his head picked up a ray of light shimmering for an instant through the boy's fine fair hair.

Witheby stood very still, entranced, as the boy reached out for another sheet. As he stretched out his arm the wine coloured velvet of his coat gave off a sheen where the sun fell on his sloping back. Round his neck was a white close fitting collar. His skin was pale and his nose seemed too large. He was thin and small. He looked up towards the window as if in thought and the humming began and then ceased. The scratching resumed.

Suddenly without looking up the boy exclaimed "Sei tu papa" and then "Bist du das Vater?"

Witheby could not speak or move. He watched the scene as a dream unfolding.

"Papa?"

The boy suddenly turned his face lifting his gaze towards the open door - expectantly still for an instant.

Again - "Papa?"

With a half smile he then turned back to his work.

Witheby was utterly motionless - as if with any movement the boy would vanish.

Then taking a shallow breath, whispering, each word set apart from the next

"Ben. My dear boy. is that really you Ben?".

Then, fearing he had not been heard but not willing to give alarm

"Ben it's me my dear boy - here — just behind you"

A voice broke into his consciousness.

"Signor Professore - Va tutto bene. Professore? Ti sei perso?"

A chamber maid was leaning over him her hand resting lightly on his shoulder her head inclined towards him with evident concern. She had laid down her pile of towels on the stone floor. His confusion, on being aroused from his vision, was obvious as she assisted him up from the hard iron seat.

He looked at her blankly. Then, awareness slowly returning to him, he mumbled "Oh – so sorry – do forgive me – it was just that ...."

Then seeing her puzzled incomprehension he smiled awkwardly and moved gently away towards the flight of stairs. Turning as he reached the second step he saw that the woman was opening the door to the room across the mezzanine her free hand clasped around the towels.

His room was cold. He looked out over the furrows of the orange roofs below him. Then, closing the pair of shuttered windows overlooking the Adda river, he pulled out the little notebook from his jacket inside pocket dropping it on the dressing table which stood between them. He was surprised at how exhausted he had become. He sat on the edge of the creaking bed his head lowered. After a while he took off his shoes.

He felt that he had just intruded into a precious private place. But the dream – for could it have been otherwise —had not vanished with reality. All was still vivid, impressed in living detail upon his mind. The shock and joy of the illusion disturbed him deeply. Sharp outlines of objects before him appeared to blur and dissolve. He felt weightless as if afloat. He rolled back as the mattress dipped under his weight.

Daylight had almost gone when he awoke. He saw that there was still time for supper - even the promised Campari. Arriving in the hall he saw that the Signora was still serving drinks so he had had plenty of time after all.

The warmth of the hall and undertow of voices were pleasant. The Campari sodas filled him with goodwill. He enjoyed his conversation with an English couple at the next table who in stilted Italian had helped him with his order from the evening menu. They seemed quite interested in his account of his morning excursion. He finished the now flat Franciacorta and ordered a large Strega.

He felt a sense of comfort and security as he closed the door to his room. The bed has been turned down and the dim bedside lights glowed through their silk shades. He would have a bath in the morning. Distant cheerful music and the muffled sounds of traffic were oddly reassuring as sleep descended on him.

Some kind of concert seemed to be taking place nearby. His ears became attuned more clearly and he realised the sound was coming from lower down in the Inn itself. He could tell that it was for stringed instruments. Probably four of them he thought. The music was not all disturbing. It was quiet but very clear. It began to enchant him. It was slow – an Adagio he thought. It was full of such longing and grace. The strains of the two violins were intertwined in loving harmony and seemed to embrace each other with childlike innocence. He gave himself up to the ineffable beauty that still informed the silence when all fell quiet again.

* * *

I had just turned over the last page of the letter when my father in a voice shrill with excitement called me to come into the kitchen. He was triumphantly holding a bottle of wine.

"I found it at the bottom of an old wine box Mrs P uses for her dusters, polish, kitchen scourersm bars of soap - that sort of thing. It's not a Burgundy as you can see. It's a '61 claret! Chateau La Dominque – next to Cheval Blanc. We had a case for my father's 70th. What a find. I just hope the cork's not gone. What a find - what a find!"

All thoughts of George Witheby and Lodi had been displaced by the St Emilion. He decanted it with infinite care.

Our last hour together that memorable day were spent round the dining room table. We turned our chairs to face the fire. My father rested his eyes for some time upon the sinking embers, remaining quite still as the fire died.

A long sigh closed his recollections as he looked up and gazed at me benignly for a long while.

"My dear boy – did you find the envelope? Oh yes - you said"

I explained that I had almost finished reading Witheby's letter.

"Oh but that was not all – not all. Didn't you take out the prints?"

Before I could respond he continued, as far as I can remember his words.

"You see, George explained at the end of the letter that at breakfast the next day – the day he wrote it - he had asked the English couple if they would enquire of the Signora about the boy dressed in what seemed to be theatrical costume and the music being played during the night. However they'd given him such a curious look that he made his excuses and got up from his table".

"George later sent me a further letter when he was in Verona asking me to send him a power of attorney, to be notarised over there, empowering me to complete and execute the documents required to fulfil his instructions and to arrange a facility for him with Banca Monte dei Paschi di Siena. He said he was not sure when he'd be back in England."

"Shortly after that I was walking back from the Covered Market to the St John's Street office. I decided to call in on Joe Benjamin to see if he had heard anything from George. Joe appeared overjoyed to see me – he put his arms round my heavy coat embracing me without restraint."

He was a little tearful. He called loudly for Ida.

"Yes, Tom, Yes. We did hear from George - we did. He sent us a postcard from Lodi. I have it here somewhere I am sure."

He fumbled in an open box on the counter of the shop. As he did so, his head still bent over bric a brac in the box, he continued.

"You know I was very interested as to why he was in Lodi. He told me it was for his studies – but how could that be? Who knows Lodi anyway? Only dusty old classical music freaks like me".

He pushed the postcard over to me but I remained caught by his comment.

"How do you mean, Joe? – is there a festival or some such there?"

"No, no – I'm surprised Constance didn't tell you – she was so fond of that piece""

"Joe – what piece?"

"Well, it was at an Inn in Lodi that Mozart stayed with his father Leopold when he left Milan on his journey to Parma when they were going round northern Italy. It was in 1770. I know because…"

'Joe had stopped speaking and was pulling out some worn wooden steps from under the counter, still talking as he shakily mounted and stood on the top his knees pressing against the stacked shelves with his worn boots close to my face. He began to ease out a block of scores and papers, some falling from his grasp.

"Ah yes, yes!" he said looking down at me eagerly "Here they are – "I knew I had them".

Descending uncertainly down the worn treads of the steps he placed before me a copy of a facsimile of a manuscript musical score. The score looked as if it had itself been copied out from a draft for it had no sign of any alteration.

As I looked more closely I saw that it was inscribed in autograph at the top.

"di amadeo Mozart à 1770. le 15 di Marzo / alle 7. di sera."

Joe was evidently delighted at finding it.

"I have many facsimile scores – my father collected them - you can get them even today – but then who wants them now."

"See this!" he continued, gripped by his own boisterous enthusiasm.

With a grunt he bent down below the counter to pick up a document which had fallen on to the boards of the floor. He puffed as he stood up turning it right side up on the counter.

It was a coloured print. Depicted in the print was a round faced youth with a large nose. He had a half smile. His right hand rested on a keyboard. Around his neck was a form of cream coloured chemise and stock. His coat was wine coloured with gold filigree to the collar and cuffs. His eyes rested on me with an almost unnerving calm.

"It was painted in Verona a few months before he got to Lodi. The print says it is by Saverio della Rosa though now they say it is by Giambettino Cignaroli. Who knows!"

"But what about Lodi?" I said

"Oh Tom – forgive me – didn't I say?"

"Well!" he said, as if presenting me with a prize, "it was in a little room at the Inn at Lodi that Mozart composed his first string quartet. He was only just 14. Such a simple but enchanting piece. I don't think there's any recording of it. K 80 it was".

Dear Joe and Ida would not let me pay for the prints.

He said they were a gift from their departed daughter and grandson.

* * *

From deep inside the house came "Lunch! Lunch!!" from Gaye.

"We'd better go in, Tom, if we know what's good for us!" said Paul.

With that he led the way out of the sunlight into the cool of the dining room.

100

BERRIES

Anne Gray was early for her appointment with me.

She had telephonedFishburns asking particularly to see me. I had retired from full time legal practice some years before. However my nephew had been kind enough to keep me on as a consultant when he took over as senior partner. I retained a few private clients but I had no acquaintance whatsoever with Anne Gray.

It was only much later that I discovered that Anne Gray's first calling was as a shepherdess. As her life evolved she devoted herself to the world of sheep, cattle, geese, horses and every kind of country trade and skill. Lambing, rearing, shearing, slaughter, skinning, and salting hides, calving, de-horning, milking, log cutting and splitting, goose and turkey plucking all fell within her competence and care. She had deep insight into the nature of things which made her articulate beyond expectation. She was not at all cultivated. Her power of expression came from sharp perception and an emotional intelligence. She was direct. She spoke loudly. She was uncomfortable out of her milieu of farm stalls, yards, barns, birthing lays, sheep dips and slurry pits. She was a force of nature.

I knew none of this as I walked up the two flights of stairs to the first floor to meet her.

What she told me in the elegant boardroom on the first floor of Fishburns was so singular that it has not been eroded from memory by time and succeeding experience. Indeed recollection has sharpened the more I have reflected on what had been revealed to me in those short hours now 10 years ago.

Whilst there is still time I feel bound to record the events that she described. Not as a mere narrative but as an attempt to illuminate, free I trust from preconception and judgment, the true character of a man revealed through the turmoil and sorrow he endured and of Anne Gray who brought him final solace and redemption.

* * *

Shortly before his death Michael Wynstick sent me a letter explaining that he was about to enter the Weldmar Hospice here in Dorchester. His handwriting was erratic and feathery. He asked me to see one Anne Gray. He had a certain disposition he wished to make for her benefit. I was unable to arrange anything since he had not given me any address for her. A letter that I sent to his last address was returned marked in an envelope with a short note "Not known here" and signed 'James Wynstick.'

A week after that received a letter from Anne Gray herself asking to see me about a card she said she had received. She enclosed a picture postcard. She explained it was from Michael Wynstick. A message was written across the back in what seemed to be the same script as his letter to me. It read as follows

"Bluebell, my dear, remember Berryland? Now get hold of Berrys. Go and see George Fishburn – solicitor Dorchester M"

Anne had called my office shortly after we received her letter. I arranged to see her.

My firm had acted for William Wynstick CBE and his wife Amanda since they had settled in Sherborne on returning from India in 1949. He had been a distinguished diplomat. William's parents also confided their business to us. William and Amanda had just one child – Michael. He was born in Madras at the beginning of the War – 1940 I think.

My father was senior partner at the time. He heard from William that they were intending to send Michael to England when it was safe to make the passage. They felt it was their duty as the heat in Madras would, they believed, stunt his growth and generally be much less healthy for him than England. They arranged a trust account at Fishburns to fund the costs of Michael's accommodation and keep. He was to stay with a great aunt in London. The school fees for his education were to be met by the Foreign Office. At any rate we were not required to hold funds to meet them.

It seems harsh today that such a severance of a young and only child from his parents could possibly have been less damaging to the poor creature than the midday sun of Madras. But such was the custom of those times for those in the Raj.

Just before his grandfather's death he had settled a considerable sum in trust for Michael with income until he was 21 when it vested absolutely in him. His parents died in the early 1990's. We acted on the sale of their Sherborne house and on the administration of their estates of which Michael was sole beneficiary. By then Michael had three sons himself. When we had realised all the assets he instructed us to apply part of the amount in setting up a trust fund for his sons and to retain a tidy sum on deposit pending his further instructions.

Michael had a troubled school life. I recall his mother telling me how miserable he had been at the Seaford preparatory school. It seems the only thing he took away from his time there was his lifelong love of poetry. He ultimately became rebellious and resentful of all discipline and restrictions. His parents were disappointed, I am sure, that he decided on a rural existence - not really as a full time farmer but more as someone whose life was to be taken up with animals, insects and plants - as if he was turning away from human kind.

It was fortuitous that he first became involved in farming at all. It was when he was in his second year at Oxford. There was a scandal which brought down all the weight of authority on to him. The Dean had taken on an au pair from Denmark. Michael had an insatiable desire for young women and he prevailed over this one. She went back to Denmark bearing his child. To his credit he followed and married her. I cannot recall what kind of farming they carried on but it was I understand quite successful. They had three sons and he and Britt seemed well set.

But he could not find the strength and discipline to cease his obsessive pursuit of intimacy with women. It was as if he could never find ultimate approval and fulfilment but was nevertheless unable to resist the temporary satisfaction of union or conquest – who knows which.

I understand that he had so many liaisons that for him they were like visits to the cinema. He and Britt tried to make a fresh start in England but the curse of his promiscuity ended it all. She took the boys and never saw him again.

Such was my understanding of Michael Wynstick's life and character when I entered Fishburns board room to greet Anne Gray as she sat at the long mahogany table covered with green baize.

* * *

Fishburns have been in Dorchester since the late 18th century – indeed in the same building. I was facing the floor to ceiling sash windows often found in classical houses of that period. This made it difficult to see her with her face being in full shadow. She had a handkerchief in the fist of one hand which she pulled out as I approached – she tried to put it in her other hand as she made to take my hand shake only to drop it on the floor as she did so. She bent down to retrieve it pushing her chair right over as she got up.

I suggested that we both sat at the end of the table opposite each other. I thought it best just to sit with her until her anxious disquiet fell away a little. She looked at the glazed mahogany bookcase behind me guarding leather bound Law Reports never referred to. The longcase clock by the door was the only sound as we both waited for what might arise.

"I'm Michael's cleaner Or that is I was ...."

"I looked after him – as best I could. In his last months."

Long pause.

"Had to drive him to the shops and hospital as well. Cleaned his cottage before his skin cancer got hold - helped with his steers and heifers."

There was a further long pause as she pulled the little handkerchief from one hand to the other while looking at the green baize below her eyes. She glanced again at the bookcase as if intimidated by its weighty volumes.

I could see that the experience of those few years were such as were yet beyond her power to describe. I did not attempt to explain to her what I took to be the meaning of Michael's note to her. I simply asked

"Do you think it might help if you say how you first met Michael? We might be able to see how we go from there perhaps?"

She looked up at me and held my eyes for what seemed a long while as if weighing in her mind whether she could trust herself to confide in me.

The door to the boardroom burst open.

"Oh! so sorry!" said a voice as the door was instantly shut again.

The seemed to shock her into response once more. She took a sudden deep breath as if finding her voice again.

Haltingly at first, then allowing the momentum of her recollection to carry her forward, Anne Gray began to speak freely. All that follows is what Anne Gray said to me that day, as best that I can remember. My hearing and sight are now failing and arthritis is gaining slow ascendancy. But so deeply incised in memory is the account that I heard from her lips that it is as clear before me as when it was first delivered by her. I have perhaps allowed my lawyer's pedantic expressions to creep in but not I think to change the sense of all she said.

* * *

I've worked all my life with farm animals and doing cleaning jobs when I could. I was living in Milton Abbas then and working on the Delcombe estate. I was cleaning for the two sisters who owned the valley. They'd inherited the estate but had no idea about farming. The woodlands and downs above and around Milton Abbas are one of the glories of Dorset. The estate was surrounded by them. Michael Wynstick lived in an estate cottage. He had a half share with the husband of one of the sisters in the Red Poll beef cattle reared there. I sometimes helped with the herd. I also went to the estate cottage once a week to clean.

That's how I met Michael.

He was a well spoken man and elegant. His was a very upright almost military posture – well built and not at all fat. He had black hair with no grey sprinkling. Being a good bit taller than me he habitually looked down with disdain – it was his common expression. His dominant characteristic was endemic rudeness. It was a means of keeping people at bay as much as defending an ego. Like the hostile smell of an animal.

Some two years after I began cleaning the cottage for him he burst into the sitting room with a friend, slamming down a document in red tape on the gate legged round table.

'Had to make a Will. There it is. So sign there!'

I had no wish to get in the least involved with his affairs and had never signed a Will. He saw my reluctance.

'George here is signing. I go first, so you have two of us to show you. As I am in the departure lounge now I went to Fishburns and got them to run off the damn thing'.

I had no idea what he was talking about.

But he went on 'Got melanoma. Found out on Monday. Skin cancer that is. They hope they can stop it going inwards. They didn't seem too hopeful'.

Michael had under three years to live. The melanoma began to take hold in his brain but by the miraculous intervention of an experimental drug it was held back for almost two years. But he was unable to do the arduous work on the farm. He was not permitted to drive. He was evicted from the Estate cottage moving eventually into a modern bungalow a few miles away – Michael of course called it The Bung.

It was a devastating setback for him but he uttered no complaint about his terrible affliction. He asked me if I'd help with driving him to the hospital and shops and keep on with the cleaning. I couldn't refuse him, could I?

* * *

Anne Gray paused and sat for a while before turning her head to look through the high windows out to the wrought iron balcony railings across the London Road to the tea rooms opposite. It seemed as if she had reached the end of an introduction to what was to follow. With her face illuminated by the sunlight I could see that she had a strong but finely moulded features. She was still in her 40s. Her face was quite free of lines though her hands had seen hard work She had an abundance of dark brown hair which now caught the light. She was generously proportioned but not fat.

She had an undeniable presence.

She turned her head back towards me. I could see that she had composed herself and was prepared for the ordeal of re-enacting harrowing events and scenes so recently endured.

* * *

You see, Mr Fishburn, I can only really tell you about the times that stand out for me. Looking back it was all so bizarre – I was so unprepared for it. I'm not sure exactly when the things I can tell you about actually happened – so if it's all right I'll just say what I remember even though it might not be at all what you expect. Just like pages pulled randomly out of a child's picture book.

Well ... Michael.... You see... How was it.... Well, he loved the colour blue. It was the heavenly colour he often said – always there. Something happened early on which started him calling me 'bloated bluebell'. He was terribly rude you see. All the time.

I had called in on him shortly after he'd moved to the Bung.

April had just turned into May but it was cold. I had on my farm blue overalls faded with the years and a blue woolly hat.

"Ah fair damsel – decked all over in blue – of all colours the most serene."

"Now, we're off to Tesco my good woman" as he pushed past me out of the front door to my yellow car.

"I'm not going into Tesco like this" I blurted out as he opened the passenger door.

He was subsiding with his stick into the car as he bellowed

"Oh but I don't think you're overdressed – not at all. Just right. But I could lend you some baggy shorts if you wish"

We stuttered into the Tesco car park.

As he started across to the entrance he started to sing" "Ah Tesco Tesco blessed Tesco, Oh Mecca of the gross obese!" to the tune of 'Oh God our help in ages past'.

He'd never take a wire basket. I was his serf; there not to speak but to carry. His habit was to proceed along the aisles very slowly like a general inspecting raw recruits. He'd point his stick at the items of his choice as if they were defaulters. I was there to consign them to the wire cage. He wouldn't address me nor assist.

When he'd made all his choices he simply went to the check out. The expedition had been launched by him to procure his supplies alone. I joined him in the queue. Announcing to the puzzled cashier "Let her have the change" he put down bank notes far exceeding the likely cost and then slowly left the store looking up as if silently acknowledging an invisible crowd.

"You've earned a treat" was his instant comment as I got in the car after squashing the shopping bags into the boot.

"£20 for last week's wages and something for petrol would be nice" I said pulling in the driver's door.

"We're going to Delcombe Woods. There is a wonderful sight there you must not miss."

I'd spent many childhood hours in those woods but it seemed churlish to spoil his wish to please by smothering it with my own experience.

Michael issued an order for me to pull over at an opening along the high straight road to Bulbarrow. White garlic flowers lay thickly along the verges. An estate path fell away down through the beech woods below us. The slope gave dense emphasis to the sublime mantle of delicate blue that now lay on the woodland floor. The tall beech trees were not in full leaf and their pale emerging green was caught by the sun. All around and far beyond below the bluebells rose from the soft ground – the haze of blue deepening as they were lost in the distant trees.

It was beyond description beautiful.

Michael had found a tree stump and sat down stiffly among the lovely flowers, his stick across his lap. The path took me downhill a little way over a sudden drop which was concealed by the blue and green carpet. Stepping into a void I lost balance. I leaned back to avoid falling but toppled over on to the waiting ground.

I sat up among the bluebells. They had no real scent but they released a subtle fresh smell which was so beguiling that I sat there for a few moments.

"What delight – a bloated bluebell listening to the pipes of Peter Pan no less." came the loud repeated guffaws from above as he saw my upper half with blue overalls and blue hat above the blue green ground.

He was still snorting with laughter as we regained the road.

"Bonny bloated Bluebell – oh yes!"

* * *

Michael told me that after he'd school – I think he was at Charterhouse or it may have been Sherborne – he was resolved never to follow the path into banking, stockbroking, the Bar or the Civil Service trodden by his public school generation. He was intimidated by the formal and social demands of those callings which still retained the prejudices and class obsessions of the Edwardian age.

"I'd never put on a starched wing collar, serge jacket, sponge bag trousers, polka dot tie and watch chain waistcoat. Stuffed up ready to be enrolled into the establishment and grovel at the end for a gong or knighthood from another fellow pin stripe of identical views and values".

This was a mantra I often heard him sound, almost as if he'd rehearsed it for repetition.

I don't know how he had got into farming. You said it was through his first wife?

As I explained, when I first met him he'd had a half share in a herd of Red Poll beef cattle. They were fine beasts but always filthy. He was less than fastidious as to how he looked after the animals and insects in his care. He thought they would somehow manage. It was both shocking and hilarious to see him walk past his chicken runs as the wretched unfed birds cast themselves at the netting to be hurled immediately back again in feathered squawking chaos. It was as if he was taking revenge.

He was also celebrated as a bee-keeper in the bee world. He wrote articles for the British Bee Keeping Association and his bees produced intensely fragrant honey.

He often received visits from bee devotees. He was very sensitive to what was happening in the hives. Years of working with them had given him an extraordinary skill in detecting the impact of a queen bee's death – he'd keep close watch for the appearance of queen cells as a sure sign of an impending swarming. He was able to use the bees swarming impulse to breed a new queen yet still retain the colony together.

But when it came to harvesting the honey he wouldn't care too much if when removing the 'super' frame over the brood frame he squashed a few bees when capping the cells to remove and filter the honey.

I'd often see the little corpses at the bottom of the honey jars.

"They add a bit of protein. Stop your railing Mistress Bluebell and take a glass or two of wine with me" as he dismissed my protests.

* * *

Michael preferred the society of bees, cattle, pigs and geese to humans. He also loved the changing hedgerows and woodlands of which there is an abundance around the Bung. He was most knowledgeable about hedgerows. He used to send letters and donations to the English Hedgerow Trust which I posted for him.

One morning I called in at the bungalow to take him shopping. It was one of those late September days promising a brief return to the hourless sunny heaven of mid summer. A thick mist, so often the prelude to lovely days, was rising above the shaven corn fields.

"Ah my charioteer! Boadicea herself– flowing wild tresses, armoured top, wild abandon – a bit let down by the Laura Ashley long floral and the yellow Ford Escort."

"I want you to make a way for me through the great unwashed to Blandford Forum for comestibles and a nice tart if there is one."

I tried to curb his rude exuberance saying "You've been at those pick me up thingies – only supposed to have them when the Black Witch drags you down into depression."

"Exactly my chiding wench" he at once responded. "You see I knew it was you who were coming – wasn't that clever."

"Michael do listen….listen!. I must have something for the journey. You know quite well its nearly eighteen miles and twice a week plus my sallies out to the surgery at Milton Abbas. Plus trips to the hospital. All of £20 a week. That's what you pay me for cleaning - when you do pay – or rather scouring this place – do you bring in the dirt with a shovel – how does it get like this for goodness sake!"

"Better than lucre you will have my doting attentions and my pearly conversation. And anyway today I have a treat for us both."

Michael took a swipe at my backside as he went out of the front door, left ajar when I came in. Chucking his clattering stick against the inside of the back window he collapsed himself into the quivering Escort.

It takes me a little time for me to negotiate settlement on to the driver's seat of my little Escort. As I reached for the gear column he took my hand in his squeezing it gently retrieving it leaving in mine a rolled up £20 note.

The Escort prefers a stately pace and rarely permits more than 35 miles per hour. Michael had his passenger window wound down to fullest extent. He'd look, almost gaze, at the passing beauty of the woodlands as we ascended above Milton Abbas emerging on to the chalk downland above Winterborne Stickland. He never lifted his eyes from the scene he beheld.

A comforting absolute silence prevailed as the air from the warming fields passed over our faces. Then as we made the long slow descent he softly put his hand upon my arm.

"Pull in up that track" pointing to a gap in the low hedge to our left. "Fear nothing, my comely Bluebell, – you're quite safe with me".

I guffawed as I guided the car on to the verge.

The track ran off Dunbury Lane down towards Winterbourne Houghton between reaped cornfields. Flint stones had made their way to the surface of the track. Michael elegantly picked his route using his stick to retain his upright bearing. I followed dutifully. Nothing was said. Before us lay the folds of the downs above Turnworth and below Bulbarrow. The sun had begun to take dominion of the pristine sky.

At the bottom of the slope there was some woodland and further scattered trees. The trees were oak and a few beech with the odd sycamore at the edges. Michael walked quietly along the woodland and around its winding edge, calling me to follow.

I found him standing over the remains of a small stone house, long since derelict. Alarmed pheasants, newly put down for the shooting season, erupted from the ruins taking noisy squawking flight.

He sat down on a low wall his stick under his chin. I got down next to him.

"I found this when I was first brought to Dorset". Michael was speaking softly as if describing a distant scene. "My Aunt Evelyn took me here one summer by train to Blandford Forum. It was intrepid of the old girl to brave British Railways - stopping trains from Waterloo and then from Bournemouth. She thought I should meet some relatives in Winterborne Houghton. I was six or seven."

"Their son had a bicycle. He'd grown out of it and was visiting a friend in the village. When the Aunt was having a rest on the Sunday afternoon and the house was quiet I wheeled the bicycle out of the shed at the side of the house and freewheeled down the little street, Water Lane it was called. I came to a cul-de-sac. There was a rough track at the end. I pedalled down to this wood – it was only a couple of fields away. It was rough but I was small."

"I found, to my joy, this derelict house. It then still had some of its roof. It was perfect for a camp and a stockade. I could attack and defend it. If need be I could retreat into the woodland depths."

"I found that if I lay - absolutely still – not blinking or breathing even – little creatures would rustle and run around. I was entranced by a rat. He came right up to me, his whiskers quivering. He seemed to have no objection to my being there. He had most delightful little pink hands and sat up to get a better look at me before applying himself to more useful work. He used his tail to balance. I thought that he was a very clever little fellow."

"There were then the remains of an abandoned garden. Just a few crab apple trees, currant bushes gone wild - some proper apple trees as well - they're now inside the extended woodland with a white flowering cherry."

"I lay there until the sun was setting."

"Of course I got into a storm of wailing and gnashing of teeth when I got back – put to bed with no supper – all of that."

"But that day was mine and has been so always".

* * *

"It's Berryland. You see, my wanton Bluebell, at this time of the year the wild berries fulfill their spring promise in full fruit."

He began to walk with delicate care around the ruins towards the woodland. I could see now along its perimeter the pins of colours dotting the hedgerow.

"What are you ballooning around over there for – get over here woman!"

As I stood next to him he raised his stick and with infinite tenderness parted some overhanging brambles revealing the fat little ovals of rosebuds of the wild rose. Just below these were bunches of of black bryony berries– round and glossy.

"*Rosa Canina* - often found close together but *Dioscorea communis*- the Bryony - it's poisonous – like so many of her sex"

"And there's a rowan tree half hidden by hazels. *Sorbus aucuparia. Generous* bunches of berries of orange and red. Do you know they really are delicious when made into a jam."

Michael held his gaze aloft in silence holding his balance with his stick.

I nudged his arm a little. I had seen large crops of elderberries further along the woodland edge borne down by their weight over the field beneath.

"Too many of those and you take off like a rocket – worse than syrup of figs" was his comment.

We walked slowly and with care along the ragged woodland rim.

"See those haws – on the hawthorn tree over there. *Crataegus monogyna. Believe me that's its name poor thing."*

"Round this corner I think there is some Dogwood. Yes there he is - *Cornus sanguinea.* The berries look like blackcurrants don't they. And the sloes. The fruit of the blackthorn and protected by its spears *Prunus spinosa. Such a lovely* modest bloom on the berries. Lots of those all along here. Planted as a hedge in the old days to keep stock from breaking out."

Michael rested, both hands taking his weight gently on his stick, his feet apart and eyes fixed as if entranced.

"Ah well……there it is…..".

He sighed as he turned back to the deserted garden of the ruined house.

"And then the crab apples *Malus sylvestris* and their rugged jointed twigs with sheltering broad leaves" he murmured, touching the branches with his stick as if to greet them.

"Sit here for a bit Michael before taking on the hill to the road" I said, immediately realising that I had burst a bubble as soon as the words had left me.

"Mother hen stop clucking!"

We started on our way back up the track. The September sun was strong but not fierce.

As we reached the road Michael stood motionless by the car. He was looking down at the woodland below, silent for a long while.

Without turning his head he continued in a thin voice as if he was mastering some inner turmoil.

"You can trust Nature. The rats and the berries. It's always is as it is. No judgment – no blame. They don't have an opinion about you. You feel at home, you see."

"Do you know – we've not seen any person – no one at all – since we left the Bung."

I waited for the moment to pass.

A soft sudden warm breath of wind caught his thin hair. It seemed to bring him into the present as he spoke with restored confidence.

As if bursting at last from his chains Michael thundered

"Get us back to the Bung. Bollocks to Tesco. Come on trusty coachman don't spare the bloody horses! Let's crack a vile bottle of Bally Polly wine and talk of twigs and berries"

* * *

It was not long after the Berryland outing that I called to take him to the Surgery for his regular check up. It was early summer – May or June. The consultant oncologist had told him he could not expect the experimental drug prescribed for the quiescent melanoma to do more than check its ultimate onslaught. Michael had thought the ravages of his affliction would resume after a few months – it would have astonished him to know that nearly 14 months of existence awaited.

There was a slope down to the entrance to the Bung. I parked the car there next to a bright new red hatchback. Planted deep along the garden edge adjoining the slope and along the entrance way were thick banks of hollyhocks. They were in full flower – mostly a deep pink varying to magenta. They stood quite still in the calm air. They were noble, keeping their station upright and unbending.

As I got out of the car that warm evening, I could hear Michael's voice in conversation with someone in the garden. I was sure that it was coming from the small terrace area on the other side of the Bung adjoining the narrow lawn.

Borne upon the quiet air was the finely cut voice of Michael – carrying an inflection of faint amusement and self -deprecation.

"How very charming of you to say so my dear".

As I came round the side of the Bung I saw a lady of early middle age, in a wide floppy straw hat and flowery cotton dress, seated at the iron garden table. She was obviously enchanted with Michael.

He turned to me raising his Panama hat with a gracious welcome, the more to charm his guest - for it contradicted his customary form of address to me.

"Ah! Anne! I had quite forgotten it was my evening appointment at the surgery."

"This is Phoebe – a lovely name don't you think?"

"But surely we still have time for a cup of Earl Grey – would you like to take some tea with us Phoebe?" he said hopefully.

"Well" the lady explained as if to excuse herself "I must confess that I was so struck by the lovely hollyhocks while trying to do a three point turn in your drive that I just had to stop for a moment and admire them. I'd quite lost my way. It was so kind of you to help. Perhaps just a cup before I go?"

I caught Michael's eye and discreetly shook my head.

"Ah so sad – the Doctor calls" he said.

"It's been delightful to have you Phoebe. Do take the Ordnance Survey map – it's essential for all the little roads of Hardy's country – bring it back at the end of your holiday. I'm here all the time so don't hesitate – it would be pleasure to offer you tea and scones."

Michael and Phoebe made their way together over the strip of lawn adjoining the road to the little red car. He had his arm round her. I could hear the sound of assurances of affection and regard being broadcast by him as she reversed back into the road.

"What was going on there?" I said when he sat down again at the garden table.

"You've never seen her before have you. Yet she was charmed right off her branch. And you don't like women anyway. No tea for you, you goat – a jab from the Doctor is what you need to keep you down"

"Well there's no danger" he said meekly. "The old weapon doesn't fire any shots. Actually the gun can't be raised at all."

* * *

It's just two miles to Milton Abbas surgery from the Bung and we got back whilst it was still light.

"There's some macaroni in a packet on the counter and lump of cheddar in the fridge. So lay on a feast my bonny Bluebell and we'll talk of many things over a glass of awful Valpolicella Soopeerioray"

I could hear him singing tunelessly to some music hall ditty.

> *Of shoes and ships and sealing-wax*
> *Of cabbages and kings*
> *And why the sea is boiling hot —*
> *And whether pigs have wings.*

He was sitting at the garden table on a plastic chair as I put down the macaroni cheese and the black pepper grinder. He poured out the wine in his glass. I had to get my own glass. He filled it.

Nothing was said. The evening yielded to night. Our plates were long since empty and the Valpolicella was down to one or two glasses. Michael felt no compunction to talk. It was as if he could not give form in his mind to an inner state. He had such a gift for wit and brilliant banter – like a gloss over a poisonous berry. He would also seek to explode his deep disquiet with startling bouts of rudeness.

Over those times it came to me that his gift of ease and charm in the company of women was in some way a search for release from himself or for a never to be found redemption.

Then, when it was quite dark he simply said

"It's not quite true that I don't like women."

After a long while I got up to clear the plates and things from the table, turning on the lights in the kitchen. I heard him take out another bottle of wine from the rack.

When I was about to leave the Bung for my place he asked me to stay a moment with him for a last glass. We sat silent in the dark in the sitting room for some minutes with the electric light from the kitchen catching the side of his face. He the spoke, almost inaudibly.

"I've never been able to see women as safe. I mean, I'm not at all at ease with them. It's partly being strongly attracted to them but also wanting to possess them – so to make them safe as it were - safe for me."

"My Mama, you see – she sent me away. I was not yet 5. I couldn't stop feeling I'd been to blame for something – never have. But then you know about that – selfish of me to keep mentioning it but it's like a growth in my brain. Hard to ignore and impossible to banish."

A tractor and sileage trailer passed down the road lights ablaze.

"Ah well. It doesn't matter now – thank heaven. It's all receding. The ebb tide you see."

"Do you know that poem by Tennyson? "No, forgive me - why should you Anne."

"It goes like this if I can remember it - just the first verse is all the remains in memory – strangely I have remembered it all these days since I was forced to learn it at Plucks Hill school as punishment for something trivial – learning poems as a punishment that was the best bloody thing I got from that torture house.

> *Sunset and evening star*
> *And one clear call for me*
> *And may there be no moaning at the bar*
> *When I put out to sea*

"That's the sand bar you get in estuaries you see – in case you are thinking of him leaving the pub"

He looked at me his still eyes lit by the light of the kitchen. He'd often recite poetry when wine loosened his tongue.

"It was good of you to make supper and listen. Wine softens the flinty edges doesn't it".

He seemed to hesitate as if some words were waiting in his mind but then rose stiff but with grace from his simple kitchen chair.

"I think I'll head for my cot now."

* * *

On an evening in September about nine months before the cancer returned, I came to clean the Bung at later than my normal hour.

We could not know when the cancer would soon again break out from the diminishing effect of the restraining drug. But on later reflection I sensed that Michael had turned inwardly to face the impending descent into final illness that could not long be postponed. For as I came in I found him sitting silently in his Parker Knoll chair. He did not, at first, look up at me. He was deep in inner reflection as if reviewing in his mind the play and passage of past events and times.

I started for the kitchen as it was bound to be in a state. As I moved he looked up.

"Ah Bluebell. There you are my dear."

I was astonished at his endearing tone. It was as if he had been dreaming quietly and woken with an inner smile.

"I have two bottles left of a 1990 claret. Chateau Montrose. A St Estephe. Not from Tesco this one. I'll allow you a glass before cleaning and another after."

Pulling himself up with a jump he seized my hand and pulled me out on to the little terrace. An opened and empty bottle of red wine was on the table. It had been poured into a glass decanter. I was surprised to see that there was a glass for me.

Sitting on the plastic chairs we looked at each other. He seemed to be verifying if it was safe for him to utter what was emerging from his memory.

"Do you know that my father ended up high in the Diplomatic Corps? That's what the invitations to Buckingham Palace were for – the ones on my desk. My people were stationed in India and then Ceylon – what's it called now– Sri Lanka."

It was obvious that he was opening a window onto his earliest memories. He looked at me as if to see how his words had affected me. He poured two generous glasses.

We sat together in the sunlight. It was bright but not hot. We waited, but not for anything. Another glass was poured.

"A big wine. Wonderful year. Best drink it while I can. I'm being slowly reeled in you see. So Carpe Diem for me"

I didn't want to risk obstructing the trickle of recollection that had started to flow from him with the help of his beautiful wine. I'd grown accustomed to waiting for a long time in silence as he struggled to express things held within.

I could see he was drawing on raw courage to make the next advance.

"You see, the English in India – those in the Indian Civil Service or military – wouldn't let their children grow up in the intense heat. The Victorians started sending their children back to grow up in England.

Papa was in Madras. So I was put on a steamer aged just under 5 years old. I think I was in the care of a nurse who was going back to England – she was young, I remember, and kind."

"It was in 1944. The steamer went round the Cape. We docked at Liverpool".

"I can't remember much about the next few months."

"I was with my great aunt Evelyn in a large mansion flat in Bayswater for all that time – when not at boarding school. I remember it was always dark. It had a lift. Whenever I got the chance I took it right to the top where there were noisy cogs and motors clicking and clacking. There was Kensington Gardens but with aunt Evelyn always there I couldn't find children to play with for long."

Michael seemed to withdraw from the scene he was depicting.

"Well, I was in a little school in Moscow Road, Bayswater for two years, just down from great aunt Evelyn's flat. And then I was despatched to a boarding preparatory school when I was still 7. That was a very bad time. Awful. I dread thinking about it even now – for years I had bad dreams about it waking up sweating. The dark panelling, smell of floor polish and clatter of boys in the passages."

"The school was in Seaford. On the Sussex coast. A dismal place with the biting wind all winter blowing over unyielding cobble beaches - as they were then anyway."

He sat quietly as if standing again as a little boy solitary in the salty gusting wind blowing over the forlorn grey scene.

"I remember my first night. No aunt Evelyn. No one I knew at all. Not knowing if my mother knew where I was. Having nothing of hers to bring her back to me as I lay there in the dark."

"But the worst thing, you see, was this awful feeling of guilt. What had I done to be sent away by her? I longed for her to forgive me and take me home. That's all I could think of. I was beyond tears. Every night at prayers I'd say my own private pleas to God to take me home."

"I became very unruly at that awful place. I wanted to smash it to pieces. I refused to keep their silly rules. I remember that we had a film show each term – normally at mid -term. I saw the film in my first term. I did not see another until my last term 5 years later – I was always in detention.

The Matron was empowered to beat recalcitrant boys and had a butter pat which she used on my bare legs and often on my bare bottom."

"Those beatings. It just made me feel even more guilty. I felt like an outcast though I couldn't express it. You can't if you're five can you? I just knew I wasn't good enough. No one could see my fears and guilt – not even myself."

Michael leaned slowly forward resting his elbows on the table, his head lowered.

I could hear him taking in long breaths, exhaling them deeply through his nose – rising steadily in intensity until, to smother his disquiet, he pulled out the large Paisley pattern cotton handkerchief he kept in the top pocket of his cream linen jacket.

"Dear me. That's not going to help is it. After all there's no point in sorrows now is there?"

Regaining some composure Michael bravely concluded his harrowing tale.

"Then one day in 1949 the headmaster told me my people" – that's what he called them - "were waiting in his study. So she'd come after all. My mother. But when I saw her I didn't at first recognise her – not immediately. Her clothes were so different. She seemed smaller. Out of place. A stranger really."

"Seeing her there I couldn't think of anything to say".

Michael paused – his mother standing before him in his mind.

"'Hullo' was all I could manage" he said.

We drank the last of the lovely wine. It was quite dark when, in a refined and lilting voice, as if to seal the sorrows he had suffered, he spoke

> *Trailing clouds of glory do we come*
> *From God, who is our home:*
> *Heaven lies about us in our infancy!*
> *Shades of the prison-house begin to close upon the growing Boy.*

* * *

I'd known from what he'd told me, briefly, when he was still at the Estate cottage, that at times Michael found comfort in wearing ladies' dresses.

It had happened that I'd mentioned to him that I had met a local farmer whose son told me his dad sometimes dressed in ladies clothes.

Michael had looked up at me for a long while.

"I sometimes like that" he said very quietly.

After a long pause he pulled up his corduroy trouser bottoms to reveal ladies tights. I laughed and laughed. He saw that I didn't mind at all however – so it was all right. But really I ask you - two in one field as it were!

I didn't actually see him wearing such clothing until after that September evening on the little terrace with the Chateau Montrose. It was as if by opening up the secrets of his pain and torment he'd loosened some reserve clamped tight within. It was a stage in revealing himself. He had found it in himself to take the risk of my rejection.

All I expressed was mild hilarity so, with his protective rudeness on his side, we reach a kind of jocular equilibrium.

Over the next few months I'd often find him sitting through the winter hours in his chair before the fire with a dress or skirt on. He also put on tights – but not, as I recall, ladies' shoes. I can't remember if he wore a blouse but it wouldn't have been too noticeable as he wore cream coloured loose fitting shirts.

He'd no desire to be or become a woman. He was through and through a goat. There was always a glint of desire in his eye. It never left him. He often referred to it as his downfall. It was so curious – he was left by his first wife because he was always seducing women and left by his second wife because he dressed like one.

I once saw him stomping round the garden with a thick tweed jacket, tweed cap, brogue shoes and a dress. Whenever we went to Dorchester for his hospital checks he would drag me into Joules to look at the latest fashions. He seemed to enjoy brazenly ordering a dress or skirt courting the risk of outrage – but of course they always thought it was for me particularly as I'd a generous figure.

He didn't speak to me directly about this trait. But it was obvious from his demeanour and attitude that he found it most comforting to wear soft and pretty clothes. It was as if the problems of the world were for a while lifted from him. He no longer had to be brave. He no longer felt the pull to be charming. He no longer had to secrete his fear and guilt. It seemed to have the effect of dissolving hard edges and allowing subtle shades and soft tones to colour his life.

He lived in chaos in the Bung. Nothing was put away and all surfaces were smothered with things discarded. Yet, invariably. the ladies night-dresses, in which he habitually slept, would be meticulously folded and laid out on his pillow.

I found nothing offensive or even unnatural about all this. I stopped noticing and never chided or reproved him. For him it was not a matter of identity but of solace.

Can you really wonder at how it was that he sought the amiable feel of soft cottons and silk? How could he be denied such slight relief from pain and guilt and sorrow?

* * *

Michael paid a heavy price with the judgment of others.

He lost the society of his beloved sons and also of his second wife to whom he was devoted. They rejected him utterly. It was as if their own identities were called into question by his wearing a skirt so that in some way, by associating with him, they would warp their own sense of who they were.

For years Michael had tried to restore loving relations with his sons. He told me – well you have mentioned it too - that he'd set up a trust fund for them and their children with a good bit of the money he inherited when his parents died in 1991. He constantly spoke of them. He would send them gifts not just on birthdays and festivals but regularly through the years. I'd always be posting cards to them at Milton Abbas Post Office once he'd stopped driving. Never a card came back nor call was made.

I recall that he bought a flock of sixty ewes for one of his farmer sons to re-generate his flock. Thanks of any kind were there none.

I would sometime come in on the dark evenings of winter and he'd simply be sitting in his old Parker Knoll wing back chair facing the unlit fire, deep in the recesses of memory.

He couldn't free himself from the guilt of being rejected by his mother. It pierced him constantly. I well remember his anguished words on my coming from the kitchen into the unlit sitting room to collect a tray one winter evening.

"Why is it that I can't get rid of this guilt in me. I feel I have done something dreadful and not yet been punished. It's like longing with all my heart to be cleansed finally and forever. If being beaten to an inch of my life would help I'd willingly submit to it. Willingly. Just to feel redeemed. Only that. Redeemed, restored. A final atonement."

For a moment I honestly thought he was going to ask me to beat him naked with his stick.

He spoke so eloquently. It was obvious it was a catechism he had recited in some form all his life. Any comment of mine would have been trivial. So I just sat with him for it must have been nearly an hour.

He let me bring him some soup and a lump of cheese and rye biscuits. He liked the sound they made when crunched. I also left some Marmite – a favourite since childhood he said.

* * *

Some weeks after that I called on my way back from work on the adjoining beef cattle farm to see if he wanted help with his supper. Again he was sitting in the low light of evening looking as the fireplace. Without speaking to him I got together some kindling and logs from the shed. I managed to get the fire lit even though the kindling was mainly rotten twigs.

The kitchen was in a bad state. I started on the pile of dishes and pans. There were even a few flies – in November. I got the worst of it done when he called to me. I put out a warmed tin of tomato soup into a bowl with some crusty bread and took it to him on a tray that fitted over the arms of his chair.

"Ah radiant Bluebell! Take a glass of red gut rot with me. Sorry it's not a first growth but that takes too long to get ready and you will keep popping in like this. Wish I could take you to Plumber Manor – Prideaux Brune owns it. Has done for 400 years the silly bugger. A good man, even though a Harrow boy. Lovely place. Bloody good food and capital wine list. I'll get you there one of these evenings. They like eccentrics so you'll be at home. Used to take Geraldine there –she absolutely loved it."

Geraldine was his second 'wife' – I don't think they were married. She was a cleaner at one of the houses on the large estate which owned all the land around the Bung. From what he told me he was devoted to her. She seemed to present no threat. Perhaps he found the same frail security with me. All had been well for a few years it seems.

Her family came to hear of Michael's disposition to wearing a lady's dress and tights. They were Jehovah's Witnesses. They boast that 'they do their best to imitate Jesus Christ and are proud to be called Christians' asserting that 'they want to honour Jehovah, the Creator of all things'. But no room apparently is there in their kingdom for someone in a ladies dress, if not a lady. Their evangelist zeal demanded of Geraldine, their daughter in God, an immediate severance of all contact with Michael.

* * *

It was in the last week of June that the drug ceased to have any further effect.

Michael began to belch and pass wind uncontrollably as the cancer now moved to his stomach and began to consume his gut. His sense of dignity and old world poise were utterly disrupted. He was acutely embarrassed – repeatedly apologising. Then his appetite almost disappeared.

It was at this time that the imminence of his death was borne in upon him. I saw that it had fallen upon me to do all I could for him.

I used to sit at the little table in the kitchen where we had so often shared a glass or two of wine. He would be opposite – really very close to me. It was then that I began to speak a bit about how we all must withdraw from this world of created forms. I could only say how it had come slowly upon me over the years. What could I do? No one knows do they? How can they? He had no other person to comfort and fortify him.

I'd hold him steadily in my gaze. I explained that we emerge as souls into existence and we return. We pass through a tunnel into radiant light. We are assisted by other beings loved by us and loving us to make the transition.

Now, very ill, Michael reached out a withered arm to grip my hand.

I told him that, beyond all doubt whatsoever, his Mama was waiting there to help him over and that I knew this as the soul knows itself.

"All is well, all will be well" I told him - repeated and repeated.

He looked at me without blinking or any sign of mistrust or disbelief.

And then, one of those times, when I had for a while held his attention to my poor words of comfort he astonished me by saying, very softly,

'Our birth is but a sleep and a forgetting;
The Soul that rises with us, our life's Star,
Hath had elsewhere its setting
And cometh from afar.'

During those three months from June to September as the bowel cancer took irreversible dominion over his frail and declining body he displayed unyielding courage and endurance beyond what I can justly describe.

It was not resignation, for he loved the Natural world deeply until his last breath - as I myself witnessed in the Hospice. It was more a sublime acceptance of what is. An inward release of resistance to the course of things. Moreover, as the indignities of the body's slow degeneration and collapse became more devastating he maintained an aloof and constant detachment. It was as if he was walking in deep slurry but saw no reason to pay it any attention.

He remained attentive to me. He revealed no self pity or made any complaint. He was still mildly rude like the growling of a much loved aged dog. He would never chide me. Indeed his banter and rude comments seemed to keep him in a sphere of normality.

The descent from the semblance of ordinary existence into complete helplessness was so rapid that it shocked me dreadfully. I'd no experience of dissolution of the body so rapid and consuming. Nothing in my life with animals had prepared me for it.

I'd taken to coming in each morning to get him up and getting his breakfast washing his urinal bottle and returning in the evening to help him into his bed. He was almost too weak to walk. But there then came that dreadful morning when, coming into the Bung, I saw Michael standing in the doorway of his bedroom. He was steeped and covered in foul smelling excrement. It was almost head to foot since it had erupted out of his defeated body as he lay prone in bed. Poor man. It was beyond any apology or gracious regret.

It came to me that I'd have to treat the body before me like a heifer much spattered with shit being washed down completely ready for a Show. I found the strength to clean him naked all over until all trace of foulness was gone. He was beyond embarrassment. As I washed him I realised that the Michael I had known hitherto had vanished.

I would take him to the lavatory to pass wind and shit – all bursting uncontrollably out of his wretched form – he kept saying how sorry he was for all this trouble. I uttered soothing words and comforting. Michael was moving into the shadow of death.

It was then that he felt the loss of his children's society most keenly. On one brief occasion one his daughters in law called. She saw the degradation of his worsening condition. The smell of faeces and urine was oppressive. Sheets were piled up waiting for immersion in the washing machine. Flies seemed to be particularly insistent that late summer and the heat was oppressive without full ventilation which his condition did not permit. There was a pervasive odour of Jeyes Fluid.

I recall in these last days at the Bung that the Doctor called with a substantial flask of morphine which he placed on a shelf above the headboard of the bed. He was very direct and truthful.

"You've got about three weeks to go. You can have whatever death you want. You can die in a hammock in your garden or here in bed. Or we might be able to get you into a field. But it would give relief to Anne and make visiting much easier if you moved in to the Weldmar Hospice."

Michael disdained sentimental feelings. He'd no wish for a death to be remembered as if it were a wedding in the Maldives.

"It is what it is. You only suffer more if you deny what is" he murmured. That was all.

At times I just had to go outside and sit with a hankie to my eyes. It was his dignity and stoic indifference that gave me stamina.

None of his three sons came to visit him. They all lived with their families around Sherborne, just 12 miles away. By their judgment of him they ensured that a stranger, his cleaner and driver, having no more than a brief association with him, would usher their father, with her poor offerings of comfort and care, as best she could, towards his final resting place.

It was in those final days with Michael at the Bung that he came to reveal, in parts and through glimpses and reflections, the deep turmoil that underlay the crust of his existence. The distance that he'd been able to maintain from me by rude banter and evasive charm had receded with the imminence of his death. He'd at the last found it possible at times to disclose something of the pain and confusion of a four year old child at being rejected by his mother – he couldn't see it otherwise nor could his maturity heal an amputation.

The impression on a dependent little child had been deep and indelible – it was one of profound guilt for having done something or for being someone that has brought down upon himself a fearful sentence of permanent exclusion from home, love and trust.

To be so cut off and remain severed from his mother for five years was a permanent loss for a small growing boy. To feel guilt for this cruel sentence must have been unendurable. It exacted horrible pain, fear and sorrow for that abandoned child.

* * *

The ambulance came for Michael at the very end of September. He was anxious to take with him several jars of his celebrated honey to give to the nurses at the Hospice. I chose the best jars – those without squashed bees at the bottom. I made to put them on his lap but saw that that he had some picture postcards and an envelope resting there.

"Oh yes my dear, would you post these? I thought I should say something to each of the boys. The letter is for my solicitor but I didn't have a stamp. Would you put one on? I hope he can read it – rather a spidery scrawl, I fear."

The driver knew Michael well. He'd taken him to his chemotherapy appointments many times. Helping him into his wheel chair he quietly addressed the noble, courageous and dignified man that was Michael Wynstick.

"Come on old chap."

* * *

The Hospice looks over the A 35 on to the downs and fields around the Winterborne villages with Weymouth and the sea beyond. It's set in generous grounds with oak, maple and sycamore trees which were in full rig of autumn red and gold.

I saw him up to his room, looking directly over the lawn and trees. He yielded willingly to the firm and gentle words of the nurse. Smiling weakly from his propped up posture on the bed he told me

"I've arranged for something to your advantage when I'm gone. There's a card for you on the Bung mantlepiece."

I got in to sit with him on most of his remaining twelve days. Each one marked a stage in his withdrawal from existence. His hand became cool to the touch. Gradually his face fell in, revealing the form of his skull. At first he took some food and water but when I called one afternoon the oppressive dense odour of vomit and excrement told of the futility and failure of appetite. His breathing became slower and intermittent.

His eyesight failed - it may have been the morphine drip easing his pain. But his hearing was maintained until the end. In the last days he often smiled, raising his eyebrows in delight and turning his head to look at the door as if recognising a kindly visitor with his sightless eyes.

I would hold his hand on the coverlet of the bed.

On the last morning that I was with him I had brought in branches of beech trees with their golden leaves, cuttings of rowan, twigs with haw berries and crab apples bright red and green. I spoke into his ear slowly describing each of them.

Then, still holding his cold hand, slowly but loudly, to be certain he could hear, I said

"Your Mama is ready with her open arms to welcome you – she is just beyond the golden light. You are nearly home. All is well Michael. All will be well."

I must have heard something for I looked up so see the day nurse was standing in the open door – quite still.

Feeling embarrassed I explained to her that this is what I was certain would happen when he crossed over. It had been my constant assurance to him.

At this a smile relieved his gaunt and sunken face. He squeezed my hand. He was deeply content.

I did not see him again.

* * *

Anne Gray was silent, reflecting on the dark and intimate horrors of the passing of Michael Wynstick.

It seemed to me that it would trivialise her suffering and her achievement for me now to explain the note that he had left for her. But I was bound to do so for it was Michael's wish and instruction. I waited until she was ready to hear me.

"Anne, let me explain Michael's note to you. You see, he also sent me a letter explaining things."

"With his parents' inheritance Michael set up a trust fund for his children. He also left with us on deposit a substantial sum to await his instructions. Eventually he asked me to invest it all in vintage claret – red Bordeaux wine you see– thinking it would be the best investment. That was in about 1992."

"I tried to dissuade him but he brushed me off. He sent me a list of wines he thought would appreciate most. I am not sure if he ever intended to sell them. He took them out of customs bond so he must have thought of drinking them. At any rate what he told me in his letter was that he had left it too late to break into all but a few of the cases of wine. He'd hoped they would be his companions in old age. But of course he was still only 69 when he died."

"I sent the list to the long established merchants in London – Berry Bros & Rudd – or 'Berrys' as they are known. There was I recall about £15,000 to invest. I instructed them to use their full discretion and the wines they put down for him were of the 1990 vintage and the 1982 vintages. Berrys have now sent me confirmation of his holdings. Among them are Chateaux Mouton Rothschild, Margaux, Montrose, Latour and Lafite. About thirty two cases I think, as he had taken a few."

I paused to allow her to take in what I had told her. Then more slowly so that she would be in no doubt I leaned a little over the board room table towards her saying

"He gifted all these to you."

"You see, Anne these are now valuable wines. Very valuable. I should imagine they would fetch well over £150,000 given those wonderful vintages – possibly even more."

As if the shocks of her acquaintance with Michael Wynstick were not sufficient Anne now move back in her chair lowered her head as she raised the crumpled little square of her handkerchief to her eyes and wept helplessly.

* * *

At the end of his letter to me Michael Wynstick, in an almost illegible scrawl, had penned the following lines. They were addressed to Anne so I gave her the letter.

> *"Try to think well of me, dear Anne, if you can.*
> *'They say, best men are moulded out of faults;*
> *And, for the most, become much more the better*
> *For being a little bad'. M."*

Anne Gray passed out of my life, but rarely have I met one so selfless or so courageous.

Who will write the memorial of such a person?

Cast into the chaos and devastation of the gradual destruction of another human being - known to her only as his cleaner - despite his deep flaws of selfishness and sour disdain she brought him out of the grip of guilt and sorrow to a final and complete redemption.

Surely it has to be said of her that she was his very saviour.

NUTS AND MAY

This story is in the form of a letter to a dear friend I knew when we were both undergraduates at Oriel College Oxford. He died over 30 years ago from a brain tumour when still in his 40s.

It's over 50 years since we both came down from Oriel – long before Margaret Thatcher and Microsoft. I have been meaning to write to you about how things turned out for me once I left Oriel. The tide of events has kept washing away my resolution and memory recedes. But my recollection has been sharpened by a recent interview with a columnist of the New Statesman – a Mr Piers Jamieson. He wanted to find out how I had got started. He had a particular bias.

I did not expect that anything of enduring interest would emerge. Certainly I did not foresee that you would appear so vividly in my mind as to be present now as ever you were. We met but rarely after you came down and will not now. So this is an unbidden gift of gratitude for all that your friendship conferred on me during those brief months, now forfeited to time.

The New Statesman article –it was like hearing a piece of music being described but not actually played. The account was correct but yet not true.

* * *

A life peerage is often taken by the Press to signify a state of retirement. I wish that were true in my case. Time has evaporated since I arrived in the House of Lords. I no longer have the support of others I enjoyed at the Arts Council and later at the V&A.

So as a rule I try not to expend time on interviews. But Mr Jamieson had said he was an investigative journalist who was writing an article to expose what he considered to be the scandal of privilege still thwarting the claims of merit in the so-called Establishment. It seemed that I was to be the windmill for his Don Quixote. His case had a specious attraction. I felt bound to take up his invitation.

He had fixed in his mind that I had been lifted, without struggle or even effort, by a high tide of advantage and privilege over the rocks and reefs of life to reach an unmerited eminence in public life. He was convinced before we our met – and more so when he left – that as an Oxford scholar, with what he thought was a background of Edwardian ease, I was set to pluck whatever fruits of life I chose.

I agreed to see him at my club in Pall Mall – they dislike 'business' meetings and have a small mezzanine room for these, looking on to the gardens. The Hall Porter came down to say that Mr Jamieson was running late. It was over half an hour before he was shown in.

I sat in the pale sunlight reflecting on how the currents of my growing years had projected me suddenly into the broad flow of life. I realised that if I said anything to deny that it was the privilege of Oxford that launched my career it would be received as testimony of arrogance – a claim of personal worth and merit.

Yet it is beyond all doubt that when I finally left the City of Oxford I took with me a dawning realisation of the profound importance of beauty, love and stillness of mind to our life – indeed to our very selves. Not the stuff of investigative journalism of course.

It was because of this, before the end when all recedes, that I have tried to describe what passed in those few months.

* * *

Let me tell you a little bit about my life before Oxford.

Like most of us, I suppose, I just bowled along and was sometimes bowled over by what turned up in life. Is it not odd that, as we grow, no one imparts to us a simple catechism of the conditions of happiness? We all pass over the same weirs and rapids of growth and decline. So how is it that self-knowledge is less accessible than knowledge of quarks and the hadron? Suffering and misery abound but surely they are like disease and just as capable of treatment and cure?

Everyone knows that wailing self pity shows itself so soon in the growing child deprived of its expectation. But did you ever see your

Whippets acting like victims? Or meet a complaining or conceited dog? What is the nature of the human condition that it fosters suffering?

The power of sex takes hold disguised as love and as much to be desired. Who will tell us how it can bind us with desire and dependence? Nor are we taught about the search for an identity to fill a perceived but illusory vacuum.

Then there is adolescence. Is this not a step into the unknown before experience has shaped memory? There will be those who feel a thrill as they are immersed in the rushing stream of life. But there are always some for whom the unknown takes shape in their minds as a deep and awful abyss.

So it was for me.

* * *

Grandpa lived at Speen House, just outside Newbury. Speen House then seemed to me, a four year old boy, to be very large as we walked up the long slow wind of the drive for the first time. It was and remains a dominant late 18th century country house in a small estate on a bluff overlooking the Kennett Valley. My brother and I had come down with my parents from Liverpool after the voyage from South Africa where we had been born. It was 1945.

I recall only those things that a small boy found gripping. There were illicit peaches growing against a pink brick wall in the kitchen garden. Entirely forbidden.

Grandpa had tea in the afternoon at the same time each day in the tea room leading to the South garden. He slurped his tea. My step grandmother told Grandpa it was Earl Grey but I could not see why.

The top floor – there were three floors and an attic – included our bedrooms and was our refuge from Victorian cold stares and strictures. There were wide wooden planks for the floors. They were highly polished – ideal for silent pillow tobogganing away from older ears below.

There was a very large bow front at one side of the house with semi circular windows up to the parapet roof. Grandpa's bees once animated my mother with frenzied alarm. I was quite still as I watched, in fascination, the waving of her arms around her head and her cries and shrieks. We had all been playing a child's game of cricket on the Bow front lawn.

Grandpa had a sacred room devoted to "Guns" with glazed cabinets housing shotguns of hypnotic attraction. Being out of bounds it exercised magnetic force upon our interest and attention. On the top of the cabinets were glazed bow fronted cases of stuffed fish – trout tricked with dry flies by Grandpa.

There was always the sound of ticking clocks.

In the outer offices (rooms) beyond the kitchen and scullery were the game larder and the dairy and then the stable and garages. Cowdrey, the groom, made butter in the dairy. It suddenly appeared as blobs in the top of the milk. He plucked the pheasants. My step grandmother would see Cook each morning to settle meals.

There was a lovely smell as you came into the tea room which I was told was honeysuckle. In winter there was such a large fire lit in the garden room that it frightened us. We dared not say anything. On Sundays we walked down to Speen Church. Speen House had its own private pew; it had a little door.

From Speen House and then Putney, where we later pitched camp, I went to a boarding preparatory school aged 7. Harrow School came next. To the East for over a thousand miles there was nothing higher than Harrow Hill until the Urals. The world was down below.

I was urged to go to Oxford. A benefactor, Mr Briscoe-Owen, had many years before, endowed a scholarship at Oriel College capable of being awarded only to Harrow boys. I went to Oriel. I was not considered to be 'scholarship material' and did not think of sitting the scholarship exam. I manage to slip in under the net.

After the end of my second term at Oriel, after the 'Prelims', I was sitting on a straw bale in a barn on a farm on the South Devon coast working as a labourer to amplify my resources. A Velocette motor cycle arrived. It had a telegram for me announcing that Oriel had decided to deposit on me the Harrow closed scholarship. It can only have been that there was such an accumulation of funds, unmatched by Harrow candidates, that the College felt compelled to make some distribution when one actually arrived.

I could wear a Scholars gown. This marked the summit of my Oxford ascendancy.

* * *

My dear Paul, it was your quiet strength and goodness that sustained me when I slipped down, unknowingly, into the chasm of depression. You remember how it descended on me at the end of my second year. It was the time of my broken engagement and the imminence of Finals. You found out who was the College doctor and took me to his surgery in St Giles. You gave me a bed in the little attic of the rooms you shared with friends in St Aldates. You put me in the back of your van when you and our friends went to the Bear Inn, the Trout and the Rose Revived. You saw that I got up. You cheered me with your warm words. You it was who put me on the path that led to Miss May Davidson, the saviour at the Warneford Hospital.

I will not dwell on the awful affliction which you recognised, mercifully, as more than stress or sorrow. But, as you will not read this, I should attempt a summary account of those days of despair for those who might.

Under the dominion of the Black Dog even the slightest decision or response creates terror. Terror is the constant condition. Any comforting words of others seeking to re-order one's thoughts, or to give perspective, sound as if someone was speaking to you whilst underwater. Nothing exists except free floating fear. There is no stimulus from the senses that does not inspire anxiety –appetite withers – sleep cannot be admitted by the fear and panic of the mind – no gap opens between experience and dread.

Then there is the sense of losing altogether the personality and outlook on life that one believes to be one's self. They have grown to be your identity and they are altogether gone – you are a cipher, no longer having the sense of being a person.

Looking back, as it were, over the trenches into the gentle hinterland of those days before the Armageddon of depression, I can just recall a little of my personality. I was ebullient and unruly – to the despair of my masters at my first school but not so much at Harrow – to varying degrees creative, unruly, athletic, loving music, fishing, dancing, painting, cricket, football, skating, talking, leading the choirs until retired by puberty – above all confident of being able to do everything. I was blessed with success in almost every respect except for conformity and restraint.

All such attributes were sheared away by depression. It was as if there had opened up a vacuum of identity. All bearings of position and direction vanished. The underlying equilibrium of life had gone and gone for ever. I had disappeared.

In place of confidence and an assumed capacity to meet the challenges of life there fell over me a great weight of guilt. I was certain that the impressions of my friends about my ability were utterly false: that I had been fraudulent, inducing them to believe what I alone knew for absolute certainty was untrue. It was as if I had been wearing a disguise which had now been torn from me. The absolute conviction of lack of worth was the most enduring – no logic or comforting words could displace it. Others did not know what I alone knew to be true.

So it was that I first came as an out patient to see Miss May Davidson, psychologist, at the Warneford – in June at the end of my second year at Oriel.

By then my academic work – I was reading Modern History – had been impaired by the Black Dog. My tutors questioned if I would cope with the stress and demands of Finals given that the examinations would last five days with nine papers.

From that moment I was in the almost daily care of Miss D. My University and College life gave way to an existence in which I studied in College, living for a while with you at St Aldates, until being admitted to an undergraduate Ward at the Warneford after Finals. Thereafter I was a resident for the next nine months with a form of bed and breakfast tenure until I left Oxford for good in June of the following year.

I did not at the time realise that falling into the abyss would sever the cord which had sustained me in the certainties and rewards of life – life which was continuing for others in the sunlight beyond and above.

* * *

I found myself in a stone built residence in the grounds of the Hospital but set apart from the main building. It was occupied exclusively by

Oxford undergraduates. It was known as Ward 5. The second floor was for undergraduate gentlemen and the first floor for the ladies. On the ground floor was a sitting room with a piano and another smaller day room. Mrs Hargood was Sister, in blue and starched white linen. She had an office next to the dining room. The dining room had a bay window. It had plastic covered tables and noisy modern chairs. The floor was hospital linoleum. The walls were an off white buff sort of colour with a band of sickly lilac, below which was a darker colour.

The regime in Ward 5 was similar to living in College. Meals were at fixed times but optional – though loss of appetite would be a concern for the medical staff. There was freedom of movement although we were discouraged from staying out later than 10.00 at night. There were rooms in the main block of the Hospital in which one could study.

Let me tell you a little about the Warneford.

It was founded in the 1820s and funded by individual subscriptions. Its architecture was that of a Regency classical country house with deep bow windows to the front elevation and a classical pediment over its three floors and basement. It was extended on the North East side in the late 19th century.

There was an extensive lawn through which the Drive ran in a shallow curve from the gate Lodge house to the circular area in front of the main building with its imposing lobby – what would have been the carriage entrance. In the South East corner there was a wooden framed building which had been fitted out for occupational therapy. The grounds were laid out with shrubs and ornamental trees. There was a private Chapel.

'Kelly's directory published in 1935 describes the Warneford. It refers to it as a hospital – private then of course – standing on Headington Hill in a healthy and pleasant situation with extensive gardens and grounds. The hospital is *for the treatment and care of mental patients belonging to the educated classes'*. The *'appointments'* are said to be *'comfortable and refined'*. It states that *'The utmost degree of liberty consistent with safety is permitted and amusements and occupation are amply provided'*. *'Patients are sent to seaside, for change, in summer'*. *'Voluntary and temporary patients are also received for treatment'*

The sanity of the 'educated classes' was confided to the NHS in 1948. There were no more inmates outings to Brighton, Worthing, Bognor or Sidmouth. But otherwise, for those of us in Ward 5, the 1935 description was close to how it was in our time.

It may be that this conveys to you an impression of an elegant country mansion that is used as a special form of health farm. Nor would this be misleading. There were 2 secure wards – F1 for the women and M1 for the men as I recall – but aside from an occasional muffled shriek or wail from these recesses the whole character of the exterior and grounds was that of a small country estate with its mansion. Ward 5 was a kind of large stone built pavilion in its grounds.

Can you not but marvel at the selfless generosity and wisdom of those who founded the Warneford and carried forward its improvement?. £1 is worth 0.89% of its 1830 value. It is astounding to see what was actually paid by those individuals for a cause from which they could derive no benefit other than the response to duty and conscience.

Jackson's Oxford Journal for 14 June 1828 includes a description of the Hospital just after it opened:-....*a Lunatic Asylum was opened on Headington Hill, near Oxford, about two years ago...built at an expense of £20,000 [now £23m], voluntarily contributed;..... its centre-house is reserved exclusively for patients of superior condition, but....its wings are open to patients from the middling and lower stations of life."*

"Its whole system is conducted upon a principle of benevolence, and not for the profit of individuals."

Dr Samuel Warneford, up to his death in 1855, contributed no less than £70,000 or £79 million today to the Hospital and its improvement. Let his name be honoured by all who were granted refuge there from rank despair.

* * *

I had not met any of my co-inmates before. Gradually we were assimilated, particularly when, with the ending of the University term, all our days were spent together. They say you grow to love your comrades in adversity.

Geoff appeared to be utterly withdrawn and out of reach. He always wore a tie – it was woollen – and a woolly sweater with grey trousers. The most striking fact was his posture. He held his head at an angle. I think if was to the left as he faced you. Thus he encountered the world as on a listing ship.

Perhaps he thought the terrors of existence could he avoided by ducking his head to one side. It impeded his sideways views. He thus developed the habit of turning his body round, head at its usual angle, in order to hear what was being said.

When I got to know him well he had become confident enough to listen and to talk without the compulsion to turn his face round to follow his attention. Someone entering the room, when he was particularly enthused, would have witnessed him inveighing against the wall or window. As if he were declaiming to himself.

He would often appear to have ceased speaking while his thought was still active. At first I found this awkward. It was as if he was held in suspension since he would continue to rest his gaze where last it fell when speaking.

As my affection and regard for him grew deeper I was able to shake off all concerns about how odd it was that he would simply to sit without changing position. He seemed to have no impulse to break into the silence. Sometimes his thought yielded speech so that he continued along the path of discussion. Sometimes he just remained still.

A week or so after I had moved my few things into my room Geoff stretched out a timid tenacle towards me. I had a 'Hi-Fi' record player.

It had good volume and clarity for those times. I played such classical music as was familiar to me.

One evening after supper my door opened quietly and Geoff stood in the opening looking at the floor. This was a visitation and a form of acceptance. It was not a trivial social call. It is curious to say so now but it seemed of importance – a moment that was full of potential.

"That was K 355 wasn't it?" – mumbling at the floor without looking up.

"Yes. Yes it was – how did you know? – it's an isolated little piece that was a track on an LP my mother gave me in my first term at Harrow. To cheer me up she thought."

"Mmm.... "

"My mother didn't listen to music much but she loved the harpsichord for some reason and bought the record for me just because it was harp-sichord music. I'd never heard any of the pieces. It's played by Wanda Landowska."

"Mmm...." – not moving or looking up.

"It's only two minutes long but it has such sharpness, longing and compassion. Nothing could be added or taken away. I've never met anyone else who knows it. Do you?"

"Mmm...."

Pause

"Mmm.........mmyes.."

Just as I thought he was about to leave the room he looked up at me – sideways.

"Mmm........ he wrote it later than a Köchlel no 355 suggests – supposed to be at the time of K 576 piano sonata. It has no home according to Einstein. But there are one or two things of Mozart for piano that don't have a home. The B minor Adagio of March 1788 K 540 – a year earlier"

Geoff saw the LP record cover. He moved gently into the room to the chair on which I had laid it.

Picking it up softly he looked at it saying " Mmm... it's like the B minor – both have a kind of breaking of light on sorrow – in relief. Dissolving everything. You find that a lot in Mozart".

I was pricked by what he had said. Not only was it scholarly but it was also informed with definite passion and an emphatic conviction. His description was as perfect as his appearance was distorted.

That was the opening of a friendship which first took root in mutual love of Mozart's music – for me the novice and for Geoff the devotee.

One afternoon he shuffled into my room and simply sat down. After a bit he started talking about composers – it was about Beethoven and Mozart. We had earlier been listening at intervals to the Beethoven's Eroica symphony and his Emperor piano concerto. Geoff saw no need to preface what he said.

"Mmm… Beethoven's persona seems to overload his music at times. Sometimes it's as if there's too much of him in it."

I did not know enough of his music to add anything to what seemed like the opening of a thesis. But I had always thought, in common with the times, that personal expression was the essence of artistic endeavour. However before I could muster a comment on these lines Geoff carried on, without any break of continuity:-

"Mmm it's like Michaelangelo. He did quite a few Pietas but his last – the Rondanini Pietà – is the most moving. Everything is pared to the minimum. Human frailty compassion and divinity all as one. Same with Beethoven's late Op 132 quartet and his last piano sonata Op 111 – all consolation really it seems to be."

I agreed that we think of Beethoven as bound in a life of struggle and conflict but suggested that perhaps that might have been necessary to express his emotions in music. Geoff would not have this.

"Mmm…..but take Mozart. You can't discover anything about Mozart as a person from his music. There are the shadows and heavenly light but it's not of Mozart but of another form of existence which he makes accessible for a while. The person is the problem. If it intrudes you end up trying to be 'original' or worse still 'groundbreaking' – a sort of JCB of music. He said in a letter that he didn't aim for originality – Mozart that is."

Then silence. Just the noise of tea cups in the dining room and scraping of chairs. We eventually went down to tea.

It was from Geoff that I heard about Schopenhauer and his notions of pure perception as the essence of artistic genius. He had a library copy (unreturned I fear) of his 'The World as Will and Representation'.

One evening after tea before we went down to the White Horse he brought it in to my room with a strip of newspaper as a page marker. He had pencilled the passage he most wanted me to read. He gave it to me. I sat down to read it sitting on the iron framed bed.

> 'the nature of genius consists precisely in the pre-eminent ability for [pure] contemplation…(T)his demands a complete forgetting of our own person'

* * *

I used to dig out Geoff from his room whenever I wanted to listen to music – his appreciation of it was sharpened by his economy of speech and lack of any demonstrative gestures. He once explained to me that Mozart believed that music is the relationship between notes – not the notes – that it is through the relation of things that absolute beauty is known. He was very fond of repeating Mozart's comment that "*The music is not in the notes, but in the silence between*".

It was not that he was addicted to classical forms of music. He was very fond of Janacek's Glagolitic Mass. However he often referred to Beecham's quote when asked if he had heard any Stockhausen "*No, but I believe I have stepped in some.*"

This always produced at least a suppressed snort.

He did not think you needed to understand music or see pictures evoked by it. He was much taken with the notion of transcendence and music. He would sometimes mention the similarity of Plato's '*Music gives a soul to the universe*' and Lao Tzu's saying '*Music in the soul can be heard by the universe.*'

Geoff would often suggest music to me that I might find compelling. One day he said I should get Mozart's G minor piano quartet. I went down on the bus to Russell Acott in the High Street – it is now "All Bar One" – it had a tessellated pavement with the name '***Acott***' as you went in. There were little private booths in which records could be heard before deciding on purchase. I bought the LP – I think it was the Melos Quartet with Georg Solti as the pianist (the great conductor).

We listened to the first movement in my little bedroom on the second floor of Ward 5 at the Warneford Hospital.

Geoff familiar with it. I for the first time.

Commanding from the first bar, dominating, inexorable, unrelieved by little notes of grace, mounting, without respite, to an almost intolerable tension at its overwhelming conclusion – final in every respect. It fills my mind as I write this. We must thank God for allowing us to be born after Mozart.

I recall Geoff once repeating to me a saying of Mozart which, far more than anything that I can fashion, underlies all that Geoff perceived in his music. I set it out here for, as with his music, it is complete. "

> *Neither a lofty degree of intelligence nor imagination*
> *nor both together go to the making of genius. Love,*
> *love, love, that is the soul of genius."*

* * *

As the time approached for me to emerge from the chrysalis and fly back into the 'real' world I sought out Geoff's company more frequently. He had no 'social graces' and had spent his life at Oxford hardly leaving his room at St Catherine's and the college library. He would not even have been noticed by my school friends.

He had a little Vespa scooter. It was bright green. He called it Gringolet after the horse of Sir Gawain of the Middle English poem Sir Gawain and the Green Knight. He had studied it as part of his degree course in English Literature.

One afternoon I proposed to him that we go into Oxford and listen to as much music in one of Russell Acott's booths as we could get away with. His eyes glinted with amusement. We got through a good bit of Mozart and Beethoven before being invited to buy or go.

I suggested we go to the Cadena Café. At one time – until quite recently – this had been a meeting place for the better class of person, as they would then have been described. It was now in terminal decline. We sat down for a modest meal – perhaps fish and chips or eggs on welsh rarebit – I cannot remember. There had been no pasta immigration at that time.

The Cadena had kept its drinks licence from more leisured days. I ordered a bottle of champagne. The Cadena, it seems, had not served champagne for a very long while as all they had was a half bottle of Lanson, forlorn on the shelves as a display item with a discoloured label.

Geoff could not contain himself – he was engulfed by successive convulsions of laughter spluttering and snorting helplessly, his head still askew. It added a little bit of theatre for the few Cadena patrons when, in his efforts to suppress his outbursts, they turned into uncontrollable explosions and coughing. A memorable excursion.

Sometimes he would recite, in Middle English, passages from Sir Gawain. The lilting chant-like sounds emerged from his memory as strange successions of verses in a tongue forever gone.

His diffidence was almost complete but not so as to conceal his nature. For he had the childlike quality associated with genius. His calibre and intelligence was of the finest. He had an unfeigned dignity. Silence did not disturb him. He was a lover of beauty and of life. Like Sir Gawain his manner was always chivalrous and with knightly courage he faced down fear and despair. As with Gringolet it should be said of his spirit that

> *All was arrayed on red with nails of richest gold,*
> *Which glittered and glanced like gleams of the sun.*

When he left Ward 5 he went to work in a local authority.

A violet in the desert air.

* * *

'Pod' appeared for the first time in Ward 5 on one of the long days of summer Finals. I think his first name was Roger but I cannot now be sure. He had been studying for a degree in Zoology, his special subject being Cephalopods – all head and feet. Hence we dubbed him Pod.

Pod was virtually mute. Depression had crushed him. He was in full retreat from life. Calls upon his attention requiring any response drove him more deeply into the dark cavern of his existence. He had a very large lump on the side of his neck.

His landlady at his digs had got in touch with his College. Her concern for Pod had deepened in the weeks before Finals. He was not going out, not sleeping and not eating properly. He grew intermittent stubble. He took no baths. He neglected his appearance and dress. She tried to help by giving him a simple breakfast. It seemed as if he had been able to get this down. He would clear away his cup and plate himself so she could not tell what, if anything, he may have left.

Eventually the College persuaded him to see a doctor at the Radcliffe Infirmary who referred him at once to the Warneford.

The landlady kindly put together his few things and brought them up to Ward 5. On clearing out his room she found the middle drawer of the chest of drawers to be completely filled with her boiled eggs.

The time came when he was able to laugh with us at this squirrelling habit.

Pod's frozen diffidence slowly dissolved. As it did so, we all, by degrees, became quite learned as to the genus mollusc *Cephalopoda*. It was at first the only topic that Pod was capable of admitting to his mind.

The spacious freedom and respite from care afforded to us in Ward 5 created ideal conditions for embracing the most improbable learning and eclectic facts.

Thus you would, I doubt, have had the advantage of knowing that the eyes of humans and cephalopods are very similar. We have a shared gene called 'Pax 6'. Or we did over 500 million years ago. This humble fellow is a master gene prescribing how the eye is made. On reflection probably not male. Like Pod, these creatures have a lot of heart. Indeed they have three of them pumping blue blood. They are the oldest of Earth's lineage. But the blood is blue because of a copper-based molecule in its blood — ours is, it seems, iron based. The Octopus had been the first intelligent creature. They found themselves to have such satisfactory bodies they saw little purpose in extending their competences.

In the echoing dining room we would drag out of Pod sparkling facts to use later in banter. The octopus have very large brains and most sophisticated mental processes. They are able to get out of an aquarium tank slither over to an adjoining tank, descend and feed on the fauna therein (crabs) and return to base. They play ball games by squirting water at pill bottles, waiting for them to float back and squirting again – cephalopod ping pong.

Did you know that *Octopus vulgaris*, has 200 million neurons? The poor Californian sea slug has just 18,000. O V's brain grows one and half times its original size. This vulgar creature can change colour and texture at will.

How did you make your way in the world in ignorance of such things?

'Eclectic' is often the snob's term for unusual. For Pod the term was exact. He showed a private and particular discrimination as he began to disclose to us, in tentative statements, his knowledge and love of two English watercolour artists. His devotion was to the works of Francis Towne and John Sell Cotman. I had no acquaintance with their work. I had not even heard of them. Indeed I had no notion that any one cared much about watercolours.

As, very gradually, Pod was freed from fear and self imprisonment it was as if a spring, newly risen from a source hitherto solid and frozen, had begun to trickle and flow. His words were few but lucid and compelling. So passionate was his quiet and brief recitals of the virtues of Towne and Cotman that I can recall them even now as if reading from a script in my mind. He spoke softly. We all learned to let the spring flow in silence.

Pod told us that Towne was a sublime genius. It was not said in any spirit of contention or discussion. It was spoken as if axiomatic. Towne, we heard, was indifferent to the styles and practice of his time – the late 18th century – or to the tastes of its buying public. He was accorded no recognition in his lifetime. No general dissemination of his work occurred until nearly 100 years after his death.

Pod had a few coloured prints of Towne's work preserved from the Iffley Road wreckage. He was able, when gently encouraged, to demonstrate, from one or two of these, Towne's depiction of the play of light and shade in the instant of the present moment – the constant through the ephemeral. He was not diverted by any detail that detracted from the planes of tones formed by the play of light in landscape. His observation was not distorted by tempting claims of the picturesque.

Collectors regarded his paintings as unfinished and strange. He painted for posterity. He took great care to ensure that his paintings would be preserved until they could delight later generations, arranging that for the British Museum to have custody of a great body of work at his death where they it lay unseen for the rest of the 19th century.

When his watercolours re-appeared in 1907 they burst upon the world of Cezanne and emerging modern art. Towne had also simplified forms, emphasising structure and planes and the phasing of shadow upon shadow. He preceded Cezanne but for Pod he surpassed him in all those respects common to oil painting and watercolours.

Pod's love of Towne naturally extended to John Sell Cotman – also quite unknown to me. Pod would help us see in his work a kind of abstract continuum in transient Nature and how Cotman saw the planes of tones in landscape.

It seemed odd to us that Pod, like Geoff, kept mentioning the philosopher Schopenhauer. Pod did so when talking of Towne and Cotman. Some of us could not accept that Art can be explained or defined by thought. But Pod lifted us out of this pre-conception. He had found a saying of Schopenhauer on artistic genius. The true calling of the artist for Schopenhauer was to

> *"to hold fast and make permanent…the fleeting world*
> *which is for ever changing its face. To hold fast a*
> *single phase thereof which nevertheless bespeaks the*
> *whole ….. to bring time itself to a standstill".*

Pod explained that in August 1805 Cotman had executed a series of watercolour paintings in Yorkshire close to Rokeby Park and the confluence of the Greta and Tees rivers. He was just 23 years and 3 months old. Pod had prints of just 2 of them – Greta Bridge and another that I cannot now recall.

The painting of Greta Bridge is just 9" x 15". It is in the British Museum.

Its abiding impression is of restraint, ineffable calm and subtlety. There is a sense of deep stillness emanating from the work – not just out of the waters of the river but from every rock, tree, structure, from the clouds and the sky, each resting in a kind of singular consciousness – a limpid certainty – a deep and moving feeling of being at home. From the lovely variety there emerges an inexorable unity. Is there not in this lovely thing an eternal ever present perfection as if we are what is depicted?.

Pod did not embark on comparisons or discussion. He was much afflicted but his devotion was almost fierce – as if to set alight a fire in us.

Thus it was in Ward 5 that there opened for me a window on the incomparable mastery of those dear men, denied a lifetime fame, whose gifts were eternal.

* * *

May Davidson was a clinical psychologist. She rose to the very summit of her profession. A much prized award bearing her name was instituted by the British Psychological Society – of which she became President.

Oxford Provosts and Wardens regarded her as a saint. We undergraduate in Ward 5 had no notion of her professional distinction. We trusted her utterly. She had patience without limit. She seemed to devote all her waking hours to us. Never did you feel that she had anything else to do. We never discussed the Black Dog's causes or medication. She could not be tempted into the long grass by intellectual discussion or curiosity.

Let me tell you something that was quite inexplicable. It came upon me when in the early days of seeing her, before moving into Ward 5. It was this – you felt that her gaze rested on you at all times wherever you were.

She was a sure shelter and haven. To us she was "Miss D".

She had, I believe, come from South Africa just before the War. She had a faint accent. She spoke softly with humour hovering in her eyes. She was very short and had wire wool grey hair. She would not have been offended to be described as generously covered. I do not think it was possible to offend her. She drove an Austin A 30. It seemed perfect for her character and figure.

She smoked incessantly but, as with all her actions, discreetly. She did nothing to draw attention to herself. She was never surprised.

After a while I came to realise that the way she answered the telephone was a master class in attentive presence. She would first turn her creaking but still revolving chair through 90 degrees so as to address the instrument, rather as a conductor of an orchestra would address his orchestra before raising the baton. The cigarette would be laid on a burned little hill in the middle of the large bakelite plastic ash tray – much eroded by countless butts.

Then with composed attention, calmly and intent she would announce that she was there with "Yeessss".

When concluded she would return again through 90 degrees. There was no verbal gathering up of skirts or any disturbance to her tranquility.

Her profession was that branch of psychology denoted by "clinical". But neither by appearance, expression, character or disposition could Miss D be compressed into that description.

Her desk top was like a geological section showing many strata of reports, booklets, correspondence, directories, documents of every kind and date. The telephone alone had a stable base on a ledge which extended out next to her from the side of the desk. There were mounds of paper like foothills all before her.

She never put her finger tips together or fixed you with a piercing eye – her hands rested in luxury on her ample lap.

In her capacity for complete attention, present stillness, fresh perception inspired by the instant matter, she conveyed a sense of absolute detachment folded in compassion.

The erasing of all confidence by the Black Dog creates a vacuum in the mind. There is no prompt as to what should be said or done. A form of paralysis seizes any impulse to speak or act. It is very common to be indeed rooted to the spot. Hiding from view, not answering letters, not returning calls, not eating, failing to turn up at appointments, longing for the blessing of unconsciousness in sleep – all these are the daily fare.

At just 21 years of age my catechism for life had been immolated by depression. It was Miss D who erected in our consciousness the sticks and strings of insight and discipline to which the tendrils of a re-born confidence could cling as we made the way back into the world.

Forgive me if I dwell for a moment on how it was that, gradually, she made it possible for me to perceive, for myself, the structures of fear and guilt that my mind had constructed from distortions of reality imposed by depression. With infinite care she opened up insight into self knowledge that enabled me, by steps, at precious intervals, to trust again in life. It was as if by imperceptible stages I was being introduced to a new existence experienced by another person. She did not teach us anything – she illuminated our own insight.

* * *

One of the first seeds Miss D sowed in my mind was a notion of using one's senses to escape thought. By allowing attention to rest solely on our sense perceptions to experience the fact of the present moment.

She invited me to trust the present moment alone to suggest the next moment.

A typical exchange in an early interview would be:-

Self	I just can't even think about 5 days of exams – 9 papers – I can't begin to scale that cliff. It's terrifying. Just 3 papers covering over a thousand years of English History?
Miss D	[Pause]…Yeesss…[Pause]…Is that what your tutors are saying?
Self	No but they only see my weekly essays. They don't know how it really is. I don't know anything – really I don't. How can I take in thousands of pages of text books – I can hardly get myself up here on the bus.
Miss D	[Chuckle]…Yeess…[Long Pause]…You'll be doing 40 minute answers won't you?
Self	Yes
Miss D	Do you think you may have forgotten what you do know?
Self	No but – it's not enough. I don't know anything – I know that I don't.
Miss D	Yeess… [Pause]…Is that how you feel or is it true?
Self	What do you mean?
Miss D	Can you tell what is true if your feelings overwhelm you?
Self	I'm feeling terrified because it is true.
Miss D	Do you climb a cliff by one leap?
Self	Of course not, no.
Miss D	But that's what you are thinking isn't it?
Self	What is?
Miss D	If you are being forced to do the utterly impossible do you think this might bring into your mind thought of the abyss into which you are going to fall?
Self	No – it's a feeling.
Miss D	But what gave rise to it?
Self	Knowing I can't do it.
Miss D	Thinking you can't?
Self	If you like but what's the difference?
Miss D	Sitting at your desk, taking out your pen, opening your bottle of ink – is that terrifying? Reading the print of a question deliberately and quietly? – is that terrifying?

Waiting for what turns up in the mind – do you see that as terrifying? Looking out of the window of the examination hall?

Writing? Blowing your nose? Taking a deep but gentle breath – and another – and another?

Self   No– no – but will anything come to mind?

Miss D   Is not thinking the problem? Is that not perhaps what's in the way? – the thought of the precipice or abyss which the poor metabolism obediently addresses with extreme hormonal anxiety.

[Pause]

They used to say to soldiers who were to go over the top in the First World War – as you wait before you go up and over remember there is only the blade of grass in front of you.

Living in the future is living in the unknown is it not? How could it not be fearful? How can you cope with what is imagined?

[Pause]

Have you heard the fable about the Giant getting smaller the closer you get up to him until he disappears?

Self   When I was a child – I think it was in a story book How does that help?

Miss D   If the Giant was real would he disappear? The fable says that becoming aware of simple reality dissolves fear created by imagined thought.

What you are describing is thinking of yourself about to fall into a bottomless chasm – is that how it is?

Self   Yes it is. Yes.

Miss D   But in the instant of presence as you sit at the exam desk, sensing your weight on the chair, the sound of hubbub in the room – doing just these simple things – is there any thinking or any self there?

Self   No – not like that

Miss D	Resting your attention on what is there – what your senses alone tell you is there – not what is in your head – might that help?
Self	But my senses have to get through my feelings and thoughts.
Miss D	If you rest your attention only on what the senses bring to you is there anything of it left for you – for your thoughts and feelings?.
Self	What do you mean 'for you'?
Miss D	Try being seated, simply, with still silent attention, listening with no naming, no commentary. Allow disaster to be – accept its existence as a notion. No resistance. Return to your senses. Listen to all around you. See if for a few seconds 'you' are still there. When 'you' reappear see what happens. See if there is silence in your head or if you have left what is for the 'you' and its thoughts of the future and past bringing with them feelings akin to terror. See if you have a choice.

In later years when life was particularly tiresome for me I came across a Zen saying "*Before enlightenment chop wood, carry water. After enlightenment chop wood, carry water*". It occurred to me that this was what Miss D had been suggesting. As if by being entirely present with what is 'we' disappear. I think that Miss D was saying something like that. Rather like the squashed flies on the windscreen disappear from you vision when you look at the open road.

* * *

My recollection of that time at Ward 5 is unaccountably vivid. Nor was it only a time of revelation and self discovery. It was also at times very entertaining.

One of my co-inmates was a chap called McIlroy. He had red wiry hair and very delicate looking pale skin distributed with freckles. Of course he also had blue eyes. I cannot now recall what degree course he was taking nor his College. He was in the elation upswing of bi-polar mood oscillations.

What is ineradicable is the memory of a particular characteristic that he consistently displayed.

He could not cross a room without bumping into chairs and table edges.

When getting up from Ward 5 meals we would wait to see if he could achieve this without either pushing over the chair or stumbling over its legs. His arrival into the dining room was preceded by an overture of explosive greetings to Mrs Hargood and sounds of mishaps and footfalls. One could not pass him without a collision.

He had extraordinary bursting energy. He spoke with a loud voice – consistently.

He was absurdly optimistic. Nothing got him down. McIlroy was indifferent to the curious fact – for so it was – of being in a mental hospital.

One day when we were sitting at lunch in Ward 5 he spotted a coal lorry delivering coal. It was being unloaded by the side of the main building's boiler room. In those days coal was becoming discredited – it was only a few years after the Clean Air Act. The NCB (the coal board) was doing its best to maintain sales. To this end it produced little spheres of anthracite coal which were said to be smokeless.

The NCB thought that it would be a marketing advantage to publicise this new, more ethical, project by giving it a title that it thought had natural connotations with no implications of smog.

However that may be, the advertising banner that was affixed on the sides of the coal lorries was peculiarly diverting to us the inhabitants of Ward 5.

It read:

"SELECTED NUTS".

McIlroy saw this.

He leaped from his chair – with other consequences for the table – and in our full view ran clumsily, uttering loud calls, his arms waving, towards the blackened and startled colliers. It was clear that he intended to be engaged in a vigorous harangue. The coal board representatives received this deluge of gesticulation and imprecation with obvious incomprehension. The sight of a red headed inmate appearing from one of the Ward buildings waving and bawling at them was too much – they bolted into the boiler room for refuge.

It appeared that McIlroy, seeing the potential for an amusing jape, had intended to persuade the coal men to let him have one of these engaging banners but could not press home his request. He had some plan to fix it to the roadside entrance wall adjoining the Gate Lodge. So perhaps it was a bit much – but still.

* * *

One of the things that happens when young men are living under authority's guidance in a small house close to one another, scarcely venturing into the 'real' world, is that a certain childishness infiltrates into one's behaviour. As there were no grown ups clustered around us save those from another planet – the strict Mrs Hargood and consultants whom McIlroy used to refer to as Trick Cyclists – there occurred a kind of mild dissolution of our recent maturity.

When funds permitted we used to go to the White Horse pub. It was a short walk along Gipsy Lane and the London Road. I was usually with Geoff, Tony Hull and McIlroy. Pod never became at all gregarious. Tony and Geoff had gradually been tempted by McIlroy's clumsy but vigorous sociability.

We made a curious quartet.

The pub was an attractive building. Stoolball was played in its garden. Its beer was brewed by Morrells whose brewery was in St Ebbe's off Thomas's Street. The brewery was on Castle Mill Stream, a branch of the River Thames. Geoff called the beer Canal Water – a lapse of his customary precision. The Morrells had owned most of the land near the Warneford including Headington Hill Hall. Geoff would have been amused to know that a family dispute 35 years later prompted the sale of Morrells public houses to a American hamburger chain –' **Fuddruckers**'.

The beer was excellent.

One evening after a Ward 5 NHS supper we arrived at the White Horse.

Tony drank a thing called Worthington White Label. The landlady seemed familiar with this and produced it from a hidden crate.

McIlroy colliding with the bar blusteringly called for three pints of Morrells. The landlord was serving at the other end of the long mahogany counter. He deferred coming down to us which, on reflection, might have been due to his unease at McIlroy's bellowing.

Geoff joined McIlroy close to the counter of the bar. The landlord with deliberate caution arrived slowly in front of them.

McIlroy again "Three pints of Morrells!"

Then, quietly, from Geoff standing just behind him, his head angled down:-

"And one pint of Ethics".

"What's that? Essex? Essex? We don't have Essex – just Morrells. Suit yourself."

Geoff had turned back to join Tony and I at his table but McIlroy's spluttering bursts of laughter suggested to the landlord some implied slight for he stopped pulling the beer in mid-pint and was glaring at the excitable McIlroy.

I got up in haste to rescue McIlroy and the evening.

It cost me the round I remember as I could not put Geoff in play and Tony had got in his order for White Label to the landlady as soon as he arrived since it had to be poured very slowly due to the yeast sediment.

* * *

Tony Hull was very tall. Even when amused he appeared lugubrious. He had a very slow delivery to his speech and rarely turned his head to address you. He had been reading (Oxfordspeak for studying) Classics (Greek and Roman). The weight of his depressive condition caused him to appear submerged below a Plimsoll line – he lay deep in the water and moved always with slow care.

He could, however, be delightfully witty. One had to be quick to catch his quips – they were like a distant little mirror catching the sunlight for an instant.

When I had paid and sat down I asked Geoff if he thought the term Ethics was different from Morals. This seemed to bring Tony to the surface for he declared, as if giving judgment:-

"Morals is what they think is right or wrong Ethics is conduct that you think good or bad"

This was so distilled and dense as to defy ready comment. McIlroy nevertheless charged at it like Don Quixote.

"What do you mean "they"? Who are they? "

Tony – "You don't know your Mos from your Ethikos"

This came off the bat too fast for the rest of us. Tony picked up the ball and started to run in again.

Tony – "Mos, moris – Latin – customs of groups of individuals – Ethikos – Greek – characteristic conduct of groups of individuals"

McIlroy – "Tony, tell me this then – if you know someone is guilty of a crime is it immoral to conceal it"

Tony – "Morally yes. Ethically no, if you are a barrister and the client has not told you he is guilty".

Someone – "What if he has but you know he's not telling the truth"

Someone else – "What about conscience"

We began to exploit the opportunities for confusion, distortions of etymology and intellectual mayhem made available by such misty distinctions.

The second round of beer transformed the discussion into chaotic banter. But Tony's comment was like the sound of a clear bell. I brought it to mind when I got back to Ward 5. I hear it frequently still.

* * *

This was the insubstantial pageant that played before my mind's eye as I sat in that little mezzanine room in my Club waiting to receive Mr Jamieson.

How could I explain to him the intimate and moving experience of reflecting on those awful days of depression with its attendant terror and paralysis? For him I represented impregnable convention and privilege in an age which despises both.

Much less could I convey to him how that the very suffering had engendered a life's love of the forms and sounds of beauty and sowed in me the seeds of self knowledge?

As he rehearsed his prepared interrogation I did not attempt to divert him from it. I experienced a kind of growing and benign goodwill towards him. I took care to be courteous and even feigned offence when he seemed to expect it.

After a preliminary charge over the drawbridge he had found the gates were open and that there was no resistance to his assault. He spoke more slowly as if uncertain how to occupy the ground he had so unexpectedly overrun.

We began to chat about Oriel and Harrow. I described for him a view of the 'distance enchanted' which I hoped would reflect his own image of those worlds.

It was late in the afternoon that the interview concluded.

"There is a very good tea to be had at the Club – toasted teacakes and leaf tea if you would care to join me?".

To my surprise Mr Jamieson accepted my invitation to the large and beautiful Saloon. He was obviously now at ease. He would be able to depict me as one whom Oriel College, in its days of privilege, had launched into a public life devoted to beauty, taste and distinction.

There was going to be no howling complaint when his article came out. He settled down to the teacakes.

He leaned over to me as he moved forward out of his deep maroon leather club arm chair. Then, to my delighted surprise, he put his hand on mine as he said with sincere kindness,

"It's been very good of you to open for me a vista on Oxford as it was over 50 years ago. No wonder you loved your gilded path from adolescence. Oxford set you on your path didn't it."

I looked up at him as he got to his feet to leave.

"Yes. On reflection I think that is right. Yes Mr Jamieson....... It is so".

I stood up to bid him good bye. I assured him with my parting words "Yes I can truly say that Oxford did indeed set me on my path".

* * *

Up on Headington Hill in Oxford the Warneford stands: *conducted upon a principle of benevolence, and not for the profit of individuals*.

Yet what could more greatly profit a young man than loving fellowship, shelter from the stormy blast and finding a way to our eternal home.

WHAT'S THE POINT?

James Fearnley had made a few notes of what he did not want to forget. Some things that would honour and describe his lifelong friend. He wanted the brightest of the many gems which made up the story of Guy Bourne.

Guy Bourne was an exotic creature. He seemed always to be on display so that accounts were plentiful of his colourful and raucous passage through the jungle canopy of life – an extravagant image, but not to those who knew Guy well, as did all those arriving tomorrow for his 70th birthday festivities.

It was not possible to be indifferent to him. James recalled a meeting at his City law firm acting on the stock market launch of Guy's group of companies. It was all of 25 years ago. When Guy had finished expounding his eager exuberant vision of the Group's future the expressions on the faces of the modest, white shirted, prudent reporting accountants, underwriters and sponsors of the share issue were as if there had been thrust into their hands a cascading Roman Candle.

James sat at the dressing table in his bedroom looking over the riverside meadows. A marquee was being put up on the lawn. There was nothing to do – Guy and Victoria had gone to Perrott Hill school to watch their son play cricket. The sounds of preparations in the kitchen and muttered exchanges between the marquee men were oddly comforting. The still June air carried the faint sound of the river.

James shook the sieve of memory revealing bright in his mind images of unconnected things long thought forgotten.

James first encounter with Guy Bourne was on his second day at Hetton Hall preparatory school for boys. It was one of the Berkshire boarding schools - close to Bradfield. He was 8 years old.

Hetton Hall looked over the Kennett valley in Berkshire. It was a large mid-18th century country house with a long drive over a mile down to the A4. Along this drive had been planted Wellingtonian fir trees now of immense size and grandeur. There was a lodge at the road end. Half way down on the left side of the drive was the Park Lake of about 3 acres. There was a smaller lake, near the main house, almost entirely covered in water lily pads. Bamboos grew to the side of a summer house set back from the small lake's bank.

The football fields were the other side of a Ha-Ha at the end of the main lawns. James Fearnley was late for games as on his second day he ran out of the changing room colliding with an older and fatter boy who seized him by his ear. Bourne was just behind James. He grabbed the bully's wrist pulling back two of his fingers as the boy let go, howling.

"Car dealer Bourne- that's all your father is – a car dealer" spluttered the boy impotently as he stepped back.

"And your dad, Spotty Potter– what's he? A debt dealer isn't he. Buys and sells others debts. Bloody Shylock– look it up –SHYLOCK" shouting at the retreating large form.

Bourne turned to James. He spoke in a loud voice – Fearnley was to find that he always did.

"He's Potter - the newbug bully. He tried it on me when I was a new boy. He's had a go at my younger brother already. So I look out for him. I know his game. His dad's a bond dealer – my dad says that's a fancy name for debt. But give him a miss if you can."

"By the way I'm Bourne" he said smiling, his hand gripping James' shoulder.

"Fearnley, my name's Fearnley" he said as Bourne ran out.

* * *

Bourne and Fearnley – surnames only at that school – ended up together in the Cricket XI. Fearnley because, although slight and thin, he had acquired a dexterous facility with spinning a cricket ball. Bourne, well built and dominant, forced his selection both because of the violence of his fast bowling and the often destructive character of his batting.

With closer acquaintance Fearnley noticed that Bourne did not always play the game as the expression was in those days. The more precious of the boys – usually those having a refined sense of privilege – sneered that he was not one of them, though never to his face. Fearnley himself could not help the thought that Bourne let himself down by not clapping the incoming batsman. Worse still were Bourne's fast bumpers. He could only get away with a few of them in a spell of bowling but there were no helmets or chest pads to fend off assaults on anyone unwise enough to take a boundary off him.

"If it's not against the rules then who cares about the spirit. If it's not an offence then not guilty – that's what I say – no good saying it's not cricket. It is! And what's the point of clapping the batsman when he comes in. We want him out don't we – out!"

"Fearnley you softie – what's the point of not taking advantage of everything that helps you to win? Push the rules as far as you can get away with. What's the point in not?."

"What's the point welcoming someone you want off the pitch? What's the bally point?"

* * *

Hetton Hall required that boys should wear corduroy shorts at all times except on Sundays when long trousers were mandatory. They had a belt of pink and grey with a silver coloured metal S in the form of a snake as the buckle. In the summer, grey short sleeved shirts were allowed in hot weather with open brown leather sandals and grey calf length socks with a pink band at the top.

One June day afternoon Bourne was in front of Fearnley in a queue under the wide oak main stairs at the closet from which you drew out stationery, pencils rubbers and the like. Bourne's socks were round his ankles. The arm of his shirt was torn from the collar round the shoulder. Fearnley looked down at Bourne's bare legs. There was a bloody and congealing hole in the calf. He saw that one sandal had lost its strap. It slapped against the parquet floor when he moved forward in the queue.

"I say Bourne – you've got a hole in your leg"

"Oh really? have I Fearnley?" said Bourne making a big play of looking down horror struck.

"It was an assegai" he said unusually softly. "We were the blues charging the reds down to the Small Lake – they put up a fight with the bamboos – cut the ends with Scout knives – clever – had to retreat".

Miss Williams was in charge that day of stationery. She refused his request and insisted that he go up immediately to Sister in surgery.

* * *

On his third year Sports day Bourne had asked Fearnley to go over in the morning to his home near Bradfield for an early lunch before it all started. But Fearnley's parents had themselves arranged to come down to take him out for the week end exeat, after strawberries and cream tea on the wide terrace leading to the South Lawn. Fearnley waited for them outside the main entrance by the large Wellingtonian at the edge of the circular sweep round to the Portico and columns fronting the double doors.

The Fearnleys arrived in a Rover 100 black saloon parking discreetly a little down the Park drive. As James moved to welcome them, what he later learned was the latest 3.8 litre Series I Roadster Jaguar E Type convertible in British Racing Green swept gravel and grass verge before it as it rocketed round the entire circle of the drive before making a sudden emphatic dust blown stop.

Bourne got out of the open topped deep green charger, his father joining him as they helped out his windblown mother and her hat. Fearnley felt an inexplicable thrill and regret as Mr Bourne boomed at the gazing Fearnley.

"Just released to us – show room car – bloody marvellous!!"

* * *

It was the winter of 1963. Bourne's last year.

By the end of November the ice on the Park Lake was thick enough to walk on. They said it was the coldest since 1740. The Headmaster had informed parents that given the very severe cold they might wish to add skates to the List of School Effects. He was considering allowing skating and did not want any boy to be disappointed.

In the last week of November the announcement was made that if there was no rise in temperature before Saturday, there would be skating races with the Bradfield College junior school on the Park Lake. The ground was too hard for games. Accordingly boys from the higher forms and those from the lower could skate on alternate afternoons from 3.00 p.m until tea time during that week. Masters to supervise, naturally.

Bourne's skates were not the figure skating type that were normal on public Ice Rinks. Those had teeth at the front of the blade so that a sudden stop could be made even if there was no room or time for a swish and turn stop. Bourne's were racing skates. They had no teeth. They did not rise up over the ankle. They came from Canada.

By the time he got in for tea on the Thursday Bourne had mastered these fierce blades so that, at the cost of grazes and frozen hands lips and ears, he had achieved an astonishing velocity. The race was arranged to start in the morning to ensure a clear surface before the sun penetrated any cloud. Proud but anxious parents stood with siblings in the packed snow on the Park Drive which came almost to the lake's edge. There was a happy sound of small children finding fun in the cold and of a few excited dogs. Some more courageous souls moved out into the lake along the brick and stone pier used to moor the Park Lake rowing boat.

The Sports Master stood on a short wooden jetty on the far side of the lake bellowing instructions for the start. Three boys from each school in alternate lanes crouched, their arms stretched behind them – six in all. Bourne had the lane next to the Park Drive.

SKATE!!

Bourne had anticipated the shout but no call came to stop. He was not aware of any other boy as he had left them standing with his first deep thrusts on the virgin ice. His pace increased as the skates hissed. The red finishing tape rushed at him.

They said the little dog was running for a stick thrown on the ice by a little girl. Bourne leaned on his left skate to get round the creature as it slithered over the ice but the force of his momentum defeated him just as he passed it. Falling, he shot forward on his front towards the brick pier his hands outstretched to shield his face.

Bourne came into his form room on the Monday his wrists in plaster but his fingers free.

"Greensticks" he said "Just greensticks". "2d for a signature 6d for a face" he said tapping the plaster. "Gather the dog's all right" he said.

The Park Lake and the Small Lake teemed with small gold carp. Fearnley passed many summer evening hours before the bell for bed trapping these with bent pin hooks and hazel twig floats. But such trifles did not engage Bourne's energies or interest. He was certain that greater prey were concealed in the depths of the Park Lake. The groundsman Phillips had told him that a few years back a boy had caught a 5 lb carp from the wooden jetty. The boy had used bread flakes. It had created much interest and excitement. It had been presented to the Headmaster.

It was Bourne's last week at Hetton Hall. He had secured from his father a spinning rod and reel, Milward hooks with the casts tied on and round feed balls. He already had a net. He took a small catapult. He would shoot rolled bread balls from the brick pier as ground bait as part of his campaign. He cut going to tea in hall so that he could be sure no other boys would disturb the water of the Park Lake. Phillips was doing something with the wooden jetty on the far side.

Carp once hooked are not easily retrieved. And once retrieved and on the bank are not easily despatched. No boys had arrived when Bourne's float jiggled slightly before it gradually descended below the surface and disappeared. Bourne raised the rod – perhaps the float was punctured. It seemed as it the hook was caught on the bottom of the lake.

It was at least 30 minutes before he saw the fish. It seemed monstrous in the green brown water now stirred and boiled by its tail. He would never be able to get it in the net.

To his right there was a shallow shelf rising to the bank where the lake dribbled over into a stream below. He walked round with great care along the top of the bank keeping the line taut but not pulled. As he reached the shallow water he began to wind in the reel. The fish sensed the action of the reel and thrashed its tail burying its head in the mud. Bourne decided to grip the line against the cork handle of the rod and keep pressure on the fish steady - not agitated. He took small and even steps away from the lake, over the bank and a little down the Park Drive – that way the fish might follow. As the fish felt the muddy floor of the lake in the shallows underneath its fins it attempted to swim but the swish of its tail only propelled it further towards the bank until its head was lying on the edge of the bank itself.

It weighed 8 lbs.

Phillips helped him up to the house with the Carp. Occasionally it would give a sudden thrust of its body. Phillips said that carp can live for hours -even days - out of water. He took it to the scullery. Bourne went in to hall to see if there was any tea left. Phillips found him to say that the Headmaster would be glad to receive the great fish. Phillips was to bring it in to assembly after evening prayers – that seemed to be the tradition.

The Ballroom formed the South West corner of the ground floor. It was a jewel of 18th century taste and craft. The floor at the entrance forming a raised platform above the main concourse. It was where the orchestra had played for Balls held there at one time. The main area was down 2 semicircular steps. There were elegant handrails running into the side walls from finely carved Corinthian fluted columns at each side of the top steps. All was constructed in oak as perfect as it had been in 1785. It was the assembly room for prayers and daily reports.

The boys assembled for Sunday evening prayers rose as the Masters, followed by the Headmaster, took their places on the raised platform floor. 150 boys below prepared to endure the Sunday evening ritual of the Book of Common Prayer and the vinegar, beetroot and cold pressed ham that followed the Nunc Dimittis and final collect. The presence of Penny the Headmaster's 13 year old daughter was not especially diverting. The row of prefects in a semicircle at the front sat with feigned attention, holding glazed expressions. Their thoughts were entirely elsewhere as the Headmaster announced that one of their number had landed a record Carp in the Park Lake that afternoon.

The instant attention of the entire assembly fell on Phillips as he entered carrying a metal tray under both hands on which lay a Carp of such magnificence that its head and tail extended over the rim. Phillips moved with evident embarrassment bearing the glistening fish before him. It was at the moment of his passing Penny that the Carp made violent lunge for freedom. For a moment it rested on the precarious rim of the tray before descending into the welcoming lap of Penny's primrose coloured dress.

Alarmed, but not distressed, Penny jumped up, so discharging the unexpected arrival which slipped in its slime onto the oak floor and slowly but inexorably glided down the steps to rest with baleful eye at the feet of the Head Boy.

For an instant an astonished silence prevailed. Bourne was the first to move. He bent down, careless of the slime, and pressed the gaping fish it to his body as he took the two steps in one bound towards Phillips and the waiting tray. "Put it in the Small Lake Mr Phillips" – it was enough for Phillips. He made his escape.

The spurting and snorting of the boys suppressed hysteria had broken into open unrestrained guffaws and howls. The Headmaster decided that dignity demanded his withdrawal from the erupting chaos. As Penny followed she grabbed Bourne's arm

"Thanks awfully – great fun – hated that dress – all dresses actually – thanks so much – loved it".

It was some time before the duty Master imposed a reluctant silence.

Bourne went on to Millfield School. James a year later ascended the Hill at Harrow.

* * *

Sitting by the window looking over the rising marquee James tried to trace how it had been that fishing had renewed and deepened the friendship which now seemed always to have existed between himself and Bourne.

He recalled that he had been invited by a client for a day on the River Itchen near Itchen Abbas. He was not yet 30 and was ascending the bottom rungs of the ladder at Clifford Turner in Blackfriars - a leading law firm. To be confident of having correct tackle and flies he took a bus down Fleet Street to Lower Regent Street and entered Farlows. It was early May 1979. The news of Mrs Thatcher's election victory was dominating press headlines. James's mind was on the Mayfly. As he entered, he passed racks of fine rods of every length each standing loose in their slots retained by rubber nibs. There was a life size model of an 'angler' with a trout rod bent by a landed fish in a net held over a simulated pool.

The artificial flies were under a glass topped counter running the far length of the end wall in front of glazed cabinets. He could not at first find the Mayflies or even the Duns. He was drawn in by fascination as he gazed at the myriad little flies of gossamer delicacy in little compartments each numbered and named. He explored each of the descending racks.

As he bent over a lower tier of trays, easing out one of the drawers, he heard an unmistakable voice booming just at the other end of the counter.

"I'm fishing Graffham Water – I need something as close to a spinner as is allowed you see - so what have you got?"

"Ah but Sir – no spinning is allowed at any time on Graffham. And forgive me for saying but it's rather frowned on to use lures of the kind I think you may perhaps have in mind, Sir."

"I know that – but if it's made for fur and feathers then it's a fly isn't it? If it's flashing metal it's a spinner – and I'm not talking about the 'spinner' stage of a fly on the water. So if it's within the rules then I'll have the flashiest 'fly' you've got. I don't suppose it looks anything like a fly but hey! do I care? Let me see your pike 'flies' and the things you sell to our American cousins for trapping Chinnook and King salmon in Alaska."

It was Guy Bourne.

James took him across the road to his club in Pall Mall for lunch. The Chablis decided them on a joint day's fishing. The Claret and Sauternes opened wider possibilities. It was Guy Bourne who insisted that instead of just a day on a river or reservoir they should have a full week's holiday devoted entirely to fishing.

"You can't mix family life and fishing. Come to that you can't mix anything with fishing except sleep, good food and red Bordeaux – Claret as you call it. We'll never do it if we just have the odd day – far too easy to cancel if something comes up. Take a slab out of time. Then it'll happen"

It started with James suggesting they have a go for salmon and sea trout in Connemara. The trip was memorable – and not only for the fact that Aer Lingus removed a 12lb salmon from Guy's rod case before agreeing to load it in the hold. Then there followed those visits to the Inn at Whitewell on the river Hodder in Lancashire. One year they took two salmon rods and a bothy on the Helmsdale in Inverness and this became a fixture. They went to WeirWood reservoir – but mainly for nearby Gravetye Manor and its wine list. One year they took a Bonefish holiday in Cuba which was frustrating for Guy but riveting for James. Alaska's pacific salmon was perfect for Guy as you cannot miss – James escaped to wilderness lakes fishing for Arctic Grayling and Arctic Char.

James was determined to show Guy the delight of small rods, reels and lines and the joy of landing a floating dry fly with utmost delicacy and stealth just beyond the lie of a rising trout in crystal clear waters. Indeed he persisted for many years long after he knew it was futile. It was the trout and salmon fishing that first drew them together. But with the years their complementary spirits enriched their mutual lives. They came to realise that fishing was an excuse for each other's company.

Guy's essential quality was abundance. He always had enough for life. Abundant with courage, generosity, humour, invention, reckless of thin ice and propriety - he was never dismayed. James had no notion of why Guy should find him good company – perhaps it was that he was not by disposition critical and was sufficiently sceptical to be tolerant and amused by most things. Guy was very entertaining and oddly childlike.

* * *

Many images of those days floated into James's consciousness until a recollection sharp and intense forced its way to the forefront of his memory.

It was the day at Blagdon.

Blagdon lake sits below the Mendip Hills. It was created as a reservoir in late Victorian times. 12 years after it was formed a dry fly fisherman from Hampshire noticed swirling circles on the surface identical to a rising trout on the Test. Returning with his fly rod he hooked an 8lb brown trout with his first cast. No one knew that they were there.

James and Guy had stayed at the Bear and Swan in Chew Parva. A good lunch had left them sitting on sun loungers on the hotel terrace. They decided to wait for the evening rise of trout. They would take a Thermos and sit on the lawns in front of the Lodge.

The Lodge had been built out slightly into the Lake and lawns laid around it to the front and sides with woodland behind. It was a magnificent Edwardian structure. Trout of historic proportions, stuffed for ever in bowed glass cabinets, each decorated and laid out within to resemble precisely the watery realm from which they had been exiled, adorned the walls of stained pine panels.

Two ancient armchairs stood either side of a fireplace edged with blue and white tiles round a cast iron grate. Long split cane rods left behind from another era were suspended below the steeply sloping roof. Worn red and black diamond pattern tiles covered the floor.

Guy took one of the boats. These were moored to a long wooden slatted jetty that ran deep into the small bay just by the Lodge's East lawn. The jetty was a good spot in the evening in June before the water temperature rose and algae formed. The fading light emboldened quite large trout to move along the edges of the reeds and banks of weed quietly picking off the rising insects - nymphs or water boatmen - just emerging into the surface. The tail and dorsal fin of the greygreen speckled fish silently parting the water's surface revealed their graceful presence to the motionless witness. But Guy was set for rougher trade and determined to try the deeper water in front of the dam. Low cloud was coming in from the Bristol Channel from the West - which was good for fishing.

The dam was at the West end of the Lake, some 40 yards beyond the Lodge. Its parapet was about 4 feet higher than the road which ran along its entire length. In midsummer the dam was 15 feet or so higher than the water level of the Lake. It was constructed of dark coloured stone much discoloured by weed at the Lake's edge. The sloping dam wall rose up from the water to the massive stone parapet with buttresses at intervals. Even in full sunlight it had a forbidding prospect as if its Victorian architect intended to demonstrate the power of civilised humanity prevailing over Nature.

James, for his part, preferred running streams and trout rising to a floating artificial fly dropped just above the pool where the fish lay waiting, their tails moving slowly to keep them in the line of the flow. Lake fishing seemed less delicate and skillful. But he had seen some good fish taking flies in the corner of the West end just round from the dam's end. There were some willows at the corner itself so he took a spot a few yards back towards the Lodge and waded out so as to get beyond the bankside weeds. He thought it best to leave Guy to himself – he would surely rock the boat dangerously with the mighty cast needed to get out his hideous lure. It would just be too risky to have that absurdly large hook flying past his ear.

Guy rowed under the dam, some coots running noisily on the surface before him and putting up a flock of black backed gulls. The wind was now coming strongly over the dam, driven by a storm to the West. His first cast immediately surprised him. The thin strips of fluorescent plastic – gold and green with a savage hook – caught the wind as it eddied down the ramparts of the dam and hurled it unhoped for distances before splashing into the now rippled water. Guy retrieved it the instant it hit the surface stripping in the line just below the surface. He thought he saw a bow wave of a following trout just behind it. His second cast was whipped into the air by a gust of the rising wind. It flew as if of its own will toward the gulls rising and falling on the little waves of the now darkening Lake. A few gulls rose easily off the surface and hovered in the wind.

Guy, frustrated that he had wasted a cast, pulled in the line forcefully so that the lure rose to the surface flashing along behind a V of parting water. His left hand came forward to seize the line again to pull it back far enough to be able to raise it with his rod and cast again. As he took hold of the line it suddenly stripped through his fingers taking with it in an instant all the loose coils lying at the bottom of the boat. The rod leapt out of his hand. All seemed lost when seizing the end of the butt as it clattered over the seat and oars he fell with it into the bilges of the boat from where he could see the rod bent double by some monstrous predator.

The black backed gull *Larus marinus* is the largest gull in the world. Its wingspan is just under 6ft. It has a dead weight of over 5lbs. It is a savage predator and can unhinge its jaws to swallow crabs and other birds -even mice and rabbits. Storms at sea will draw it inland for easy prey. It is a fearsome creature easily offended by the least slight.

At least three of the black backs hovering just over the surface of Blagdon Lake in the lee of the dam had fallen upon Guy's gold green luminous lure as it lunged in violent jerks immediately beneath them. The leading gull's hooked beak had opened viciously to seize its unexpected prey at the very moment when Guy had paused for a second to make the next pull back of the lure. The great gull overshot the lure but as Guy pulled it through again, the opening of the hook had collided with its ankle joint above its webbed flat feet.

The gull, outraged by this restraint, launched itself into the air on powerful wings with bitter shrieking recriminations. Guy had a glimpse of his flashing lure suspended from the foot of the swiftly ascending bird as other gulls took up the chorus of affronted dignity. The gull was high above dam wall before Guy was able to arrest the now tethered monster.

Standing up in the boat, thinking it would give him more command in the developing crisis, he held the rod at right angles to the extended line, pointing it at the errant bird as he tried to turn the reel. The gull lost its equilibrium with the sudden pull of the hook on one side of its undercarriage causing it to dive precipitously to the Lake, its wings flapping helpless in the water so close that Guy could see its malevolent eyes. The line had gone slack with the descent of the bird to the Lake. Now, with no pressure of the line on the hook, the gull rose with a mighty thrust of great wings and lurched once more into the air.

But Guy had gained a slight advantage over his infuriated adversary whilst it lay for a moment impotent near the boat. He had been able to gather in some of the line upon the reel. As the winged beast rose, gratefully expecting the freedom of the heavens to return, it was forcibly returned back to the sullen Lake with a violent splash as the line resumed his hold upon its ankle. Again there was a momentary slack on the line and a further upward lunge of the black backed bird as it once again took off with smacks and flaps upon the surface of the water. The undulating progress of the gull continued with the loud splash of its descent and the flaps of its rise sounding across the Lake in bizarre succession, its circles around the boat growing ever smaller as Guy reeled in the line.

James, from his stand just out from the bank, first became conscious of the struggle for ascendancy that had erupted on the Lake when he looked up to check his line in the air on his forward cast. Ominous low cloud had darkened the scene and spots of heavy rain were falling. Before him rose the ramparts and buttresses of the dam like some medieval castle before whose battlements an ancient feud was being tried in mortal combat. He saw the dark silhouette of Guy holding his rod high with hands uplifted as if uttering a prayer for deliverance whilst, in grotesque circles of splash and flap, the black back of the winged creature moved ever closer to a fatal resolution of the hellish duel.

Distant thunder accompanied the ghastly spectacle. Streaks of cadmium yellow slashed the leaden grey of the darkened sky as the sun's rays pierced the gathering storm.

But as farce dissolves tragedy, so it happened that the knot attaching the lure to the dogged cast at last gave up its hold on the proceedings and slipped off the hook. The lure fluttered down like the samara wings of a sycamore. The dark form of the great gull rose slowly and in silence above and over the dam wall to join its departing flock.

Wisbeys was just off Fetter Lane. Its partners described it as a City law firm. Some still held that Ludgate Circus was the City boundary but its extension to Chancery Lane and the new Law Courts lent a caché to firms in the larger catchment.

It was a small firm. Punching above its weight was how its admirers and critics both described it. James had been poached from Clifford Turner for his venture capital experience. The firm had embraced the opportunities for fund raising work under the new tax break investment schemes. Wisbeys had attracted high volumes of work with fees at a discount to the market. The spice of risk and novelty began to flavour its corporate work and reputation.

Guy Bourne's father had used Wisbeys as advisers on a substantial loan advance to fund the opening of further outlets for his Jaguar franchise. Guy did not know his way around the City but he had friends in the trade who had invested in tax break projects. The investment could be set off against tax. How long would that last?

Guy had prospered on the back of the Jaguar dealership. He had diversified his business interests in line with his passion. He had opened an enlarging chain of small leisure parks offering fishing on disused gravel pits. More recently he had acquired options close to riverside sites within the M 25 on which he proposed to create trout lakes. All these enterprises were intended to attract a new market – those in the more modest income groups in London who wanted to fly fish for trout after work or at week ends. He needed to raise funds for further projects.

1988 was an optimistic year. Money was flowing into new ventures being floated on the main London investment exchanges. All was looking good for Bournesport and the future. Guy suggested that James came over to meet him at his flat in the Barbican. They could go to Gow's Oyster Bar afterwards.

James arrived just as Guy was opening a bottle of Möet Chandon. The flat was ultra modern in its interior. The surfaces were of glass, anodised aluminium, limed oak, even polished concrete. The walls were a fierce white relieved by abstract pictures without frames and of violent colours.

Guy welcomed his old friend with a hearty bellow and hug.

It was obvious to James, as Guy began to explain his project, that what he intended would have appalled F M Halford Esq the fountain head of dry fly fishing and author of the almost biblical 'Dry Fly Fishing in Theory and Practice'. The essence of fly fishing is the skill and delicacy of the casting of an artificial fly so that despite the hazards of branches behind, vagaries of the breeze, entangling weeds, reeds and rushes on the banks, the fly settles unimpeded and silently just above the swirl of a rising trout. Not with a plop - this would 'spook' the fish and waterlog the fly.

The use of nymphs had once been frowned on – these were little bugs of flies as the ascended to the top of the water before rising into the air and breaking out as winged flies– the 'dry flies' of the sport. The trout took the nymphs before they reached the surface. Acceptance of the practice came slowly. Casting a nymph was less hazardous than a dry fly but demanded skill if it was to be at exactly the right height in the water for the trout to take.

Guy's proposals broke all these boundaries. This was no surprise in itself – but James was to be shocked by what Guy seemed intent on tearing down.

"What's the point of them James – they just make it more difficult than it need be – it's all out of date – I'm all for pulling down the barriers – same in everything – art, sport, everything. Art can be anything can't it? And why split cane rods – they got rid of those as soon as carbon fibre came in didn't they?"

"Look" said Guy "I've got a prototype for a fly rod. It's part of the Bournefish brand for the sport. It goes with the trout lakes I'm planning. You see James, the casting is the problem. Take away the risks and snags and it's all much easier – especially for the new market I'm aiming at – beginners or people with very little time. It's just a form of snobbery – dry flies and all the ruddy paraphernalia. Stripping it down is what I'm doing. Just like those modern artists – same thing. Breaking out of the limits."

"Guy – what has this got to do with the fly rod?" said James patiently.

"Imagine, James – just imagine if you could cast the fly just where you wanted it? Exactly I mean. Yes? And no worries about trees or bushes behind you? And no hitting the far bank? Eh? What about that!"

Guy banged the low table in front of the sofa and continued before his friend could muster a response.

"No hooks getting stuck in your ear or your waders. Come to that no clumping waders – no waders at all! Don't even have to stand up. Can do it from a wheel chair – think of that! From a bloody wheel chair!"

"Well that's not quite the point is it Guy?" began James "I mean it's not about short cuts to a fish on the bank is it? Any way as I see it….."

"I'll show you James" burst in Guy. "Let me show you – that's why I asked you over – better than your office you see. Wait a sec."

Guy came back into the room carrying a short tube. It was similar to a tube used for rolled up plans but longer than normal – cardboard with plastic caps at the end.

"Just a temporary tube – there'll be a range of these when we've settled on what are the ideal lengths. Here, take the reel and flies" handing James a Farlow's bag and a clear plastic box in which were artificial flies.

Guy's Barbican flat looked over a long forlorn strip of grass dominated by the dismal concrete panels of block of flats in the brutalist style of the two decades after the War. The frail beauty of the saplings at each end was made more poignant by the horror of the setting.

Guy opened the tube and untied a rod case. The rod was in two parts. It tapered more abruptly than he expected. It had a longer butt than usual with what appeared from a distance to be a narrow dial or screen on the upper side with the reel catches on the under side. There appeared to be a lever just behind the dial.

"Watch this" said Guy. He had assembled the rod and attached the reel. The line ran down the ringlets and lay spooled on the lawn. The carbon monofilament cast had a fly already moulded into the cast itself. No knot.

He moved half way down the lawn. Fitting the fly into the end of the rod Guy aimed the rod at the foot of the far sapling. After a few seconds with a sharp pop the fly flew straight ahead, then lost momentum and died to fall neatly at the foot of the little tree.

Guy retrieved the line. There was a bench on one side of the strip of grass. Guy moved over to is and sat down summoning James.

"Look at these" he said opening the plastic fly box "they look just like normal dry flies don't they. But they are siliconed so that they never sink. There is a shaped little cap like a tiny badminton shuttlecock in the top of the fly – the compressed air from the bottle in the butt drives it out of its housing at the end of the rod. Have a look!"

James took the short rod by the butt. It was thicker than the butt of a normal trout fly rod. It had a little screen. Pressing the button on the end of the screen illuminated various settings. As he raised the rod a cursor moved to show the distance in centimetres from the "Target". Pulling the small upright trigger behind the screen and holding the target for three seconds discharged a burst of compressed air at precisely the volume and force required to project the fly out of the rod's end to fall over the target.

"And James – you know what? For salmon fishing it's got an even greater future. Alaska and Canada have thousands of miles of salmon fishing –a vast market untapped for new technologies in fishing. We are developing a 12 ft rod for it plus much more powerful compressed air cylinders. And we have a compressor coming to market that operates from a cigar battery or computer terminal."

James could not help being impressed by the technology – who would fail to be? But it seemed, as he stood under the lowering concrete masses above and around him, as if he was witnessing an act of gross vandalism.

Guy had not finished.

"James, come back to the flat for a bit – we've got time before our table at Gow's."

Depositing the rod and reel on the sofa he took the fly box into the kitchen calling out for James as if to witness another trick.

As the sink filled Guy picked out two little bug like creatures with antennae and tails.

"Nymphs" he said. "Though the ancient Greeks wouldn't agree I suppose."

As the water rose in the sink he dropped each of them into the water. One settled just below the surface – the other just above the bottom of the sink.

"Can't fail can you! Not with these. Land them exactly where you want and depth you want. No skill needed. No risk. No ruddy variables. Straight into the trout's mouth. No messing!"

James recoiled in his mind at the vision of the Chalk streams of Hampshire with chairs lining the bank, air gun rods popping out unsinkable silicone flies and eye level nymphs at docile stocked trout - for surely no wild trout could possibly survive such a campaign.

But it seemed discourteous and, with Sole Meunière in the offing at Gow's, a little ungrateful for him to show distaste or disapproval.

Gow's provided excellent whitebait before the Sole. Guy was fond of Sylvaner – very cold. They had a good Barsac with the raspberries. Guy was delighted that James thought he could put together a good Prospectus for the Bournefish Rod as part of fund raising for a larger project such as the M25 ring lakes proposal which would have some fixed assets. He thought that there would be appetite for such an enterprise if offered under the tax break investment scheme. James advised that it would be good if Guy could secure a few more options on sites.

So it was left that they should meet again in 12 months which would also give the market more time to mature in relation to these new kind of public offerings. Guy asked James back for an Irish malt whisky. They dwelt for a while on days at Hetton Hall before returning to technology and fly fishing.

"All that English restraint" boomed Guy. "It seems to come with life at the top. Not for me James – as you know. I am the vulgar iconoclast – that's what a customer once told me when he saw I'd put a soft top on Jag 3.8 saloon! Vulgar iconoclast! – I was flattered. Who wants icons! Do you know James – I looked it up. It means an 'Idol or object of uncritical devotion'. Not my idea of a car –of all people it is me that should be offering grateful prayers for Jags icons or not don't you agree?"

James, emboldened by the 12 year old Middleton Irish whisky, attempted to put another perspective, familiar as he was with the courage, inventiveness and bluster of his friend.

"But Guy – once you have no limits then what's skill, what's judgment, what's art?. In fact, thinking about it, what has any meaning? It's like writing on water. If art can be anything – any kind of form - then it's nothing isn't it? Form is nothing of itself – it's the effect on us that matters surely? You can't disentangle form from what it reveals and still expect no effects. I mean, to see or hear beauty there has to be form revealing it. Beauty is not a thought. Serenity, wonder – they're things we recognise in our selves - not think. The surface is there for the depths. If you're changing the visible form you risk losing the invisible which is the real point – you know – the meaning, the beauty - all that — the whole point".

"Can't see it James – you play to win, you fish to catch, you paint to express yourself, that's all it is."

* * *

After the Ford takeover of Jaguar in 1990 Guy was able to extend the franchise and this provided welcome revenue cover in the uncertain early 90's. In September 1994 Guy and James took Bournesport on to the Alternative Investment Market. Guy diluted his holdings and took the chance of raising cash for himself to pay out his second wife and fund his pension scheme.

Guy also saw yet another opportunity for diversifying into the US and Canadian sport business – this was to be by tapping the Pool market – far more popular in those countries than snooker or billiards. He had developed a cue of just little longer than the normal length. It had a ferrule that contained a digital sensor which could be adjusted by WiFi signal emitted by pressure on a pad behind the player's grip. This could make very sensitive adjustments to the cue tip so changing angles, density or convexity. It took a few hours of practice to master the options offered by it. But mastery brought with it extraordinary facility for swerving the cue ball, arresting and even reversing it - and with variations in pace as the cue ball progressed.

Guy realised that the cue would not find favour with the World Pool-Billiard Association and the international competitions conducted under its aegis. But those rules were for the elite – he was for those in clubs, bars, pool halls and working men's association halls – what would they care about the rules and spirit of the game. So the Bournecue went on the market with world wide patent rights under the Bournesport flag.

The Bournesport launch was a success – indeed it was oversubscribed. But it was to be the last major transaction on which James Fearnley acted for his lifelong friend. In 1997 he was seconded to New York to look after the venture fund capital markets business of Wisbeys – it was a joint venture with a US law firm. He did not return until 2010 after the Lehmann and credit crunch fiasco followed by profitable few years in the Jersey office acting for offshore funds before becoming senior partner in the London office in 2016.

* * *

Guy Bourne now lived in Dorset with Victoria his third wife – next to the little River Frome chalk stream near Cruxton south of Maiden Newton. It was ten miles to the nearest dual carriageway. The M 27 expired 56 miles away in Hampshire and it was 36 miles to the M5. A land of chalk downs, streams and views such as they would have been long before Thomas Hardy.

Guy had said he would meet the train at Dorchester South. He would come down with Brian, his driver and gardener. Much more convenient from the City than the 5 hour drive– probably more with the M3 and M27 on a Friday. The single track line from Dorchester West stopped at Maiden Newton but he was not sure how frequent it was and it was a twenty minute walk up to it from Dorchester South.

The train from Waterloo was comfortable and fast to Winchester. It was leisurely thereafter. He opened his own laptop as they passed Ashurst into the New Forest. Guy had said he was not far from Maiden Newton. James called up Wikipedia and Google maps. It was but a simple navigation from there to the ancient Dorset of the Romans, Anglo Saxons and the little rivers - the Frome, the Hooke, the Cerne and the Piddle.

The Anglo Saxon and Roman names seemed to protect these clear and merry sounding streams from modern life. From Evershot, then Maiden Newton and Throop and Frampton , the little River Frome passes through Roman Dorchester receiving first the Cerne and last the Piddle at Wareham before they all achieved release into the vast basin of Poole Harbour.

Roman settlements along the Frome followed the Vespasian conquest. James dug from the web a Heritage article describing a mosaic at the Roman villa at Throop:-

> *The most elaborate pavement had a central medallion of a horseman spearing a lioness, with two corner panels depicting scenes from the tale of Venus and Adonis. The whole was surrounded by minor borders in guilloche and a main border of dolphins and cormorants emerging from a mask of Neptune. James was caught by the beauty of these images. The forms of life,*

He had a momentary glimpse of Ms Emin and her dismal dirty bed.

There was charming glimpse on the web of the little rivers that fed the Frome. The Piddle rises in Alton Pancras then on to places anchored in Saxon and Old English - Piddletrenthide, Piddlehinton, Tolpuddle. Affpuddle, Briantspuddle and Turners Puddle. The Cerne emerges from the Downs at Minterne Magna, between High Stoy and Dogbury Hill, flowing through ancient Cerne Abbas into the Frome at Dorchester.

The little Hooke runs for just 6 miles from its source at Toller Whelme through the villages and hamlets of Hooke, Kingcombe, Toller Porcorum and Toller Fratrum to be welcomed by the Frome at Maiden Newton. Roman and Saxon again.

None of these lovely streams above Dorchester were more than 12 Roman Pedes (feet) wide and for most of their flows were just 8 feet or less than that.

The train pottered through Wareham, Wool and Moreton. A vague sense of taking leave of normal life arose in him.

* * *

Brian opened the back door to the Jaguar for James. As he slid on to the seat he saw that Guy's right wrist and hand were in a splint. Guy was ebullient in his delight at being again with James his friend since boyhood. He had some wonderful schemes in pilot stages and wanted to take them to another level – James to do all the legals. He was still talking as he got out and carried on into the house over the lawn by the river.

It was the early evening when, unpacked and changed, James joined them under the verandah overlooking a sloping lawn that slipped into the Frome. The wisteria blossom above them was nearly over. Guy and Victoria were in wicker chairs. There were glasses of champagne on the cast iron table.

Guy and Victoria had a twelve year old son – she had just got under nature's net when she was already 37. She was 18 years younger than Guy.

"Ah James well done" boomed Guy. "Look – before we lose the sun come and have a look round. We only have a few acres – just enough for Vicky's horses but it's quite nice – start with the river of course"

Guy moved his glass slowly across the table to his left with his right splinted hand.

"Every drop of Krug is precious after all isn't it" said Guy.

They took their filled glasses down to the river's edge. The stream was shallow. There were drifts of long weed moving slightly from side to side in the flow. Above them a few large stones had allowed a small pool to form and higher still the water was darker and faster as the river bed narrowed between enclosing banks. Small flies danced above the surface. Below where they stood the river glided along the far bank by a shoal of gravel before passing from sight round a bend, some pollarded willows just beyond.

As they moved back over the lawn James heard a plop as a fish rose in the river.

"Good little spot that" said Guy "A short cast just up above the fast water and mend it to this side very quickly. Only get one cast – two if you're lucky. I put in some brown trout each April and September – get them from an excellent chap in Hooke just upriver – only a few small ones – there's not enough feed in the river for more you see."

"It looks too tight for a fly cast" said James. "How about wind? And why not cut back the growth on the bank?"

"Ah, but the trout like it right under the bank – flies and grubs fall in from what grows above them. Too exposed for them to stay in mid-stream unless deep or in weed."

Victoria broke in

"Fishermans' tales James – don't get him going just yet if you want any supper. And you have to see my stable beauties."

They crossed over the gravel circle in front of the house. James saw that the house was Regency with windows down to just above the ground. It had a shallow slate roof extending well beyond the elevation with timber shaped brackets under the soffit. To the side of the house was a yard with stable doors on one side and at the far end a barn with high double doors.

"I have these for eventing – you know – cross country, show jumping and dressage. Oh! so sorry James - I see I needn't explain! They're normally out in the field but they hate the flies."

She pulled some carrots out of a paper sack in front of the stable wall. We stood listening to the chomping and crunching. It was hot and still.

"Did you rise that one Dad?" a young boy's voice came from the lower half of an upper sash window of the house.

"No rod with us Derek – and say hello to James Fearnley - a good friend of many years – be careful though – he's a law man."

"Hallo Mr Fearnley."

They had supper in the kitchen. Derek went upstairs to some project he had on.

James noticed that the decoration, paintings and furniture were restrained and restful. There was nothing strident or claiming attention. Looking more closely he could see that many of the paintings were of river scenes.

"But what of your modern art Guy – you had it all over your Barbican flat"

"He took a while to get over the disease" said Victoria. It was just after I'd met him. I sent him a Valentine with a picture of a little river and willows by someone called Thomas Moran. It was called 'Cloudy Day at Amagansett'. It's such an English scene but it's on Long Island New York. Painted in 1884, just before it was spoiled for ever."

"I couldn't stop looking at it" said Guy. "Things were a bit rough at the time – wife no 2 creating and my Sports business stuffed by the credit crunch. I kept the Crown jewels – the Jag dealership – but it nearly went.

"The painting was just so full of atmosphere – you can tell it's just been raining – I didn't know it then but the river is just like the Frome. Really a little creek, as they call it in the States. Not at all wide but opening out in places. Cattle and sheep grazing in deep peace and the signs of a worn path. In the far distance the sun lighting the roofs of an indistinct village. It just seemed to have caught an instant – fresh and changing all the time with the light and wind – but with a kind of constant calm about it."

"Then on our honeymoon Vicky dragged me into a museum in Paris – all its walls were covered in water lilies – would you believe it – painted of course. Like being in a cathedral. But I suppose the Moran painting was the game changer. It's why I ended up here. Then I got this ruddy arthritis in my wrists – worse in the right than the left but only just. I smashed up my wrists at my first school and so….."

"I was on the ice with you that afternoon you ass – I saw it happen – we thought you were finished."

"James old chap, yes of course – of course you were there as well. My God, so long ago."

"So then I was splinted up and plastered. I don't know how but I still opened the bowling my last term there. But it's caught up with me now hasn't it?"

James expected his old friend to descend into a morose reflections on all these challenges. But he burst out

"Bloody grateful I am for it too. It's painful of course but it's been a hell of a trade off."

"Trade off?"

"Well you see, it was only when I became unable to chuck a fly out 20 yards or more that I had to bloody well accept things. Pointless fighting it. Not just the wrist – the business as well. Need to manage it of course but once you know the limits you can really enjoy yourself. Who was it said "A rich man is one who has enough." Vicky would know."

"Seneca?"

"If you say so - but what I mean is that I found I could enjoy the little I could manage only by not trying to get anything out of it. Just actually doing it – nothing else. After all I could do so little anyway. D'you know James – I found more pleasure – no, not really pleasure – more like satisfaction really - in landing a fly on to a small rivulet just five yards upstream on our tiny stream than I had on any day on the Test at Stockbridge."

Derek had come down for a late piece of cake, cheese straws or whatever was on offer.-

"Dad's getting quite good – waves the rod around like a fly swatter but not bad"

"I'll swat you!" said Guy reaching out as his son jumped just out of reach.

"So you see James, that's how I came to the idea of this new venture – we'll go into the detail after the binge tomorrow. But what I've manufactured is fly fishing rods much smaller than normal. And they're not carbon fibre or phenolic resin or any other ruddy resin. They're split cane. Yes, beautiful split cane. Same as the old Hardy Palakona rods but much smaller – only 6ft 9 inches – 2 metres to you I suppose. works of art they are!"

"And not only that, I've got hooks which are not only barbless but have the nylon cast - only 2lb breaking strain, mind - actually moulded into the hook. The flies are on a very fine surgical tubes so can easily be run down from the top of the nylon cast down over the eye of the hook."

"But the best thing isn't the barbless hook – it is the hookless fly. You see if you are only talking about brown trout of no more than ½ lb then it should be possible to trap them with a fly that has tiny spines that catch in their teeth or gills for long enough to know you have them on but no longer. And why not little dace or perch?"

"You see I found the more I wanted to get a fish the less I enjoyed the river. Like the monkey with his hand round a sweet in the jar. Had to let go you see to get free? People say they love fishing because it gets them into Nature- but actually they are so bent on getting a fish they might as well be off the A3 in one of my Bournefish sites."

"So why not have tackle that requires good skill but doesn't trap you into wanting something – which is all the trouble. You need to have the skill – the trout taking the fly – but not be locked into the result. So it is the takes of the duped trout that become the thing. "

Guy leaned over and slapped James knee. "It's 'takes' without taking!" he exclaimed loudly in a burst of self approval.

"And they're going very well at the tackle shops. So what I want to do – for young boys and girls who can't get to a river – is to get a complete set up so that not only do they have the kit but they also have the lake – of course it's just a pond. It only works if you've got a good garden but then all that's the same for a swimming pool. A morning with a JCB, fit the Butyl liner, backfill a bit with soil to encourage fly life and there you are. Needn't be big – just a cast to the middle – 18ft overall would do it. The real deal!"

Victoria had Derek next to her on the sofa in the drawing room after supper. The glazed doors out on to the lawn were still open. The evening light had not finally retreated. Guy seemed to have withdrawn into reflection.

"Does Derek ride as well?" James asked Victoria.

"He did for a while, but he's not a Pony Camper. And you've got to love your horse to do the eventing."

"Is it very competitive?"

"Well not for me or most of those I know who are into it. It's about your horse, seeing how well the horse goes. Like, in dressage, when your horse has a fault of finding it difficult, to stand still in front of the judge or when transition into canter is too clumsy. It's so satisfying when your horse is still or slips into canter. Climbing up the competitive list isn't the point. The horse is not bothered. The rest is conceit really isn't it?"

After a pause "Come on young man, up with you" said Victoria quietly leaning down over her son.

Derek said good night and went up with his mother. The silence of the evening extended into the silent space they had left. Guy sat with his old friend and lawyer as the room gradually darkened. Then, very quietly, from Guy

"I was always defying the limits, the rules wasn't I – you remember? – yes I can see you do!"

"But look at me now – the split cane, the hookless flies, the very light line and the narrow rivers – all these boundaries. But without them there's no sport is there? The limits make the play as it were. It's how you keep it a game isn't it."

"Change the limits and you change the game – isn't that what happened in the Jardine Test series – you know Larwood and bodyline? The Aussies were right weren't they? We still call it cricket but it's not really – not when it's just a primitive defence from intentional serious assault on the face and head."

"And what about the new tennis racquets – new thirty years back – no more net play except the killer serve-and-forget-it-volley – all baseline grunting, pumping of fists, violent force on the ball. It's more war than it is lawn tennis. No grace at all. Look at the warrior Nadal and his intense violence and pumping, bawling coups de grace. Nice chap I'm told. But well on Court – well I don't watch it."

James could not bring to mind any apt response. He knew there was more that his friend had waited for a long time to impart to him. Great changes in Guy's life had wrought a shift in the underlying mantle of his existence.

"Talking too much I'm afraid – just so good to have you here" said Guy.

"So, just to finish – well, you know James, you remember I always used to say there's no point – you know how it all was. The real thing was success at whatever you were up to at the time. But there has to be a point for everything doesn't there? Or well… what I really mean is… behind it all. You see. Isn't that it? Otherwise what's the point?"

Guy waited – as if he had now trespassed on unknown territory uncertain of his bearing and direction. He reached for words to give shape to his insight.

"But the thing is James – well isn't that the thing about life – you know, there has to be a point but it has to disappear when you reach it."

Unsure of what he was saying and now uncertain of everything, Guy muttered brokenly,

"As if you have… I mean if you think that the point of what you're doing is really all there is then…. well then…. then actually… you missed the point. So if there's a point isn't it just a kind of prompt? Into realising it's not really the point is it? – only just what is?"

"You start by being in nature – the river's sounds and smells, the light and breeze… you know – well all of it. Then at times – well you see, James, at times I find when, quite still, it's as if just being - just the very fact of being was nature – like as if there was no difference. I used to find this very unsettling at first – like as if I'd disappeared. But now it's – well it's kind of like the point isn't it – the point of it all isn't it?

"If you see what I mean, James?

PUPA

The County Courts of England used to be uncongenial places. Lawyers, who have their own terms for anything judicial, call them "venues". For the most part these Courts of civil justice were to be found in solid Victorian public buildings built for the purpose with the name "COUNTY COURT" carved in a stone panel above the solid mahogany doors that admitted its litigants and lawyers.

There would be the prevailing sound of squeaking linoleum as Court clerks, barristers (whom lawyers call 'Counsel), solicitors, witnesses, claimants, defendants, a few spectators and, of course, journalists from the local newspaper – all hurried to their duties and places. The rooms for barristers to put on their costume – lawyers call them 'Robing Rooms' – were generous since when built it was not supposed that more than one Court would be in operation – or 'sitting' as is the legal term. With the coming of Legal Aid and the expansion of the economy after the War the original spacious facilities were replaced by small and graceless closets to make room for additional Courts within the Victorian structure and new extensions of ugly utility.

For those who had practiced in these buildings in their original state, the destruction of the stained glass windows and panelling in the entrance hall and of the massive marble urinals, might have signalled a loss of *dignitas* or at least of tradition. It was not as if convenience had replaced what was now outmoded. People still crowded the confined entrance hall, the narrow corridors, and waiting rooms. There was a sense of disorder and pressure.

But today, a generation later, the County Courts are modern halls of justice, with all the facilities and dignity required for its administration. Such was the Bournemouth County Court to which Matt Burton had been assigned as junior Court reporter right from his first day of joining the staff of the Dorset Clarion.

* * *

Matt enjoyed his regular visits to the County Court. It was pleasantly air conditioned, there was a restaurant, many interview rooms and free extensive parking. It was on a riverside site. This was the easiest of his responsibilities. He had done the hard yards at Portsmouth Poly – the name his mates called it even now. The University was well regarded for many of its courses and particularly for its Honours degree in Journalism. He was small fry of course – comment columns in the national dailies or Sundays were up at the top of a very long ascent. He liked the atmosphere of quiet respect of the Judges' Courts. The Court ushers had got to know him now.

But it was all rather bland with, so far, no really contentious disputes. He had been on Court reporting now for a few months and had been hoping for some sort of news interest that his sub-editor would notice. His Court reports were like repeat prescriptions for readers. Expected but already assumed. Only noticed if missed or mistaken. Did not his three years degree course and the burden of student loans qualify him for steeper slopes than these?

He could still hear the lecturer's last words on Court Reporting "Check on it or Choke on it". Verify your conclusions or have them stuffed down your throat. But what was there to verify? There was just the drone of formal legal process. For the first few weeks he had accustomed himself to sitting in Court watching the stream of civil claims flow past. But surely he could manage to find a personal angle to just one of the succession of mirror image orders of the Court.

On that August day the Court lists showed that the morning was to be taken up with various uncontested hire purchase default claims. There were a few possession claims in the afternoon which appeared to be contested. Crown Court was not sitting. He thought he would sit in on the h.p. cases but these appeared to be formalities. He decided to get a sandwich and a pork pie and sit by the river. It was just over Riverside Avenue through the end of the car park. He had discovered the way over to the river bank on his first week in Court. He had plenty of time. The sun was warm on his face as he lay down in the grass by the bank.

It was well into the afternoon when he woke. He sprinted back to the Court buildings where the Court usher was speaking to witnesses in the entrance hall. The contested possessions were the last to be heard so he was not too late. He slipped through the double doors of the Court past the frowning usher on to the side bench reserved for the Press as the Court clerk announced the next case.

The Judge in wig and violet robes had just opened the hearing.

"Mr Elder it looks as if you are appearing for the Claimants in all of the contested possessions – is that right?"

"Yes your honour. The first is only technically contested as the Defence was filed but not pursued. It appears that it was drafted on behalf of the C.A.B for the Defendant when she first was served with the Claim. There has been no mediation but it has not been requested by either party."

"Has the contractual tenancy expired? I assume that is the case so we are dealing with an old style regulated statutory tenancy?"

"Yes your honour".

"Is the Defendant in Court?"

"No, it seems not your honour."

"And you are seeking an unconditional order for possession. I see that there are arrears of rent. Over what period have these accumulated?"

"They arose over 15 years ago your Honour. They represent an accumulated balance over that period. Housing benefit has helped but the historic arrears remain amounting to £5,649.35p disregarding any interest. I understand that Miss Wynnstay has been unwell for some months. She simply could not keep up with heating and cost of food after she lost her employment – though the rent is very modest."

"Mr Elder I am not sure there are any grounds on which I can refuse the order for possession in those circumstances but I would nevertheless still like a bit of background if you could oblige".

"Certainly your Honour. The tenant is a lady of 83 years of age. Her mother took the flat on the ground floor some fifty four years ago and Miss Wynnstay succeeded to the statutory tenancy on her mother's death fifteen years later. Until prevented by poor eyesight she worked as a seamstress in a household furnishings workshop leaving there when she was well over retirement age. The Claimant company acquired the freehold of the property a little over a year ago together with others in the street. Miss Wynnstay has no means of discharging the arrears I fear your Honour. That's how the matter stands."

"Very well Mr Elder. As I say, I have no jurisdiction to refuse relief and it is clear that in the circumstances of this case mediation or time to pay is not going to help. I trust that something is in hand to aid this poor woman."

"Order as sought. I take it Mr Elder that you are not seeking costs?"

"No your Honour and we waive any right to recovery of fixed Court fees for issue of the Claim".

Matt moved silently out of his bench to the double doors leading to the entrance hall. As he approached the row of waiting witnesses and litigants sitting on the wall benches he saw a lady holding an obviously used supermarket bag sitting at the end. An incongruous clear plastic raincoat covered a long faded blue skirt and grey woollen stockings. She was looking at him. As he passed she got up in front of him. She was small, elderly and had lost much of her hair.

"Young man – you just came out that Court didn't you?"

Matt nodded and stepped back a little.

"Well, it's saying here on this paper I got – it says…..Oh…. I can't read it without my glasses. Where are they" as she looked anxiously into her tilted plastic bag holding it by one handle and resting it on her bent knee.

"I can read it if you like". Matt took it gently from her little veined hand.

"Well it says you've a case on today here at the Court. I'll go and check on the list."

"Thank you ever so much dear – my name's Elsie. Elsie Wynnstay."

"Oh but they've done that one. I was in the Court you see."

She gripped his arm with surprising claw like force.

"Am I out? Did the Judge say I'm to go? Is it over?

"Well Elsie – you see I'm from the newspapers. I'm not a lawyer. But how can I say this – Elsie I am sure that you've been told to go by the Court. I'm really sorry."

"Ah no, bless you dear, bless you! It's come as a great relief after all this worry. I was that worried I couldn't sleep or eat some days. It is really over now is it?"

Matt could not bring himself to say that it was only just beginning, as far as he could see. She seemed to be pleading him to say Yes.

He waited for a while as if some other response might appear.

"Yes Elsie it's over, I'm sure of it.

* * *

Matt was shocked at what he had seen and heard.

A frail and apparently destitute woman had been ejected from her lifetime home. He knew Wyncombe Road. It was not as if it was a Georgian terrace or lined with Bournemouth Edwardian villas. The terraced houses were mean and uncared for with front steps directly on to the narrow pavement. And here was this bottom feeding, property company buying it up and straight away turfing her out, literally into the cold.

And there were still the arrears of rent – £5,649.35p – a fortune to her – hanging over her for life. She was of that generation that would not accept charity but could not bear the shame of debt.

If that did not deserve to be exposed then what was the point of having a Court reporter. You might as well just have a computer link to the Orders made each day in the Courts.

Here surely was something he could do as a reporter that would have a sharp edge: make readers realise that the eyes of the press fell on injustice and wrongdoing. He would file his copy that evening to get in the Clarion's next issue. He rehearsed the text in his mind as he sat on the bus back to the office. It had to be tight and snappy. Suppose his sub was not there? He could still file it he thought. You shouldn't suppress news for the sake of office process. It would set his foot on the next rung up. He could get it in on the Friday edition so it would be on breakfast tables over the week end – and it was Bank Holiday on Monday.

* * *

Rupert Maddock and his family lived off Hartfoot Lane, Melcombe Bingham. It is still unspoilt. Hardy's Dorset lies all around. Its new flint faced new houses were well built with brick arches and quoins. Some were thatched. They do not detract from the charm of the village. With Martha, his wife, and their son he had moved into one of these in 2011. It had not been easy to find a suitable house, even a modern 3 bedroom one in what is called a 'Close' – just a small estate. A blood clot stroke had recently left him with 'foot drop' on his right leg so that only by swinging it out could he walk at all. He needed wheels and had bought a "Powerchair". It could easily ascend the ramps into their adapted Ford Transit.

The stroke had finally made up their minds to move house. They would look for one which could easily be modified for him. It was a relief in one sense. The national financial crisis – the credit crunch – had caught Rupert when his residential investment business was overstretched. Lloyds had called in those of his loans which exceeded loan to value covenants. The personal guarantees took him nearly over the edge. Downsizing could no longer be postponed.

He still had a few joint business ventures, mostly with Alan Sorrell whom he had known since they were both at Foxleys in West Kensington starting out. When Alan got going in residential investment he had ridden the surf of the Thatcher years so well that he had moved down to Dorset. He had also acquired a house off Lancaster Gate to placate his wife Raisa – she was addicted to Harrods– and now carried on his business in an office converted from an outhouse. He had been able to finance his projects without the PGs that had brought down Rupert.

Alan had persuaded them to come down to Dorset – there was no need to have an office anywhere but at home. Even he had found his way round a key board. He had advanced to scanning and cropping and mobile phone e-mails. The systems did all that was needed except make the tea. It was Alan who found the Melcombe Bingham haven for them both.

Alan himself lived with Raisa, his Russian wife, in deep countryside a little way outside Melcombe Bingham down a drive off Aller Lane– on the way to Bingham's Melcombe. That was just a hamlet – the Lane expired just past a farm further on in open fields.

It was very beautiful country.

* * *

The article – it was more than the usual news report – appeared in the Dorset Clarion on the Friday before the Bank Holiday week end. It was on the second page.

"83 year old evicted from home of 40 years"

There was also a short piece in the Wessex World – the local Freebie.

The report asserted, correctly, that the claimant Alsor Investments Ltd had bought the property only 12 months ago and had given notice of eviction to Miss Elsie Wynsstay the sole tenant of a terraced house in Wyncombe Road, Pokesdown.

The piece then descended into damaging innuendo.

No one had represented the defendant and no one from the landlord's had turned up to give evidence. She was not in the Court. The landlord had evicted her as soon as they could after their recent acquisition of the freehold. She had been the tenant there for nearly 40 years after her mother had died. The solicitor had explained that there were arrears of rent which had built up but the landlords had refused to allow further time.

The report ended with the comment "The days of the rapacious landlord have not yet gone it seems".

Raisa was in London for a few days – shopping and socialising. Alan Sorrell walked down to the outhouse office in the morning sunlight thinking of his 4 days of solitude, horticulture and lepidoptera. He could hear the insistent ring of the telephone within as he approached. He slowed down hoping it might stop. There was silence for a few moments before it broke out again. Reluctantly he let himself in and lifted it from its cradle.

"Alan is that you? Now listen. Marcia took me over to Blandford this morning – to the Dentist – I picked up a Dorset Clarion while waiting. Never usually look at it."

"Is that you Rupert?"

"Yes, yes of course it's me you ass. Stir yourself will you. Listen – there's a report in the Clarion about one of your Alsor properties in Bourne-mouth. Says you have evicted an old lady and makes you out to be a harsh and grasping"…

"All true my dear chap – all true!" chuckling "Are you sure it isn't one of yours" – guffawing.

"Well when I got back I couldn't raise you on the blower. So I called him and told him he'll regret what he's done as it's libellous. I told him Alsor was a reputable landlord and would never have behaved as his report implied. He started to justify himself but I was so angry I put the phone down."

"Back in the cradle?"

"Alan be serious – what would your bank funders say – have you thought of that?"

"Knowing mine they'd probably send me a Valentine" – snorting .

"She's 83 and you chucked her out as soon as you got the freehold – let me see – a Miss Wynnstay – out on the street"

"And straight into a sheltered flat kindly provided by the dear old Stourside Housing Association".

"Alan – really? That was a piece of luck wasn't it?"

"Yes – with one bound Elsie was free – just like that as it were – not like that – like that!"

"Can't you see how serious this could be?"

"Not on a day like this and specially not when I'm wearing my red tassled Fez – which I am."

"Look she's got to pay over £5,000 back rent – you'll be shown up as Shylock Sorrell to all who know you!"

"There's a butterfly species named Sorrell Shylock – did you know. Australian. They haven't decided on the Latin yet – not too many scholars in the Queensland rain forests".

"You're bloody hopeless – you know that. This chap at the Clarion – he's just a very junior reporter I gather. Get him to put in an ruddy apology – you've suffered an injustice – stand up for yourself – and what about our joint ventures – we'll get a bad name."

Alan realised his frivolity was a kind of ingratitude for his friend's kind concern.

"Well my dear chap – you've obviously put a rocket under him. Why don't I get him over here for lunch. Did you say it was my company?"

"No actually – we didn't get that far. I cut him off."

"Well you're obviously worried that there might be some sort of backlash for our joint projects. If you think an apology might help then why not call him back and ask him here for lunch tomorrow – if he gets here an hour before I could show him round. I've got to get down to Wimborne and Bournemouth that afternoon. Better you do it as you've already started in on him with your tin opener. I can then explain things to him and blame you Roo – no need to upset the Press. I expect he's just a new boy trying to get on. I don't like battles – always look for the way round."

"Oh I forgot – Raisa's not here so it'll be me in the kitchen" he added.

"We don't want to risk that" said his friend. "Marcia loves coming over – the butterflies and wild flowers you know. We'll do the lunch while you sort out the Clarion"

* * *

Matt got to Aller Lane, Melcombe Bingham in one of the Clarion vans. The property was down a rough drive bending to the left out of view of the Lane. There was a blue Transit van parked on some hardstanding in front of some double garage doors. He parked next to it.

The house was built of stone with a thatched roof above casement windows of diamond panes right under the deep projecting eaves. There were small dormer windows in the thatch. The house had a welcome and comforting feel . As he lifted up the iron knocker the planked oak door opened before him revealing an attractive woman in an apron over a matching pullover and skirt.

"Hallo – well done for finding us. I'm Marcia Maddock, Rupert's wife. Do come in. You got here in very good time".

It was dark in the entrance hall.

She led the way down a corridor to a kitchen. He followed her from there into a kind of conservatory forming part of the house but also projecting into the garden. He saw that it was close to a lake extending along woodland on one side and at the distant end. There was a glass table and some cane chairs round it. A door led out on to what looked like a stone patio and a lawn beyond. A sort of vine was growing up one of the walls up to the glazed roof.

"Ah there you are Roo" she said as a tall figure emerged silently on a wheelchair through a door to the adjoining sitting room. Mr Burton's here".

"Good of you to come Mr Burton" said Rupert. "So glad you could find the time. Forgive me it I don't get up – safer for you actually as I'm apt to fall into people's arms – not ideal exactly."

Matt shook Rupert's raised hand.

"You need to meet Alan – he's the one who controls Alsor and can fill you in on the background. We have a few joint projects but Alsor is all his. He's in the garden – he laid it all out you see – everything. Can't get him out of it. Remarkable chap. Lives for his lepidoptera – butterflies that is. We love what he's done here."

Matt felt he should say something.

"Who runs the operations of his property business – where's it based?"

"Just Alan – in his outhouse. He converted it to his office. His secretary – not really a secretary – more Girl Friday – not really Girl either – she's a good bit older than Alan – she comes to his office now and then when needed."

"Marcia – see if you can pull Alan out of …..Ah Alan!! come on in!" exclaimed Rupert as the door to the little terrace opened.

Matt looked round to see a genial looking man in a short sleeved sweater – holed in places – and a khaki shirt with ravelled cuffs. He was beaming at him. His shirt had escaped his trousers on one side. His eyes had crows feet as if he was smiling most of the time. Matt shook the hand extended to him.

"Alan Sorrell – so sorry I was caught up in the butterfly house – overheating a bit. Well done getting here – good of you – and early as well."

"Rupert tells me he gave you a bit of a raspberry – in my best interests of course. All about Elsie Wynnstay wasn't it – Oh that thank goodness – that reminds me – you need to witness this, Roo, before I go down to Canford this afternoon."

He put the document in Rupert's lap and down at the table. Matt sat opposite him.

Rupert reviewed the document and nodded.

"Well" said Alan addressing Matt again "I've not actually read your bit in the Clarion but Rupert tells me you think I am the Ugly Troll."

"My friends would all agree of course" he added.

"But seriously – let's sit down and I'll give you the background".

"You see it wasn't quite as I gather you said. It actually took me 9 months to persuade Stourside Housing Association to put Elsie at the top of their lists. There are so many people who are paying full rents who are desperate for a sheltered housing flat. So those on low regulated rents haven't got the loudest shout. It was only when we offered to keep her flat available to Stourside rent free for a period of six months from Elsie's leaving that we were finally able to persuade them to let her in. It was a temporary licence but it helped them out – there's such pressure on them. Not enough affordable housing – nowhere near enough and its getting worse."

"She was in tears when we told her. Overjoyed. I thought she was going to kiss me but she took a closer look and thought better of it."

"But we had to get the possession order – the Stourside needed this. She had to be homeless you see. Officially."

Rupert move his Powerchair back into the doorway of the sitting room saying

"Alan forgive me for butting in but why don't you take Matt outside for a chat – and he must see the garden and butterfly house as well. There's an hour before lunch. Marcia can bring out some tea."

* * *

The conservatory opened on to a terrace. It was laid with irregular stones. Daisies, small flowers. Alchemilla mollis and mosses had claimed the gaps between them. Catmint and blue geraniums flopped over its borders. To the left as they came out was the lake. Matt thought it was longer than a football pitch but not so wide. There were pads of water lilies. They walked along the stone path across the lawn and sat down on a shaped garden seat under some untidy willow trees leaning over the end of the lake just beside them.

Marcia brought out the tray. The tea had been already been poured into cups and there was a biscuit in each saucer.

"Rupert tells me that he read your piece in the Clarion about the eviction order. I gather he called you about it – he's a great one for taking on what he sees as injustice – even with the local garage – especially with them. I don't know what the letters page of the local Freebie mag would do without his contributions!"

Matt waited to see if Alan would continue.

"Well, when you think about it, we're really the good guys. You see what you call "fair" is something no one would disagree with but which no one seems to agree on."

"Who wouldn't want to help those we seem push to the rim of society? But what is fair is just wishful thinking if, in reality, it's more harmful for those who are supposed to benefit. You don't get something for nothing."

"Zero sum is that what you mean?"

"Do I? Not too sure I know" said Alan laughing. "Well I'm no economist. I can't even do my accounts and tax returns without my secretary on one of her days.

"It's just that after a long life I've seen how rent controls dry up spending on building or improving homes to let, creating shortages, forcing poor families to live in degrading conditions. Repairs are kept to the legal minimum. Everyone loses, not just the landlord".

"It's easy to step in with virtuous outrage and sever the normal processes of supply and demand. But wherever this happens on any sort of scale it has to be paid for in unintended consequences – or so it seems from what I've seen – after many years that is you know."

"But you're not drinking your tea – it's a first flush Darjeeling – see what you think of it."

Matt looked at the lake as he took up his cup. Up from the far side of the house Buddleia grew unrestrained in deep banks falling across the grass path along the lake. He could see hints of pink of the distant water lilies beneath orange branches of willows over the dark water at the far end. Behind the lakeside path high oaks and ash rose over the dark waters below them, the sun lighting only their tops. He saw that hazels and brambles had been cleared allowing a few autumn crocus and early cyclamen to push through the woodland floor.

Tall spikes of purple verbena were in flower and stood among pink sedums and monarda in wide beds along the stone path from the house.

"All for the nectar" prompted the watching Alan as if to deepen Matt's evident interest.

After a while, returning to rents, Matt started to question what he has heard.

"But when there are housing shortages then don't you need to keep rents down below excessive levels?"

"That's another word for unfair isn't it?" said Alan.

"Do you know, when I was in Melbourne looking at a Butterfly exhibit project a few years ago – by the way, there are over 400 species of butterflies in Australia and would you believe it many varieties in the suburbs of Melbourne itself – they like native tussock grasses and mistletoe – some like nettles – the caterpillars of the Yellow Admiral feed on them."

"Well…. as I was saying….. what was it?…. Yes – I was told that after the War when all the troops came back to Melbourne they put on strict rent controls. You know what happened? Not one block of flats was built for years after. And in this country, when rent controls came off for new lettings the supply of rented housing was explosive. Rents fell – people got places to live and so on."

Alan sipped his tea.

"But, Matt, I try to keep well away from politics. As for economics – well who knows?"

"I spend almost all my time now with butterflies and the gardens here. A day away is a day wasted – as Churchill said. Come on –let me show you the rest of the grounds."

Leaving the tea they moved down the path from the lawn down along an overhead pergola. Below there were beds of nasturtiums and nettles co-existing in slight chaos. Tumbling over the top of the pergola itself were hop vines in heavy gold and emerald trusses. They seemed to be exuberantly out of control.

Alan started to speak in tongues as if reciting a catechism.

Nasturtiums – Tropaeolum majus – good hosts for all the Whites – Small, Large and Green Veined butterflies.

Urtica Dioica – the common stinging nettle – a favourite of caterpillars of the Peacock, Red Admiral, Small Tortoiseshell and Commas.

And then the Humulus Lupulus Aureus – the golden hop vine itself – family Cannabaceae. Delighted in by the Comma caterpillar.

There are the vetches, of course, but these are in the wild flower garden just ahead. Horseshoe – Hippocrepis Comosa – for Adonis and Chalk

Hill Blues and Anthyllis vulneraria, common kidneyvetch or woundwort for the Small Blues.

Alan stood still for a while silently gazing at the scene. He seemed unaware of the waiting Matt.

"So sorry" said Alan suddenly realising he was speaking to himself

"The older I get the more I flutter off – or so my friends tell me. This all must be rather bizarre for you. Did you say something?"

Matt hoped he would not offend by pressing his questions further.

"Well it was what you were saying about good guys. What do you mean you are the good guys?"

"Well, we try to stay in touch with the market. The vacant possession value you see. A dilapidated property in an unfashionable area is going to mean we lose on our investment. On those sites that don't have development potential. And only a very few do. So we keep them in repair – makes sense even though the rents go nowhere to set off the cost. They sell more quickly when we get v.p."

"Come on Matt – that's enough about rents and flats – you must see this –I bet that you won't see another one for a while".

Alan had stopped by the nettles at the end of the pergola walk.

Before them was a circular expanse of what looked like wild flowers of every kind. Their petals moved slightly as the breeze caught them. They were simple little things. With childlike colours such as would be seen in kindergarten 'paintings'. There were grasses growing with them –and lace like fronds of green. Bordering the encircling gravel path were spikes of verbena and drifts of lavender. Fennell plants with little yellow flowers and finespun green ferns of unimaginable delicacy grew amongst them.

The scene was strangely disordered yet appeared complete and whole. It defied attempts to classify by naming or knowing. It all seemed so natural, so free and graceful.

They walked slowly along the gravel path. As they reached the other side of the round garden Alan took hold of the arm of a garden bench and gratefully let his weight subside on to the seat. Matt joined him.

"We took off some of the richer topsoil to make this garden – stops the rampant grass and weeds taking over and wild flowers like it better"

"You see most of the plants here are for the butterflies. A few are for the house. There are the bees as well. But butterflies need many more different plants."

"It won't take a minute to explain – if you have time?"

Matt could not disappoint him – things were not turning out as he had thought. He had come about rents and evictions. But the Clarion wouldn't expect him back until his briefing last thing that day.

"Well putting it simply – the butterfly changes from egg to caterpillar and to chrysalis before it is freed in the glory we all see. The eggs have to be laid on plants which the caterpillars can feed on. And these have to be what they like."

"The serious foodies are the caterpillars. They need certain plants. So Red Admiral, Peacock, Small Tortoiseshell and Comma caterpillars all eat nettles. Common Blue caterpillars like bird's-foot trefoil or Lotus Corniculatus– there's a lot of it in here. Brimstone caterpillars need the small trees we call alder buckthorn or Frangula Alnus – it does well on clay – best where it's moist so we plant it round the end of the lake".

"Tall wild grass is good for Meadow Browns. The Orange-Tip and Green-Veined White caterpillars eat lady's smock – that's Cardamine Pratensis. They also like garlic mustard. Lady's smock is a beautiful little pink flower but likes it a bit damp. Garlic mustard or Alliaria Petiolata is good also – it too likes damp and shade but can grow in drier areas. It has fresh green leaves and little white flowers. We have some by the lake."

Alan paused, looking at some butterflies dancing and sipping among the petals before him.

"They need to eat – actually they need to gorge. Do you know that a caterpillar bursts its skin at least 4 times. A Monarch will grow one hundred times its size. All that food is stored you see. For the coming butterfly."

"It then turns into a chrysalis or the pupa – a fat blob under a branch or under leaves or the ground. I was often teased by my daughter saying silly "Fat Papa Poopa" – always with giggles."

"And then the butterfly. They don't eat that much. Butterflies I mean. They sip nectar and reproduce. Sounds good doesn't it! But it's over in a fortnight."

"There has been some good news about butterfly stocks – it looked very bad a few years ago. There have been terrible falls for some species. The Common Blue, Adonis Blue, Green-veined White and Large White have all fallen in abundance by at least 40%. As for the rare Heath Fritillary its numbers have now declined by 90%."

Alan leaned forward and looked down on the path at his boots, hunching his shoulders over his elbows. Then abruptly he looked up turning to Matt.

"I do what I can. I bore the pants of people of course. But I have a butterfly visitor attraction near Salisbury which does very well as the children bring their parents – so good for them both. And I invite wild life clubs and groups round in the summer. Sometimes I get interviewed about all of this. It's not much."

"But it's my duty isn't it Matt? How can I do nothing knowing what I do?"

Matt was moved by the obvious devotion that inspired what he was hearing.

"It's your passion isn't it – that's obvious." Matt sensed he was being taken into some other world. He was a little bewildered. He could not think of how to get things back to his interview.

"Yes you're right – of course. Since I was a boy. Well there it is. One just has to do what one can."

Alan pushed himself forward hand on the arm of the bench as he eased slowly up onto the path. He tucked in his flapping shirt as he smiled down at Matt.

"Come on – we'll peep in to the butterfly house on our way back in".

* * *

Behind the wild flower garden was long old fashioned glasshouse. It had misty looking windows which on entering were explained by the polythene panels laid over the frames.

The door opened outwards. Its hinges were rusty and complained. There was a barrier of thick clear overlapping plastic strips suspended down to the bare rough concrete floor. The heat and humidity felt solid as they pushed through the heavy barrier. Heated pipes ran the length of the glasshouse sides. Water was trickling into a central rectangular trough extending along the middle of the floor with racks over it. More racks stood over the hot pipes. Glistening wide leaves, fronds and pads competed with vines and vigorous plants to gain ascendancy.

The atmosphere was dense and utterly silent save for the tinkle of the running water.

Matt become aware of a constant silent fluttering. There was no sound. Nor did it appear to be in any place. It was like a movement of the air itself.

They stood together in silence gazing at this colourful and fragile world.

"That little chap is Dynamine artemisia – the small eyed sailor" Alan announced as if opening the show. "It's not a front runner box office hit as it were. But look at the soft blue of the transparent wings. You can see the stones on which it's resting quite clearly through them. Such a modest creature – a favourite of mine."

A flash of scarlet, white and black burst from behind thick passion fruit vines and vanished.

"Ah Diaethria Anna! They call it Anna's Eighty-eight. You might just have seen the red under its forewings. Did you catch the white undersides with the 88 shaped black circles? Very like Diaethria Astala – the circles stand out more it seems.

A butterfly landed for an instant on Matt's purple polo shirt fluttering away unconcerned above him. The stillness enveloped them. For some minutes nothing was said.

"Of course I expect you know the Blue Morpho – there's one on the vine above you. Morpho peleides. Very popular. Sometimes called the Common Morpho – though its everything but. Keeps predators away with its iridescence. Done by refraction not the colour of the wings themselves – so it's like a blue mirror for predators – puts them off."

Alan sat down carefully on an old slat backed rush seat chair just down from the door.

Matt stood next to him. He began to feel enchanted by the silent magical existence of these beautiful beings. The close heat and humidity were intense but did not oppress him.

Suddenly Alan took Matt's sleeve saying softly,

"Look down the side there – see it? Just on those lilies. That's the Blue-grey Satyr or Magneuptychia libye. Its blue grey wings set off by terracotta stripes.

Then as if addressing himself, quietly "You could weep it's so lovely".

They waited a long while. Matt felt his shirt damp with sweat on his skin. Alan sat motionless as if entranced.

"Ah good" he said quietly, leaning up to look at Matt "Such a lovely thing – do you see it on the slats next to the lilies over there? The little Klug's Clearwing or Dircenna klugii as you might say. Deep honey coloured and transparent wings with little pale blue jewels decorating its tips."

Some more time passed. Alan sighed and rose slowly. He looked kindly at Matt.

"I'd have liked you to see our swallow tail. They have a kind of forked tail and – even for Belize – exotic wings".

As they came to the door he glanced round – then alive with excitement he whispered

"Yes – yes – quick there's one just settling on those rotting bananas. It's the Dark Kite-Swallowtail – Eurytides philolaus. See – quickly!"

Matt had missed it.

They emerged into the cool of the garden.

* * *

Lunch was a mix of various lettuces, pimentos, artichokes, strips of Parma ham and anchovies. Elderflower juice with ice and grated ginger stood in large glass jugs on the table.

Just as they sat down a clock striking in the adjoining room brought Alan to his feet pushing back his chair.

"My gosh – it isn't 2 is it! I should've left half an hour ago – got lost in the butterfly house – always a danger. Look here Rupert have you signed that deed?"

Alan picked up the document and leaned down slightly towards Matt.

"Look I'm awfully sorry Matt. What must you think of me! I know you've probably more questions and I've rudely pushed you around the garden instead. But Rupert can tell you all you want to know."

"You see, as Rupert will tell you, its Joshua's last year at Canford. As I've got to see Elsie Wynnstay with this before she moves out tomorrow I thought I'd call in on Canford on my way down there. I did promise Joshua I'd get down to watch him play his first Squash match. They're playing Wellington I think."

"Dear Alan" said Marcia "Always catching up after lingering with lepidoptera. Just you now watch out with that BMW beast you keep chained up in the garage".

Alan looked sheepish. As if he had to give an excuse he continued

"It also gives me the chance to see some Real Tennis – I did once see it at Hampton Court. Very strange but exciting – incredibly fast. I once read a thriller about it. The serves have strange names as I remember "bobble", "poop" and "piqué". And making or defending volleys into what they call the dedans at the back – does it mean inside I wonder."

Rupert swivelled the Powerchair towards Alan.

"Push off old thing. Good that you are seeing Josh – we'll savage old Matt here when you're gone"

* * *

"Did I hear him say he was going to see Elsie Wynnstay – I'm sure she came into it as he was speaking" said Matt after the flurry of Alan's exit died down.

"Yes that's right" Rupert explained. "He had a deed drawn up by his solicitors for her. It's what lawyers call a Deed of Waiver. His company waives all the arrears of rent. It's not that the Housing Association need it – though they will be glad to hear of it."

"No, it's just that he wanted her to have an official document to prove she was free of debt. You see Alan got to know her well. As soon as he'd bought the Wyncombe Road reversions he did all he could to get the tenants into sheltered housing. Well they're all elderly – being in old regulated tenancies arising many years ago – in some cases not long after the War with the children succeeding when parents died you see. Many are on their own. They've no on site care. They've no modern facilities – I mean things like dishwasher, central heating, double glazing, electric hob, built in eye level fridge – all these things mean so much – and with no steps down to the pavement. Such small things. But the difference between comfort and survival."

Matt could not think of anything he could aptly say.

Marcia came in with a tray carrying a jug of coffee, milk and brown cubes of sugar. She poured a cup pushing it quietly over to Matt.

"How did he come to put in the butterfly house for you – and the wild flower garden?" asked Matt.

Rupert put down his cup.

"Oh no Matt – we don't own this. No, this is Alan's. He's done this over the years. I can see why you might have thought it was ours – Marcia letting you in and Alan not being around. And it was me that called you and – I'm ashamed to admit – bawled you out."

"Alan might have mentioned that he had created all this but not perhaps that he was the owner. He doesn't like drawing attention to himself. He's just like his plants and butterflies. He greets you as if for the first time. He really is a child of nature. But very shrewd in business dealings – as many have discovered."

"I suppose" said Matt "that – not being unkind – it was not a big deal for him to waive the arrears as he knew he couldn't get them from her and he was getting possession early – so it was not quite as generous as it looks."

"But even that's not right – he's deferred getting possession for another 6 months and is paying for Elsie's move, such as it is. And he devoted hours and hours to getting her a nice ground floor flat to have for the rest of her life."

Matt held on to one last loose thread saying

"It seems that he's done very well for himself anyway. He's got a son at Public School hasn't he – and a successful business – like you have" said Matt as if to tie it up.

"Matt" said Rupert after some while "You're looking at the surface ripples not into the depths. If you're to be valued as a reporter then you'll need to develop insight as otherwise you'll just be shouting up high in the stands. No one will hear you. Didn't anyone tell you in your training to verify what you assume?".

Rupert continued but more slowly, defining what he said with quiet emphasis.

"I don't have a successful business. I have just 50% of it. The Bank sold all my best investments when I hit the wall during 2009. It was Alan himself who made good the net value of those properties in my company – he paid 80% of its value – for only one half of its shares. I'd still be bankrupt if that hadn't happened."

Matt interrupted him.

"Mr Maddock, sorry to interrupt. But it's not what you think. You're right. I didn't check the story. I rushed into it and see that now. I'll have to face the music at the Clarion for that. But you mustn't think that I grudge him anything he has worked for and achieved."

"I was only with him just a little over an hour but when I came out of the butterfly house it was as if I'd been in some sort of trance. I thought he'd be a fat bottom feeder picking up the scraps of peoples' lives. I can well see you as a tough egg, but walking round with him – well, I could hardly remember why I'd come over in the first place. He seemed only to want to show me flowers, plants and butterflies. What was I doing here for goodness sake. He was like a smiling genie conjuring up for me fantastic things. Not at all the fat Papa Poopa."

Rupert, looking puzzled, began as if to speak but Matt anticipated him

"Oh sorry – you see he told me his daughter used to call him Fat Papa Poopa. It was when he was telling me about the Pupa of the butterfly. I had this very sharp image of him before I got here. It was of a greedy bulging Pupa – just as he described."

Marcia had come unnoticed into the Conservatory as Matt was speaking. She sat next to her husband and held his hand.

"Ah Matt – the miracle of metamorphosis – that's what's happened to your image of him isn't it – I can see that it has – he's no longer the greedy bulging Pupa. He's now the very butterfly isn't he?"

She looked at her husband. Then quietly, with infinite care, as if touching a wound, she said

"When Roo had his stroke we didn't know how we could go on. All our hopes and plans abandoned. No way out – no way forward."

"It's true, Matt. There is a son at Canford.

And it's true that Alan indeed pays all the fees."

Matt felt the sudden still silence.

"You see Matt, Joshua is our son".

BIRTHDAY TREAT

Have you ever had dinner in a club with two complete strangers and found yourself at Covent Garden with one and pheasant shooting at Tollard Royal with the other within the space of a month and all at their expense?

So singular was this encounter that I have tried to recall, as precisely as memory allows, all that happened on that extraordinary evening a few years ago.

I had gone to the Reform Club where I was staying overnight in order to be on time for an early meeting the following morning in the West End. I got there at about 7.00 in the evening and having taken my overnight bag to my room descended to the vast and important morning room where drinks are dispensed on a large mahogany table.

As I walked through the magnificent paved Saloon I could hear the sound of loud guffaws coming from the morning room. On entering I could see at once that these emanated from the far end of the room, looking over Pall Mall, where sat two gentlemen who seemed to be of late middle age but whose appearance made it hard to say. One of them was in a wheel chair and had evidently been speaking loudly to his companion who himself was holding his hand to his ear. Both were rendered almost helpless with laughter. They were finding it hard to catch their breath. As I watched them each of them took out handkerchiefs to wipe eyes and blow noses whilst snorting and making futile attempts at speech.

Discreet members were casting glances at the convulsing pair.

I was drawn in by the gusts of uncontained hilarity and approached the wide and deep Victorian sofa on which one of them was sitting with the wheel chair drawn up against it. I had no notion of what to say to them.

I had misgivings as I got near to them and was about to turn back when the wheel chair called out to me.

'Have you come to throw us out! Never been thrown out of the Reform. They took me in when Boodles thought it best I found another berth – most indulgent is the Reform.'

'Do join us' said the deaf aid. You'll have to bellow a bit at me – copped an incoming practice shell burst in training – mortar set wrong – don't hear high or low notes – a blessing when you're listening to Desmond!'

'Forgive me for butting in but…'I began.

'No, no not at all. Not at all. We haven't met you before but then – well – James and I haven't met for over 30 years, so much the same really' said the wheel chair.

'Desmond Wiley-Stiffe' said the wheel chair.

'James Lampbull' said the deaf aid.

'Roderick Wagstaff' said I.

'You see it's our birthdays – not twins – God forbid! – just happened to get out on the same day – 50 years ago' said James.

At that I called one of the stewards who was collecting glasses from tables and asked him to bring a magnum of the Club's champagne, three glasses and bowls of cashews.

'That's very civil of you Flagstaff' said Desmond leaning over towards me.

"Very civil indeed!.' I noticed that he had a yellow leather glove on his left hand.

To distract him from my tactless gaze I quickly responded

'How is it that you've found each other after so long? What's could be so hilarious about it? You've acted like an egg whisk on the atmosphere in here – just what it needs. Too many accountants and not enough unreformed members. Lost its way a bit the Reform I fear. No one to reform – all rather wet safety-first merchants.'

'A soul mate no less!' bellowed Desmond.

'A soul mate would you believe! "Minime ferendum patiens ad impatientes". The inscription to be carved on my gravestone. 'Intolerant of the intolerant.'

The champagne arrived in a vast bucket with a cold mist and drops on its sides. The glasses were large wine goblets – just perfect I thought.

'Slange Var' they each called out as they sank the first delicious draft.

James turned to me and began to speak loudly – as if it were I that was deaf.

'Well it's an extraordinary tale". It was James Lampbull who spoke. "It needs to be told to the accompaniment of fine wine and food in the best of company – so you must join us. Be our audience and our spectator. We've booked the Garden Room – got them to put in a round table. It'll help us to recall those events that brought us together if we have to recite them to you. Don't you agree Stiffy?'

'Absolutely – I can hobble to the table for a good Margaux and Reform beef. I'll need your arm Flagstaff. Got my foot stuck in the tracks of a peat digger – nasty mess – passed out.'

'On condition that I provide the wine – not otherwise' I objected.

'Of our choice or of yours?' was Desmond's instant retort.

'Margaux 1990?'

'Bloody hell!' was all that Desmond could say.

I got up. 'Better get it decanted now. They'll need to keep the bottle level in the rack as they do it. I'll go down to the cellar as we can't risk an upright bottle.'

When I got back the tide of champagne in the large bottle had ebbed quite a bit but there was enough for half an hour. It was then that Desmond took a long look at me as if to affirm that I was sufficiently unreformed.

After a little while he put his leathered left hand on my arm saying

"It's really very good of you my dear chap" he said as his eyes met mine.

'Oh my hand! – that – ah yes – well it took a full barrel of shot from a 16 bore at a clay pigeon shoot. Not even a proper bloody shoot. Chap swung too early next to me as the clays went overhead. All the bones and bits are there somewhere in my glove but not of much use now'

"Now! Flagstaff! you see these envelopes?" he said stifling further comment as with his good hand he picked up two envelopes that had been lying on the round table between us.

I looked at each of them. They were addressed respectively to each other. James at an address in Devon and Desmond in Yorkshire. I could see the postmarks for dates in June that year. They were unopened.

Desmond continued

'I got a letter from Lamps a few weeks ago – quite shook me – hearing a voice from one's boyhood as it were. You see I was stuck in NZ for a good many years until Pa died and I then took over in Yorkshire. I lost contact with Lamps. Had no idea he had become a land agent and in the West end of all places.'

'Well the letter was posted to Wileys Wine Merchants at Borough-bridge from where it eventually washed up on my shore. It proposed that we should go to the Isle of Jura for our 50th birthday. In the Inner Hebrides that is. James knew that my family had a good sized house there when we first got to know each other.'

'Now why James proposed that will become clear over the caviar and beef. But he also thought it would be agreeable if we were to do something which reminded us of those days in the distance enchanted. So I responded to the effect that it would be delightful to have his company again but that we should each propose to the other what the celebration gift would be for him'.

'To lend spice to the arrangement we agreed that we should send each other a token of the gift in an envelope to be opened when we met. My family had sold out Jura house 10 years ago so I suggested the Reform as our meeting place – the only Club that would have me by then. James was a member of the In and Out – Scots Guards officer and all that you see. But they have a mutual arrangement with the Reform – he can bed down here – so this was our venue."

At that James Lampbull stood up and held me by the arm.

"Don't let Stiffy start down his run – you'll never stop him. We ought to get to the Garden Room – the beef trolley stops at 9.00."

"Look, Flagstaff" Desmond called to me "if I lean too far forward James'll get me in his lap. Winch me up will you?"

I went to stand in front of the wheel chair. As Desmond rocked forward I lifted him under his arm as he propped himself up on the arm of the now locked wheel chair with his other hand.

The little caravanserai made its way across the great Saloon under the magnificence of its glass canopy, with sundry explosive comments from Desmond to his friend about being perfectly able to manage, at last arriving, with gracious help from the Club staff, at the Garden Room now bathed in warm evening light.

After the Puligny Montrachet was served and the caviar despatched James began to turn the pages of their little history.

'You see, Roderick" started James "it began just 32 years ago when Desmond turned up at Blundells. That is where I was at school – in my last term but one'

'Yes – know it well' I broke in. 'Used to fish the Exe above Bickleigh with one of the Factor's sons who went there'.

I could see that James wanted to have the field to himself. He was waiting silently for his recollection to give shape to memory so that he could describe what was actually before him in his mind.

Because he was mostly deaf – at least in higher and lower registers – he spoke in a loud but very clear voice as if he was listening to all that was being said with abundant interest. It is because of this, I think, that the remembrance of all that he unfolded that evening in the Garden Room remains so clearly incised in my memory. All that I have done is to treat myself as an unseen observer and narrator of all that he recounted.

* * *

Peter Blundell had prospered greatly as a clothier. He died in 1601 leaving a great fortune. Among gifts to many he left an endowment to build a school in the borough of Tiverton Devon *to maintain sound learning and true religion* – today's Blundells School. He funded scholarships for boys from the school to go to colleges in Oxford and Cambridge.

Among those who benefitted from Blundell's generous foresight were Peter Schidlof and Bamfylde Moore Carew. Both achieved distinction in their life's work. Let me take a little time to speak of them for they foreshadow the characters of James and Desmond.

For Schidlof the path to celebrity began when as a 16 year old boy he escaped from his native Austria following its seizure by Nazi Germany in 1938. He was saved by the British Government's Kindertransport programme. A few thousand Jewish refugees escaped the death camps of the Final Solution by this means. Schidlof was given a place at Blundells. He was an accomplished violinist. He was cruelly interned in the Isle of Man on outbreak of war so his stay at Blundells was short. But he had cause for further gratitude to the Government since it was there, in the internment camp, that he met the violinists Norbert Brainin and Siegmund Nissel. Schidlof changed from violin to viola to make a place for Brainin. Together with Martin Lovett they formed the great Amadeus String Quartet – the most celebrated of modern times.

So Schidlof's misfortune became a portal to prosperity and fame.

Bampfylde Moore Carew's life story was published in 1745. It was very popular.

He ran away from Blundell's School where he faced expulsion for chasing deer. He developed into a skilled confidence trickster. He posed as a shipwrecked sailor, a clergyman, a rat-catcher and then as a woman whose daughter had been killed in a fire.

He ran off with the daughter of a respectable apothecary of Newcastle on Tyne but resumed a piratical life living off the land poaching when he could both salmon and game. He was convicted of being an idle vagrant and sentenced to be transported to the English colony of Maryland. He escaped, was captured, escaped again and found refuge with friendly native Indians. He made his way to Pennsylvania, swam the Delaware, disguised himself as a Quaker, got to New York and back to England. Having tracked down his wife and daughter his last adventure was in 1745 when he accompanied the Bonnie Prince, Charles Edward Stuart on his forlorn march down to Derby. He settled at Bickleigh on the River Exe near Tiverton having won a lottery.

'A fine example of a model old boy' was Desmond's apt comment.

* * *

James Lampbull had lived all his 18 years at Mawes Gate, his father's small farm of around 80 acres lying above the Iron Bridge on the Bampton road north out of Tiverton. It straddled the river Exe up to Cove. Colonel Richard Lampbull, his father, had been a widower for 10 years. He had brought up James cherishing the hope that he would follow him into the Scots Guards. But by the time his son had reached his 11th birthday it was evident that his precocious talent on the keyboard was flowering into an almost prodigious gift. When the time came for him to move into the Blundells senior school he had also begun to master the violin with an ease and modesty that aroused admiration and affection.

The Colonel had not shared his late wife's love of chamber music to the same intensity but he had responded to pieces by Handel and Mozart that those of his background could recognise if not name. He accorded them the same kind of respect that was due to regimental banners in the Guards chapel.

The Colonel grew to accept that his only son was sure to embark on the precarious career of a classical violinist. But he did not live to be disappointed by this for he fell from his horse with a heart attack and expired whilst out with the Tiverton Foxhounds on the opening day meet two months after James's 18th birthday. James's uncle came over from Barnstaple to arrange everything. It was decided to lease the farm for two years. James would become a boarder at Blundells and in the school holidays live in the farm cottage down a lane off the Bampton Road. The river Exe ran along its boundary. It was used for letting to holidaymakers. Mrs Brunny would come in each day during the holidays and do the school run at the beginning and end of term and exeats.

So it was that James Lampbull found himself an orphan and a boarder in Old House Blundells School Tiverton.

He had the manners of an earlier generation. His family on his father's side were strict Presbyterians. The sons had served in the Scots Guards for three generations. They had maintained a modest but privileged existence in Inverness on the upper Findhorn river until post War taxation drove them out of the house of their ancestors. Having relatives near Bampton they moved to the Mawes Gate farm where twenty years later James was born on 14 July 1970.

James had inherited the restraint and social polish of his parents. Though gifted he was also self effacing. He had been schooled in the manners of a gentleman officer which had set an indelible impression on his personal conduct however much it ran against the current of the times. When you spoke to him he had a feint half smile that drew you in. He appeared immune to slights and intended insults. He gave you the impression that what you were saying was full of interest and deserving of attention. He never seemed to hurry.

In stature he was tall – so much so that he walked with a slight stoop as if the better to see and hear others. He spoke little and moved gracefully. His skin was pale and his face rather long. He had long fingers and delicate hands. He had pale blue eyes and a shock of unruly very fair hair. His gestures were graceful. He lived very much within himself.

On the second day of his last year at Blundells James was leaving the Chapel after a preliminary run through on the organ of the anthem and voluntary for the coming Sunday. As he emerged on the path outside the West door he collided with a boy who was obviously in his last year but whom he did not recognise.

'You're must be in the God squad! – Are you?'

Not waiting for a response his new acquaintance continued

'Bended knee on prickly hassocks. Victorian folk songs served up as hymns. Should be used as national anthems for liberated black colonies. I was just going into town to get some necessaries from the tobacconists. Do you want to come?'

'Oh by the way I'm new here. Got sacked from Eton. No one else would take me for my last VIth form year so here I am at Bloody Blundells! Well are you coming or not?'

The speaker was dressed in the official Blundells jacket and trousers. But James could see that the jacket was lined in maroon satin. His shoes were the regulation brown but were suede brogues. He was wearing a cream shirt – not the glaring white of the school clothes list. His hair was parted in the middle as if he were out of Brideshead. He seemed utterly out of place – as if he had wandered in error into a convent carrying an open bottle of champagne.

'Well' said James 'You see I was playing the organ. I was going in to tea. My name's James Lampbull.'

'Lampbulb! What a name. And with that hair! Yes Lampbulb! Excellent. Well I'm off to the corner shop whilst all are at tea. By the way I'm Wiley-Stiffe – Desmond Wiley-Stiffe. Pronounce 'Whylie – not 'Willy'. Pity really. I've always thought 'I'm Willy-Stiffe' would be a good conversation starter.'

"Got to go!" he said and went.

Desmond was in Petergate House. His paths did not cross James's except at School assemblies and Chapel. Neither had any disposition to Rugby, the sporting preoccupation of the Winter and Easter terms. It was music that brought them into strange alignment. Desmond had a fine baritone voice and condescended to join the Choir on the basis that it absolved him from an hour's study time in his house during Choir practice. He almost at once became the lead upper bass voice. He had a facility for sight reading that was unaccountable for such an unruly free spirit.

It was therefore in the unlikely forum of the School Chapel that James first made an acquaintance with Desmond Wiley-Stiffe. Strangely this grew by stages into regard and reluctant affection. It was Desmond's truthful rudeness, initially startling but undeniably apt, that drew James to him for it was never intended to offend – he seemed surprised that offence was taken. If what he said was true then why let feelings obscure it? If it was not true then why mind? So spoke Desmond.

James found himself exhilarated by the sight and sound of Desmond's flashing blade and his belief that risk was the essence of life's experience. He did not allow resolution to be' sicklied o'er with the pale cast of thought'.

James began to seek out the company of this extraordinary character whom no school could easily contain.

The half term exeats at Blundells in those days allowed only two nights away from the school. This was sufficient for most of the boys since only a few lived in other counties. Desmond's 'people,' as he called them, lived near Boroughbridge in North Yorkshire. There was little to attract him to Yorkshire in late February with journey time of seven hours door to door. He decided to ask James about booking a room at a suitable hostelry on the River Exe.

'Lampoil!' he bellowed across the football pitch on which a rugby match was being violently contested. James was standing on the opposite touch line. Desmond was wearing one of the fashionable Barbour jackets. He had managed to persuade the suppliers to dye it a kind of British Racing Green.

'Like the coat? Goes with the new chariot. Got a spanking new Jaguar XJS V12 Convertible all in BRG. For my 18th. The date of maturity according to the Government. I have no intention of maturing. Well, you see, I keep it in a garage just across the road in Popham Close – chap there thought it was worth £200 to keep his own car in the road for a bit. Best say nothing as its strictly verboten.'

'Look Lamps I need some local know how. No point my going to Yorkshire for 2 days so thought I would pitch up at some welcome inn if there is one'

'Well I'm not sure Stiffy. I suppose there's the Fisherman's Cot down the river at Bickleigh. But I can't see you in there. I don't think they could stand the shock'

'Too early for salmon I expect?' Stiffy enquired hopefully, looking up at me.

'Fear so."

There was a pause as James rubbed the back of his neck. For a while nothing was said.

'Look why not come home with me? I mean home is just a cottage but it could be fun. I canl call Mrs Brunny to get all ready. Too early for salmon but not for pigeons. We have two copses on our small farm and on the last week end in January we join up with neighbouring farmers for a pigeon shoot. Very difficult birds. Always spot you and fly cleverly. But if you stand just in the woodland edge you can get a good shot in as they come gliding in to roost in twilight. With guns in all the nearby copses the birds keep on moving between them. So you keep going till dark.'

'Not sure if that is your thing is it? What do you think?'

'Bloody hell Lamps – can a damned duck swim! Brilliant. No gun though.'

'I've got a 20 bore and there's a double barrelled .410 hammer ejector. It's quite old but it was proofed when I was given it. But you need a good eye and swing with plenty deflection – good sport – only brings them down if it's a perfect shot.'

'Strewth!' was the only response from his friend.

Then Desmond took up the chorus as it were.

'We'll go up in the Jaguar. I've got a couple of cases of 1970 Margaux. A very good mouthwash. Chateau Palmer. Courtesy of Wileys Wine.'

* * *

Mrs Brunny had made not only a large fish pie but also a steak and kidney pie enough for a regiment.

The fire had been lit on their return in the dark from the woodlands. Mrs B had set out everything with the pie on a low flame in the oven. There was just one ceiling light in the day room so she had set out a few candles in saucers. There were candles in their holders on the black upright piano opposite the outside door.

Upstairs the smell of starched fresh sheets softened the air of the two bedrooms and early snowdrops were in drinking glasses on the wooden table next to the beds.

Desmond came in with bottles from the Jaguar going straight to the kitchen with his own Wileys Wine corkscrew. He decanted a bottle it into a glass jug, cleaned out the sediment at the bottom of the bottle and with infinite care poured it back in again.

Banging the bottle into the wine coaster that he was surprised to find on the sideboard. He spoke quietly as if confiding in James

'Got the sediment out OK. Bottles were upright in the boot so sediment jumped about a bit but still at the bottom. Took them out of the wooden one at home and put them in an empty Pimms cardboard box. Unusual wine coaster you've got there?'

'Yes it is nice isn't it' said James 'A present from my father – when we were living up in the main house'.

Planting his slight frame astride one of the wooden spindle back dining chairs Desmond suddenly burst out

'Great God that was some sport. Frosty clear end of January day – long evening twilight– perfect! just bloody perfect! – Eh Lamps! Perfect wasn't it!. Far better than driven birds. No comparison. You have to be rigidly motionless as they flight in down to the trees don't you. No smoking – they see the burning end. I found I had to have the gun ready at the shoulder. God almighty we could've gone on into the night with that moon – what a couple of hours. Even being hit on the back of the neck in the dark by a stricken bird – wouldn't have missed that for larks.'

'You can bloody well use a shotgun Lamplight" he said. "Thought you were with the angels with all the violin and piano malarkey.'

'Well I hope you'll not mind me saying Stiffy but I didn't think you'd do much with that little .410' began James.

'There's such a small charge and no real spread. And it's not everyone can get used to a hammer shotgun. Risky in the dark in a wood. Trip and you're in for a big surprise. God isn't it great when you only just hear them flighting in and catch just a glimpse of them in the air against the moonlight. Where on earth did you learn to shoot like that – and with just a little .410'.

They sat down to the pie. Desmond poured the Margaux. The fire warmed the modest little room next to the little kitchen at the foot of the steep narrow staircase. The wine had not had time to get its breath fully but was still magnificent.

'You're a strange bird yourself' said Desmond. 'Thought Blundells was for the gnomes and grey men. Didn't expect to find a good mucker there'.

'Well what's there to say about me?' he continued. 'I suppose I'm what they call a chancer in Yorkshire. As my father put it, before he pegged out, it means I am a reckless, improvident, unscrupulous opportunist. Mostly right. I'm not sure that unscrupulous is quite fair – I just have no scruples about the consequences to myself. Is that unscrupulous? It sounds more like a skin disease than a fault.'

'As to shooting – well we have a small estate in Yorkshire on the river Swale – still get a few wild birds plus a few salmon up there – also barbel, God bless their whiskers. But the real family asset is in Jura.'

'Jura? In France? The mountains?' put in James.

'France! Lord no. France my God! Jura is one of the so-called Inner Hebrides. Means deer island in Gaelic, so I understand. Called Diùra in Gaelic– some still speak Gaelic there you know . Sing in Gaelic. I've heard them recite ballads in Gaelic – lovely lilting themes and sounds. Still a wilderness up there. Especially on the west. Heaven to me it is really – it truly is Lamps. No limits you see. I spend all the time I can there. Easier now with the car – you get to a place called Tarbet on the west of Scotland a good way above Campbelltown – there are a lot of Tarbets up there – and take the car ferry over to Islay, then a wartime Tank Landing Craft to Feolin on Jura – that's only a few hundred yards across the Sound but it's a different world altogether. Different ecology and wild life and few humans.'

Desmond took a good slurp of Margaux and fell silent for a few moments recalling visions of the beauty of that little known island. The wind had got up. James got up to shut the banging kitchen window returning with a plate of something under china cover.

'Well what happened at Eton Stiffy?' said James guiding his friend back to the warm room.

'Oh they weren't too keen on my having a chain of boys as distributors of wine in a few of the houses. I was doing well when I was rumbled. Some idiots in D block got severely inebriated and broke the spell as it were. I thought I'd extend the family wine business to the wealthy South. Wileys Wine importers are big in Yorkshire – Wileys Wine Bars as well. My grandfather floated our fortunes on alcoholic beverages – no Norman blood involved.'

James produced a small Stilton and some digestive biscuits from under the china cover. They used the same plates. Desmond had brought in the second Margaux. As he did so he looked more closely at the wine coaster. It was silver. It was in the shape of a fish. Its head curved round to meet its large tail. It was obviously a salmon. The coaster had an oval plaque on one side in which were incised the following

14.07.1988

Tight Lines!

'Well now Lamps, why have you got my birthday engraved on your wine coaster I wonder?'

'Stiffy please, please don't tell me we're twins!'

'If you say so Lamps – but perish the thought. And why tight lines on my birthday?'

'Well you see I landed a 15lb salmon last year on my birthday two months before my father fell of his horse and died. Very good for this river. He wanted me to have symbols of good living and great sport in one gift on my 18th.'

'Sounds a good man. Very good man. You must have taken a tumble when he died.'

'He left like a sound suddenly silenced. A severing in an instant. So yes, a terrible shock but no pain –but a lot of wondering since then.'

'Stiffy you did mention that there are a few salmon in the Swale. Do you ever fly fish?' said James wanting to snuff out the remembrance of his loss.

'As if you do you must have a few evenings with me on the Exe. The fishing belongs to the local Estate but the owner was also a Scots Guard and allowed my father to fish a few pools when no other rods were out. I've been able to step into his waders as it were. Would this amuse you?'

'It would you silly sod. It would. I'm beginning to think I should move in here.'

'Well what about half term in the Summer? We get 5 days and I could arrange it with the Factor of the Estate if you're not going up to Yorkshire'.

'I'll bring down my rod and flies next term – it's just a small sea trout rod – single handed. Would that do? Waders as well?'

'Ideal. Do you get any fishing in Jura? Apart from sea fishing that is'.

'Not what you'd think of as fishing, Lamps. The island is narrow – three to four miles wide – eight miles at its widest. There are two small rivers – only about twelve foot wide even at the estuary. The Corran runs into Jura bay and there's a river– the Lussa – that drains out of Ardlussa loch further to the north. There are a few sea trout. But nothing like the Exe. Mind you I've had good fun on the Corran. I don't think you'd approve Lamps – your rectitude would get in the way.'

'I can't see how rectitude could come into it – and I've got used to your turpitude – it's an engaging quality of yours – so open up Pandora's box'. The wine was releasing the flow of tales and memories.

'Well it was like this' said Desmond. 'Catching sea trout –mainly sea trout up there but also a few salmon – on a fly or even a spinner is very difficult on the Corran. It's so small you get no room to cover the fish and if you do you lie too high in the water. You don't have time even with a sinking line to get just below the surface. And always you're bitten to death by the midges.'

'It occurred to me that what might work was a seine net in the bay itself. That's a net about ten foot deep with corks at the top every six feet or so and weights at the bottom below them. I got one in Oban and brought it over to Ardbeg – our house there.

'But it was seventy five yards long. That's very long indeed.' He said looking up at me.

'What gave you the idea? Had you done anything like this before at all?'

'No but I'd heard that the lads up at Inverlussa did it – I couldn't resist the idea when it popped into my mind. To get out the net from a boat is quite tricky you see Lamps. You have to fold it into a wide deep box and feed it gradually out of the stern as your boat moves along – not

too fast as the net will tangle or too slow or it will gather up. No good
having an outboard motor. Have to row. I got my younger brother Jack
to feed out the net. He did it well – a steady chap he is – I pulled on
the oars. We had to do it at night, for the tide, but also to avoid being
spotted by the ghillies of the Leargybreck estate which owns the Corran
fishing. The idea was to form a net barrier close to the estuary across the
runs of the fish in the bay as they prepared to go upstream. If you stood
in the estuary waters just in front of the river's mouth you could see the
fish in daylight – they would knock into you if they were moving up to
the stream – beautiful sensation I have to tell you. Actually standing in
the water with the fish.'

Desmond filled his glass and pushed out his chair.

'Our first effort getting out the net went well but we didn't realise
we had to put it out an hour before high tide. We put it out at low tide
thinking it would rise with the tide and be there when the fish started
to run whenever that might be. Bloody hell when we dragged it on to
the sands of the beach it was moving all over the place. Do you know
why Lamps?

'Fish?'

'No! Crabs –bloody Crabs! – hundreds of them –all tangled up in the
net and in seaweed – God what a mess. We had to smash them all to get
the net clear – it took hours and hours on that beach – and the mess! I
suppose it was then that we were seen by the ghillies up in Leargybreck
which looks directly down on to Corran Sands.'

'Well a few days later we put the net out again – this time at high tide.
We were sure we'd got it right – there were fish moving all round as we
paid out the corks and weights. There was no need to wait more than
a couple of hours so we went up to the Jura hotel and had a few drams.

'Jack got squiffy and was starting to sing when we left the hotel. I am sure someone had tipped off the ghillies. Jack had been loosing off about our little caper so that must have been it. Anyway we found the boat and pushed off to lift the net. We rowed about for over an hour before we found the end float. It was a red plastic air filled ball. We lifted it into the boat. There was just 15 ft of net left. The rest had gone. It had been cut right through. We rowed back and hitched the boat to the pick up. Didn't go back into the bar though.'

'So what was the fun in that Stiffy? Can't see it' I asked.

'You mutt! There's nothing more exciting than illicit trapping of salmon, sea trout or game let me tell you. It's the risk of apprehension that spices it all. And, in any case, we had the 15 ft of net so we weren't out of the ring yet – no not at all.'

'But that wouldn't trap anything surely Stiffs?'

'No – not in the bay or estuary. But what about the river Lamps? – what about the bally river!'

'Well" said Stiffy, enthused by the wine, "Jack and I tied ropes to the ends of the remnant net, top and bottom. We added more weights to the bottom. We tried it on the lawns at Ardbeg. If each of us stood opposite each other and held the top rope tight up at shoulder height but allowed the bottom of the net to bump along slightly behind we found that we could slowly bring it along in such a way that a fish would either have to turn back or be caught in the moving net. Sea trout that have started to move up don't get put off easily – they're drawn upstream by a force of nature. So unless we ourselves were caught – which would be tiresome of course – we were 'sucking diesel' as the lads up there say'.

'In the early morning on a high tide – must have been after 2.00 am – it was a few weeks later just to be prudent – we took the pick up and parked it on Corran Sands just by the edge of the estuary. You could do that in the summer. We walked up our side of the bank to well above where the river met the incoming tide. Jack then waded to the far side of the river. I kept station on the near side. We carefully took up slack on the ropes and started to inch very slowly down the banks on each side – really very slowly as any faster would lift the net off the bottom. Jack tripped and cursed – there were tussocks and heather roots on his side all the way down. We'd taken quite a few minutes – it seemed a very long time – I remember holding my breath. We'd only gone a few yards when the net lurched violently upstream.'

'Pull the bottom rope Jack towards you – pull! It's going to slide under the net. Go on lad pull the bloody bottom rope NOW!'

'We had a 12 lb sea trout. It still had sea lice on its sides. It was purple and silver. More beautiful than I can possibly describe. Jack had fallen in the river as he was bringing over his side of the net but was rejoicing as he gathered it up under the fish. We couldn't linger as we'd allowed our excitement to overpower our discretion and anyone awake within half a mile would have heard the commotion. So with the great fish down my trousers into the top of my gumboots I flapped as best I could back to our pick up and then home to Ardbeg.'

'The minister from the Manse came next day to call on my Pa and Ma. He saw the great fish on the marble slab in the hall which was the custom of the house.'

'"Curious" he said "I canna see any hook marks on the beastie at all – is that not a wee bit strange dy'e ken now Desmond?".

'It was hooked deep, Minister' was the best I could do.

* * *

They cleared the table – piling it up for Mrs Brunny next day. There was an ancient sofa against the wall next to the outside door but they went back to the table and opened the next bottle to go with the cheese.

The excellence of the first bottle of Margaux was now being slowly superseded by the mellow dissolution of care and restraint that is bestowed by the second bottle.

'Your father, Lamps. He was a Scot wasn't he? From the western high-lands wasn't it?'

'Not the west – Inverness actually – Near Forres. Yes he was a Scot for sure. Born there.'

'Did he go in for Highland dancing or singing at all?'

'Both – specially the singing. The only music that stirred him. It was the laments that took him to other worlds when he'd had a few malt whiskies. Thin reedy voice he had – not how he looked at all. Rugged red faced – always in tweeds and stinking of pipe tobacco. But a voice like an oboe. I used to accompany him on the piano. He picked out the words very well – with snorts and coughing between verses – his pipe you see'.

'You know Lamps" said Desmond after a pause, quietly, as if admitting something which would invite ridicule.

'I've done quite a bit of that sort of thing in Jura. Ma and Pa don't approve. Nogging with the locals down at the local village hall. Not much they do fancy about me – not since I was 5 that is. I'm rather a 'disappointment'. I'd like to please them, really, but I just find it more amusing to drive on both sides of the road.'

'Yes, well about singing laments and ballads and such'. Desmond paused again.

'You see there's a hall – more of a hut – across the road from the Distillery on Jura. It's an Edwardian I gather. It's just above the little mooring bay facing the sea – just across form the shop. Stone outside and stained pine timbers on the walls and up the underside of the roof. It has a little stage at the end. Every Saturday the island comes down to Craighouse – that's the name of the village – just a few houses and the Jura Hotel plus shop – for the cèilidha – a cayli its called –sort of a dance and get together. Its gaelic. Much the same as the Irish.'

'Anyway, Lamps, at one of those Saturday caylies I had had a few drams of Jura – many few – and my sister bet me I wouldn't dare sing the words of The Wild Mountain Thyme when the accordion squeezed out the first notes for a waltz – he was doing it in slow 3:4 time so that was a help. I shot up and slithered about a bit on to the pine strip floor –a few of the locals stamped their feet as I got my head over my shoulders again and picked up the lines of the lovely song. The few who were on the floor stopped to look and laugh.'

'Must have been a good bet Stiffs– getting you up in front of well lubricated crofters and fishermen' interrupted James.

'Ah but you see James they don't drink too much at all. The islanders are restrained and quietly spoken. They have a lilt in their voice. No malice at all. It's a gentle place Jura, dominated by nature. No one has yet spoiled it. There are three estates on the East of the island with their own big houses. Ours is one of the three. But none of them farm – only interest is the deer – there are supposed to be over 7,000 head on the island. Just 200 people'.

'No one goes over to the West. What a place that is. As it has been for millions of years. No trace of human existence. No change of any kind – except for the raised beaches.'

'What do you mean – raised beeches?'

'Stones you clown – not trees!'

'Bring to your mind an utterly uninhabited land with no trees and little vegetation other than tussock grasses and heather. And the wild goats. Above the shore line many yards inland are these countless large stones worn smooth by eons of water erosion in long rows up many yards wide – much wider in the north west of the island.'

'Apparently the sea levels fell in ice ages and rose when it warmed up. The ice must have been bloody thick as it pushed down the land but when sea level rose with retreat of the ice the land didn't rise at the same rate. So the sea level was higher than it is now by a good bit. Where the ice was thickest the rebound of the land was greater so the beaches are higher they say.'

They helped themselves to more Margaux allowing the images of such a forlorn land to play in their minds.

'Lamps– sorry – left you there for a while.'

'Well I managed to get past the first verse and was starting the chorus when a few began to join in. I suppose they couldn't bear the mangling of the song but it was beautiful to hear one voice then a few more and then the lassies and then the whole hall giving loud unsentimental voice to the enchanting words:-

> *And we'll all go together*
> *To pull wild mountain thyme*
> *All around the bloomin' heather*
> *Will ye go, lassie, go?*

For a while the two young men sat in the light of the candles and fading fire.

'Stiffs' said James I think I've got sheet music for some Scottish songs. What about it? I brought the upright down from the main house when we leased it out so I'll cover for you on the piano.'

The music sheets were in the piano stool, mainly of Scottish dances. There was the Wild Mountain Thyme and The Wild Rover – as you would expect. What caught James's eye was 'Lady Anne Bothwell's Lament'. He had no acquaintance with this. It was in single stave treble clef written for violin and voice. He was arrested by the last two lines of the first verse

Baloo my boy be still and sleep It grieves me sore to hear thee weep

'Stiffs do you think you could manage this? I'll pick out the tune on the piano so you get it – it's simple but – well you'll hear. I'll then get out the fiddle. – it's not got a piano part.'

'No need old thing. I was taught it by Alastair McInnes – now deceased. He used to sing solo at times at the end of the evening in Jura, sometimes in Gaelic, though not for this one. There's so little to it. But very sad. Like so much up there – beautiful but forlorn as if it's not meant for us at all.'

So the friends stood together honouring the baby boy of the lament, the violin adding flourishes to the steady drone of the Desmond's lower notes and rising with his in unison on the higher than octave leaps – a wistful distant sound.

When it was over they looked at each other as if they had been elsewhere

'Well Lamps' said Desmond softly 'That's why we eventually has to leave the islands – its beauty is not for us. Not really.'

James wondered at the depths of his friend. So little suspected.

They sat in silence, James now sitting on the sofa Desmond still at the piano.

Desmond turned his head around to face his friend. He spoke slowly and intently as if disclosing something intimately personal.

'James, I'd like it if you came up to Ardbeg for our birthdays – after we escape into the world from the shades of the prison house. I don't ask people to come up there as they wouldn't get it at all. But I know you would. We can emerge into manhood in step as it were – Jura malt whisky helping us on our way. You could fly Loganair to Glasgow and on to Islay. I think they fly from Bristol. I'll meet you at Islay. Get up on the day before – 13 July. Remember James – Loganair – 13 July. Remember.'

James returned for his last term at Blundells. It was a day or two before he realised why Desmond had been so insistent and specific about the Jura invitation.

Desmond had decided his school days were over. He had just had not turned up. There must have been a bust up in Yorkshire because just before half term James received a postcard from Christchurch in New

Zealand. Desmond had been sent out by his father to a small winery in the Marlborough region owned by Wileys Wine which they were intent on expanding.

There would be no birthdays in Jura. They were not to meet for over 30 years.

* * *

So concluded the account that James Lampbull gave on that evening in the Garden Room at the Reform of the days of their transition to manhood. We were by then well into the Eton Mess and the Bread and Butter Pudding. There was an excellent half bottle of Barsac, I remember, to go with all that.

It was only when we pushed our chairs back for the port and cheese that I felt I could probe a little into what it was that had so amused my new and generous friends.

'Did'nt we mention that?' said Desmond.

"Oh well you see' he continued 'When with the help of the kind Porter I got up the stairs into the Saloon and then into the morning room I saw James sitting at a long Victorian sofa at the Pall Mall end of the great room. He hadn't seen me. So I trundled over and called out to him but for some reason he didn't hear me. Just as I got close to him I saw that he had a a bloody great hearing aid in his top pocket which was attached by wires to both ears. It was then that he saw me. He didn't at first recognise me in my chariot.'

'There was a kind of pregnant pause – if that's actually possible'. 'We looked at each other saying nothing. Stanley and Livingstone kind of thing.'

'I think it was James who first burst. He started with a sort of snort but could not contain the guffaw that was erupting as he looked at me in my chariot with my yellow gloved hand.'

'I didn't notice all this too much as my cheeks had exploded after vainly suppressing what seemed to be unkind mirth at realising what his hearing apparatus had made so evident.'

'By then we were helpless. That was when you came in.'

'But forgive me' I interjected 'what on earth was it that should have instantly rocked you both with laughter to the point of helplessness?.

'Ah' said James. 'For that you need to open the envelopes. They will reveal all'.

'But, I must ask, how do you know that? They're unopened.'

'Have faith, dear Roderick, have faith' intoned Desmond.

I opened each of the envelopes. In the one from Desmond addressed to James were two tickets for a box at Covent Garden to attend a performance of Mozart's Don Giovanni. In that which James had addressed to Desmond was a letter from the secretary of the Tollard Royal shoot confirming allocation of two guns for two days driven pheasant shooting.

It was only after holding the letters for a few moments that I realised they had known as soon as they saw each other that their generous gifts had already been rejected by fate.

They did not need to open their envelopes at all.

BLIEISTER'S BUBBLE

Nathan Bleister's ego was gross. He kept it in constant incubation within a bubble that he maintained around him – invisible but potent. He was gifted, brilliant and courageous. He was immune, it seemed, to praise or rebuke. His fees were mountainous and had elevated him to the top of his profession. No one could be indifferent to him.

Bleister erupted into my life as a consequence of the Control of Office and Industrial Development Act 1965. The Act was provoked by the scandal of Centre Point which Harry Hyams built on the back of a deal with the old London County Council. Control of office building was a palm for Harold Wilson to carry to the temple of virtue. He could demonstrate how he was putting homes before profit. The outcomes were the opposite of the intention. Limitation on office space produced an explosion in rental values. Insatiable demand fired rocketing asset values. At the same time the Rent Act slowly throttled the supply off rented housing leaving a dearth of flats to let and rents that did not even cover repairs and basic improvements.

It was one of these two showpieces of virtuous law making – the ban of office building – that enriched both the owners and the tenants of No 1 Rawlinson Street, London SW1. It also projected me into the bubble of Nathan Bleister and Goldbergs the Fetter Lane law firm.

I had spent ten balmy years at the seaside at Eastbourne in elegant double bow fronted solicitors' offices opposite the exotic Pavilion of the Prince Regent before necessity of school fees and divorce legal costs bore me away from the sea front into a partnership at Reevely Merstham – a second division firm just within the City of London.

I had chosen the firm because its offices were in Lincolns Inn. The Inn was and remains a beautiful place. It is composed of 17th century and early 18th century 'chambers', a medieval hall, 16th gatehouse, a fountain falling into a lovely pond, camelia trees, lawns, a stern but striking Victorian library and the ravishing Stone Buildings of classical purity in Portland stone. Outside its gates lay spacious Lincolns Inn Fields, with its plain trees, tennis courts and open lawns for resting in the summer sun.

It was at my first the meeting with the delightful senior partner of Reevely Werstham that I learned the firm was 'consolidating' into some modern glass and concrete accommodation off Fetter Lane. Practical and sensible but dull. It was a little disappointing.

My own practice was limited by what I had been able to garner in Eastbourne. My firm had acted for the family that owned the local brewery. We got the family's trust, probate, property transactions and some liquor licensing work. These were too small for the London law firm that dealt with the brewery's commercial work.

Liquor licensing sessions sat every month or so in Brighton, Lewes, Hailsham, Bexhill, Eastbourne and Worthing. Thus when the brewery was sold to Metropolitan Breweries this trickle of trivial work enlarged to a good flow with a wider spread of public houses. Liquor licensing in Sussex towns was not – even for Eastbourne – a source of large fee income. There were the odd disputed applications for licences – most memorably when the police and local residents objected to an application by the Evening Star public house for a new licence of premises whose patrons would have the diverting experience of being served by topless waitresses. We got it to the High Court before Metropolitan Breweries' head office found out and pulled the appeal. They thought it was likely to bring down ridicule upon it – my partners were mildly amused throughout – to their credit.

One of the last appearances I made before the Licensing Justices was on behalf of Heavenly Hotel Limited. It had a large Victorian hotel of that name on the main promenade in Eastbourne not far from the Grand Hotel. It was seeking a full on licence for an extension to the back of the hotel. I got on well with the owners Felix Mattleib and his wife Rosa. When I moved to Reevely Werstham I used to go down to Eastbourne to do their licence applications. They recommended me to others. This brought in a few investment agreements and minor acquisition deals.

* * *

I had been a partner at RWs for a few years. I had a grip on whatever Town and Country Planning work came in. We had a large Utility pension fund as a long standing client. It was owner of no 1 Rawlinson Street S.W.1 subject to a lease granted in 1946 for a term of 75 years. The tenants were property developers. The lease permitted use for residential purposes. The pension fund's managing agents had reported that it appeared that the property was being used as offices. I advised that if office use occurred well before the prohibition on office uses had come into force a certificate of lawful established use might be obtained. Consent of the pension fund to the change under the lease would be needed but was certain to be given – at a premium of course.

I suggested that I should go over and speak to the tenants, Rawlinson Land, to find out more. A certificate would have an explosive impact on the value of the lease and of the freehold.

I passed an interesting morning at Rawlinson Street. The various explanations as to the extent of office use were not consistent. I could not confidently advise they would satisfy the local planning authority as to long term office use. I prepared a draft affidavit on the basis of what I had been told. The pension fund, ever cautious, declined to pursue the matter. But it had no objection to my contacting the solicitors for the tenants. The solicitors were Goldbergs. The partner at Goldbergs who dealt with Rawlinson Land was Bleister. I sent him the draft affidavit with no comment except as to my client's position.

By this my stock as Reevely Werstham had fallen steeply. I had for months been insisting that each department should have weekly financial reports of basics – bills delivered, work in progress, unbilled disbursements – that sort of thing. I was told I was opening Pandora's box. My application for increased share of profits was passed over.

I had also recently been taken to the USA by top management at International Cables & Communications, by far our most important commercial client, to negotiate a fibre optics development agreement in Maryland. My second wife was about to give birth. C&C agreed to put me on Concorde for the flight back if I agreed to stay another week on the deal.

This also frightened the horses at Reevely Werstham.

About two months later, shortly before Christmas, the door to my office opened and Bleister steered himself in like a Thames barge. Behind him was Fred Hawes his planning assistant – one time planning officer of a London Borough. Bleister had simply told Reception he was there to see me and asked for directions – there was no question of his having to wait and warn or of any appointment being made.

Fred stood by the back wall. Bleister descended into the sole but inadequate chair. His hair stuck out over his jacket collar. He had a light grey suit which, though new, was now shapeless and creased. Bleister sat with his hands in the distended side pockets, his legs sticking straight in front of him. He leaned over slightly towards me at my desk. Spitting a bit he announced

"Watson, now listen – I've spoken to the two that matter and the others'll just have to find out. I'll give you twenty grand more than you're gedding now".

Silence.

Bleister pulled his hands out of his pockets and blew his nose on a large cotton handkerchief stuffed up his sleeve. He had not shaved properly – it was, I found, quite common for him to appear with unintended patches of stubble. He had dandruff all round his collar and some down his lapels. He had an incongruous pale blue V neck sweater under the suit jacket. The sweater seemed too big, even for him. When he got up and took off his jacket it reminded me of a loose tea cosy as it descended his frame vertically, leaving his stomach to find its way back to his waist. It looked as if it had been hand knitted by an aunt. He thrust his hands into the little pockets of the distressed sweater. It would not at all have surprised me if he had been wearing trainers. It did not concern him that he looked so singular.

"So you got the lawful use certificate?" I said, to gain time. "Office use all fine now? Was it kosher? Don't tell me! Please no! Best I know nothing! Well what's that done to the value of the Rawlinson Road Lease – 25 years left on it too. Harold Wilson's still keeping the market at an all time high 20 years on – eh!".

"Yeah yeah. Got it. Piece of cake wasn't it Fred?" said Bleister turning his head to him.

"Fred went down to Westminster City Council – didn't you Fred. Tidied up the affidavit a bit of course – once Fred had been through it with the blokes on site that is. Thought it best for Fred to see the Council – not to bang the drum too loud if you see what I mean. Got the certificate yesterday. Easy as anything wasn't it Fred?"

The timidity, caution and propriety of RW, my first berth in the City after Eastbourne, had been stifling. I had tried to persuade them to link up with a Brummie firm. That caused them to rise like roosting pheasants. Then there was the partners lunch with Sir William Grunt, the very civilised Chairman of valued property client –fully listed of the Stock Exchange – who was also a patron of the London Symphony Orchestra. We discussed Mozart and violinists. Grunt was still there at 3.30 p.m. My partners were appalled.

Grunt was a delightful man. I later tried to get him to sponsor a young lady violinist of Jewish Russian blood – superb virtuoso and enchantingly beautiful. He declined with grace and wit.

And there was the flight back from Dulles Washington on Concorde. I had sat next to a mid West entrepreneur who was flying to Poland with a Senator and other back up sitting behind us. Poland sits on vast Silesian beds of coal. Yet here was this bulldozer from Cheyenne selling Wyoming coal to eager Polish state buyers. He was also looking for UK legal representation. I declined most reluctantly.

This was more like it.

How could Bleister have known that the fruit was ripe for picking? I had just done an investment deal for an entrepreneur intending to turn round a UK power tools manufacturer. Joseph Blundell at Goldbergs had been the lawyer for the company. I had spent many late hours over there. We completed the deal just before I went to Maryland. I would certainly have remembered Bleister. I am sure we had never met.

It was one of his gifts – the instinct for what move to make at what time and in what way. It was not just seeing the weak points in others – he excelled in that. It was the ability, even as he undermined an opponent, to illuminate in simple terms why he would be far better off adopting his own position. Taking no prisoners was not his way. He would always try to make it easy for the salmon to swim into the net – his gift was sensing the very moment when the fish was ready. He bullied with his ability and instinct.

Propriety demanded that I did not immediately bite his hand off. I winkled out a very good dinner at Wiltons in Jermyn Street and a few bottles of champagne with Goldbergs partners. I was able to persuade RW that all round it was best for everyone if I slipped away. I did so within a few weeks. I felt I had been swept on by Bleister's bubble.

* * *

His bubble contained a vast ego of self certainty. It did not allow him to appear less than he saw himself to be.

It explained what to many seemed absurd acts of self promotion. How was it that he never worked with others in Goldbergs? Major work required some delegation – so much was procedural or administrative. Yet Bleister's system was to have assistants dedicated exclusively to his matters – he would never disseminate his practice within the firm. His assistants would be those with no hope of partnership. He would rarely share praise or offer gratitude. He needed to keep a *cordon sanitaire* around the goodwill of his own clients and ensure that he obtained credit for all the billings – which were gross. Even at that time he billed at £700 an hour. He was reputed to earn more than any partner of any law firm in the City of London.

So I was not surprised when, instead of wandering into my room not long after I had joined Goldbergs, he called me to ask me to get down and see him. It would concede a scintilla of status for him to come up to see me.

His office was the largest by far. Since the building had been constructed to Goldbergs specification Bleister procured that his room should be a corner of the first floor next to the lift. It was fitted with 'bespoke' sofas along the far wall, a large 'Rosewood" table and a set of reproduction Hepplewhite chairs. Enthroned before a colossal partners desk sat Bleister – surveying the field – like a fat landlord before his tenants. The walls were entirely covered in limed oak panelling. In the individual panels were prints framed in black and gold depicting the various stages of manufacture of Aston Martin Lagonda luxury touring cars.

I was once with him when clients were shown in and were ushered by Bleister's shirt sleeved arm toward the green buttoned leather sward of the sofas. Bleister had got me down on some technical point about removing a director. His client owned a thriving Waste Disposal business – he was used to Bleister's bubble – I recall he once called Bleister "Frigate Bird" due to the vast orange bubble below its beak. The client was a privateer– bold and rude. He had not been in Bleister's new room before.

"God almighty Nathan – it's like a Berkeley Square new car showroom. Suppose it makes them realise what it's all costing doesn't it. But why'd they rub chalk in the wood panels? And the motors – they're all last year's models."

He sat down upon on the expanse of sofa. "Lord – I can hardly see you down there – and that's saying some, there's a lot to see after all isn't there. Well here we are then Nathan – ducks in your row? Out of spitting range anyway I suppose."

The acolytes chuckled briefly as they sat down expecting Bleister to yield in some way to the banter of a valued client. As I left his office I heard Bleister saying

"Well you do realise, Greg, that if we're going to get a look in for planning on this new site I'll need to get to lobby each of the planning committee members – that's going to cost – you do realise…"

Bleister was not in any way offended. His identity was so anchored in his possessions he had no interest at all in other's opinions of them. For Bleister they were like moorings in deep water by which the security of his fundamental identity and status was assured.

His bubble was so compressed that it actually repelled. It accounted for his apparent ingratitude. It made it both very difficult to thank him and also for him to express gratitude. It was obvious beyond question that he had everything. For him to give thanks for something might imply a lack or need.

It seems now so simple but these notions only formed in my mind slowly as I reflected on them in the months following our last encounter.

* * *

Bleister called me a few days later.

"Who's this bloke James Fitch then? What's he get up to?"

"Client of mine – property developer, residential investment, zoo keeper – good friend."

As I had hoped it would, this wrong footed Bleister for long enough for him to back off a bit with his bubble.

"Residential investment –that's rented housing to you and me" he said pushing back.

"Nathan they do it upstairs on the sixth floor – dear Claire Watson and her 'team' – you know you need to offer 'planning gain' Nathan – planning gain for your multi use developments – offer affordable rented housing with the deal – that sort of thing – you need a sprig of holly on your Christmas pudding".

"Only thing I do have at Christmas – plus a whole Stilton. Christmas! It's Seasons Greetings only for me – that's all."

Bleister again ran in with the ball letting fly a bumper.

"Zoo keeper – bloody hell! – where's the money in that, Pets yes! You can sell pet food – you can sell jewelled dog and cat collars and leads – or not jewelled – and bowls, bones and biscuits. You can scale it all up. But a ruddy zoo! You'd need acres to get the numbers in. Anything less and you're pissing in a pot. Why are we wasting fee time on him?"

"Property developer" I said.

"Well what's he doing with a site in Stratford on Avon with a potty little zoo on it?"

"It's rather profitable in fact. It's for children. They bring their parents you see. Just a big aviary and a house for small rodents with a larger one for meerkats. He breeds them all. Why do you want to know?"

"Avonglebe. They're looking at options for multi use development sites in historic towns – have been for a few years. Got one going near Salisbury – on the Nadder there. Looking at Chester – that's on the Dee. Just been looking at Stratford – not at the site itself – just internally at the strategic side of things. But if they need to talk to someone who'd it be? Is it this James Fitch?"

"Too early Nathan. James hasn't yet got total control. He's been trying to get 100% of his zoo business for nearly 20 years. He got me in on it a couple of months ago. I've put up a scheme to him which would do this. "

"No harm setting up a meet?" he said.

"Wrong. If the idea is just a vision in someone's mind at Avonglebe then leave it there. Don't let them even send round inter office e-mails about it."

"What if they're hot to trot?"

"Shoo them back in the stable. Once I get James control over 100% then get them out again. They've got something of an inside track with you after all. So leave it at that. If Avonglebe contact James then the awkward squad in his company will make life very tiresome. I'll call James to see if he has any problem with my explaining things to you."

I was able to raise James there and then. He had no objection provided I only explained the mechanics of the scheme.

James's company had a minority shareholder, Eddie Egan, who had come in at start up. Egan had used the know-how he acquired from James to launch his own butterfly exhibit in Tewkesbury. He had obstructed rights issues that James had proposed. He had challenged actions of the Board as unlawful, alleging unfair prejudice to him as a minority. He made groundless allegations of bad faith and misfeasance.

The footwork on this one was rather neat. To get rid of Egan a general offer to all shareholders would be made by James – but not directly. It would be through a shelf company controlled by him. To ensure Egan was not able to exchange his shares for new ones in the shelf company – which would defeat the purpose – the offer would be in shares but if that would mean more than 80% of the shelf company would be held by the old shareholders then the 20% would have to accept cash. Due to the proportions already held by James and his amenable co-shareholders this meant Egan would only get cash. He would be out of James's hair.

Normally such a general offer has to be made by a third party – somone who is not already a shareholder – which James was of course – or an entity controlled by a shareholder. But in this case the Articles only referred to existing shareholders. There was no further limitation. A new shelf company controlled by James was not precluded from making the offer. It was a new entity in the eyes of the law.

We had a recent share valuation by City accountants. The transaction was completed at that price. Clive made a loan to his shelf company of the cash element of the price. Had discussions with Avonglebe been opened and reached a stage when their interest was more than speculative it would have been necessary to disclose it in the offer document and obtain a revised valuation – James would have had to stump up a good bit more cash. A power of attorney appointed by the directors to execute the Egan stock transfer was permitted under the Articles. All was seamless and effective.

Six months later I met the Avonglebe directors at completion of the development and finance deal for the Stratford project. There were the usual pizza slices and champagne.

"I gather you dealt with the investment and development agreement on Stratford?" said one of the Avonglebe party.

"For James Fitch – of course. Yes that's right."

"Course if it wasn't for Nathan's nifty footwork in reorganising his company we couldn't have done the deal. Had to have full control you see. We've used Nathan for planning and commercial property deals for a few years. Didn't realise he could do it with mirrors on corporate stuff. Brilliant wasn't it! Cheers!".

"Good luck with Stratford – I gather you've got others in the pipeline." I said seeing the opportunity for further corporate legal work.

"Yes a couple on the go. On rivers you see – all ecology and environment now isn't it. Adds to the mix you see. Dee at Chester and Nadder at Salisbury. Great now that Nathan can serve up the full menu – corporate, property, funding – always wanted a one stop shop we did!"

A cold shiver passed through me with contemplation of Bleister inflating his bubble as to his part in the deal. Perhaps his skill had extended to explaining how he could have acted for James as well as Avonglebe? What had he told Avonglebe about not disclosing interest in the site? Why were they so happy to stay with the deal while James got 100% control? Did James himself know all along?

Deep waters. But all was foam and bubbles on the surface. Bleister was not going to l have me attracting any of the magic dust of his Avonglebe goodwill. Even at the cost of appearing unethical. It was his way. Oddly, I was amused. I even warmed to him.

He was pushing his bubble against a bemused lady from ANZ Bank as I joined him by the windows overlooking the Thames.

* * *

When I joined Goldbergs it had only seven partners. There was no 'corporate ethic" or "mission statement". Partnership shares were decided by the three highest fee earners. The firm had no formal meetings. Lunch in the partners dining room, which doubled as a meeting room, was where information was exchanged. There was a record of bills delivered and information for compliance with Law Society rules but that was about all. In my second year there I billed nearly three times the amount I had at Reevley Werstham. Year 4 and I was third in the Goldbergs billings stakes – never to be repeated.

My entry into Goldbergs was entirely down to Bleister. If I flopped I would be flipped. I was not invited to act for any existing clients of the firm. Swim or sink it was and I had no complaint about that.

But I was lucky.

I had been at Goldbergs for just over a year. Ben Mattlieb called to say he was going ahead raising money to acquire a group of seaside hotels to complement Heavenly in Eastbourne. He had got the support of three City institutional investors. There was a strong asset base of the freeholds of the hotels, income tax relief on entry subscription price and capital gains tax relief if shares held long enough. It transformed investor risk.

Over the next ten years Heavenly hotels grew to own twenty hotels and had long term management contracts over twenty more. It ended up with being listed on the main market of the London Stock Exchange.

It seemed to others at Goldbergs that Bleister had picked a winner just by following his nose. He had plucked me out of the air was how it looked. I gave the impression of another maverick – less of the breed than he was – who grew clients out of his fingernails.

It all ended silently with the 1991 recession. Heavenly was caught overextended. Its Banks called in secured loans. It was found that there had been poor corporate governance and there was a DTI investigation. Heavenly collapsed.

Bleister stepped in to represent Goldbergs and myself specifically. The DTI were investigating all Heavenly deals over the past ten years. All files had gone to the DTI.

Bleister had a very serious head cold. It was the winter of 1992. He was running a high temperature. The utilitarian rooms at the DTI were overheated. Sweat glistened on his pink poorly shaved face and ran down his fat neck. The DTI sat long hours. It was not possible for Bleister to stay in contact with his office. He had at least 12 lever arch files to review. He had to set aside all other work. Above all he had to attain such a mastery of the facts so evidently superior to the investigating panel as to command respect, at first, and, later, acceptance.

His conduct of the investigation was superlative. He never expressed forensic shock or simulated anger. Despite his chaotic personal appearance, billowing stomach, sniffing and blowing on a succession of handkerchiefs he maintained absolute decorum and courteous patience. Above all by the final day he was in complete command of the respect of the investigators.

The DTI did not disclose what their suspicions were concerning my role until the last few days. It was then that questions began as to whether I had been aware of Heavenly's use of new secured loan advances to fund interest due on existing secured loan advances by other Banks. The following morning Bleister referred to a letter from myself to the company secretary he had turned up the previous evening on getting back to the office.

"It does happen, regrettably" he addressed the enquiry "that when a company is running out of road, as it were, in order to deflect enquiry and financial investigation, capital is used to maintain interest payments on due dates as if all was well. But that can only be done if there are at least two distinct sources of available funds. In this case until February 1991 there was only one – the Central and Commercial Bank."

"Exactly Mr Bleister" came back the DTI. "The second bank came on board then and we have a letter from Mr Ben Mattlieb to Mr Watson requesting him to act on that secured loan. We have no response but we know that the loan advance was made at the end of March."

"Sir it may assist you if you refer to the correspondence for that month. It is in File 10 I believe – a letter from Mr Watson to the company secretary dated 9 March 1991"

"Wait one moment Mr Bleister – no that's not it –forgive me while I find it ah! here we are. Yes here it is."

"I only have a copy of the file copy. You, Sir, will have the original I suspect?"

"Yes, that is so Mr Bleister."

"Does it not state that Goldbergs could not accept instructions as to the National Fidelity Bank's secured advance since we had acted on the Central and Commercial Bank's advance earlier that year and the potential for conflict of interest precluded our involvement".

It was the end of the inquiry. It was obvious that the DTI had missed the letter. But Bleister had not. Nor did he produce it. He simply identified it leaving it to an understandably unsettled inspector to flurry the files until it was found.

It was impossible to thank Bleister. He just grunted "All in the line of duty Watson" as he closed the lift doors. Nothing was mentioned by my partners or by Bleister. It was as if all that had happened was the opening of a window to let out a bad smell.

I ordered a Jereboam of champagne from Berrys. It was 1990 vintage – a very good vintage I was assured. I left it late one evening on his desk with a note. I heard no more.

* * *

I had lost 80% of my practice.

It seemed certain that I would fall off the branch at Goldbergs. I was not political and was regarded as slightly off limits in character. My share of profits was being eyed by others.

Just before the end of the DTI inquiry, through the recommendation of a close friend, I was asked to act for the author of a book by a former EU employee. He had alleged wilfully misleading statements by EU officials as to the cycles of economic activity of member states and rigging of data to fit the criteria for convergence of the economies under the Maastricht Treaty. The EU had applied for an injunction to prohibit publication. The hearing was due in six weeks and publication had been voluntarily suspended until then.

I agreed a fee basis that was attractive to the author and to the three UK funding backers all of whom had written open letters to the Press disclosing their financial support. We worked late each night putting together the case. We had two Queen's Counsel and a brilliant junior barrister. It was just at the time of the conclusion of the Maastricht Treaty and the hearing attracted much Press coverage. On the day we announced the filing of the defence to the EU claim a Press conference was laid on at Goldbergs in the public ground floor reception area. Press comments and interviews followed. The Commission withdrew the application once it became obvious that much of the material was already in the public domain. There was buzz of interest and excitement for all of us including clients arriving for meetings.

The settlement was announced in Court a few days later. On that morning I was included in a front page photograph in the National daily press coming out of the High Court with our client the author and a leading public figure of our supporter group.

Bleister himself told me that there had been a meeting with the Goldbergs Senior partner and Managing partner to consider if the DTI – Heavenly affair had made it necessary for me to consider my position. Bleister had simply produced the cutting from the front page of the Telegraph. It somehow preserved my Alladin like reputation.

Providence Oil came to me just after that. It was well named.

I had bought a mile of salmon fishing in Kilkenny with a small riverside cottage. I got on well with my immediate neighbour – he had comical attitudes to extracting salmon from the River Suir. He was CEO of a Dublin based oil exploration company and wanted a UK quote for its securities. There was too short a track record of results and insufficient probable recoverable reserves of hydrocarbons to qualify. But I acted for the company on a rights issue in Dublin to raise funds for a Siberian oil field joint venture. After a switchback of events none of which we could have foreseen and many of which were hilarious the company secured sufficient funds to move the project forward.

It was only much later that I discovered that Bleister had challenged all the doomsayers among my partners facing them down by demanding of them when did they last get a front page on the Daily Telegraph on a client's case and land a Stock Exchange rights issue within six weeks of each other from entirely new clients never mind whilst mired in a DTI enquiry. He approved of both luck and also the tenacity to survive. He also would have retained his reputation of picking rainmakers.

But it kept me as an equity partner much longer than merit or performance justified.

Bleister became immensely rich for a City lawyer. He had no difficulty in attracting a great flow of work billing even then at close to £1000 per hour including premiums for highly contentious matters. He distributed his wealth between supercars – he had at least 12 when I left – Belgravia freeholds, antique clocks and Rolex watches and fine art. He was tactfully excluded from any part in the management of Goldbergs. His bubble was too destructive. He was accorded the sinecure of being in charge of Partners Cars. He was discouraged from attending the yearly partners meetings. One of his proposals was to convert the ground floor of the City offices into a Car Showroom. He had done all the costings and was quite serious about it.

His voracity for high profile highly paid work was remarkable. His day started at 6.00 and ended when there was no one else to badger or persuade. He was moderate with wine –Sancerre or sparkling water were his staple.

He was a force of nature – a concentration of exuberant energy. He would warm you but not admit you. He was to be admired and applauded – but from afar. He had the confidence that if he could close with officials they would ultimately succumb to his bubble and his brilliance. He admired many buccaneering spirits but surpassed them all in boldness and tenacity.

* * *

Light and shade – artists call it chiaroscuro. It suggests subtlety of a kind as would not light upon such a gross and dominant creature. Yet it seemed to do so on the day of my last time professional contact with Bleister. It was late in April 2004 just before the end of my time at Goldbergs. The well of my client goodwill was nearly dry.

Bleister had called me down to explain that clients of his had their eye on a site on the Sussex downs just to the North of the A 27 near Shoreham harbour. To get to the site there was an access road through the adjoining holiday camp – Skiplands. It had been built in stages over the years. Its entrance was from a road that ran along the western perimeter along which ribbon development had spread. On each corner of the entrance were a few pebble dash detached little villas with small lawns and privet hedges facing the access road.

It appeared that the access road was owned by Gadslip Ltd. Searches had revealed that a Mr Joe Winterman was sole shareholder and director but it turned out he was a nominee for a Mr James Fitch – my client and close friend. Mr Winterman was just the company formation nominee – nothing sinister.

"Is this bloke the same Fitch we had on the Stratford project 12 years or so back? Be good to know before wheels start to turn. He was a developer when not with the children's zoo wasn't he?"

"Gadslip's one of his" I said. "Don't think it's trading. It just holds residual interests in developments of James's left over after sale of the houses."

I called James. Gadslip had bought a company with a subsidiary which had put up a few houses on land adjoining a holiday camp – Skiplands – and still held the freehold of the site access road. It was subject to rights of way for the benefit of Skiplands granted for each new area of land on each occasion the camp site was extended. Gadslip had to keep it in repair. James was delighted that Bleister had interested clients.

Skiplands were building a large extension to the holiday camp to provide for many more chalets. The owners of the little villas at the site entrance were distressed by the large buses bringing in and extracting the holiday makers. The buses were modern with seats high above the luggage and engine compartments. As these leviathans negotiated the entrance to Skiplands the passengers could see into the interiors of the villas. It would get worse with all the new holiday chalets. James was being harassed by their owners to stop what they saw as an intensification of use of the roadway.

Bleister was acting for Lanwor Land. They could obtain access from the perimeter road by acquiring one of the roadside houses. But that would be at some cost. Far better to use the existing site roadway if possible. But the roadway did not extend to the boundary of the Skipland site – just to the various of the individual parcels of land comprising the camp site. I discovered on making searches that the new chalets were being put up on land which had no grant of right of way to it. There was a right of way to the area of land immediately next to it. But a right of way can only be used for access to the land identified as the land to be benefited. If the right of way is to plot A it cannot be used to get to adjoining plot B.

Deep foundations were being dug for the new chalet centre. It was a major project. If Skiplands could be pushed by the threat of injunction proceedings into a settlement under which Lanwor secured access over the roadway to the adjoining land it would be worth while letting Bleister loose to see how far he could get. He thought it might be fun to growl at them.

Bleister would go down with James and myself to the site for a recce. We could go back via Brighton for lunch at English's Oyster Bar. It was early May when we picked up James from Edburton under the South Downs. He had arranged for us to call first on the two sisters who lived in one of the villas by the site entrance – Elsie and Winnie Hardiman. These ladies were expecting to meet a learned London lawyer who was going to help them stop Skiplands using large charabancs whose visitors would peer into their homes.

They were confronted with Bleister.

He had parked his Aston Martin Vantage supercar model V 600 brake horse power metallic blue twin supercharged V8 registration **BERN 100** on the verge of the roadway. Its bulk and menace seeming to threaten the sisters as they parted the curtains of the sitting room with the final explosion of the exhausts.

Bleister was wearing an already crumpled pale blue linen jacket with open neck pink shirt. It was a wonder that the buttons held for it was far too tight. Its cuffs were above his wrists a weighty glinting Rolex watch strapped on one of them. He had red felt braces holding up some generously cut pale grey flannel trousers. On his feet were a pair of blue and white large trainers. He had no brief case or papers. His grey hair blown by the breeze from the sea stood up from the back and sides around the bald and shiny arena of his head. As he advanced upon the elderly ladies, a tooth filled smile opening wide on his stubbled face. He looked like a drunken leering monk.

James endeavoured to introduce me – but the sisters astonished eyes were fixed on Bleister. They appeared to be expecting him to growl or rear up before them. They were still gripped with fascinated awe as he said to them in kindly tones

"Ladies" he said "I'm Nathan Bleister."

"Somewhere between Blister and Bluster – both true" he said.

He held out his hand for a moment before letting it fall, seeing they were still in a trance.

"Sorry about the noise – the car can't help it. I've tried to train it."

"Well I can see how you must both feel your privacy invaded – you're really close to the roadway aren't you. Have they been doing this for long?"

A sense of great relief passed over the sisters' countenances as if their call had been answered.

"Oh no, no – not until recently, have we Winnie – just one or two – it's not yet the season you see. But do come in. We've put out tea and biscuits. We asked our neighbours over the way to come over – they're so looking forward to seeing you."

I wondered now how Bleister would cope with what was sure to come. I was surprised that he even remembered the peering holiday makers in their coaches. No case in law could be made out of unlawful intensification of use. It was often alleged but could not be sustained. So would he waste time at £700 an hour on tea and sympathy.

We passed through the front door with its panels of 1930s coloured glass lilies. Bleister and his bubble filled the sitting room. It seemed impossibly crowded. A trolley with tea things was in the little bay window area. Around the walls were six stained wood single chairs and in between them an upholstered Knoll armchair. The sisters steered Bleister's bulk into the Knoll chair – taking the single chairs on either side. An elderly couple, who had to be the neighbours, were sitting expectantly on the other single chairs, green Minton tea cups on their knees. James perched himself next to the door. Bleister was in the middle, sitting back and beaming as if he were himself entertaining visitors.

"How do you like your tea Mr er…er..?" said the fearful but thrilled Elsie..

"Bleister! Think of Bluster or Blister!" he said again, confidingly.

"Tea as it comes dear Miss Hardiman – as it comes" he said.

Now tell me all about Skiplands and the buses – I've never stayed in a holiday camp – have you? Is it always full in the summer? – what about winter? Any indoor entertainments? What do they do for goodness sake? I suppose there's Lancing beach?"

Now completely at their ease the Hardiman spinsters and the neighbouring couple warmed to the task of releasing the frustration of not hitherto having found anyone willing even to listen to them much less take up their cause. I was half in the room and half in the hall. I discreetly slipped out and retreating into the front garden. I could see Bleister leaning forward nodding as he listened and smiling – like a cheerful fat abbot listening to confession. He accepted another cup of tea. James caught my eye, smiled and shrugged his shoulders.

It must have been nearly an hour before Bleister emerged with the Hardiman sisters closely in train. Their faces were bright and a little pink. They had been entranced by Bleister and his bubble. Quite thrilling. As he reached the gate he turned round only to find Winnie immediately behind him – impelled by her gratitude she rose as if to kiss him but seeing his rough stubble and the sprig of cotton wool on his chin compromised with a shake of his hand.

Bleister took out from back seat a yellow plastic hard hat. It was too small. It would be trite to describe his appearance now as that of a Pier-end Clown.

"Always put this on when site visiting. Look the part! Don't look like the nosy lawyer see!"

James snorted as he stifled a snigger in the front.

The Aston took off down the roadway into the site. To the right could be seen the English Channel and Shoreham harbour. The sun was over Brighton in the distance, a morning sparkle on the sea. There came into view a concrete mixing silo and an excavator mounted piling drill. Bleister stopped the beast. I handed to him the Pentax with telescopic lens attachment from the other back seat. With a push and grunt he stumbled out walking up the road and back taking pictures of the operations and the deep concrete reinforced slab.

Falling back on to the driver's seat he said we would need GPS shots of the site to compare with the scale Title plans and planning application plans. Catching sight of a mini roundabout ahead distributing further roadways over the site he slowly rolled the mighty Vantage down and round to return to the main road. As he passed the working area he was waved down by a hard hatted man in a suit but before he could utter any protest Bleister bellowed through the rolled down driver's window

"Excellent progress. On time and on budget. I'll report to the Bank. Thanks!"

The Vantage slipped its moorings and sailed out of sight round the bend on to the A 283.

"Seen everything haven't we?. You live up this road don't you James? Edburton isn't it? I had some smoked salmon from there I think. It's only 11.00. Have you got any meerkats of mice there? Didn't you have a children's zoo at Stratford? Never saw any on that deal. Wasn't there an aviary? Poor little blighters."

"Well we do have some North American blue Jays. Plus gerbils, voles and such like – even dormice – when its summer anyway. Meerkats too as you say."

"Tea with two spinsters, a walk on the South Downs, sitting with rodents and Jays, Sole Meunière at English's. A heavy days legal work for me that is" commented Bleister.

It was a short drive over the lovely downs down to Edburton. It was actually at the next village Fulking with its pub – the Shepherd and Dog. Edburton itself was just a Saxon church – rebuilt in the 12th century – in utmost seclusion – and also the fish smokery. The clear chalk stream that burst out of the down outside the Shepherd and Dog also fed the lake on James Fitch's 50 acres to the north of the Fulking – Upper Beeding road.

James directed Bleister down a lane just past the Shepherd and Dog. At the end were a pair of slender brick piers with what appeared to be stone birds with outstretched wings on the capping. The drive formed a large circle in front of the house with what looked like a kitchen garden wall projecting from the West elevation and facing the Downs to the South. There were openings in the middle of these two walls with semicircular arched doors painted dark green.

The house was second quarter 18th century. It had a parapet with a shallow breakfront central bay of two upper sash windows and a dummy window above the doorcase. In each of the side bays was a large sash window. The brickwork was typical of its period – Flemish bond with the grey glazed ends of the headers created by the salt in the firing of the clamp of the unfired mudbricks. In panels below the windows were cut flints hand knapped with precision to perfect squares. This delightful pink and grey façade was embellished by wisteria just coming into flower and climber rose stems trained over the graceful doorcase of just two slender Tuscan columns under a moulded canopy.

A middle aged lady in a pinafore and gumboots came out of the side of the walled garden.

"James – how very nice – didn't think you'd be back till 4.00 at the earliest – specially with a free lunch and wine!"

Bleister's plastic hat fell off his head as he leaned out of his car seat to gain lift-off.

"My treat this – so free only to them" said James. "This is – or that – is Nathan Bleister – when he extracts himself. You know Geoffrey of course. Nathan – Katie"

"Bloody hell – forgot it was on – Hello!" said Bleister picking up the yellow plastic hat.

"Couldn't get more rural could you" he said looking round. Yet just over the Downs the A27 and the sprawl of bungaloids from to Little-hampton to Hove. Had to see James's menagerie – never did get to see the perishers when we did Stratford."

Katie followed them into the walled garden. As they opened one of the green doors through its arched opening the sound of distant calls and screeches at once caught their attention. Looking towards the source of the sound they saw along the North side, facing the rising Downs a series of three connected glass houses of Victorian origin. Along the entire length of the structure it had the typical iron and lever devices of the period for operating upper windows. The central glasshouse was a much higher edifice rising to form a transept over the two sides of the building. It had a raised belfry having louvred slats for ventilation and a clock on its South facing side with blue dial and gold numerals. It was obvious to Bleister that the entire structure had been completely and dutifully restored without thought of compromise. He was clearly impressed both by the quality and also by the lavish expenditure that the work had demanded.

As they approached the main transept building the sight of brightly coloured wings and forms within revealed an aviary of considerable scale. It must have been at least twenty five feet high to the apex.

They entered through a heavy door below the 'belfry'. Beyond the door were thick suspended strips of clear plastic. Passing through these Bleister found himself assaulted by a cacophony of shrieks, chattering and calls. Blue and white birds, excited by the promise of acorns, nuts and seeds, were swooping and diving to feeding trays and little roosts in the lower part of the crystal structure. The birds were all varieties of North American Blue Jays. The flashing and whip of their wings created a sense of sparkling agitation in the air. There seemed to be countless numbers.

Bleister stood motionless for a few moments as waves of blue and white flew past his face rocketing to the sunlit arched glass roof and immediately plunging down to just above the black and red tiles on the floor and soaring in steep ascent again.

Katie pulled at Bleister's sleeve. "They'll calm down when they see there's nothing for them. They don't normally behave like this. Normally they just slowly flit about in the branches of the potted birches."

Bleister could see that the entire far end of the transept was full of birch trees planted in vast black plastic containers. A drip hose lay over the base of the trees. All around the floor below were twigs, grasses, moss, seeds, dried mud and droppings. There were also large amounts of what looked like broken chicken egg shells.

The intense and varied blues of the birds, set off by the pure bright white of the underside of their flitting bodies in the summer sunbeams, enchanted Bleister. Each had a crest. The display of open feathers as they settled on branches was of captivating beauty.

Katie was pushing a creaking cane and wicker chair towards Bleister. It was of woven wicker arms and back. It had a thick rather grubby cushion.

"Nathan, you might like to sit for a while to let them get used to you. They're very clever creatures and curious. I often just sit and watch. The heat from the Meerkat house next door keeps it all warm – can get really hot in summer so we need to keep the ventilators open."

"Oh by the way don't open the little hatches along the Mouse house on the other side! Friendly Freddie is OK – the ferret – he gets in an out as he pleases. There's a ferret flap by the front door. Just behind you. Brilliant for the rats. The jays will have a go at a gerbil, vole or dormouse – just look at their black beaks. They're just crows after all you see!"

"James and I'll show Geoffrey the walled garden and rose walk. You'll be better off in here I suspect. More going on as it were. More comfortable."

Bleister sat down in the ancient cane chair that eased and creaked in protest. He loosened his collar and two of his shirt buttons. He pushed out his legs and surrendered to the enveloping warmth. It seemed that any movement created springs of sweat. Perspiration formed on his forehead and ran down his neck.

The heated wide Victorian cast iron pipes running into the Meerkat house gave off faint cracks. Bleister heard the boiler fall silent somewhere in the structure.

Gradually he became aware that the air was still. The sound of birds settling above had quietened and ceased. The voices in the walled garden were faint and restful. The flutters in the birches seemed distant and pleasing. A sense of deep calm pervaded the sunlit void. All was silent save for the trickle of water from the sides of the tree containers on to the tiled floor.

He seemed utterly at rest, as if entranced.

* * *

"Just look at him!"

It was Katie looking in from the walled garden perimeter path. I moved up beside her.

Bleister was sitting facing us at a slight angle to the entrance door. His arms had slumped on to his lap. His head was resting on the high back of the cane and wicker armchair. His mouth was open a little. Sitting on the near arm of the chair looking away from us was a blue Jay. It was looking beak down and crest up at the glinting face of the Rolex watch. It twisted its head as if to see if it was just sunlight. Back again went the crested head. And again.

We moved as silently as possible through the door and slatted plastic screen.

"Bloody hell!" erupted Bleister as with a piercing shrieking call the blue Jay regained the canopy of the birch trees.

"Pecked my hand. Look at the hole it's made" he said holding up a bare and pudgy wrist.

Katie saw a red pin like prick just next to the strap of the massive watch. It was then that she saw that it had rose diamonds around the rim. How gross she thought. Like having gold plated bumpers on your Jaguar. The bird had thought to pick one out but its beak had slipped on the hard glass face.

Katie suppressing the eruption of laughter as she looked at the now bewildered Bleister.

He had brought his hand down and was trying to get it into the side pocket of his jacket just as Freddie the Ferret put his nose out of the warmth of his recent resting place and for a moment stood up in the pocket, his front paws pushing down the side, his pink nose twitching with expectation.

He then, with a delicate bound, landed on Bleister's lap curling himself at once in his other hand upon his lap. Bleister was motionless as he looked down at the silken fur of the coiled creature now resting upon him. Slowly to my astonishment he brought up his other hand and rested it with infinite care upon the ferret's back.

Katie stood for a while and then made to move closer to the chair – as if to witness the delightful scene more closely – the still and perfect moment. It was then that Freddie spied her and leaped out of the gentle fat hands of Bleister on to the tiled floor. Humping his back as he ran towards her he jumped into her lowered arms.

Frozen in my memory was the image of the corpulent glistening Bleister his great head twisted and looking down at the side pocket of his tortured jacket at the quizzical and sprightly ferret. And of his hands resting gently upon the trusting creature.

"Nathan" I said "You'll miss the lunch" as he extricated his bulk from the suffering chair.

* * *

We all agreed that Bleister had the greatest clout for the Skiplands foray. Skiplands would be very sensitive about anything that undermined their development. Bleister's clients were on the high ground. They could get access by other means. James himself could not threaten litigation too vigorously as it would soon appear that his companies did not have the deep pockets needed to pursue an injunction claim. But James was still anxious to offload the access road. So it was settled that Bleister should open the negotiations.

But within a few weeks Nathan's clients went cold on the site. It became obvious that planning permission was very unlikely to be granted for any further development on land north of the A 27. Even so Bleister extracted an offer of £100,000 which he cranked up to £150,000 to include settlement with the spinsters. Skiplands got the roadway.

James was delighted. He had achieved a generous exit and had done the right thing by the residents. There was just the matter of Bleister and his fees.

Just before Christmas, some eight months later, he called me to say he had received a fee invoice from Bleister. It was marked "Fees waived". No covering letter or call.

* * *

Over the years immediately following the collapse of Heavenly I had partially restored my place in Goldbergs. The EU injunction case and the Providence Oil fund raising had given me some remission at Goldbergs. However I could not conceal from myself the fact that long term repeat work had disappeared. I was 60. It was time to go.

I went up one Friday evening in February to see Nathan at his house in Cumberland Terrace, Regents Park to thank him for all he had done for me. I had with me a gift of an original Drivers Handbook for a 1926 Lagonda Speed 16/65 model in the lengthened chassis version and a six-cylinder 2.4-litre engine. I had found it with other classic car memorabilia in an auction sale in Putney.

Bleister was not expecting me. He was wearing a form of house coat in midnight blue silk with dragons and exotic birds sewn in gold thread with fantastic shapes and colours. He had matching slippers with what looked like a mink frill round the feet. His hair was absurdly untidy. He had a loose fitting shirt round his ample form. The Bleister bubble inflated before me as I stood there.

Before I could say anything he stomped into the morning room to our right facing the Park "Look at these" he said gruffly.

He was bending over a mahogany cabinet with serried drawers secured by vertical rods which ran into the floor. They did not seem very secure. They had padlocks at the top. He said the floor around the cabinet was alarmed but it did not seem to be working.

Like Aladdin, Bleister began to bring forth the genies from the cabinet by releasing the padlocks and pulling out the rods. When all was ready he summoned me to behold the top drawer which he was just opening.

Before me arrayed in their original boxes were rows of the most elegant wrist watches. It was obvious that they were Rolex. Bleister saw that my eye was caught by one very pretty example in what looked like a pink metal. It was displayed on its own in the centre of the drawer.

"Pink gold that is. A war time watch made only between 1939 and 1945. First Rolex to be fitted with a water-resistant 'Oyster' case with screw-down crown. Supplied to captured Allied aircrew would you believe it. £300k or thereabouts. Piece of history."

Bleister had pulled up a chair and was gazing at the contents of the drawer. There must have been 12 watches on display.

"Six more drawers of these" he said as if intoning a chant.

We looked on together in silence – he in wonder, I privy to a view allowed only to few.

Bleister continued, quietly, as if in a cathedral

"One that has so far escaped me is the 6062. Came out in 1950 and made for about 10 years. You see, it's only one of two types with a triple calendar and moon phases. But the 6062 had the 'Oyster' case. One was sold for over $1.m"

Reverently he opened the next drawer.

Occupying a discrete place – like a Queen bee in the hive – was a watch with a deep yellow dial.

"It's the Rolex Day-Date. Came out in 1955. You can get one for under £10k but the best are the ones with brightly coloured 'Stella' dials like this one. Do you know that the colours are all hand mixed – layer on layer – none the same. Lovely isn't it? £100k of anyone's money."

"All the others are Rolex Submariners. All different bezels and bands some date some no date. Green the best."

"This drawer is Yachtmasters" he recited as he gently opened the next one. "Lovely blues and also greens and all with box and papers – £20k for a good one in Everose Gold"

He stood silently as if within a sacred place then walked slowly out of the room – assuming I would follow.

"Up here – the best is in my bedroom. When I wake up – no nagging wife – no post – no phone. Just Thomas Tompion and George Stubbs. They say gold is best. It's OK for hedging – I've got some physical in the cellar. But it's not that interesting is it?. Not like English clocks and paintings – proper painting not 'groundbreaking installations' crap – bricks and steels – all that bollocks."

We had come into a bedroom much smaller than I had expected. There was a small double bed or it may have been a large single. Above it was a striking portrait of two spaniels at play. It had a commanding brilliance of subject set against a very dark green and brown background of a tree and thick woodland. This projected the delicate feathery fur and rich golden brown and white of the dogs' markings with great effect. There was no sentimentality – just a sense of the exuberance of life.

It occurred to me that very few such paintings were still in private hands. How could one begin to estimate the value of such a lovely work.

"Got to be £1 million – Stubbs – got to be" said Bleister seeing my astonishment.

"Got to be" blowing his nose theatrically.

In the wall beside the bedside table and lamp was a niche deep into the fabric with a slender moulding around its edge finishing on a plinth base. It had been fitted with discreet lighting. Upon the plinth stood a clock of dignified restraint. At the top of the dial plate were incised TOMPION + BANGER over **LONDON"**. It was a bracket portable clock. Bleister allowed me to regard it silently before declaring its virtues.

"It's a repeater – can strike on the quarter hour and hour. Has a pull repeat to the last strike. There's a Strike/Silent mechanism on the dial plate. Ebony was used for the case as normal. Set off by gold and silver of the dial and spandrels. It's got the original verge escapement and twin fusee movement. Date around 1696."

Then-

"Got to be £250k. I've got a Daniel Quare and an early Knibb in the study downstairs but the Tompion is the prize."

I followed him down the elegant staircase with its continuous handrail in mahogany with a satinwood central field and fine ebony stringing. The Portland stone treads were cantilevered from the curved wall so that one came down in a perfect half circle into the generous hall and outer lobby. As we descended I paused by a niche in the wall in which sat a bronze bust of a lady. It appeared to be early 20th century – Bleister looked up at me from the hall.

"Brancusi – a Mrs Pogany . Not that you'll meet her."

Bleister gathered in his garments turning his head briefly towards me.

"Got to get ready for people this evening – good to see you Watson. Dorset's a good place to go and die. Best of luck."

With that he shuffled off into the back of the house. The housekeeper, Leah, came out from a side door and put down her tray on a hall side table. She handed me my overcoat and showed me out. I walked round the Park limits and emerged into the Marylebone Road. It was as I started down the stairs at Baker Street station that I felt the Lagonda manual still in my overcoat.

I knew he would be at a Chelsea football clash on Saturday. I would catch him after lunch on Sunday.

Leah let me in. She put her index finger to her lips. But I could hear the snores from the study. I carried the manual into the little room looking out over the Park just next to the lobby. I found Nathan Bleister sitting in the opposite corner on a faded orange leather covered Gainsborough chair. His head was resting on one of the side wings. He was fast asleep his mouth noisily ajar.

Silently I stood before him. So often had the exuberant display of his bubble and the noise of his ego obscured him.

It was then that I noticed the two clocks.

They stood one above the other in a corner cupboard behind Bleister's chair. The Daniel Quare – with a marquetry case and delicate silver mounts. The Joseph Knibb with rare walnut case and silver gilt spandrels and mounts. They looked down on Bleister below as if blessing him with their subdued and constant tick. Tokens of timeless security.

He looked so still. As he had been when I glimpsed him sitting in company with the Jays and the ferret.

He was such a generous soul who hated to admit weakness or want.

I moved over to the desk to put down the Manual with my note to him.

As I turned away from the desk I could see into the lower shelf of the corner cupboard behind him below the priceless clocks.

Standing there, unopened, was the Jereboam of Champagne with the Berry's label for 1990.

Forty Years On

Liz, my wife, and I live in Sussex near Barcombe on the river Ouse. We are down a long track through maize and wheat fields. The Ouse is just a hundred yards or so from the house. You get to it over a hump back bridge crossing the disused Victorian railway line, now overgrown. The track is flint and chalk. In its hedges honeysuckle and dog roses flower in early summer. The river flows slowly down to Lewes and the sea at Newhaven. Sometimes a sea trout is caught in the Pool a little upstream from the house.

A few weeks ago a letter arrived for me from the my old School Association. It keeps in touch with old boys, making regular appeals for funds – the school has no great endowment of funds or assets. As I opened the letter I felt the guilty disquiet that comes upon me when having to regret my incapacity to help after a life of interest but much expense. However the letter itself was a delightful one.

It appeared from it that Michael Montague – who I was astonished was still alive – was arranging a cricket match. It was to be held on the 40th anniversary of a match which he himself had arranged. That fixture had been for members of the school cricket eleven of 1959. He had been the captain. His family then lived just outside Adelstrop in Gloucestershire for many years. The match itself had been played at Adelstrop in 1979 on the 20th anniversary of the 1959 MCC match. Those who played in the fixture were still possessed with the vestiges of youth. It did not seem at all nostalgic at the time – we were too immersed in the torrents of life for sentimental reflection.

Montague had been unable to trace the addresses of the survivors of the 1959 eleven. He had got in touch with the School Association sending it a letter of invitation to be forwarded to each of us. The match was to be played on 2 July – 60 years after the original contest. Montague had moved to Nether Clympe in Dorset a few miles on the Clymington Road south from Clympe Down. The match was to take place against Clympe Valley Cricket Club at its ground just above the village. He was rounding us up for reunion before the remnants of his side all disappeared – finally. None of us could be under 80. We were not expected to play in the match. We were asked to provide sons and grandsons who would.

There was a kind personal note. Montague had arranged for rooms be booked at the Fox Inn and at the Royal Oak at Clympe. But he could put up five of us from the 1959 eleven at Nether Clympe. We should let him know with our response – e-mail was preferred.

I was standing by a kitchen chair next to the long kitchen table. I sat down still holding the letters. I forgot what I had been intending to do. I sat motionless for what seemed a long while.

I became aware of a deep quiet. I was for a moment unsure of who or where I was. I felt as if I had been pulled, as it were, out of the stream of events and thoughts. The dogs were sleeping on their vet rugs. The spring day was bright outside. There arose in my mind, as I sat utterly still at the table, a clear and instant image of what had been the world for me nos sixty years ago. It did not come upon me gradually but all at once and as if all together.

I will not attempt to describe the scenes. They were too vivid and numerous to bear any rehearsal. Visions of faces and sounds of voices came before me sharp and distinct. I could feel myself smiling as they arose. I will not conceal the sense of gratitude and joy that came over me as they arose in memory and passed. I confess to being strangely perturbed. I found myself defenceless to the sentiments of the song we all sang in Speech Room about looking back at fleeting youth from 40 years on. We thought nothing much of it then – bawling it out as loudly as possible – it was always the last one to be sung. It now came clearly to mind as I sat there alone in the kitchen as those far off days returned.

"Then, it may be, there will often come o'er you,
 Glimpses of notes like the catch of a song –
Visions of boyhood shall float them before you,
Echoes of dreamland shall bear them along,

Oh the great days. in the distance enchanted,
 Days of fresh air, in the rain and the sun,

How we rejoiced as we struggled and panted –
Hardly believable, forty years on!

Love is often simply disguised as sentimentality. Is it demeaning or the mark of the feeble minded to recall the fleeting days of youth in the recollection of old age? Why should such reflection be poignant?

I reflected as I sat there, having reached that pass in life, on why there is no song of longing for the distant blessings that come with age. After all the struggle diminishes or so it has seemed to me. Nature begins to inform your existence. Animals and humans seem as one. The days are shorter but the moments longer. Possessions and status lose their grip. The advance and recession of human folly is of less concern. Acceptance comes more readily.

Are these but natural preparations for death?

There was the sound of a car drawing up and a door closing. I could hear Liz moving with careful steps over the gravel path towards the kitchen door. I resolved to respond to Michael Montague accepting his kind invitations to Clympe Down and to Nether Clympe. Perhaps Francis would be able to play.

* * *

I had set up a lounger of canvas and wood –a deck chair with extending legs. I was next to the score board by the Scorer's table. The lounger creaked a bit. I was delighted and surprised to see that a tea urn had been put out on a trestle table with cups and saucers and biscuits. There was a pleasant tinkling and a murmur of voices as the players and visitors met each other cups in hand.

"Visitors are batting".

It was Chris Pitt the captain of the village side. He was leaning down over the Scorers giving the names of the opening bowlers. Montague had told me over breakfast that Chris was a devotee of cricket who plays in one – or even two – of the Dorset cricket leagues. He looked incredibly fit. He managed all the kit, the groundsmen, scorers, umpires and tea makers: the fixtures and finances and teams. A powerful man in every way. I could not help noticing that he looked at you steadily without moving when you spoke to him or when he spoke to you. His presence was oddly reassuring. He is reputed to be an excellent electrician.

"That's best for the Village" he said in a rich booming Dorset voice. He had paused to speak to me as he passed. He was looking down at me a little quizzically.

"You must be Chris Pitt" I said as I raised up an awkward hand to him. "Good to be here. I'm Simon Savill. Yes you're right. Our chaps'll find it hard running around fetching the ball in the afternoon sun from what I've seen of the spread they've brought for the teams' lunch. They intend to make the day memorable whatever the result on the field"

"Well" Chris came back "Memorable lunch may be enough for some of them – but I'm told that they've have a few good young Club players so it could be a good scrap. Hope you don't mind me asking" he said "But did all the – how can I put it – all the more senior of you here today play the MCC for your School?" he said a little diffidently. "

"Five of us. I'm one of them would you credit it. Some have died. Some have lost their wits. But five isn't bad when you think it's 40 years since our scratch side played last at Adelstrop. Actually one of my sons – Francis – is playing today – he came along rather late in life thanks to my third wife. Last of six. Sons that is – not wives – only three of those".

"The Visitor players today are all sons or grandsons of the five of us and of those still alive who couldn't make the journey. Rather nice that – sense of a continuing line. Following tradition and family over three generations – all outdated now of course."

After a long pause Chris smiled indulgently. He then slowly straightened up looking down at me. Putting on his cap he turned and loped off to take his side on to the field of play.

* * *

The Visitors' captain James was the youngest son of Michael Montague. He was captain by virtue of being his father's son. He over 50 years old. He had played a bit of cricket for his house second X1 at school. His father had been my older contemporary there and it was his generosity and benign nostalgia that had brought us together on the cricket pitch at lovely Clympe Down.

His father had lent to James his old club sweater, cap and kit to wear for the Clympe Down match. The club had been I Zingari and James Montague looked in fancy dress in such splendid assertive costume with its black red and gold. The motto of that the oldest amateur cricket club was 'Out of darkness, through fire and into light'. Colours had to be worn to display gold at the top. James' half moon rimless spectacles sat oddly under his loud cap.

He had spent his life as a partner in a firm of solicitors specialising in Church of England diocesan legal matters and with the family trusts of wealthy landowners of the South West. He was the author of a few slim volumes on the Perpendicular in English ecclesiastical architecture. Being both tall, thin and scrupulously courteous he had the habit of bending down slightly when he spoke to you as being condescending to a child. But he had the great gift of conveying to you his sense of privilege at having met you.

James had decided that he himself should open the batting. His father's IZ cricket blazer, garish and magnificent, dominated his reserved disposition as if it was an embarrassment. He seemed relieved when he slipped out of it to put on his sweater and pads.

He had explained that he thought it best for him to go in first. The opening bowler for Clympe Down was known to be fierce and fast. Will Sharp had a well disseminated reputation for destructive treatment of the batsmen who faced him. There were just five overs that the Clympe Down CC allotted to each of the total of six permitted bowlers. James Montague was offering himself out of a sense of sacrificial duty by facing the first over. He reasoned that his evident want of skill – indeed his lack of acquaintance with the functions of a batsman or even knowledge of the basic laws of cricket – would induce a Christian mitigation of aggression in the Lilley of the village and so limit the exposure of the few experienced batsmen of his team to his destructive assault.

James Montague left the Pavilion for the crease with William Walderberry, a very fine batsman of the Harrow XI of fifteen years ago. Those years had not diminished his skills. It has to be said however that they had considerably increased his girth. Walderberry was reluctant to acknowledge that he had been in any way disadvantaged by his love of the table. He wore around his considerable stomach an extravagant and vulgar yellow and orange MCC cummerbund which he admitted to having had specially made by Gieves & Hawkes outfitters. His long sleeved cable stitch sweater had been produced for him in Hong Kong.

When he took his guard he was compelled to hold his bat far away from his body which put him risk of toppling over – prevented only by his allowing his weight to rest on the bat. He made no concession whatever to his lack of mobility. His dignity seemed to depend on paying no attention to matters concerning avoirdupois. He was determined to appear – at least on the cricket pitch – the same exponent of the cover drive and hook of the bumper ball as had been in his pomp.

The rumble of conversation, while the two openers moved from the Pavilion towards the place of trial, carried to me as I sat by the scoreboard. It appeared certain to those watching that Montague would promptly be dismissed back to the Pavilion having lost his wicket and probably needing medical attention.

Combat commenced with the onrush of Will Sharp down the east slope, strides lengthening with hostility, arriving at the crease with his front foot rammed into the turf and bringing his great chest and thick arm over with such power as to hurl the red ball bumper past the innocent ear and vision of Montague and of the wicket keeper standing five yards behind the stumps, maintaining its trajectory until it disappeared into the long grass.

Montague seemed uncertain of the passage of events and was looking over his glasses at the bowler, now standing half way down the wicket, bemused as if Will Sharp was expecting something from him.

When hostilities resumed Will Sharp accelerated down the slope dispatching the ball fiercely at Montague only to find that it hit a crack in the pitch and rocketed up once more, this time catching the top of the handle of his bat which raw protective instinct had caused him to raise up as he himself turned around and ducked. Knocking the bat out of his hand the projectile shot off the handle, just avoiding the fielder standing at Gully. Montague could see the deep fielders retrieving it from the long grass as he picked up his bat and took up a revised stance.

He explained later that he thought that from then on he should stand with his feet apart facing the bowler as this would enable him to see the incoming missile with both eyes and to leap to one side or to the other depending on its trajectory.

Thus when the third ball was fired at him he leaped to one side in time for his body to escape injury but not so speedily as to bring his bat with him to safety. The ball struck the top of the bat in mid air. The missile flew over the head of the slip fielders in a great parabola through the air landing in the long grass. Montague's leap meanwhile had propelled him into a close fielder standing just a few yards away at Point who was graciously assisting him to get to his feet and retrieve his spectacles and abandoned bat.

The fourth ball was directed at the stumps.

Montague's new stance was such that he was holding bat with the face open to the onrushing bowler. He could not lift it back as he himself was standing behind it. He could only move it sideways. Being unable to see the incoming ball at all Montague held the bat firmly without moving it. The ball struck the edge of the bat with such violence as to cause him to totter back and begin to hop as he sought to avoid collision with the stumps. Not being able to regain his balance Montague hopped with acute presence of mind away from the crease falling again onto the patient fielder at Point. Meanwhile the ball with a ricochet motion had shot off his pads down to fine leg where the fielder, being diverted by the antics on the pitch, saw it too late to arrest its entry into the long grass.

Montague bravely resumed his unorthodox stance.

Clapping, braying laughter and shouts of 'Good man' and 'Stick to it Monty' and such like could be heard from the Pavilion.

This might perhaps have mollified Will Sharp for his next ball was his 'slower' ball. It would have been slower to a seasoned batsman. However to Montague it was a testing delivery. It rose in a graceful arc descending just before his waiting bat. Montague raised his bat upwards just in time to connect with the ball a few feet above the pitch. The ball rose gently into the air and fell into the hands of the now astonished fielder at Point and out again.

At this a loud shout burst out from Walderberry. Frustrated at being detained at the bowler's end he was also resolved to relieve Montague. Yelling "Run! Come on Montague Run!" he advanced down the pitch his bat in the air rolling as fast as his weight and gravity permitted.

Montague was not sure what was expected of him but, willing to obey the command of a proper batsman and pushing back his glasses with his left hand, began a shambling run to the other end of the pitch past the breathless Walderberry.

Sharpened by shame the fielder at Point seized the guilty ball and hurled it at the stumps just three yards away. The bails flew and a stump fell prostrate before Walderberry reached the white line of the crease, his momentum taking him well beyond the standing stumps into the arms of a slip fielder.

It was now eighteen runs for the loss of one wicket. For another six overs Montague confronted the wrathful opening bowlers. He was intent only on self defence. He moved his bat a little to the left or to the right in hope but with improving instinct. The ball occasionally collided with the bat but with such force as to knock it backwards so depriving the ball of the kinetic energy needed to reach the waiting hands of the close fielders.

The runs and byes accumulated with the increasing frustration of the bowlers. It seemed that only injury could dislodge Montague from his tenure of the crease. So it proved. A ferocious discharge from Will Sharp hit Montague's bat at an angle so causing the ball to fly up and strike him above his right eye dislodging the half moon spectacles once more. He seemed surprised as he fell back over the stumps and embarrassed by the consternation he had caused among the fielders.

Will Sharp looked with relief at Montague as he was helped on his way back to the Pavilion.

* * *

"Hullo Savvers!. Only just recognised you. Very good to see you Savvers!. Quite a few of us have turned up. I live just a few miles away so easy enough. Rather good turnout isn't it. I say poor old James Montague!"

It was Graham Buick. He had been the fielder at short leg for my in-swingers when I had bowled for the X1. He was an Old Bailey judge – now retired.

He pulled up one the white plastic round backed chairs that were scattered around.

"Sacrificial lamb wasn't he" said Graham. No clue about batting at all. Got guts though. Stuck it out until honourably discharged due to injury."

"Very good to see you Buick" as I stretched to meet his welcoming hand. "My God I remember you with your great hands at backward short leg. Still got a press photo of you."

"Ah well" I continued "James Montague never was a cricketer but he has 21 runs to his credit and broke the back of the opening attack. But it's not really cricket is it! Going out to bat without any means of defence or prospect of scoring."

"Cricket's a great leveller though don't you think Savvers?" said Graham. There's Walderberry, you know. Very fine batsman but somewhat living in the past. He's still thinking he can take the quick but risky runs. Take advantage of the mistakes of a fielder. I wouldn't be surprised if that is how he is in Court – he's another barrister you see. Pouncing on hesitations and uncertain answers of the witness. But that's a dangerous trick if the witness is honest and genuinely not sure – can backfire badly as it shows you in a belligerent light attacking a witness whose doing his best."

"But listen, Graham, we all knew that Montague couldn't possibly cope with a very fast bowler bent on his destruction. He was lucky to get away with a black eye."

"You know Savvers" said Graham, "it was once considered very bad form to bowl so fast that the batsman couldn't play. The bowler was not there to intimidate but to deceive and confuse. I think the Australians were right in the 1933/34 test – bodyline bowling with Larwood and Voce. Bend the rules too far and you deny the spirit of the game".

"It's part of the game now isn't it? 'Chin Music' it's called isn't it?. Got to learn to cope with it surely Graham?"

"I'm not sure about that. Fast bowling is a test of a batsman's skill of course – judging the pitch of the ball and its trajectory – swing and line of the stumps and movement off the pitch and so on. You should know Savvers!. But surely it shouldn't be a test of skill at avoiding serious injury or in inflicting it? If a bowler hurls down a ball intending that it should fly up at the batsman's head or upper body that cannot be more than intimidation. I'd amend the Laws to forbid it altogether. Prescribe a no ball or a free hit, for example, or deprive the bowler of further overs during that innings or add runs to the battings side's score. Something like that."

This took a bit of digesting. He was obviously sincere. I was surprised at his strength of feeling.

"But Graham how can the umpire possibly know if the bowler intended to aim for the head or upper body. 'The thought of a man is not triable' or so it is under English law as you should know – still is, even if only just".

He would not have this. Leaning towards me he said

"But a judge would say that you can deduce the intent from the act and the circumstances. It's degrading to watch a bowler wilfully intimidating a batsman. It's as bad as trying to distract him with coarse comments from the slips. If you allow offences against the spirit of the game then in the end you are left only with the husk. The spirit has vanished. So we get the vulgar slog fests of T20 in the dark under artificial lighting in a gladiatorial arena"

"Aren't you going a bit far with all that? I mean does it matter really Graham?"

Buick sat back again in his plastic chair. The legs straightened a little as he tilted it back. There came a shout of an appeal from the fielders and claps from spectators.

"Well, Simon" Graham leaning forward again now in his chair and looking directly in my eyes

"It's like war – some say it's inevitable for humans. Perhaps it is".

He was looking at me doubtfully as if not sure if he should say any more.

"Go on Graham – you're surely not saying cricket is a form of war? And what if it is – doesn't it act as a safety valve for aggression?".

Thinking I was still with him he decided to carry on.

"Turning a game into a war means losing one of the most delightful means of learning how to live – or so it seems to me. A game becomes a war when the opposition is seen as the enemy – the 'other'. Doesn't that create a kind of separation so that victory alone becomes the point of the contest? So it's you against them and me against him. It's a small step to cheering the batsman's failure and putting him off by malicious comments."

I had to pause to consider what he was saying – it deserved reflection.

"Graham I must admit there's something in what you say. Do you know that Jardine, who captained the bodyline England test team in 1933/3, told the players that they had to hate the Australians in order to defeat them? He actually instructed them to speak of Donald Bradman as "the little bastard". Bradman – the greatest and most artistic batsman of all time!

"But, even so Graham, it's how the game is today – why not just accept it?"

"I know that's how so many people think and I've thought about it a lot over the years" he said. I think it's because it destroys the joy of life that the game can reveal and replaces it with a result."

Graham looked at me as if he had said something shocking or very stupid. He battled on against my soggy responses.

"A game is really time at play surely?. It's both a test and also a display of skill under the dominion of chance. It's about taking part and playing one's part. Treating each other with appreciation and regard. Not displaying conceit or triumph in success. Accepting the decisions of the umpire. Shunning individuality– including as to dress. Applauding good play of whatever side. Having a kind of indifference to the score while doing one's best."

"I know I sound like a vicar's sermon. Of course it's old fashioned but all that really means is we've forgotten the old golden rule. You know – play up and play the game. No one dares say it because it sounds cheesy. People laugh – but isn't that just the crackling of thorns under a pot – as it says somewhere? The vicar would know!"

"Well, Graham that's a mouthful though I have to say competition can bring one together – in the play as it were as you were saying. I often experienced that at the end of a day's cricket. I'm sure you found the same."

He looked at me smiling as if he was still patiently listening.

"Didn't you?" I said.

He turned to me as he got up with a grunt and a heave.

"I did Simon. Just so. That's the point of it all as it seems to me. Sounds very out moded old chap. Doubt if anyone in the ECB would agree with us – not now."

* * *

Cricket on a Village cricket field in the vale below the bowl of downland hills such as in the parish of Clympe Down affords the spectator entertainment entirely distinct from the famous grounds of Lords or the Oval.

The run of play does not command undiverted attention.

It is as if the little groups sitting in the Pavilion or on the boundary or by their cars with hampers at their side have come because of the cricket but are absorbed by the little incidents of the day and the company of others. It is rather like a Private View of an artist's work – talking and meeting is everything: no one looks at the pictures.

There is the spill of players and their wives, friends and children in front of the Pavilion – the noise of boots on wooden boards as batsmen mount its steps. Dogs run loose among each other and children. Calls and squeals are heard of excited boys pushing each other to be the next one to bowl in the cricket net down at corner of the ground by the heavy Roller. Cars coming into the ground at intervals over the rough flint and gravel entrance setting down new spectators with folding tables and folding chairs. Laughing young ladies darting away from mocking young men. The umpires shouting demands for the telegraph score board be updated or calling the names of new bowlers. The crying of a child with a grazed bare knee. Clapping of runs scored or wickets falling or of an incoming batsman as he takes the field. Lying on deck chairs or sitting in the Pavilion's shade. Some content simply to regard the great beech trees on the chalk downs, their pale grey powerful trunks silently majestic.

In all, the benign and gentle swell of life and people all together.

So it was that I did not follow much of the morning's play except as
a kind of continuum or background drop to the diverting scenes. There
was also a sense of delightful pointlessness. Nothing was demanded or
expected. Even though it was an hour before Lunch my head rolled
slowly on to my chest as I lay back on my creaking lounger.

* * *

Wickets had started to fall quickly after Montague had left the field.
Then we broke for Lunch.

We sat at trestle tables outside the pavilion. All mixed up together.
Montague had arranged for the Royal Oak to provide jugs of Clympe
Down Brewery Ale. He himself had provided chilled Touraine wine both
red and white and elder flower cordial, Scotch eggs, pork pies, slices of
thick cut cold beef and honeyed ham and wide bowls of lettuce and
rocket and cold Eton Mess for pudding. For those with the taste and
head for it there was some Barsac in ice buckets.

I had got up from my lounger as the Umpires led the players off the
field for Lunch. They took two places next to each other at the end of
the trestle table at which I had claimed a place. No one else having yet
joined us I moved up to sit opposite them. They were still in their white
coats and straw hats. I wondered how it came about that the Clympe
Down CC was able to provide two dedicated umpires – certainly the
Visitors had not brought one.

"How good to have you both as umpires. I was half expecting to be
on umpire duty for a few overs. Do you turn out for all Clympe Down
matches?"

"Well" said one "it's unusual to be sure, but you see we are twins. We
prefer to be in each other's company like. So if one goes the other comes
you see. That's the way of it. We've got a builder's yard in Clymington.
We live in Clympe Down and at week ends and evenings we go umpiring
you see. That's right isn't it Paddy".

"That's right it is Dermot" said the other.

I could see when they took off their hats that they were indeed images
of each other. They had a faint brogue to their voice.

"By the way I'll be Patrick and this be Dermot"

273

"My name is Simon – Simon Savill."

"Grand!" he said. "Look we should be loading our plates before the crush I'd say" said Paddy as he slid out of the side of the bench.

We had the best pink cuts of the beef – sirloin it looked like – cold potatoes and rocket salad on which Dermot and Paddy squirted Salad Cream. There was horseradish sauce and Clympe Bakery bread baked that morning. Paddy brought over a jug of elderflower juice – diluted and cold. I helped Dermot with glasses and tools.

I was obvious that the Umpires were Irish. My wife I had once had owned a house overlooking the River Nore in County Kilkenny. We bought it shortly after we were married as it came with a mile of salmon fishing. We spent all school holidays over there.

"Tell me how did you get into it?" I asked after taking a cut off the beef on my plate.

They both made to reply. But with the practice of a life time Patrick took the lead.

"Well you see now it was like this it was. We came over to England in the 1980s from Ireland when there was no work at all, not at all. We had a rough time getting started. Had to navvy a lot – on building sites that is. We were both brickies so we had the skills to be sure. But hard to break into the contractors see. But then we got a job at the Convent just a mile or two from here – refurbishing it was. The nuns – many of them – were from County Cork – where we come from. So they took us on may Mary bless them. The work lasted more than a year would you believe it?"

Dermot took over from Patrick like a solo jazz trumpeter yielding instinctively to the piano.

"We had digs in a semi detached house in Clympe. We got so attached to the place – Clympe that is – we decided to stay. We had a lucky break so we did. We got into building of new homes in Clymington. So good it was that we took on men and bought the yard. But there wasn't much doing at the summer week ends until we found out about the cricket."

"We seemed very Irish to all over here then if you take me. Cork we were and no mistake. Had a job to make ourselves understood we did. They say it's rough brogue you see. Even in Galway they look blank at you – sure they do. But we'd done a lot of hurling at home. That's the great game over there by God. Mixture of hockey and cricket you see."

I broke in saying "I was often at Croke Park – Kilkenny – DJ Carey and those great teams. We had a house on the River Nore for many years you see."

"Can you beat that now Paddy! Kilkenny Cats! And you going to Croke Park. Holy Mary! Someone like you – with that fruity English accent – mother of God!"

"Paddy took us" I said "Our Paddy that is – a neighbour. Man in a million. After a few matches they got to accept us – the Kilkenny crowd from Thomastown. What a day out with all the cars streaming black and yellow flag and scarves up from all over – joining us. Huge steak and chips and tea in Naas on the way home."

"Go away!" said Dermot "Go away! Isn't that just grand Paddy?. Lord save us!"

They took bites out of the still moist brown bread. Each in unison as it were – it was quite arresting to watch. I noticed that they were drinking only the elderflower cordial.

"Well" Dermot continued "so you'd be knowing all about it would you not. We thought we could do well at the cricket if we got the chance. But having two broad brogued native Irish labourers in their side, as they saw it, with no idea of the rules of the game was too much for the Secretary at that time you see. Too much it was".

"So we used to go up to the home matches and make ourselves useful – sticking out the little flags round the boundary, getting out the benches and what you will. After a bit we got to looking after the telegraph score board. We were after making a few mistakes but one of us would stand by the Scorer and so by the end of the season we'd got the hang of it had we not Paddy"

"To be sure" he said softly.

"Well it was after the final match that year, with the village team, when we were at the Guinness in the Oak. We were not actually sitting with the team like –a good crowd mind but a bit at arm's length – so it is was. At that time Jake's father it was who was the landlord and Secretary of the club too. Well yer man comes over to us and said he'd like to be buying us each a pint. I'd say he had had one or two himself. Well anyway he brought over the Guinness and he said that he'd seen us at almost every home game. Then by God – would you believe it – he said would we like to become umpires. We couldn't credit at all. Judging of the game of cricket by the Irish over the English. We were bowled over – in a manner of speaking you see."

Paddy took over from Dermot as if by arrangement.

"So Dermot says to the landlord 'We'll do it if we can have lunch and tea and a pint – or maybe two'. And Dermot him not speaking to me about it at all, at all!"

"So we spent that winter learning the Laws of Cricket. There we were two Fenians sitting in our semi in Clympe Down Dorset over in England learning the game of the wicked British Empire. By Jesus that was something to tell them in Cork to be sure! And yer man the Secretary was delighted he was – delighted. We only did the home games but we got so to like it and all that we often went to the away matches. And that was 15 years ago it was, or more, was it not Dermot?

There was a rest in their lively ebullient account as we addressed the rest of the Lunch. I had taken advantage of the chilled Touraine Gamay provided by Montague and the wonderful soft brown bread. It was all unexpected and pleasant.

I got up to get some of the pudding asking them if they would like some

"No, no – you work away, work away yourself!" they each chanted.

"How do you find the umpiring?" I asked sitting down again as they were finishing the last of the Lunch.

"Ah well you see t'was like this now – we were great readers of the Laws so we were" said Paddy. "We knew more than the English we did – took pride in it to be sure."

"A big problem we often got caught by was the state of the pitch. You'd find the ball nipping and leaping about unexpected so to speak, as it had a mind to. There'd be no telling where it was going to bounce on some days or if it would bounce at all to be sure. But Dermot and I took it that we were there to judge the game not to stop it. So there was this great Law which we learned in our heart you see, so we did. It was in Law 2 about the Umpires. It says this.

"It is solely for the umpires together to decide whether either conditions of ground, weather or light or exceptional circumstances mean that it would be dangerous or unreasonable for play to take place.

Conditions shall not be regarded as either dangerous or unreasonable merely because they are not ideal."

"Now then! What a statement!" said Paddy leaning over to me. "We got to saying out loud the last sentence of this Law when the visiting side objected to the pitch – which they sometimes did if they'd been bested by the devil in the ball. After a bit, as the season went on, when we were after reciting Law 2, the close fielders would break out with the singing they did".

"Conditions not ideal! – Conditions not ideal!" they sang so they did.

"Great crack – all in good heart" he said quietly.

Dermot took up the rope as it were saying

"Of course we thought at first that we could always rely on "exceptional circumstances" meaning "it would be unreasonable for play to take place". When we first read that Paddy said that we could stop play if there was no way of the Clympe side winning. But the Secretary thought that it was more for when a hot air balloon landed on the pitch or such like you see."

They were putting on their straw hats and easing their legs from under the table. They seemed to be acting as one – it was curious and delightful.

As they buttoned their white coats I asked them

"What's the best thing about the umpiring would you say, after twenty years?"

Dermot was checking the counting stones in his pocket. Paddy had finished buttoning his coat and was standing for a moment quite still, ready to go on the field.

Then after a glance at Dermot and looking up as if trying to hold a mirror to his mind he said reflectively

"It's not something you can quite catch. But it's like each and every ball is the key to it all. If you've something on your mind it's hard. I find that once you are full on with your attention time it doesn't drag at all. It all seems so peaceful and everything in place so it does. Each ball – one at a time. Six in the over but only ever one in each moment."

"You'd say so Dermot – would you not?"

After a pause

"To be sure" he said.

* * *

The Village side began to reassemble for the remaining overs on the field. The opening bowlers still had a two more overs each to bowl before the slow spinners came on to the end of the innings. Will Sharp had been saved for this moment. Into the lists went our two batsmen – only three more of them after this.

After Lunch I had sat for a while next to Brendan Connolly. I had liked him a lot when we were both at Harrow. He was in another house but we had also been at the same preparatory school. He was wild and very amusing. He lived on the edge of life. He was a carefree spirit not having undue respect – or contempt – for others. He was still as Irish as ever he had been. His family came from County Waterford – they had a very large country mansion indeed outside Kilsheelan – it overlooked the River Suir. They had a private cricket ground bordered by the river and grew melons in great glass houses. They lived extravagant lives.

His son Arthur Connolly was now going in to bat at number 8 with only 38 on the scoreboard.

There was mild concern that the Visitors side would scrape a score which would shame them. Connolly told me that Arthur had played a good bit of hurling as a boy. There was a hurling pitch on a bend of the Suir at Kilsheelan. He had braved the initial hostility of the Irish lads. He would practice with them at every opportunity. The Connollys were accepted by the town and in the County – they had been great benefactors at the time of the famine and those things are remembered in Ireland. They were Catholics and spoke with a slight Irish brogue. They had been in Ireland since the end of the 15th century.

Connolly was in exuberant spirits after his plunder of the beef and chilled wine. It was obvious he was going to educate all in earshot about hurling. He had a rippling laugh which broke out among his elegant phrases. There were smiles on quite a few of the faces of the spectators now sitting on the benches and plastic chairs.

Connolly was delighted to squash any retort by asserting that the captain of England's one day cricket team was himself a Dublin man

– had played hurling twice a week and owed his skills to the sport. Which was all quite true.

By the conclusion of Arthur's short innings, facing just six balls and one no-ball, he had struck no less than forty runs – all but four of them in sixes. It seemed as if he played the same shot for every full length ball. He got right under the pitch of the ball keeping his head down as he rammed the bat straight up and through the line. After the first four balls he had to face successive short pitched bouncers that were hurled down rearing up half way down the pitch and flying just above his head. These he simply tilted over the wicket keepers head with one hand holding the bat high over his head and swatting the flying ball.

When the first over finally came to an end he was left at the bowler's end. There was a break in the ascent of the score for two or three balls as the batsman at the other end sought to find a single which would bring Arthur down to his end to begin a new assault. Arthur was leaning on his bat at the other end when the batsman struck the ball very hard in his direction striking him on the boot and rocketing into the off stump. There was a loud appeal from the bowler standing now immediately next to him. Arthur was out of his crease but his bat was on the white line.

The next thing we saw was Arthur returning to the Pavilion. I confess that all watching – and there were none who were not – exchanged comments of varying severity about the injustice of the appeal itself and the palpably false judgment of the umpire. Indignation had reached a seething consensus by the time that Arthur strolled easily up the Pavilion steps and descended into a plastic chair.

"That was fun! Bloody good fun! Great crack I must say. Funny way to get out though. Irish umpires too!. But then I'm not sure of the laws. Any of that pudding left?".

He did not seem at all discountenanced as if getting out was as much part of the game as knocking the ball out of the ground. But he had tilted the scales in favour of the Visitors and they would not be tilted back.

* * *

It was a little while after Lunch that I thought I would find a spot under the beech trees on the far side of the ground where the downs descended to the village below. I'd had a good share of the cold roast beef and Montague's generous chilled Touraine Gamay Fleurie – ideal for the warm day. I could not resist the light Gamay. So perfect when chilled. But I find it's best now after wine to allow sleep to descend.

There was a spectator already slumbering in a deck chair near to me when I pitched camp with my extending chair in the shade just in from the boundary edge.

The Clympe downs sloped gracefully to merge into the cricket field affording a clear view of the game even when stretched out under my straw hat. My neighbour was uttering quiet guttural snores which were oddly restful. He had a crumpled cream linen jacket and a Panama hat much travelled. He was certainly elderly. His legs had fallen wide in his slumber and his large and mottled hands rested on thin legs which showed like large sticks under his dark grey trousers. He had a dog collar above his clerical blouse. It seemed to be rather crumpled by perspiration. A large cotton polka dot handkerchief was almost falling out of the top pocket of his jacket. There was what looked like an old fishing bag lying at the side of his deck chair.

The distant clapping, the calls of batsmen and fielders, the smack of bat striking ball and the feint summer drone of insects and coo of a distant pigeon were slowly lost to sleep.

* * *

"I say my dear fellow – so sorry to disturb you – you were happily gone to the world but you see the players are just going in for tea and I wondered, perhaps, if you wanted to join them?"

As gradually I came to life I became aware of him under his hat as he leaned over, his knees slightly bent, his long fingers resting lightly on my shirt cuff as he tried to rouse me. He had large sprouting white eyebrows and his white hair stuck out at right angles from under his Panama. A kindly diffident smile creased his reddened face.

"Do please forgive me for waking you but I thought perhaps you might like to join the players as you look like one of the Harrow older brigade – they've concluded their innings you see."

"No, no, not at all – most kind of you" I spluttered "I trust I didn't wake you with my after lunch grunts and snores?"

"No – in truth I found them quite restful I must tell you – more like the quiet release of sighs really."

"Look – if you like" he continued as if he had just lit upon a solution "do please have some of my tea. My wife always makes me far more sandwiches than I can conveniently consume. I would only dispose of the excess to others –for the sake of not disappointing her you see – or to that well meaning Basset hound I saw as I came in – dear creature stepping on its own ears – too priceless it was. The sandwiches are cucumber thin sliced – we grow our own you see – the cucumber. Come to that my wife bakes the bread – do join me won't you my dear chap?"

"Oh my name is Everard – John Everard" he said. Then peering at my face he continued enthusiastically

"Forgive me but are you not Savill? Time's winged chariot you know – may have mixed up faces in my recollection –there are now so many you see. Were you not the opening bowler for the Eleven when I was a junior beak? Classics and divinity with the VIth form – in 1958 it was – at least I think so. I remember that you had this sudden leap in the air just before you released the ball – you were fast – very fast. Cruel to the Masters the one time that I was playing – couldn't see the ball at all before it caught the inside of the bat on its way into the hands of short leg. Merciful really."

"Simon Savill" I said. Then, memory flashing bright again.

"Yes, good God you're Everard!– Mr Everard I should say! Of course – I was up to you for divinity O level – the only one I failed – other than Greek of course – so I didn't cover myself in glory with you did I. I'd never have known you – you look so venerable and worthy. Well, well – are you quite sure about the sandwich? Nothing could be better than the crunch and cool of thin cucumber for a summer's afternoon cricket tea – that really is most kind – I accept!"

"But didn't you end up as a Bishop – I heard you'd taken the purple cloth – you must have despaired of us boys – you'd gone from Harrow when I went back for Founder's day a year or two later"

I pulled up my lounger near to his deck chair. He opened the fishing bag taking out a square of a cream coloured table cloth – it had lace worked corners I remember. He spread it between us on the mown grass. Out of the fishing bag he pulled two packets covered in metal foil. Held by a string bag attached to the bag – presumably for fish – was an historic Thermos flask. It was unusually large and had a yellowed cup as the cap with another smaller one fitting underneath.

"I'd afraid it's only tea – rather good though – first flush Darjeeling. No milk or sugar. But the plastic cups add a little more flavour – 'Stain of ages, Left by me, Let me hide my lips in thee!'"

He opened one of the packets and unloosened the squashed brown bread sandwiches with the translucent green of the peeled cucumber just showing as the edges. He opened out the metal foil wide taking one himself and pushing them over to me. Pouring the tea into one of the bakelite plastic cups he offered to squeeze a quarter lemon into it – I accepted it not wishing to disturb the settled ritual of his cricket tea.

"Did you enjoy Harrow?" he said suddenly.

"Every blessed moment – except the time I was caught smoking and had to sign a death warrant – you know 'next time and you're gone'. Ended up a big-wig even so. You can well imagine what it was like as a 16 year old taking the field for the first time up against grown men of the MCC and the other great amateur clubs. Rather like your ordination I suppose?"

"Yes that was a big day – back in the distance enchanted".

Everard looked out over the cricket field, now without the players, slowly finishing his sandwich. Then turning towards me he continued

"I gave it all up you know".

Everard paused as if wondering whether to burden me, a stranger, with further explanation.

"I floated up the hierarchy ending up as a suffragan Bishop of a Midlands city. Very Reverend and My Lord Bishop and what not. Too much seaweed on the rock for me. How can you progress in simplicity or humility? It seemed to me that religion is not much than a theatrical performance if it didn't show the way to our eternal home – as it says in the hymn. So I got a diocesan dispensation and took a small parish. After a few years I retired.

"What drew you into it? Did you have a strong belief in God?"

"Not really – it was more that the Church of England seemed like a worthy tradition which seemed to hold an imperishable inner beauty. I've often asked myself the very question you have put to me. Really I suppose it was a sense of long tradition and of beauty – very much to do with a sort of Englishness if I can call it that".

"Do people feel that any more? – I do hope so. There such reassurance in tradition – it holds us together really."

"I so agree. Latin Tradere young Savill! – to hand down. From generation to generation. You know, the silence of the ancient stones in a village church and in the church yard. The long centuries of faith and duty. When leaving after Evensong having sung Nunc Dimittis. Now let us depart in peace according to thy Word. What does that really mean? Does it matter? Isn't simply beauty? Do we not know what it is – beyond thought. Where does thought take you after all. To feelings and more thought mostly."

After a pause to see if he was going to continue with his reflections I said

"But aren't you really speaking of the comforting English church architecture and its simple monuments – its yew tree churchyards and snowdrops on graves – its simplicity and its centuries'".

Cries of "Catch it, catch it" broke into our exchanges. A heaving breathless fielder reached the fallen ball well after it had rolled to a stop a little in front of us and begun to roll back down the slope.

"Goodness my dear Savill" said Everard "we've slipped into deeper water haven't we – but I find it happens on those few occasions when peaking to someone who, if I may say so, loves such things as you clearly seem to do. Usually people keep to the shallows don't you find?. It's as if they might find out something about themselves or perhaps lose their moorings in some way. Not willing to perceive what is."

Wishing, by contributing to our exchange, that it would encourage him to go further I said

"Convention goes deep with us doesn't it. It forms a cast over our conduct as it were, don't you think? As if being superficial is itself a form of good manners. But without perception what is there but shapes and shadows."

"Pilate's question wasn't it. I do agree that belief isn't enough. For one thing it depends on some concept or being. And it shuts out revelation. I mean a realisation of things, if you can follow me?. That didn't come to me until very late. I came to find that thinking was not really helpful. It seemed that realising things was more valuable than anything. Hard to explain as it is not about explanation".

I did not wish by any comment of mine to trivialise his comments. We sat in silence for a good while.

"For myself" I said eventually "it seems that belief itself is pernicious. Not like faith. You need faith at times but it's trust really isn't it. After all one can believe in anything. How did you cope with belief as you made your ascent in the Church? "

"Well now you see Savill" he said but paused for a while as he pulled out a white handkerchief from inside his jacket sleeve and wiped his lips and returned it with great care up his cuff.

"At first I thought that what was missing from the Church was guidance as to finding inner peace. But after a time – after many years actually – I came to a kind of deep stillness which I found in silently sitting in those simple English buildings. It was more than peace – more than the absence of conflict. It seemed like a sort of presence. And I found it when standing perfectly still in the oak woodland near our home above the river. Do you know I find it when finishing in my small workshop after a day 's carpentry and look around at the tools before leaving. Nunc Dimittis again! "

"So what was the point of remaining in religion?" I interjected. "Weren't you simply finding comfort from the Englishness of the countryside and village people. I do hope you won't think me impertinent on such short acquaintance but we seem to have both embarked on rather an unexpected tour don't we? "

"No, no of course not Simon – may I call you Simon? Better at our stage of life than just Savill!"

"Well you're are right of course. I do think that there is a kind of Englishness which is a continuum of tradition. But isn't it also closely bound up with a sense of the beautiful? It seems to me that the beauty of an English village is that, like nature herself, it has a spirit that is greater than its form. After all is that not the very stuff of music? Not the notes but the spirit of the piece?"

"So you see that's really why I went back to the parish – it seemed to me that simply doing one's duty and not seeking or thinking too much, as it were, was more in line with how we should be in our true nature. Everyone is so concerned with originality, with authority and authenticity. But how can all that be found? Outside yourself I mean? We can only realise that it is. In the end all this seeking and gaining is without end – if you see what I am trying to say."

"I'm not sure for the moment what you mean, quite. I can see that you're telling me of discoveries you've made over many years so bear with me if I'm a bit slow"

"Well it's like this isn't it Simon? Us two, now, just sitting under Clympe Down here, now, the lovely tower and clock of St Mary's below, the little sounds of nature and of man, the warm and gentle air, the sense of timeless tradition and beauty – changing but in a sense ever the same. Isn't that why we love village cricket? All held for an instant – the eternal instant as it were? Being drawn through changing scenes of life to the constancy of it all? And us of the same stuff, as it were?"

Everard sat for a long while and then pushing up his hat a bit, said, with a slight start

"Ah! they're coming out to bat – the Village that is – Visitors in the field now. Full of cakes and ale" said Everard

"Oh Lor", he said "look the sandwiches will begin to curl so do have a few more won't you?. Then we can open the other pack – it has buttered scones with Mrs Everard's home made damson jam."

* * *

We were sitting behind what would have been Third Man at the end closest to us. It gave a good view down the line of the pitch at a slight angle. This was a blessing. I knew it was going to be Francis who was to open the bowling for the Visitors. Everard was entranced that I had a son who had played a few matches for Oxford. I said he had been put in last to bat and hoped I had not missed too much. He told me that

Francis had not faced a ball – as soon as he got to the pitch the other batsman had got out next ball.

I was not sure if the Village home team were aware of the assault that was now about to be directed at their best batsmen. There were just eighty five runs to get to pass the Visitors score. There was a confident air about the opening batsmen as they reached the pitch twirling bats and bending knees. We were sitting behind the line of fire.

I waved to Francis as he approached up the slight rise towards us marking out the steps of his run up. He did not seem to notice. He was intent on loosening up – arms swinging and back bending.

Play! came the clear call from the umpire.

Francis had a graceful and deceptive run up to the wicket. It did not seem that he even gathered speed. It seemed almost laconical. There were no sudden bounds or leaps. I watched with intense care, sitting upright on the edge of my lounger. The first ball of the over was released with a whip of his right arm at merciless pace. It ambushed the batsman. The ball swung in sharply to the line of the stumps just at it reached the deceived batsman striking him on his pad with a dull report. He was standing directly in front of his wicket. He had to return to the Pavilion.

There was a gathering of fielders around Francis. With just one ball of the Visitors innings bowled it was obvious to them that they had unleashed upon the Clympe players a most formidable fast bowler. The outgoing batsman could be seen speaking and gesticulating to his successor. A covey of excited fielders surrounded Francis as if seeking to verify what they had seen. An expectant tension at once arose.

The next two balls swerved in the air out away from the tempted batsman. The first eluded his whirling bat altogether. The second caught an edge and flew to first slip where it was struck the alarmed fielder on the wrist spinning down to the grass.

For a moment Francis looked at the dismayed fielder, raising his arm – in forgiveness perhaps or relief of frustration.. He turned to retrace his steps to his mark. For an instant he raised his eyes to us and pointed his index finger toward direct at me then down. It was clear to me that he was going to target the stumps with fast yorkers.

His third ball was so fast that the batsmen had scarcely raised his bat before he was struck on the toe directly in line with middle stump. The next two balls got under the base of the bat with no stroke being played the leg stump jerking back and bails pinging upwards.

The home side was 3 wickets down with only 6 balls bowled and not a run on the board.

My fatherly spirits fell as the over ended and I saw Francis with Montague taking a few steps down the pitch– he was polishing his glasses and looked ill at ease. He patted Francis on the back. There was a slow crescendo of clapping among the fielders and to my astonishment the not out batsman came down the pitch to shake his hand as Francis took his place in the field.

Honour and fair play indeed. Francis did not bowl again.

* * *

After a few more wickets had eventually fallen I left the now sleeping Everard and walked slowly round the boundary until I had got back to the Pavilion and score board.

Another wicket fell as I eased out my legs onto lounger.

"My dear Jerry"

A voice from 60 years ago. In an instant it carried all the connotations of those school days including my dislike of the awful "Jerry". How extraordinary that my distaste should not have tarnished with age.

It was David Forrester. He had a habit of belittling others to enlarge himself. I remembered that so clearly. I recall once speaking about a Mozart symphony at a match lunch at school with one of the visiting team who was also a violinist. Forrester sat next to me. He tried intently to pull things up to the shallow waters where he could feel less vulnerable. His could not help but trivialise with ridicule or smothering bombast.

"Hello there's a change of bowling" he said. "Isn't that young Dunster? His father was with us in the Eleven you remember Jerry" as he pulled a plastic chair towards him and dropped into it. He was wearing a faded cricket blazer of the Free Foresters cricket club. It had pleasing broad green, off white and purple stripes – it was rather tight around his shoulders.

"I well remember him David. We were at Oriel together as well". "Seems as if his son's a leg spinner as well. Do you remember how Dunster would move awkwardly exactly like a sideways crab before lifting a claw like arm gripping the ball. He never ran – just a kind of shuffle."

"That's right Jerry. Hardly took more than a step up to the wicket before bowling – had fat fingers too I remember" he said.

"I've always thought it was the greatest of skills – leg break bowling. Like dry fly trout fishing".

David broke in saying he could see no connection.

"What twaddle Jerry! Just more of your old twaddle! I'd forgotten how you rambled on. You use a very long stick in fly fishing. It's called a rod and you wave it about in the air with a line attached. Plus you have to do it in a river."

"Ever done it David?"

"Had more sense! Have you?" he said.

"Never successfully. When I was a small boy my grandfather had a stretch on the Kennet at Hampstead Marshal – Carew water it was. When he died he left me his split cane rod – Hardy Palakona – and a beautiful small net and silvery gaff. Also a stuffed trout in a glass case."

"I remember I first used the rod on a lake in Devon. I used far too much force getting out the line as far as I could and bust the bloody tip. Had to go to a chap in Marnhull on the way back home to get a new tip made. Great skill making split cane up into a rod piece."

"Waste of time Jerry. Can't see the point in it. Why use a fly anyway. Worm is just as natural or maggots they say. Lot of nonsense."

"But David the point of dry fly fishing is to landing the fly just where you intended with a parabola of line that allows the fly to drop precisely just above the lie of a rising fish. I never mastered it. Do you know I knew a chap who would – still does actually – make up a fly on the bank to match rising flies attracting the trout. With his fingers – can you believe it?".

"Just being cleverly stupid it seems to me. Can't for the life of me see what that's got to do with cricket."

"Isn't that the skill of the leg break bowler David? Dropping on to the spot. It's so difficult to twist the right hand to give the ball sufficient spin to the left out of the back of the hand and still be able to drop it on or just outside leg stump. On top of that to flight it in the air so as to deceive the batsman as to length and bounce. Surely you'd agree?"

There was a roar from the pavilion as the ball was struck high over the rough grass around the boundary into the adjoining cornfield. There was a partial exodus from the field in the hope of retrieving the ball from the standing barley.

"You're making comparisons that don't hold up Jerry – just flighting a kite. Always were doing that I remember – never the middle of the road for you".

"Ah! but isn't the delight in finding the patience and skill to cast a dry fly or bowl a leg break the same? Endless flops of the line and the ball, I mean, but with the perfect cast and delivery in mind?. Or for any one else with a vision? Wasn't that how Frank Whittle or Monet persevered and broke through fixed ideas?"

"Too deep for me my dear Jerry – it's just a cricket match when all's said and done. You just want to get the chap out or have the fish on the bank – that's all there is to it. Nothing particular profound in that is there. No need to be poetic!"

"Well what about all that goes into it David? After all,– you know – concentration, practice, determination, patience, delicacy, perseverance and all that. Aren't they what we need in life? And what's so deep about talking about life? It's all in front of you – not down some mine shaft!"

"Why bother with all that Jerry. I just like to keep on going. No time to waste on looking at life – not when you've got it to live. And we haven't got much left.

But David aren't you missing something? When you are totally focused on bowling or casting – there isn't any time – it's very odd. You're not wasting it – you're free of it for a bit. The challenge is more important than the result – I sometimes think that really the best things are pointless."

"Don't you think?"

David was silent. He was ill at ease but did not at once return to the surface.

A fielder in pursuit of a ball rushing towards them crashing against the scoreboard, knocking off some of the hanging numbers and bruising his shoulder, as we scrambled ungainly up and out of the way.

The game resumed and for a while they watch Dunster minor bowling his flighted slow leg breaks which appeared so tempting to the batsman – like a fat mayfly to a rising trout.

Forrester sat for a good while watching the cricket with me. He then turned to me saying quietly.

"Good to see you in such good form Jerry."

Then in jocular voice "Have you been slurping the Chablis?"

"Tempted I must say – but hanging in there until close of play. You see if you think about is what spoils it all of course is claiming the result. The result is actually the death of the play. How often has it been said the point of fly fishing is the perfecting of the cast. "

"Lord Jerry – you've spent too much time in Ireland – talking gilded nonsense. Riddles and twaddle. You've got to have a result – a fish on the bank or a winner of the game."

I left him with the last word.

"God he's struck another bloody six into the barley" I said. Won't he have to retire when he gets to 50? Not hogging it is he? Give the others a go?

"No fear Jerry. Being fair doesn't mean equal shares does it – nasty outbreak of liberalism there Jerry. Very nasty. No equality in nature – good thing too. Keeps the weak culled I say".

There was a throaty gravelly rumbling coming from the entrance to the ground from what looked like a vintage motorcycle and sidecar throwing up an eddy of dust behind it.

"Look Jerry it's very good to talk to you and everything but I must see Phil D'Abbaye – he's just turned up. Collects vintage cars and so on. Look at him making an entrance!. Squashed into the sidecar of a vintage motorcycle – must be nearly 80 now. What a fellow he is. Drives on both sides of the road – always has".

Forrester leaned forward pushing himself up out of the plastic chair. Steadying himself he turned to look at me saying

"Phil lives somewhere near Sherborne. His son's playing for the Visitors. I expect that's one of his grandsons on the bike – Royal Enfield it says on the tank. See you for a beer after stumps Jerry!"

Forrester move off unsteadily as he waved at the new arrivals.

* * *

The village had accumulated sufficient runs to afford them some hope of success. They were 50 short of the Visitors total with 7 overs left. They could still do it.

It was at this point that as captain it fell to James Montague himself to turn over his arm. The expectations of the Village team were aroused by the prospect that opened up before them.

Throwing a ball requires the sudden straightening of the arm. Bowling a ball in cricket requires an entirely straight arm. Montague was able to fulfill this condition but he found it impossible at the same time to direct the ball as he wished – sometimes not at all since he found that it often thudded on to his foot.

He had concluded that to ensure direction when delivering the ball he would need to keep his right arm extended in a plane or circle of movement in line with the middle of the stumps. He could not do this with a sideways posture as it involved turning his left side to allow his right arm to project the ball. He found that he could not turn as well as bowl. He thus determined that he would face the batsman with his body square on and as he brought his right arm round he would allow his left side to fall down as it naturally was inclined to do.

This enabled him to keep his arm over his head but it also brought his head down towards the ground so that when the ball was released he was facing backwards looking at Mid – Off's feet. He would of course be unable to see the outcome of his effort as he lost sight of the batsman at the other end when half way through the manoeuvre.

He shuffled up to the wicket and stopped dead on the line. He then addressed the batsman at the other end face on and with a sudden whirl of his right arm and twist of his left side down to the ground set the ball on its journey. The ball remained as if suspended high in the air before suddenly landing directly just a few feet in front of his bat. It had insufficient energy to bounce up more than a few inches in his direction. The batsman tried to play the ball far too early not taking account its lack of kinetic energy and found that his weight forward was greater than the pull of gravity. He fell in front of the stumps upon the rolling ball.

The umpire relieved him of his wicket as soon as the fielders deafening appeal for LBW was heard. Montague, his glasses dislodged by his dive to the left and not entirely clear as to the succession of events, was walking down the pitch apologising and enquiring after the batsman's welfare as he levered himself to his feet and stumped off to the Pavilion.

The remaining five balls of Montague's over produced further bizarre outcomes. The ball either did not have sufficient velocity to reach the bat at all, or it rose so high in the air as to defy attempts to judge its fall, or it was released too late and bumped gaily over the turf without ascending at all. The end of the spell came with not a single run being added and with another over gone.

Montague resisted the insistent pleas of the slip fielders to resume.

"Oh no I've done my duty as captain – I've let you all down I fear. Still it was quite exciting in its way. Yes indeed – yes. Not my line of country you see. Hope I've not disgraced my sweater and cap!"

* * *

The Clympe Down CC side now had just two wickets standing with just the final over in which to score the six runs they needed for victory. They had reserved their most powerful offensive for just such a critical state of affairs. It arrived in the person of Will Sharp whirling his bat as if it were a broadsword. His arrival at the crease was greeted by the traditional mild clapping of the fielding side. As he reached the wicket he muttered to the Visitors wicket keeper.

"They won't be ruddy clapping when I go back I'll be bound. Fancy having schoolboys to patch up the side."

The new bowler was James Dalrymple's twelve year old grandson. He played cricket for his preparatory school. He had been recruited to fill a gap in the side. Despite the good wishes of the nearby fielders he was obviously nervous. Dalrymple was a tall boy – very tall for his age. He had an extensive reach. It seemed from the whirling of his arms as he loosened up and the length of his run up that he was determined not to be intimidated. He stretched his calf muscles by touching each of the toe caps with his legs straight. His face was set. Montague had moved all but the close slip fielders out to the boundaries of the field expecting a mighty and devastating onslaught.

Young Dalrymple walked back to the line of the stumps turning with extended stride back to his mark and without pause ran in with a light step to the bowling crease where he released the ball from his high extended arm.

The wicket keeper later described what then occurred. As it approached the eager batsman the ball moved in the air from outside the line of the off stump to the middle of the pitch where immediately upon hitting the turf it cut back again to the off stump line catching the edge of the lunging bat of Will Sharp now utterly confused as to its whereabouts. The ball was deflected behind towards the wicket keeper who in his excitement spooned it up in the air to hit first slip's chest where with admirable presence of mind he arrested its fall by pulling out his sweater as he subsided backwards to the ground.

Will Sharp's expressions of disgust could still be heard as he entered the Pavilion.

The last man in for the Village was the Vicar. uniformed in clerical collar and clergy shirt. He was a traditional member of the side – an ex officio inclusion. He was always posted in the deep while fielding. He was never trusted to bowl. He was the number 11 batsman. It was for him a day spent well – an excellent lunch – tea and sandwiches brought to the ground by his sister – beer with his straying flock in the evening. He had never been known to contribute to any extent to the outcome of the game.

The Vicar faced Dalrymple with the pluck of an early Christian.

As the ball bounced up sharply from the pitch he launched his bat to meet it only to find it had struck his gloves and rolled towards an open space to his right. Satisfied that he had survived he became aware that his fellow batsman was rushing towards him shouting "Yes, Vicar. Yes come on Vicar – come on run!!". It was not until they were each standing together at his end that the Vicar started his hopeless trek towards the other end. I think it was Dunster's boy who ran to collect the waiting ball and hurled it at the unoccupied wicket towards which the Vicar was making his uncertain advance towards certain defeat.

The ball missed the bowler and the umpire standing by the stumps and the fielder behind. It ran down the slope unimpeded to the boundary by the Pavilion. It was then that the interest of the Basset hound became engaged. The ball, losing its momentum, rolled towards him as he lay in front of the Scorer's table. He rose ungainly and slow. He sniffed the ball. Satisfied with his find he seized it and with a lolloping gait ran underneath Montague's large and ancient Rover saloon which was parked against the long grass on the other side of the Pavilion.

The imprecations of his owner fell upon his magnificent ears to no effect. Montague refused to risk an injury to the Basset which might befall from moving his car. The sloppy grinding sounds emanating from beneath the Rover spoke of the slow demise of the ball. Barking and yelping of dogs attracted by the melee and the poking of sticks under the Rover by the rougher element of village boys added to the diverting scene.

It was deemed to be unfair to the village to use the substitute ball it being a new ball with all that implied for swing and bounce. Law 2 was invoked by the Umpires.

And so it was that the match was declared a draw.

* * *

There was no Scorer for the Visitors' scratch team. It was just a gathering of old fogeys and their sons and grandsons. The Clympe Down CC had their regular Scorer. She was June Sellar, the wife of the landlord of the Royal Oak. Jake Sellar had provided a barrel of Clympe Down Brewery Ale. It was brewed in a barn just outside the Village. The River Clympe ran down from Clymping Magna behind the White Horse carved in the chalk of the Down, through the Village to Nether Clympe and on to Clymington and the River Flumen. Its little stream went directly by the brewery barn and supplied the water for the incomparable beers created there.

June Sellar was marking up the scorebook at the close of the match as Chris Pitt organised more trestles for the glasses, beer, sausage rolls and pizza strips that were being unloaded from Jake's pick up – more elderflower cordial as well. There were one or two bottles of Montague's Touraine wine left over from lunch. Chris tapped off large white jugs of the Clympe Down Brewery ale from the barrel and thumped them on the tables.

As he passed us he called to us "Simon this is June – June Sellar – Jake's better half. June meet Simon Savill – a veteran fast bowler so watch his swinging balls."

Loud guffaws arose from all around.

"Boisterous bugger" she said.

I sat down on the bench next to Mrs Sellar but without disturbing her rubbings out as she corrected the record of every over and every run for every player of the entire day that she had dutifully set down in the Clympe Down CC Scorebook. There was a cup of tea for her on a plastic tray. Chris had put out a plate of a few sausage rolls, leaving her to her work.

"Got to tidy it up a bit" she said without looking up.

"There's a lot to do with my pencil when things get exciting. Got to get it all down and all correct. Always find I have to check with the batsmen and bowlers see. They don't let me forget in the Pub if I've made a slip. You might think it's the total that counts. But then that's for the scoreboard. Gosh what a fuss grown men will make over such things. Can't miss a run or put in a wrong extra. Ever so important it seems – you wouldn't believe it really you wouldn't . But it helps being a woman and pulling their pints – it does too!"

The players were still in their whites and sweaters. Some began to sit down. Chatting and laughter began to rise and fall as beer was poured and the day's play receded.

Mrs Sellar smacked shut the score book.

"There – that's done and when they've had a pint they ain't going to pry. Mind I make sure it all adds up – one way or another that is." she chuckled.

She looked up at me. She seemed to be a very definite sort of person. She was wearing a faded brown linen jacket. It had a pencil in the top pocket and was a little short in the sleeves and the cuffs were frayed. She had a floppy wide brimmed hat of what looked like palm leaf. It had a ribbon with a few limp artificial flowers attached to it rather bleached by the sun. She took if off as she spoke to me.

"Come far Mr Savill?" she said then rising suddenly with a shout "Get down Oscar – get down at once you wicked dog!"

The Basset had managed to pull himself on to the bench opposite and had made an optimistic lunge for the sausage rolls almost dragging down the plastic table cover.

"He'd be right up here on the table if I weren't here the devil. Think a dog as low down as that wdn't be able – have to hold the plates up high at the pub I tell you. Still he's very popular with the customers – spoiled of course."

More trestle tables were being set up a little way out into the field from the Scorer's table. A few more benches were being brought out from behind the Pavilion.

"Well as it happens I've come over from Sussex – staying with the Montagues. I've been watching you follow the match with your pencil getting the names of all us foreigners as they come on to bowl. Must be quite difficult to get the fielders names as well – when there's a catch I mean? Or a run out?"

"It's strange this scoring thing" she said. "Only got into it 'cos Jake's Club secretary you see. Thought it'd be very difficult at first – you see if a batsman hits a ball from the bowler and it's a no ball and a fielder runs him out on his second run then I've got to know all three names, then I have to put in the run and the wicket and the no ball on the left hand side in different places and then on the right hand side put in the no ball, the run and the wicket and the extra."

"But after a few seasons you see I got to like doing it. It took me a while mind. You get no time to make mistakes like. Have to be all there all of the time. Right there like – can't let your attention wander see. Can't catch up see".

She took a sip of tea. Putting down her cup she looked at me.

"You lose the moment if you lose attention and then you're lost" she added.

This seemed suddenly to me to be so perceptive I was taken aback. Did she mean it or was it the tumble of the words? It was as if I was swimming from a little boat in the sea and suddenly being told that there were 5 miles of the deep below me.

June Sellars continued as if to explain.

"The players come up to you don't they. All the time. Like to see their score even though it was for a while on the score board telegraph. That doesn't do somehow – it's just the running story of the game so to speak. Need to have it, of course you do – can't be shouting all the time from the pitch to find out what the state of play is – overs bowled and so on."

"Scoring's different see?" she said looking sideways at me.

I was much taken with her comment as it was either trite – which I did not think it was – or it implied a surprising insight.

"How's that Mrs Sellar? They're just tallies aren't they?"

"June it is. Call me June. They'll think I'm putting on airs if they hear you with your Mrs Sellar."

"My name's Simon. Simon Savill."

"Glad to meet you. Well Mr Savill – er Simon that is, as I was saying, the tallies of the scoreboard – they're gone with each change in the game. No one can say how things stood at each change can they – it's the whole point of the game isn't it – that no one knows what the score is except for the moments when there's no score being made. As soon as there's a run or a ball the score changes and will never be the same. Seems so obvious doesn't it?"

"Do you know June that reminds me of some one who once said "You don't step in the same river twice".

Mrs Sellar looked up at me again, not speaking for a few moments.

"That's good that is. Yes I do like that — not in the same river twice – very good. Stops you somehow doesn't it?"

Then looking down before her as if bringing it further into mind she said

"I've often as a girl stood in the Clympe below the Village and also in the Clym at the ford by Clymping St Nicholas and watched the rills of water run over my feet – seem to be always the same stream but never the same if you get me? That's what your friend was saying wasn't it?"

"Something like that I think" I said.

"Well scoring you see – is like seeing the whole game but seeing it changing all the time like. It sounds funny but in a way when the teams go down to the Pub after the game is over and the day's done as it were – well when they're in the Pub and then at work next week and so on. Well then, you see, how do they know that there's even been a game of cricket at all? I mean they can remember their bit for a while and the bits they saw when their minds weren't taken up with something else but that's all. It's become like a dream sort of hasn't it? It's sort of gone from what we see and hear and so on into an invisible thing?"

"Yes I see what you mean – very clearly if I may say so. But isn't that what happens with every experience? It flies forgotten as a dream as the old hymn says doesn't it?"

"Well now isn't the odd!" she exclaimed emphatically.

"Why that's just what old Mr Tisdale used to say – he was organist at St Mary's for years until he passed away last May – heart was bad I was told. Collapsed in the nave after organ practice he did. Head music teacher at St Joseph's boarding school he was you know – for years he was. Took St Mary's choir each Sunday and sometimes for sung Evensong – St Mary's was known for that years ago you know. It's a fine church – proud of it we are. Something to look up to what with its tower and clock – like a small cathedral they say. After all Clympe Abbey was a famous monastery known all over Wessex it was – as you'll know I'm sure."

She looked at me as if to check she had not been presuming.

"Now Mr Tisdale he used to umpire for us – he was a very gentle man. Spoke very well and softly. Some said he'd been at Oxford – at one of them colleges as a teacher or what they call it. He used to write little poems for the Parish magazine – about the countryside and nature and things. Always had a good word for everyone."

Mrs Sellar was looking down at the closed score book but seeing the kindly Mr Tisdale clearly before her. There was a long pause. Someone sat down on the bench below us making it move.

"Now look here Simon" she said "You're missing the fun – you don't want to be listening to my prattle – you've got to try the beer – it really is the best I've ever served. Bitter hops held back by a sweet subtle taste like – can't describe it – have to taste it, like all the best things it seems. He's a marvel that man Vic – he started the brewery you know. He's an artist with his beers – all kinds he makes. And saying that, you can bring me over a half if you like!"

I pulled my legs from under the table over the bench and stood up.

"Glad to" I said "Hope you won't mind me joining you again – I'll bag some sausage rolls and pizza if there's any left."

Mrs Sellars took the tray from me, heavy with two pint glasses of beer and a plate of rolls and pizza. The beers slopped a bit as she got hold of the tray. I prized my legs again under the table.

"I expect a few of them will be down at the Oak after this. Are you coming? Or you going to the Montagues?" she said.

"They've got a late supper organised with those few of us still alive from the Harrow cricket elevens that played at the end of the 50s you see. That's how this match came about. Nostalgia really. Shall I tell you something June? You see we had School songs you know, when I was at Harrow School that is – used to sing them in Speech Room and also in our houses – we were all boarders you see – in various houses. It was a sort of tradition. Well one of the songs is about looking back after 40 years. In it there's a line which calls the past "the great days in the distance enchanted".

June Sellars; to my great surprise, looked suddenly at my face. She then put her hand on my arm. Her grip was firm.

"Oh I say that's nice –that's lovely – the distance enchanted. Old Mr Tisdale would've loved that he would really – the distance enchanted. Is that what the past is? I'm not sure – is it? I hope it is – such a lovely thought that is."

She paused but was quite still as if seeing something arising in her mind

"That's sort of how I think of what happens when the game is over and the scoring's done. It somehow vanishes as it were. Gone for ever. But the distance enchanted is still there isn't it? – if we know how to find it? That's what I find with the scoring you see. After it's done then you look at it all there – everything in dots and squiggles and little lines. All that remains, see?

"But it's more than that 'cos when you read it carefully – when you know how – you can bring to your mind like – the shots and wickets and all moments of the game. It's there as a record of what's really happened – not just what the numbers hanging on the telegraph score board tell you 'cos that's all gone hasn't it. It's the scorebook that's the way back to the game as it were isn't it. Even though no one looks at it – still you know it is there. So it must have happened. It hasn't just vanished has it?"

As June Sellars finished speaking there occurred to me something that was said of Churchill when speaking late one evening to one of his daughters.

"Do you know June, I said, that what you have said reminds me of something Churchill said to his daughter Sarah.as they sat looking over a beautiful lake – it was Lake Como I think. It was a few years after the War."

"He said to her, 'the most valuable piece of experience I can hand on to you is how to command the moment to remain.' But of course no one can do that can they really?"

"No that's true" said June Sellars. "But then at the same time I know what he means. Did he say that really? Must have loved her very much I'd say."

June took her glass of beer and drank down a good bit. Then re – assembling her thoughts

"But what Mr Tisdale use to say was that the score was the way to the music you see."

"We was always in a puzzle like when we got in for choir practice and he handed out them sheets of music. I'd no idea really about it but then you see I was a treble so always had the tune. Got difficult in descants and when only us had the tune and God knows what was going on with the altos, tenors and basses – not to mention the organ. But once I had the tune I was all right. There was a good many who worked out how to read the score as it were. Not having any training mind – they picked it up over the years. Wonderful really."

"I can remember one old chap – he had a very thin tenor voice. He was retired. He'd been a tractor driver would you believe it. Used to keep the churchyard mowed. Did a few repairs. Well he'd get the music and look at it right through if he didn't already know it and then he'd hum it to the end. He could hear the music there in the score you see. If there was time I'd get him to hum the treble part as well for us – octave lower of course. He was always ready to help. And then there it was. The music. Nothing to fear from all them notes and lines and dots you see. The music was in my head – the music itself."

"Do you think you need the score for the music" I said wondering if this was stretching the elastic a bit tight.

"No. No I don't really" She looked ahead a while. "After all the stream babbling along is music. And some say that them famous music writers had it all in the head anyway – we sang a lot of Handel and such. There was also a lovely one by Mozart it was– always were asking for that thing by him."

"Ave Verum"? I suggested.

"Yes that's it. That's the one. No idea what the words were as we sang it in Latin. But oh my dear we always felt as if a spirit had entered us when we sang that. As if we were all different for a little while. And him hearing music all the time in his head. There's no accounting for it is there now?"

What she was bringing to her mind was so obviously from her sincere observation. June was not persuading or arguing. She was reciting from images in her mind – just as she was describing to me about Mozart.

"But you need the score to actually play the music even if you don't to write it down like. You can hear it and then write it down. He did that Mr Tisdale used to say. That Mozart I mean. Scribbled out from his head. But to play –to remember – well you need the score"

The Basset dog sniffed hopefully around the bench. The evening was approaching. June Sellar was still with the thoughts in flight in her mind. I remained impassively silent as she continued – now speaking so quietly that I leaned, slowly and without distraction, towards her. Eventually she resumed

"You can't see music can you? Seems funny to say that. It's invisible but it comes to your ears through the score doesn't it really? Hard to say which is real isn't it when you come to think about it. What you can hear but not see or what you can see but not hear?"

"Something like that with cricket scoring isn't it Simon? Like what Churchill said. It's trying to fix the game in time as it were. Doesn't do it of course. The moment's the thing. Once you try to claim it then it's gone. All you've got is the score – what you were saying weren't you. It's gone to the distance enchanted."

She paused, waiting. "I'll not forget that, Simon– the distance enchanted – makes you calm it does – just saying it".

The glasses and plates were being cleared and the benches stacked behind the Pavilion.

"June just where've you go to girl!" called out Jake from the pick up the other side of the field as he retrieved the last of the benches on the boundary. It was twilight and cars were starting. Chris Pitt had stacked the tallies of the scoreboard and was starting to put up the shutters on the Pavilion.

With a look around her June Sellars slid sideways out from the table. I followed her. She stamped her feet as if to get the feeling back.

"So that's all about scoring then! Seems to have taken a lot of time and hot air to explain it. It's simple really."

"Off in the clouds I've been. I don't know what I must have said and what rubbish it might have been. What would Jake say. Here, Simon, what's this!. You've not drunk your beer! Don't you like it?"

"Well, June, I think we've both been somewhere else for a while."

Then very quietly she said

"Yes. Yes you could say that. We have. Been somewhere else."

She sighed and smiled.

"The distance enchanted!"

"Funny coming back though isn't it?"